Canoodling Up North

— BOOK ONE —

The Canoodling Series

Shawn M. Verdoni

ISBN: 978-1-957351-43-8

Library of Congress Control Number: 2020909062

Canoodling Up North
Written by Shawn M. Verdoni
Edited by N. Amma Twum-Baah with Amma Edits LLC.
Cover Design: Meredith Hancock
Interior Layout & Formatting: Griffin Mill

Published by Nico 11 Publishing & Design
Mukwonago, Wisconsin
Michael Nicloy, Publisher
www.nico11publishing.com
mike@nico11publishing.com | 217.779.9677

Printed in The United States of America

Dedication

For the pioneering women who came before me and taught me how to be formidable, independent, and resilient. These women are my role models for balancing a strong work ethic with buildin nurturing and compassionate relationships.

These women believed in me and my dreams:

My grandmothers, Rose Clare and June; my mom, Kris; and my godmother, Sandie

For the fearless woman who is my daughter.

The one who taught me to believe in miracles and unconditional love: Erin

Canoodling Up North

Chapter One

It was the kind of morning she had been dreaming about since February. Isolated from the hustle and bustle of her everyday life in the city, Catrina, or "Cat" as she preferred to be called, woke to the whippoorwill's song echoing through the big woods. She looked at her watch for a sense of timing. It was 6:55 a.m. in the big woods. You see, the day starts much earlier than it does in the city. In the big woods, the whippoorwill begins its morning song around 4:00 a.m., followed by the toads croaking their good morning, and then a menagerie of other birds begins to say "hello." Cat always suspected that the sun only rose after it heard the good mornings from all the woodland creatures. There were a few woodland creatures that Cat could do without: horseflies, deerflies, mosquitoes, and ticks.

Everything else was just a part of the experience.

After tapping on her watch to get the time, Cat rustled in her sheets. Now the real party was about to begin. Mia, her two-year-old black lab, took the sound of rustling sheets to mean that the day had started, and Cat must be up to feed her. Sure enough, Mia's cold, wet nose found a section of Cat's uncovered arm and began the morning ritual of nudging Cat until she got out of bed. "Okay, okay, little one. I'm up." One big yawn later, lacing up her tennis shoes on top of yesterday's socks, T-shirt, and leggings, and Cat was trudging toward the cabin door to let Mia out to do her duty and to do her own.

Two hundred and fifty acres of virgin woods surrounding a sixty-five-acre crystal-clear spring-fed lake was Cat's utopia. However, it came with a few sacrifices: 1) the dratted bugs, 2) no running water except for the old-fashioned red hand pump at the kitchen sink, 3) no electricity—only gas lights, 4) and no toilet—only a two-hole outhouse located fifty steps away from the cabin. In Cat's view, these were minor inconveniences that could be overcome. You want flushing toilets? Make a run into town for gas or food. No electricity? Read a book, go for a hike, swim, or shoot the shit with friends. No heat? Make a fire. Bugs? Insect repellent and a fly swatter work wonders.

As she shuffled her way to the outdoor toilet, she wondered, albeit briefly, whether it was all worth it—driving four-and-a-half hours to go to the bathroom in a hole in the ground and making sure the toilet paper went back underneath the old tin can so the squirrels didn't get to it. But she already knew the answer to that question; it was most definitely worth it. "Hmm, someone left reading materials in the privy," Cat pondered. "Looks like an article on Yellowstone National Park." Afterward, Cat replaced the wooden hole cover, grabbed the magazine, and headed toward the cabin for some hand sanitizer and an ice-cold can of diet soda from the cooler. Sure, there was a gas refrigerator in the cabin, but there was just something about a can of diet soda emerging from a cooler full of ice that got Cat's insides all tingly, as if her body was getting ready for the caffeine infusion to start the day.

After a long drag on the soda can, Cat was woken out of her caffeine stupor to feel Mia's body wriggling with anticipation to be fed. "How can something so little be so bossy?" Though Mia was a female dog, confirmed by how she fawned over all the men in the family and they fawned over her, Mia was also a bruiser when it was time for food or play fetch. No-holds-barred for this little lady. She could show a few good wrestling moves to the women of *Glow*. Cat's favorite move was the one where Mia would jump up on her hind legs, wrap her front paws around the necks of her opponents, and twist them around so the other dogs would flip helplessly onto their backs!

With a quick flick of the lighter, the small, white-enamel stove came alive with blue flames. Cat always started with the breakfast meats because then she could use the grease to fry eggs, French toast, or blueberry pancakes right after. Though she had counted calories and steps for as long as she could remember, she was more relaxed about what she ate and drank when she was up north. With the bacon sizzling, she opened the box of pancake mix and began making her favorite meal of the day, breakfast. How did people not want to eat breakfast? She'd never understand that—dropping blueberry smiley faces into the cooking batter. When it was time to sit down and enjoy her feast, a deep sigh escaped her lungs as she poured the pure maple syrup over her happy pancakes.

Cat thought about what she would do this first day of her up-north weekend while she savored the smoky flavor of the crisp bacon and the sensuously sweet maple syrup. Occasionally, her thoughts were interrupted by a series of splashes down by the boats. "Mia must already be down at the lake playing in the water. How long did it take her to get from completely dry to soaking wet this morning? Ten, fifteen minutes?" Cat just shook her head and chuckled. Mia was all tomboy.

With breakfast done, Cat did a quick cleanup. The dishes could be done at the end of the day. For now, she threw paper plates in the fireplace and eggshells into the woods, and then she put on her swimsuit. She brushed through her thick chestnut-brown hair and French-braided it into place. Her blue-striped halter top fastened, she slipped on the black swim shorts that completed the suit. Weight had always been an issue for Cat, but this last year proved that when she focused and made her health a priority, she could succeed. While she knew that looking like Jennifer Aniston would totally be out of the realm of possibility, a curvy Sofia Vergara body could be a possibility. She swept lip balm on her full lips and wiped the sleep out of her hazel eyes. Packing a beach bag with a book, sun lotion, insect repellent and a beach towel, Cat and Mia were ready to walk the quarter-mile or so down to the swimming beach.

The beach was deserted, as expected, and the sand was still wet with last night's rain. The blue sky had just a hint of white puffy clouds floating past, which reflected in the still lake water. The only movement was of a water bug or two flitting and making ripples around the surface as if they were ice-skating. Three purple plastic Adirondack chairs were nestled in the sand overlooking the lake and the almost-submerged swimming raft. With so much rain this spring and summer, there was hardly any beach left, and the yellow plastic slide nailed to the raft was three-quarters underwater.

Mia flew past Cat as soon as she recognized the beach. The young lab threw herself into the crystal-clear water with such force that ripples wafted all through the bay and waves rocked the raft. Cat smiled and shook her head. Definitely, not a girly girl. Mia turned around and wagged her tail while smiling at Cat. "All right, all right, little one. I get the hint. Time to play ball." Cat fished around in the tote bag and came up with a yellow tennis ball and threw the ball as hard as she could. Mia danced around and plunged back into the water to retrieve her ball. No question about it, Mia was all lab—a love of water, a passion for playing, and a wicked-intense focus on retrieving whatever was thrown for her. When Mia began taking in more water than she was swimming in, Cat put the ball away so Mia would start to calm down.

Going to Loon Lake in the summer was a family tradition. Her mom and dad took her to the cabin when she was barely six months old and every summer since. Twenty-six years of packing up the night before, driving the four-and-a-half hours from Mukwonago to Loon Lake, and living out of duffel bags, beach bags, and coolers. Some of her friends shook their heads and asked her why she didn't just go stay at a hotel or at the family cabin just down the road. But Cat just shook her head back and told them that this place *was* her family cabin.

When she was still in diapers, Marshall Luther, who owned the 250 acres, main house, and cabin, told her the rules of the cabin, "There's only one rule up here. Kids rule," and gave her one of his famous bear hugs. Standing at 6 feet 6 inches and weighing 300 pounds, Marshall was surely a man to be reckoned with. Add to that, his white hair sticking out in all different ways, his full mustache and beard, and a voice that sounded like he had been smoking cigarettes and drinking whiskey all his life, he sure could scare the strongest of men. But Cat knew better. Inside all that harshness, there was a heart of pure gold and a genuine love for family, friends, and his land. No one else she knew had ever had loons sing to them when they came home. Marshall would hear them sing their song, and he would sing right back, "Halloo, my loons! Did you miss me?" And they'd sing right back that yes, they had missed him.

Today was different, though. This weekend at Loon Lake was different because she was alone with Mia. Mom, Dad, and her little brother, Ryan, all had other plans and Marshall was gone. It felt different, a little lonely if she was honest, and the loons weren't singing. Still, Cat could use some peace and quiet time. Too much drama and stress on the work and home fronts, and she needed to just be. Mia was a good distraction and was ready for any type of adventure Cat threw her way. The minute Cat said, "Let's go," Mia would wake up from a deep sleep, scramble to her feet, wag her tail, and be ready to join her.

Cat dipped her toes in the water and cringed a bit. The lake water in June had a tendency toward being a bit cold. Still, she was feeling a bit grimy and wanted to take a lake bath to freshen up. Wading toward the large silver mailbox on the stone ledge, Cat opened the mailbox door and fished out lavender-scented soap. She recalled how Marshall had given her one of the many important lessons about caring for nature. "When you bathe in my lake, always use a biodegradable soap so it doesn't hurt the lake or the creatures that live in it." Now anytime Cat packed for a camping trip, she googled shops that carried biodegradable soap so she could be a good steward of nature and make Marshall proud. She took the lavender soap and her beach towel over to the raft and went to work washing her hair and body until suds started dripping into her eyes. "Don't be a wimp, Carneri. One, two, three!" and she plunged under the water. "Holy shit that's cold!" she screamed as she came up for air.

Mia woke from her nap, cocked her head, and took that to mean it was time to play ball again. Cat felt her hair and realized that she needed at least one more good dousing to get all the soap out of her thick, medium-length hair. "Okay, okay. I can do this," and under she went. Because she was already in the water and Mia came out to join her, Cat decided to do a bit of swimming before she hung out for the rest of the morning on the beach. Mia was great fun to watch in the water. Her whole body wiggled like a water snake and her tail acted as a rudder guiding her around the bay. When Cat felt like she had had enough of numb body parts, she walked out of the bay and into her pink beach towel to dry off. The sun was already shining, making the wet sand feel warmer than the lake. She opened the towel, closed her eyes, and lifted her head toward the sky. No better feeling in the world than being kissed by the sun after a swim.

With her eyes still closed, Cat tried to clear her head. However, being a firstborn child, that was hard to do. Always trying to pay attention to the details, always trying to be the best, always trying to be perfect took a toll on her in more ways than one. At least she granted herself this moment to not do anything or be there for anyone else. This was her time and her time alone. She deserved it. She deserved to not do anything at all. Though she was no longer a kid, in Marshall's eyes she would always be one, and therefore the one and only rule for Loon Lake, "kids rule," was guaranteed to Cat if she came to the cabin to visit.

After her sun-kissed meditation, Cat squinted her eyes open and looked at the sky. If she had to guess, it was getting close to dinnertime. She felt something prickly on her leg and looked down. A pale-blue dragonfly with black wings had landed on her thigh. For such a beautiful creature, she was surprised at how coarse their legs felt on her skin. Cat smiled, noticing how the dragonfly's coloring matched her swimsuit. She wondered if the suit attracted it to her. Since no one was around, Cat talked to the dragonfly as if it could understand her. "Hello, Mr. Dragonfly! I want to thank you for eating up the mosquitoes up here. Eat as many as you want!

You can land on me anytime. As a matter of fact, let your friends know, too. The more the merrier!"

It felt like a good time to read a fun summer romance novel. Cat reached into her beach bag and retrieved her copy of *Luck, Love & Lemon Pie* by Amy E. Reichert. She had picked it up at the library the week before when she stopped by to see if they had anything new to check out and found a display of books written by Wisconsin authors. Enjoying the mental escape that the storyline was providing her, she had completely lost track of time when she felt something scratchy on her cheek. Whack! While Cat may not be the star athlete, no bug stood a chance with her swing. She looked down to see if she had killed the pest—she had—the light-blue dragonfly lay motionless on her leg. "Damn!" She scooped up the dead creature and laid it on the stone ledge. "I'm so sorry! If I would have known it was you, I would have left you alone. Please don't be dead!" She watched for any sign of life. None. Deader than a doornail. It reminded her of one of those crazy family stories that riddled her memory bank. Back when Cat was about ten and Ryan was eight, they had got a surprise present from Noni; the whole family was going to Disney World! Noni paid for the airfare, condo, and park tickets. They just needed to share the experience with her and their parents. On the way to the airport, it was clear that Mom and Dad were already stressing out. Mom had her packing lists checked off and ran a tight ship to get to the airport early. However, Dad didn't need any stupid list and felt that time would stop for him while he chose to do chores that had absolutely nothing to do with leaving on time for the vacation.

After Mom lost her cool for about the twelfth time, everyone was piled into the minivan, barely talking. Cat remembered it was an early morning flight, so the sun was just rising over Lake Michigan as they barreled along I-94 to General Mitchell Field. Cat was looking out the window and saw a large bird land on the expressway right in front of their minivan. "Dad! Watch out!" she screamed. Thump, bump.

"What was that?" Dad asked.

Cat started crying. "Dad killed nature!"

"No, I didn't!" Dad was looking into his rearview mirror. "See? It's still alive." She looked back to see the bird was trying to flap its broken wings and jump around when they heard a thump, bump. Another car hit it. "Umm. Now it's dead."

While she was mortified at the time of the bird accident, it became one of those favorite stories to regale to new members of the family or when they were up north. Truth be told, that episode was the start of Cat's path to her career as a wildlife rescue and rehabilitation grant writer. Blood, guts, and broken bones made her feel faint. However, she was a skilled writer, having learned from the best about how to tell a good story. She knew early on that she loved animals. She also enjoyed sitting on the ancient wood-and-rustic fabric sofa in the cabin listening to the tales woven over the many years her parents came up north. Some were sad stories, others had her laughing so hard she cried, some were mad stories, yet they all tied together. Her family was a challenging one, but, in the end, they loved one another. That love, sometimes only the size of a mustard seed, was all that was needed to keep the family together during those difficult times.

Cat had her share of heartbreaks, failures, and difficult times. As someone who strived for perfection, she knew each one of her faults intimately. But when she had the opportunity to come up north to that cozy red cabin with the white trim, it seemed that the trees, wind, water, and creatures were there to soothe her pain and give her the sanctuary she needed to get through the yucky parts of life. No, it couldn't take the yucky parts away, but it gave her time to recuperate, lick her wounds, and get up and fight the good fight.

The last few months at work had been agonizing. Her new boss, Rose, was absolutely the opposite of what her name represented. Rose was in her early fifties and had been a veterinarian for most of her life. However, she had recently had a change of heart and accepted the executive director position at their wildlife rehabilitation sanctuary.

The woman was pure evil and found complete pleasure in taking turns in ridiculing each of her employees in front of the rest of the team. Now, instead of waking up early to get to work because she was excited about the day ahead, Cat was hitting the snooze button multiple times, driving with white knuckles for the twenty minutes it took her to get to work, and then practically holding her breath for the eight to ten hours she was required to be there.

Cat absolutely loved the animals and the team she worked with. In the past, when she was notified of a grant, Cat would pass out candy bars to the team, and they had an impromptu dance party to celebrate. Now that Rose was there, that practice was eliminated, and instead of hearing "way to go!" or "well done!" Cat heard Rose's deep sigh and "Is that all they could do?" Cat wondered if Rose had ever said anything nice to anyone in her whole life. Did she have any idea how much work it took to research donors, get them excited about a project, write the grant, and still not know if they would fund you? It was damn hard work. There were lots of "we received numerous qualified applications but can only fund a limited number of them. We're sorry, but you were not selected for funding. Good luck in your future endeavors!" A solid fundraiser would only get 50 percent of his or her requests funded and an even smaller percentage of those funded at the dollar amount requested. However, when a grant was funded, it helped pay for important medical supplies, a critical operation, or training for the clinical staff. Once funds came in, she could see almost immediately that her work was an important part of rehabilitating the animals. Still, it was very disheartening when your boss belittled what you did every day. Was it worth staying there? Where else would she go? So many questions were still floating around in her mind that it gave her a constant headache. At least the knot in her stomach had subsided, and she was sleeping better since she'd been up north.

Cat looked down at her watch and saw that it was almost 5:00 p.m. "Come on, Mia! Momma's gotta go. Tonight is snowshoe baseball and pie. Can't miss that!" She grabbed her beach bag, slipped on her black rubber flip-flops, and trotted through the woods on the dirt path back to the cabin.

After feeding Mia her dinner, Cat opened up her grill stove and started preparing a quick leftover meal of pork and veggie kabobs with wild rice and craisins. Once she attached the propane tank and pressed the automatic igniter switch, the griddle started to hum, and blue flames danced below. She quickly sliced and diced last night's grilled pork chop and slid cubes of the meat onto the skewers in between fresh snow peapods, red and yellow peppers, and pearl onions. On one burner, she poured three cups of water and a tablespoon of butter into a 2-quart pan to get that boiling for the rice.

In the meantime, she ran a brush through her hair and put it into a hair tie for an easy ponytail. She put on a little powder foundation, brushed some blush onto her cheeks and eyelids, fished around in her purse for her jade-colored eyeliner, and finished off with her bronze-shaded lip balm. Slipping on a blue dress and Americana patterned leggings, she was ready.

Cat ate her two kabobs and wild rice meal with zest. She didn't realize how hungry she was, but she wanted to make sure that she had room for pie. Lake Tomahawk was known for two things: 1) snowshoe baseball games were held on Monday evenings every July and August, and 2) the Lionesses pie fundraiser was held before and during those games. Since she was up here by herself, the idea of drinking and then driving on roads in deer country did not appeal to her, but good old-fashioned family/small-town fun was something she had been looking forward to all weekend.

Snowshoe baseball was played on the baseball field built right behind the businesses on Main Street. It had the look and feel of a little league field with bleachers on both sides of the fence and a wood-and-cinderblock two-story tower right behind home plate. The tower held the media box on the second floor, where the announcer called the game in a voice that sounded like he must have been around since Lake Tom was founded in the eighteen hundreds.

Spectators could also walk into the lower level of the tower to buy raffle tickets or snowshoe baseball hats, T-shirts, jerseys, and sweatshirts. To the right of the field was Lion's pavilion where the Lionesses were working like crazy to cut up hundreds of homemade pies that cost $2 for a single pie piece or $8 for a whole pie. If Cat was lucky, she would get there early enough to get a slice of strawberry rhubarb pie with whipped cream to eat while watching the game. The last time she made it up north, it was the Fourth of July weekend and she had to wait in line for forty minutes for a piece of triple berry pie because strawberry rhubarb was long gone by the time she got up to the pavilion to place her order.

When she talked to her co-workers about snowshoe baseball, they would sit in disbelief. They actually thought she was making the whole thing up. "No, seriously! It's two teams of players who wear old-fashioned snowshoes buckled onto their own shoes," she would explain. "The field is covered in sawdust, and they play with a baseball the size of a small melon. During the sixth or seventh inning, the home team will pitch up a real melon, and when the opposing team hits it, the melon and the audience explode! When the ball is in play, they all run in snowshoes and catch the ball with their bare hands." She bet them it was real. She even won all her drinks for their night out when one of her colleagues googled it and they had to concede.

Tonight, she found parking right behind the butcher's shop. The line for pie was only about fifty-people long.

"Not too bad," she thought as she joined the tail end of the line. The guys behind her kept her entertained while they waited. "Yeah, they actually do wear snowshoes and the pie is a part of the experience," said the man in a baseball hat and sunglasses.

"I don't believe it," said the other guy.

Cat smiled and joined in, "It's true, and tonight's game will be even more fun because they play against the local media, and they don't know how to run in snowshoes."

As the line started to move, a young Lioness came out of the pavilion to update the night's list of pie flavors. The guy in the hat said, "This is the part of the evening that gets stressful. Since the ladies only make a limited amount of homemade pies, you never know what will be left by the time you get your turn. I'm holding out for the rhubarb cream pie. During the Fourth of July, it was so busy that I swear I saw them start to serve anchovy pie." Cat chuckled a bit.

"I'm here for the strawberry rhubarb. I was here on the Fourth of July too, and it was painful. I was in line for forty minutes, and I had five people in front of me when they took it off the board. I was crushed." The new guy got really interested now and started reading the pie selections out aloud.

"Oh, I see a lemon pie. I haven't had one in ages. Do you think it has meringue?" he asked.

His friend with the hat responded, "It probably is just a crust with a bunch of cut-up lemon wedges in it, and then they slop some whipped cream on top." The new guy started to really get into the whole scene and was focused on what the Lioness was doing with her eraser and dry-erase marker.

"Don't take off the lemon pie! Leave the lemon pie alone!" he started to chant and then whoosh! Lemon pie was off the list, and the new guy said, "Oh man! Now what am I going to have?"

His buddy with the baseball hat smiled and said, "Don't worry, I hear they have plenty of cabbage pie left in the frig." When Cat's turn came, she ordered her strawberry rhubarb pie with the whipped cream and went off to find a seat in the bleachers. Many of them were already covered in blankets, but she did find a spot near the railing that she could sneak onto. Opening the bottle of water that she had brought with her, she dug into her pie, closed her eyes, and almost let out a sigh when the sweet and sour tastes exploded in her mouth. Yum. This was worth waiting for.

She had just taken her first bite of the pie when the umpire yelled, "Play ball!" Seeing the seriousness of the home team and their impeccable play brought a smile to her face. They ran in those snowshoes like they were in a commercial with the motto, "Snowshoe Running Rocks," on the screen. However, the best part was watching the radio announcers try to walk in snowshoes. The way they lifted their legs up high, just to move forward, mimicked stepping in dog poop; then they had to try and run. So many of their outs were because they tripped over their own feet and fell face-first into the sawdust.

Then something even more unusual happened. The announcer was out of the news box and near the bleachers for some announce-ment. Cat's team was in the outfield and ready to pitch the ball when an elderly woman walked up to the announcer and gestured for the mic. The announcer handed the mic to her, and she started to sing the national anthem. The pitcher stopped in mid-pitch, took off his hat, and held it over his heart. Cat looked around and saw that every member of both teams was standing straight and following suit. She felt the wave of people in the stands doing the same, so she joined in. When the song ended, the elderly woman gave the mic back to the announcer, and the umpire yelled, "Play ball!" Cat smiled to herself. Where else could someone disrupt a baseball game, have everyone join her in singing the national anthem, and do so without anyone getting mad or yelling? It was a beautiful thing.

Of course, the home team won the game, but that wasn't the point. It was just plain fun to hang out with a bunch of strangers and enjoy a slice of homemade pie and good old-fashioned family fun. Cat walked back to her SUV and drove the few miles back to the cabin. Because it was dusk, she drove with extra caution. It was oftentimes the most popular time up here for the deer to come out of the woods and start grazing on the sides of the roads.

When she got back to the cabin, Cat let Mia outside while she packed up the non-essentials for her trip back home in the morning. After breakfast, she would drive the four-and-a-half hours back to Mukwonago and get back to reality. This time when she sighed it was a bit wistful.

Cat pulled into her driveway a bit past 1:00 p.m. The trip hadn't been too bad that day with only a few spots of heavy traffic and, of course, a potty stop or two. Mia was jumping around outside, glad to be home. "Home again, home again, jiggity jig," Cat said as she stretched out her legs, grateful that the drive was over. Anytime her family went on a road trip, her mom would quote that saying when they finally got home. Cat was happy to continue the tradition. She didn't know when it started or why, but her mom had told her that as a little girl her mom would say it, and it would be a solid bet that her Grandma June would have done also. She looked around and found Mia sniffing after a bird that had flown into a blue spruce tree in the front yard. Her black body wriggled with excitement, and her tail seemed to be going at sixty miles an hour. After working out all the kinks that came with driving in a car for so long, Cat grabbed the cooler and headed toward the tan bungalow to let herself in.

Cat's parents still lived in the Town of Mukwonago in the original saltbox house they had built on a land of 1.5 acres when Cat was just a toddler. After attending college out of state and studying abroad, she had felt a strong urge to come back home. And when she had suggested that to her parents, they had been thrilled, but with conditions. 1) She could move back home temporarily, 2) pay rent, 3) keep up her room and bathroom, and 4) help out around the house when needed. That worked out great for a few months, but then she had felt the need to get out on her own again. After all, they had raised her to be an independent woman, and she had started feeling claustrophobic in their house. "Where are you going?" "What time will you be home?" "Who are you going out with?" And heaven forbid she would want to bring a guy home for a drink; then there was good old dad. Not a great way to end a good date when your dad is at the kitchen table in his D.A.D.D. T-shirt (Dads Against Daughters Dating) cleaning one of his rifles. After the last time they had a huge blowout, she knew it was time to move out. Now their relationship was back on track. She called or stopped in once a week, which was just enough to keep everyone happy.

For the past two years, she had been renting an upper-level flat in a bungalow near the library in the Village of Mukwonago. Mrs. Romansky, the owner, lived downstairs and only rented the flat to single young women. When she found the place, her friend, Melanie, had been living in the two-bedroom flat but was getting married and moving out.

"It's $400 a month for rent plus utilities," Melanie had said. "Mrs. Romansky doesn't drive anymore, so you have access to the detached garage. The apartment is furnished; there is a twin bed in each bedroom, a closet in one, and a dresser in the other. The stove and frig are old, but they still work just fine. You'll have a back porch, kitchen and pantry, dining room, and a family room in the front of the house. There isn't any air-conditioning, so you'll want to invest in that. When rent is due, make sure you don't try to pay it when she is watching *Wheel of Fortune*. She won't open the door for anyone during her favorite show. But when you do pay, she asks you to sit down at the kitchen table with her for lemonade and cookies. Her sister, Edna, and brother-in-law, Gus, live next door, so if something isn't working, Gus is her handyman. He can fix anything. She is a bit old fashioned, so if you are bringing men home or want friends over, be respectful about it." Cat recalled moving around the space and falling in love with it right away. Since she didn't have much furniture of her own, she could certainly use what Mrs. Romansky had provided and slowly add her own touches over time.

Their living arrangement had been going very well these past two years. When Cat was looking for more permanent work but could only find part-time jobs, Mrs. Romansky asked her to do odd jobs around the house and yard and keep track of the time for each job. Then when it was time to pay rent, she would say in her thick Polish accent, "Let me see your ledger. Well, it looks like you did about $300 worth of work for me last month. Give me $100 for rent and we'll call it even. Would you like some lemonade and fresh-made snickerdoodle cookies before you go?" Cat was truly grateful to her landlord who was a tough cookie but had a soft heart. Mrs. Romansky was a widow whose son had moved away to start his own family. He was the reason the upstairs had been turned into a flat. Cat didn't think it had changed much in the twenty to thirty years since Mrs. Romansky's son had lived there, but it was clean, in a decent neighborhood, and it was home.

Cat climbed the back steps to her door and stepped into the kitchen. Sunshine was pouring into the cozy space and brightening up the buttercream walls and yellow curtains covering the windows overlooking the back porch. She set down the cooler by the white-enameled sink that had matching curtains drawn from its base to the floor. Then she went back down the back steps and brought up the laundry basket that carried all her dry goods. She placed it onto her two-seater kitchen table. Once everything was upstairs, she would put everything away in the pantry that was built into the back dormer of the flat. The camping equipment was stored on shelves she had installed in the two-car garage, and the only thing left to unpack was her duffel bag filled with various levels of dirty clothes and her toiletries.

Once Cat had brought everything into the flat, she went back downstairs to collect Mia. It was a blessing and a sign of trust that Mrs. Romansky had agreed to let Cat have a dog on the property.

She had agreed after they had spent several hours talking at her kitchen table about Cat's work with animals and family stories about her parents' dogs. Mrs. Romansky had determined that they needed some extra protection. "You know, Catrina … ," she was very formal, "… times are changing even here in Mukwonago. I keep reading about cars and homes being broken into, and I sometimes worry that two women living alone need some extra protection." Cat looked at her landlord, quizzically. What was she getting at? "I think it is time we get a dog. I understand that fewer break-ins occur in homes with dogs." Her face had a stern expression, but Cat knew she was waiting to see her own reaction to the news.

Cat's hazel eyes grew wider than they already were, and she tried very hard not to shout for joy. With a nod of her head, she said, "I couldn't agree with you more, Mrs. Romansky. Now to scare away thieves, we would need at least a medium-sized dog. A small dog wouldn't have any effect on someone thinking of getting into the house." She could see Mrs. Romansky wrinkle her forehead and nod in agreement.

"Now, Catrina, you must make sure that the dog behaves and is looked after. You know how I feel about my yard, so it must be cleaned every day. I never grew up with a dog, so you must train it. However, when you are at work or running late, I would be willing to let the dog outside and feed it while you are gone. Agreed?" Mrs. Romansky squinted her grey eyes and looked above her wire-rimmed glasses, but Cat saw a slight smile coming through her pencil-lined lips.

"Agreed." Cat nodded in agreement, hugged her landlord, and ran upstairs to call her parents. Mia came home to live with her a few weeks after that conversation and had been her best friend and companion ever since. Mrs. Romansky was a bit standoffish at first, but Cat could tell that she had grown fond of Mia. Now, when Cat went downstairs to pay rent, not only did Mrs. Romansky put out lemonade and fresh cookies for Cat, but Mia got a special treat from the pet store in town.

Once the car was unpacked and Mia was back upstairs, Cat went to work organizing her long weekend's worth of unpacking.

The dirty laundry pile was growing in the middle of her dining room, as it was the most central location to unpack. Toiletries were neatly put away and so was the duffel bag back in the closet set into the family room. While the flat was a bit stuffy, it smelled clean—thanks to her favorite air freshener it always reminded her of visiting Grandma June's apartment. Boy, did she miss hanging out with her grandma! But looking around, she realized she had plenty to do. First things first, she wanted to take a real bath with hot water and bubbles.

Shedding her camping skin, Cat turned on the silver faucet on top of the claw-foot bathtub. While there were a great many things she loved about her place, it was the bathtub that clinched it for her. Cat always loved baths compared to showers. To be able to soak neck-deep into a sudsy tub was pure pleasure. She sprinkled a handful of Epsom salts and started to sink into the tub. She closed her eyes and felt the kinks slowly dissolving. Washing her hair under the handheld showerhead, she scrubbed her scalp until it tingled. In the background, she could hear Mia's deep breathing turning into snoring. Her puppy was pooped. Sweet.

After a nice long soak, Cat towel-dried herself and walked into her bedroom for a clean set of clothes. Throwing on a red tank top and jean shorts, she walked back across the flat to her bathroom to twist her damp hair into a clip for the rest of the day. She threw the dirty laundry into the laundry basket and grabbed her laundry detergent bottle to go on top. Cat looked down at Mia and concluded that Mia could use the nap, so she left her home while piling back into the SUV for the short drive to her mom and dad's home two miles up the road. While they all needed their space, her parents were still willing to let Cat do her laundry there. It gave them all an excuse to see each other once a week or so.

When she got back to her car, she noticed that Mrs. Romansky was in her gardening hat, short-sleeved yellow shirt, and beige crop pants. "Hello, Mrs. Romansky! Mia and I just got back home from our trip. Did we miss anything?"

The elderly woman brushed her hands off on her pants and looked up through her glasses and a stray gray curl or two blowing into her face. "Ah, it's good to see you, Catrina! Looks like you are going to see your parents and do some laundry. Wish them well for me. Not much happened around here. My sister and her husband came over to play cards the other night, and I slaughtered them," she said with a twinkle in her eye.

"Will definitely tell Mom and Dad you said 'hi.' I'll have to remember to be careful when you ask to play cards with me. I'll need to make sure I still have enough money to pay for rent!" Her landlord chuckled and waved her away.

Hopping into her silver SUV, Cat drove the two miles to the home she grew up in. She pulled into the driveway and saw her mom puttering in her garden. She thought she heard her talking to her plants. Cat would never understand her mom's passion for flowers and plants. They just wither and die, lots of wasted time and money, she thought. Still, they made Mom happy, and it sure was an easy Mother's Day gift: a gift card to Yerke's Frog Alley Greenhouses.

"Hey, Mom! Is it okay if I do a little laundry over here tonight?" Cat asked as she dragged the overflowing laundry basket into her arms and kicked the door shut. Her mom looked up and smiled.

"Looks like I already said it was fine. Need some help, Munchkin?" Claire Carneri wiped off the dirt from her hands and pushed up on her kneeler to get to a standing position. Ever since her car accident, her back would bother her if she stooped over too long. Still, Claire had the best garden in the neighborhood. She was never one to care about what she wore or be much impressed by expensive -brand clothes and shoes. But in her garden, she made sure that a quality fertilizer, and she always bought her plants from one of the local greenhouses, like Yerke's Frog Alley Greenhouses, because she trusted that the staff there put the time and energy into making stronger and more unique flowering plants than those available in mass quantities at one of the big box stores. She didn't mind spending the extra money that it took to get her garden to its peak perfection. Today was no exception to Claire's rules on what went in her garden or what she was wearing. Today, she wore her graying dark brown hair in a ponytail poking out the back of a ratty baseball cap. She paired it with an oversized blue T-shirt, jean shorts, and bare feet.

"No thanks, Mom, I got it. Hey, you shouldn't be barefoot out here. The doctor told you to wear your inserts all the time for your back," Cat scolded her as she made it to the garage door.

"I know, I know. It's just that I love the feel of grass between my toes and on the bottoms of my feet. It feels like I am getting a massage. You know I was a tomboy as a kid and I never wore shoes in the summer. It's hard to break such an old habit." Claire shifted and slowly got upright with her hands supporting her lower back. She walked to reach the inside garage door for Cat so she could drop her basket inside. "Will you be staying for supper? Dad's making homemade pizza."

Cat dumped the contents of her basket onto the laundry room floor and started separating what would go into the washing machine first. "Yeah, that sounds great. Where is Dad anyhow?"

"Where do you think he is? Down in the magical basement doing some woodworking." Anthony Carneri was retired from his job as a store manager at the local hardware store. Since his retirement, he seemed to spend even more time working downstairs in what the family lovingly called the "magical basement." It was called the magical basement because you could never find anything down there, making it the perfect spot for Anthony to hide things he didn't want his wife to find. There was a time when he hid an entire fifty-two-inch television downstairs for almost a year, and she was dumbfounded when he brought it upstairs to replace their thirty-six-inch television. However, it did have its downside. Anthony would buy things throughout the year on sale for his family to give as presents at Christmas time. Unfortunately, he oftentimes forgot where he hid the items, and when it was time to give out the presents, he was at a loss where many of his presents had gone. As often as things magically appeared from the basement, they frequently were lost in its abyss as well. "Hey, Dad, I'm home!" Cat yelled down the wooden steps.

The sound of power tools subsided, and a gruff voice yelled back up, "I'll be there in a minute!" Soon Cat heard footsteps pounding up the basement steps and saw a familiar face. Anthony was the picture of a woodworker. He was covered from head to toe in sawdust, including his thick glasses. While his hair looked tan, she knew that it was more silver than dark brown these days. His lean build led people to believe that he wasn't very strong. They were wrong. For twenty-seven years, he had been hauling boxes, bins, wood, whatever was needed to keep the store's merchandise on the shelves. The only stronger person she knew was her younger brother, Ryan. "Hey there, do I hear my little girl's home?"

"Hey, Dad." Cat reached out her arms and took him into a great big bear hug. When she closed her eyes, she could smell the type of wood he was working with, oak. There was no denying that deep rich smell. When they were little, Dad would take Ryan and her downstairs to play while he did woodworking and taught them how each wood looked and smelled differently. Her favorite part, of course, was when he would stop what he was doing to pull her into one of his famous bear hugs and say, "Who's Papa's sweetie?" and Cat would answer in her little angelic voice, "I'm my Papa's sweetie!" and then she would gather all her strength to give him a great big squeeze and a sloppy kiss. Once she hit the teen years, that small tradition went by the wayside. She never called him Papa anymore, only Dad or Father if she was very upset with him. These days, though, he and Mom had been more of a sanctuary. With work and everything else, it was great to come home and just fall into a bear hug once in a while.

"Mom says I can stay over for pizza. Do you need any help?" "Of course, I do! No one else in this family gets the amount of cheese just right, except for you. You can be the cheese police." Just as Anthony completed his sentence, the bread machine on the granite countertop by the refrigerator went off. "Beep!"

"Dough is ready!" Anthony let go of his daughter, walked over to the white enamel sink, and started washing his hands, careful not to splash any water on the oak windowsill above the sink.

Anthony took great pride in their home, as he should. Almost every piece of wood in the house was crafted and stained by his hands. He let his mind wander a bit to a time when Cat was about three and a half years old and waddled through the empty structure of the house. Anthony and Claire never had a lot of money, and so when they decided to build in Mukwonago, much of the finish work was done with their own hands. Claire painted every room while Anthony stained all the woodwork and put in ceiling fans in all the bedrooms, the great room, and the kitchen. There was still a photo somewhere when he had the kids hanging out in a playpen while he was standing on a ladder putting the finishing touches to the wood-and-brass fan in the great room. While there were more times than not these days that things were breaking down, he never regretted the blood, sweat, and tears he and Claire invested in building a home for their family. He knew it was wrong, but sometimes he still saw Cat as the three-year-old toddler waddling around with a bow on top of her head of curls asking for a paintbrush to help.

Anthony brought out the darkened stone jellyroll pan and sprinkled cornmeal on the bottom to make the crust crispy and not stick to the pan. Next, he grabbed the wooden rolling pin, sprinkled flour directly on the counter and a bit more onto the rolling pin, and began the chore of rolling the dough to the size and thickness necessary to make the pizza crust.

Claire entered the kitchen and set the oven temperature to 425 degrees. As quickly as she came into the kitchen, she swiftly left to leave the two pizza masters to their task. Cat added the browned and crumbled sweet Italian sausage to the pizza sauce that she carefully spread onto the dough Anthony spread over the baking pan. Anthony took thinly sliced tomatoes and placed them in rows on top. Next, Cat sprinkled the diced onions, and Anthony took charge of the sliced black olives and mushrooms. Finally, it was time for the cheese. For a true Italian pizza, cheese is a minimal component of the whole pie. In the Carneri household, cheese was the feature. The more the better. Cat went to task to sprinkle four cups of shredded mozzarella cheese on top. The goal was to make sure you couldn't see any of the other ingredients. By the time they had completed their task at hand, the oven preheat alarm went off to let them know it had reached peak heat. Anthony slid in the masterpiece and set the timer for twenty-five minutes. Now they could take a deep breath and catch up a bit before the next tradition began, dinner and a movie. If they were lucky, they would choose the movie before the pizza got cold.

"How was up north?" Claire asked.

"It was good. Great, in fact. No bad weather; the mosquitoes and flies were tolerable, and I saw a snowshoe baseball game in Lake Tom." Cat started picking at her cuticles because she knew that her mom had just begun the inquisition.

"Did he try to reach you while you were gone?" Claire's eyebrows lifted along with the lilt at the end of her sentence.

After a pause, Cat answered. "Yes and no. He tried to reach me at first, but when I wouldn't answer, the phone just stopped ringing."

"That's good, right?" Claire was trying to determine where her baby girl was in the grieving and healing process of this most recent heartbreak. Out of the corner of her eye, Claire could see Anthony's eyes pained at the thought of someone hurting his baby girl.

"Yeah, it's good. I know I was right to break up with him, but we'd been together for two years and now we're not. It'll take a while." Cat looked down now at her folded hands. Was she embarrassed? Was she sad? Angry? She was still sorting everything out, and having a bitch for a boss was just a bonus to help boost her confidence. She was wishing she could come up with an excuse not to go back to work right away, but unless she was quitting, it was unlikely that Rose would be willing to approve any more vacation for the next few weeks. It was almost the end of the fiscal year, so it was critical push-time to get out as many proposals as possible to boost the numbers for the month and year closing.

"At the risk of sounding like an old-fashioned, overbearing father, Jansen was never good enough for you. I didn't trust him from the start." Anthony was letting his ire up and gaining more steam to tell everyone what he really felt about Cat's ex.

"I know, Dad." And then Cat let out a sigh. "It's just that I am in my twenties now, and as hard as it is for me to make my own decisions, I need to do that, okay? You can't keep making decisions for me. I'm an adult now, and I have to manage my life my own way." Cat had never told her parents the details of their breakup; that would just add fuel to the fire her dad was stoking, but she needed to let them know right away or else they'd be hurt if they didn't hear it from her first.

Anthony's Italian temper was on simmer now, and he looked over at his Irish wife for a clue as to what to do next. They'd been married enough years that almost by telepathy she let him know he needed to let it go. It was time for unconditional love and past time for the "I told you so!" talk. Anthony cleared his throat and said, "We know, Sweetie. And you are doing a great job of it. Sometimes we need to learn to back off a bit. We're still learning how to be parents of an adult, you know? No matter what, we love you and are proud of you. You can come to either of us for a hug, a talk, or a safe place to just take in the quiet if you need to. Remember, family sticks together." As he said that last affirmation, Anthony shook his head, and little puffs of sawdust escaped his carefully parted and feathered hair.

"Well, I will get over it, I always do. Thanks for being there for me. I love you guys," Cat said, as a tear snuck its way down her cheek. It was just enough of a break from her tough exterior that Claire needed to poke into her innate nurturing need. She got up off her chair and wrapped her arms around her daughter and snuggled Cat's face into her plentiful bosom. Not wanting to be left out, Anthony pushed his chair back and gathered his baby girl into an embrace on the other side. Cat felt the love and support flow through them and into her. She could have stayed that way all night, except they were cutting off her access to air. "I. Can't. Breathe," she squeaked. As quickly as they came to her, they let go and were about to sit down at the kitchen table when the alarm went off on the oven again. This time to let them know the pizza was ready.

"I got it!" Anthony sprang into action. He grabbed a hot pad for the pan to sit on and cool. Claire focused on running around

Anthony to get to the blue and brown ceramic plates and utensils. Cat snapped out of her sadness and went to the refrigerator to get a fresh piece of Parmesan cheese and a handheld cheese grater to fill a small bowl with the aromatic cheese to sprinkle on top of the hot bubbling masterpiece coming out of the oven.

"Do I smell pizza?" A bear of a man came waltzing in through the garage door in dried mud-covered work boots, stained carpenter jeans, and a short-sleeved buttoned-down shirt with a Lone Pine Contractors logo over the top right shirt pocket. Ryan may have been eighteen months younger than his older sister, but that was the only concession he gave to her. In typical little brother fashion, he always rattled off a list of reasons why he was bigger or better than she was almost every time they got together as a family. With his 6-foot 4-inch height and linebacker build, he was sure a sight to reckon with. He always reminded Cat that he was bigger than she was by saying what he said at this moment, "Hey, little sis. Welcome home." He would have liked to do more, but as big as he was in mass, he also had that size of a heart. Ryan had an innate sense and felt that he walked in on something very personal and tender. Knowing that Cat had recently broken up with that rat bastard, Jansen, he put two and two together and felt there was no patience to pick on her much more than calling out his pet name for her. He would pick on Cat incessantly, but no one else could lay a hand on her or say anything bad about her because he would have something to say and do about it.

Ryan heard a faint sniffle and then heard his sister's pet name for him in return, "Turd." Good, she's not in too bad of a state. Maybe he could coax a bit more teasing out of her tonight.

"Looks like you all got everything covered. If it's okay with you, I'll go upstairs and get cleaned up for dinner." Ryan didn't wait for anyone to answer. He began the chore of unlacing his boots and kicking them off into the hall closet. Next, he walked over to the stairs and took them two at a time to get up to his room and the bathroom at the top of the stairs. Since it was dinner-and-a-movie night, Ryan knew not to expect the family to wait for him to shower up before they began to eat. Besides, seeing the scene he had walked into, he realized that Cat would be christened to choose tonight's movie out of the hundreds of movies his parents had collected over the years. No need to hurry downstairs because he knew Cat would get their support in whichever movie she chose. Also, he knew all the words and music in most of the movies they owned. The purpose of seeing a movie was not necessarily for its impact. Dinner-and-a-movie night was more about the family connection. It just felt right to have everyone sit in his or her preferred chair or couch and watch the movie together. Sometimes they would shout out when a character looked or acted like a member of the family. For the movie, *Moana* for instance, Ryan knew he would always be chosen to be Maui. Not just for Maui's size, but also because he could make his pecs dance—a perk due to the three hours a day he weightlifted at the gym.

Downstairs, they carried steaming-hot square slices of pizza on plates out of the kitchen to arrange on top of pillows, which were placed on top of their laps, along with bottles of water, beer, or soda cans strategically set on handmade oak-and-tile sample coasters. God forbid Anthony would catch anyone with a drink set down directly on a piece of wooden furniture. "Okay, sweetie, you can pick out tonight's movie."

Cat thought about her choice carefully, closing one eye in a squint while the other looked up at the ceiling. "How about *RV*?" A classic in the Carneri household. With a lot of slapstick humor, it was the perfect end to her day and her vacation. Mom and Dad sat on the brown leather sofa, she sat on the brown recliner, and Ryan sat on the brown office chair in the corner when he came down.

Laughing at all the same parts and singing some of the corny songs while eating pizza helped ease some of the sadness and tension that had come back into Cat's body. After the movie, it was time to gather up her clean laundry and say goodbye to her family for now. Because she helped Mom and Dad make dinner, she knew that Ryan would automatically begin cleaning up the kitchen and boxing up any leftovers for lunch tomorrow.

The sky still showed signs of summer sunshine with hints of pink behind some of the leftover clouds although it was almost

9:00 p.m. Cat arrived in her driveway just in enough time to see some lightning bugs flicker on and off in her yard. She pulled into the garage and shut the wooden door by hand and locked it with her key. She balanced the weight of her purse on one shoulder with the laundry basket on the hip on the other side, holding her key in her mouth until she could get the motion light to turn on to see the keyhole. By the time she made it up the stairs to her flat, she could hear Mia's tags tinkling behind the white-painted door. Mia would need to go do potty and eat now that she'd been asleep for several hours. When the door opened, Mia's slick black coat glistened in the artificial light of the kitchen, and her body wiggled in anticipation and excitement for what was coming next. Cat wished she had the same anticipation. Thinking about what was coming next just made her tired.

Chapter Two

Damon MacGregor was the kind of man people noticed. Towering at 6-feet 6-inches with a shock of red shaggy hair that melded into a closely trimmed beard and mustache, it was easy to see that he would stand out in a crowd. It also helped that his preference of clothing made him look like a lumberjack most of the time; jeans, brown work boots, and a plaid cotton shirt during spring and summer switched to flannel in the fall and winter. Damon took up space when he entered a room because of his broad shoulders and muscular thighs that showed through his jeans. He didn't deliberately wear tight jeans; it was just that he always found it difficult to find jeans long and wide enough to fit his build, and he wasn't about to spend an obscene amount of money on clothesthat he could easily buy at a big box store.

As much as his appearance screamed, "Notice me!!!" he had other features that were just as intoxicating. Against his creamy white skin and shocking red hair, his ice-blue eyes were striking. A person could look at them and feel like they were looking out into an immense ocean, the color so crystal clear that you could see to the bottom. Just above his beard line lay another surprise. When Damon smiled or laughed, twin dimples appeared in his apple cheeks. No matter how old he was, once those dimples came out, they made him look like a mischievous little boy.

These physical features got people to notice him, but it was his voice and laughter that stopped them in their tracks. Like a cherished Irish whiskey that had been meticulously blended with just the right amount of smoke from a peat fire and set to age in ancient oak barrels, his voice rolled over his tongue and filled the immediate area with warmth. And when he laughed, his whole head bent backward so that his mouth faced the sky, and its sound echoed off each wall and the ceiling. When he smiled, it almost always reached his eyes, which gained twinkles to change one's impression of his eye color from the bluest ocean to the most star-filled sky.

In all, Damon was a force to be reckoned with. If he was in a good mood, it enveloped everyone near him, and added a perk to their steps and pasted a smile on their lips. Were he to be in a foul mood, everyone stood clear.

As a child, he had a wonderful life living in Erin, Wisconsin. While there was a small-town center hugging Highway 83, most of the township residents built homes and farms among the rolling grassy knolls that became God's quilt when fall was in peak season and all the trees blossomed into vibrant reds, bright yellows, and warm rusts and melded together to form the most breathtaking patchwork quilt design anyone could imagine. Jutting out of this picturesque community was Holy Hill. Built by early Irish settlers, today its impressive two-spire red brick cathedral is a destination for religious pilgrims and tourists, as well as a focus for local artists. Damon just thought of it as his home parish.

In his thirty years, he had seen many changes in the area, most in the name of progress, of course. Milwaukee's wealthy were buying up property from elderly farmers whose children didn't want to work the family business any longer and had moved away. They got it at a steal and then proceeded to build grand homes and host lavish parties for their peers and business associates. The area got its next wave of change in 2006 when Erin Hills Golf Course opened and became the course for the 2017 US Open. However, Damon was nonchalant about the celebrity status of the golf course. He was more interested in the people who had a true connection to the land, its people, its animals, and its legends.

Damon was a pretty easygoing guy, being the middle one of six children who were raised on a horse farm. He could let things slide until he couldn't and then watch out. As slow as he was to anger, once he hit Irish temper mode, get out of the way because he was going to explode. The nice thing about his temper was that because the rage came on so explosively, it was very quick to dissipate. It was a solid coping mechanism because being a part of a large farming family, there wasn't much time allowed for unproductive behavior, and there were just too many MacGregors around to spend time coddling. It wasn't that his parents were uncaring or unloving; it just was they had to be practical. They chose to farm and had a large family. It took a great deal of energy, time, and money to take care of both. They needed to be practical 90 percent of the time. However, when it was time to let loose, Pat and Heather MacGregor could party like there was no tomorrow until tomorrow came, and then they'd rub the sleep out of their eyes, put on their work clothes, and get to it without a complaint.

Oh sure, he tried to sow his wild oats in his late teens and early twenties. He had a huge row with his Da and swore he'd never work on the farm again, then packed up all he owned in a duffel bag and refused his parents' help to take him to his dorm at UW-Madison. His size, flexibility, strength, and a solid intuition of knowing his opponents' next move led him to a full-ride scholarship to wrestle for the Division 1 school. School was very easy for him as well, so the 3.8 grade point average requirement to get into the university was a piece of cake. While Damon looked the part of the star athlete, he found he had an interest in the performing arts and literature. His bass voice was on pitch and melodic, so he was often chosen to sing solo parts in the school choir. He also found that he loved reading classic literature. He hadn't really paid much attention in high school English classes because he was honestly bored. However, at the college level, his professors challenged him and taught him to think provocatively about what he was reading. He became fascinated by the authors he was introduced to in his English Lit 1 class.

If he was honest, and most often he was, it didn't hurt that Paige was a true beauty and was in the same class. Paige had wavy blonde hair, a year-round golden tan, and warm brown eyes. He fell for her hard. When they were assigned to a group project in English Lit, he thought all his years of going to church were finally paying off. Paige was a pretty good student herself and was soft-spoken. She was impressed with his ability to remember passages and recite them verbatim. When Paige showed interest in something that Damon said or did, he just worked that much harder to impress her.

As their freshman and sophomore years went by, Damon and Paige were inseparable. Paige was not only his first serious girlfriend but also his first lover. Where he could educate her in her studies, she provided the same level of expertise in the bedroom. She was never afraid to tell Damon what she liked or to show him how and where to touch her. If it were up to him, they could have stayed in bed all day, every day.

Unfortunately, because he was spending so much time on Paige, his wrestling and grades paid a hefty price. Interestingly, Paige's grades improved, and she seemed less interested in his needs and goals while building on her own.

When Coach sat Damon down to let him know he was being cut from the wrestling team, he was dumbfounded. Damon had no clue things had gotten so bad. Without wrestling, there was no scholarship. Without the scholarship, there was no way he could afford to stay at Madison as a full-time student. After walking around the quad for a few hours and drinking a pitcher of beer in one of the brightly colored sunburst chairs lining the Union Terrace overlooking Lake Mendota, Damon thought of a plan. He walked back to Paige's dorm room and knocked.

"You look like hell, Damon. What happened to you?" Paige asked quizzically when she opened the door.

"I was let go from the wrestling team today. Coach said I've been too preoccupied, and I wasn't pulling my weight." Damon ducked his head to make it past the doorframe and sat down on Paige's pink geometric-shaped comforter covering her dorm bed.

"Oh, baby, I'm so sorry. What are you going to do now? Didn't you need that to keep your scholarship?" Paige said while she sat down beside him and began to rub his back.

"Yeah, it was quite the shocker, but I figured out a plan to stay at Madison and still be together. We can look for an apartment, and I'll get a job here. After I get enough saved, maybe I can go back to school part-time." At that, Paige stopped rubbing his back and stood up.

"I don't think that's such a good idea, baby." She was looking at the floor and fumbling with her hands.

"Why not? It sounds perfect to me. That way we can still be together, and it won't affect your schooling at all because I'll be working during the day and then I can have meals ready for you when you get home. We're rarely apart most days anyway; having two separate places to live in is just a waste of time and money. Look, we love each other, and it just makes sense now that my situation has changed." Damon looked at her with his clear blue eyes, observing her murky brown ones for some sense of what she was thinking.

Paige stopped pacing and kneeled down in front of Damon, taking his large hands into her petite ones. "Damon, we've been good together, I agree. But I don't know that I can say that I love you like that. Living together is a huge commitment, and I should concentrate on school. Grades don't come as easily to me as they do to you. You know that I started getting extra help from Dr. Richards for my English class, right? My grades are really important to me, so I can't be distracted." Paige paused, and Damon didn't like what he was feeling her next move would be. "As a matter of fact, I have been thinking that we've been spending so much time together that I need to step away from us, so I can concentrate more on my classes. I'm sorry, but I think now is the best time for you to just cut ties with this place and find your new purpose."

Damon remembered leaving her room like a zombie. He wished he had been drunk and that it was all a bad dream, but by the next morning when he tried to reach her, he knew it was real. Her phone went directly to voicemail. She didn't answer any of his texts. Things went from bad to worse, and he couldn't sleep.

Damon's world was in chaos. He couldn't sleep, and he had no wrestling practice, class, or girlfriend to go to. As he was walking around campus on a night when he had insomnia, he found himself walking the paths between the nontraditional student and faculty apartments at 3:00 a.m. He looked up when he heard a door opening to one of the faculty apartment buildings and saw a slight blonde woman in a skintight black dress that barely covered her ass. She was reaching up to wrap her arms around an older man and gave him a long and lingering kiss before she turned around to walk back to the parking lot. Damon squinted to get a better look at the guy and recognized him as Dr. Richards. His intuition kicked in, and his eyes followed the young blonde to her silver convertible. Paige had found his replacement in the bedroom and in the classroom.

Damon was twenty years old, broken-hearted, with shattered dreams, and penniless when he took the bus to Goerke's Corners to be picked up by his da. That was eight years ago, and Damon had grown up a great deal from that experience. He was in a deep depression for a long time and refused to get medical help. Then one day his mom took him in her car into the city. There was a place that she wanted him to try.

"Listen, I made this appointment for you because you have us all worried sick. I know what depression looks like and feels like. Mental illness is no stranger in my family, you know that. Now you may refuse to want to talk to anyone about what happened and how you feel, but you will do something to try to get better. I made you an appointment with my acupuncturist at the Jensen Health & Energy Center. You don't have to talk about your feelings, but you can talk about how much sleep you're getting, how you're eating, or if you have physical pain anywhere. You are going there and that's final." Heather started to cry, and her voice shook a bit.

"I refuse to have another person I love hurt themselves because they are unhappy and refuse to get help!"

Damon remembered that he felt his mother's pain and anguish, and it was enough to get through the wall he had built around his heart. He nodded in agreement and walked into his first of many acupuncture appointments.

"When God closes a door, he opens a window" was an absolute truth for Damon. With his love-life door slammed shut in his face, he found another opportunity to be successful. Equine acupuncture therapy.

After that first session, Damon was amazed at how much less grief he felt and how much calmer he had become. While he couldn't recall how many sessions he went through, he could tell that over a period of twelve months the time between sessions was becoming longer. After about one year, he felt confident that he no longer needed regularly scheduled appointments but that he would willingly come back if he felt he was going into a deep dark place again.

If acupuncture was a powerful tool for his well-being, what could be accomplished with horses? Could it help with their pain? Temperament? Difficult pregnancy? Age? Damon threw himself into learning as much as he could about horse acupuncture and what he would need to do to become a certified acupuncture therapist. It meant going back to school to get his bachelor's degree and a Doctor of Veterinary Medicine degree first. Besides getting his life back on track, getting a veterinarian degree would mean the security of his family's farm and its horses. With the added acupuncture certification, it also meant that he would have a unique marketable skill to sell to those families who didn't care how much it cost them to care for their prized horses.

Next, Damon went back to his coach and fought for a space on the team to get his scholarship back. With his newfound dedication, he also found his way back to UW-Madison's veterinary program and got his grades back to the upper 10 percent of his class. Once he graduated with his DVM, he completed a fellowship in Florida to learn the practice of acupuncture therapy on horses.

Two years after he graduated, his hard work and dedication paid off; Damon was now a successful equine acupuncturist only about thirty minutes away from the farm. He threw himself into his acupuncture therapy practice and was doing very well. So well, in fact, that he could afford a few of those high-end jeans that his clients wore, but his frugal upbringing just couldn't get him to cough up the dough.

To everyone else, he was back to his old happy-go-lucky self. He sang in a community choir and went out with his bros to the local pubs for a beer or two. His personality and the fact that he had a strong reputation for his business landed him a steady stream of young women to take out to dinner, the movies, or one of the many festivals in Milwaukee. When a woman started to think seriously about their relationship, though, he would smile and wish her well as he got in his truck and left.

Paige had torn something in his heart that wouldn't go back together. In eight years, he never once told anyone what he saw that night or why he was no longer with Paige, except for once to his best friend and business partner, Pete. His parents and his siblings tried to get it out of him at some point. They were very persistent, but Damon wouldn't budge. He was willing to go for acupuncture therapy and started going back to church but talking about his life with Paige was off-limits.

While his heart put up a fortress for human connections, it seemed to increase its capacity to connect with his equine patients. It was becoming more and more frequent that he could sense what was troubling the horse before its owner or trainer told him. Sometimes what the owner or trainer told him wasn't what he was getting from the horse. In those instances, he followed his instincts, and they were always on target.

While his three older siblings moved on and started their families and living their lives away from the farm, Damon and his two younger siblings still lived on the farm. The money he made from his practice helped pay off the mortgage, remodel some of the buildings, fix the fencing, and even remodel the family home. After a while, it was clear that he needed his own space, so he and his dad designed a new home and a pole barn that was turned into an onsite clinic so Damon could provide basic clinical care to the large animals. For anything more serious, they all agreed it was best to take them to the equine hospital. The location was great because he was still on the forty-acre homestead but far enough away from everyday family life that he could live his own life. He still enjoyed Sunday evening meals and occasionally went to church with the family, but he also needed his alone time.

His twelve hundred-square-foot two-story log home was built in such a way that the front of the house faced the rolling hills of the farm with Holy Hill in the distance. A covered porch was decorated with bright-red geranium pots hanging between the beams and on either side of the French doors. The doors had been a gift from his parents. They were originally a part of the first homestead built by his beloved grandfather. The rich oak doors were paneled with six 6-by-6-inch glass windows on both doors and aged bronze door handles. When the doors opened, you felt that you were entering a rustic yet classic home. The whole first level was rich with polished hickory floors dotted with warm-colored rugs placed throughout. On the left, the great room's chocolate leather sofa, love seat, and matching recliner provided the best views of the hills, and the fieldstone fireplace in the center hid the staircase. On the right of the open-floor plan was the dining room. Damon and Pat had spent many hours using old barn wood to build a suitable dining table and benches.

In the back of the first floor and across from the dining room was the kitchen. The countertops were made of soapstone and dropped into a large single-basin sink. The cupboards were simple single cherry raised panel with aged bronze drawer pulls and cupboard handles. His stainless-steel gas stove and French-door refrigerator rounded out the rest of the space. The first-floor full bath was set between the kitchen and a smaller room that was the perfect space to house a mudroom/laundry room. Completing the first floor was an alcove that worked as his office space.

Up the stairs were the master suite and bath. This was Damon's sanctuary from long days at work or overzealous girlfriends. The hickory floors continued from the staircase and into his room. A lush beige rug was placed underneath his king-sized missionary-style bed. It was made with solid oak and covered in an emerald-green down comforter with cream accent pillows. The master bathroom was tiled in cream with emerald-green accents. He had a supersized walk-in shower with a bench, and next to it was his favorite quiet place, a clawfoot bathtub that was long and deep enough to let him sink up to his chin in hot soapy water. Actually, he used this tub mostly to soak his sore muscles in foaming Epsom bath salts. Across from the master suite was a second bedroom used mostly for times when Pete had tied one on and needed a safe place to sleep it off before going home to his beautiful wife, Angie.

His routine was fairly simple. Get up at 6:00 a.m. on work mornings and have a quick hot shower to wake up. A hot cup of coffee and a three-egg scramble with whatever vegetables were on hand and he was out the door by 6:45 a.m. to get to work at 7:30 a.m. With the clinic opening by 8:00 a.m., it gave him a little time to get through emails and paperwork or an overnight patient. When the clinic closed at 6:00 p.m., depending on the night, he would work out at the gym for an hour, go on an evening date that started at 7:00 p.m., or take in a 7:10 p.m. baseball game with his buddies. As long as he was home by midnight at the latest, he could still get up the next morning and start the day without any trouble. On weekends when he didn't have to work, he tried to help out Mom and Da a little, especially with a new project or if something needed fixing. All in all, Damon was pretty happy about his uncomplicated life. As long as he steered clear of another heartbreak, he was as good as gold.

On this particular early Monday morning, Damon was still damp from his shower when he heard a horrible screech outside his front porch. He walked out of the kitchen and opened his front door to the same awful sound that seemed to be coming from the creek that ran through the property. Putting on his work boots, he set down his cup of coffee and started out toward the sound. As he did so, he looked up to see his da's truck coming down the gravel driveway to meet him.

"You heard it too?" Damon asked.

"Never heard anything like it. I was afraid one of the horses got stuck in the crick, but that's not a horse's cry." Pat jumped out of the truck and matched his son's gait toward the sound of an injured animal. He had brought his 22-caliber rifle with him just in case they couldn't help it or it was a dangerous animal that needed to be put down.

As they crept closer to the creek, they also heard some fluttering and saw the object of their concern. It was a mature whooping crane with a broken wing. It was trying to fly, but the wing was so damaged that it was inflicting more pain than helping itself get to a safer place and it was in danger being out in the open and vulnerable to the local coyotes that roamed this region. Damon crept near the bird and started to talk softly to it while Pat stood in front of it in case it would try to get away. Careful not to injure the crane further, Damon slowly removed his flannel coat and gently covered the scared animal. "Da, go back to my clinic and get a large crate; fill it with towels so we can transport it to the wildlife sanctuary. They're better equipped to handle it than the horse hospital."

Pat hightailed it back to Damon's place and quickly got together the necessary supplies to get the animal into a safe place for the thirty minutes or so they needed to get to the sanctuary. Putting the crate on the tailgate, Pat assisted Damon in delicately placing the crane into the crate and then used bungee cords to hold the crate in place so it wouldn't be knocked around while they drove to the center.

Driving as carefully as he could maneuver his truck, Damon took a little longer than usual. When they pulled into the parking lot, only one other vehicle was there, a SUV. Pat hopped out of the cab and quickly walked to the door. It was locked. He started to knock and yell, "Hello! Anybody in there? We've got an injured bird we need your help with!" A young woman with chestnut-brown hair unlocked the door and opened it up for Pat.

"Hi, I'm Cat. I'm the only one here right now. Dr. O'Brien should be here in a few minutes, but I can at least get you all started."

Chapter Three

Cat opened the door, noticing movement by the truck that had just entered their lot. "Need any help?" A second man appeared from behind the truck and stood before Cat. When she looked up, she found herself lost in the bluest eyes she'd ever seen before. They were so crystal clear that they looked as if she could see into them for miles. She caught her breath and then she stopped breathing. Her mouth opened wide and formed a silent "Oh!" She gained back her senses quickly enough to notice the man staring just as intently as she had been. The only difference was that he was carrying a very large bird in a crate.

"Um, no, I think I got it as long as you tell me where we should put it." Cat noticed he looked a little flustered and wondered if he wasn't used to being around animals. However, he had all the basic characteristics of being a farm boy: jeans, muddy work boots, truck, and a plaid shirt. "Did he just shake his head? Look at all that wavy red hair! He looks like a ginger lumberjack," Cat thought to herself. She realized that she was standing still although he had asked her where to put the bird down. "Sorry, let me take you to the exam room 3. That's where all the larger animals get to go." She turned around and briskly walked down the hallway to the largest exam room in the center. He gingerly set the crate on the exam table, then rested his arms on his thighs. After a deep breath and a shake of his head, he began to stand up straight and then looked straight through her.

"Thanks for opening up for us. I'm Damon and this here's my dad, Pat. I was just getting ready for work when I heard this god-awful sound near the crick and found this poor thing screeching away, trying to make its wing work. It is definitely broken, by the way.

Wah, wah, wah, wah …"

"Oh shit," Cat thought to herself, "he's trying to tell me something and I can't concentrate. I keep getting stuck looking at his eyes. Focus on his mouth. Focus." So she started looking at his mouth. His full lips were surrounded by more of that fascinating red hair and his teeth. Do men whiten their teeth? Oh wow, what that tongue could do to me … Suddenly, Cat realized that he had stopped talking, and she was beginning to have very naughty thoughts about a man she had literally just met no more than five minutes ago. Next, she heard another car drive up and saw the luxury vehicle that Rose drove and knew she needed to get it together.

"Listen, I am just the grant writer here. I don't know anything about fixing the animals, just how to raise the money for everyone else to do that. My boss, Dr. O'Brien, is coming in now. She should be able to help you." With that, Cat walked past the two men and almost right smack into Rose.

"What's going on, Catrina?" Cat knew Rose was perturbed because she was using Cat's formal name. Or perhaps it was so that Rose looked important and Cat was the underling?

"These two gentlemen found an injured whooping crane on their property this morning and brought it here to see if we could help it. Dr. O'Brien, this is Damon and Pat." Cat stepped out of the way and let Rose get closer to the two men.

Rose reached out her hand for formal handshakes, and when she got to Damon, she stopped and stared at him a bit and stalled in shaking his hand. "Damon, you look familiar. Have we met before?" she asked quizzically.

"I'm Dr. Damon MacGregor. I have an equine practice here, in Lake Country. Maybe we've run into each other at a conference or something," he offered with a slight smile.

Rose's eyes opened wider with recollection. "Yes! I remember going to one of the sessions at the national conference in Indiana a year or so ago and you presented on equine acupuncture! It was fascinating!" Rose was animated now, almost flirtatious. Cat knew it was time to get out of sight as Rose was going into high gear to promote herself and impress their guests.

"Yes, that was me. I'm glad you enjoyed it. It was my first time speaking at a conference and I was nervous, but the surveys that came back were full of great feedback. Maybe someday I'll present again." Damon caught Cat slinking down the hallway and wanted to make sure he could keep her around a bit longer. "Cat has been very helpful so far with our situation. You must be very proud of your staff." Cat turned around and looked right back into those blue eyes and stopped dead in her tracks. Was she imagining it or was he trying to get her attention?

"I'm so glad you ran into Catrina this morning. She certainly is one of the special ones." By the way that Rose inflected on the word "special," it didn't sound like she was giving Cat a compliment. Great, it was going to be one of those days, again. "Well, I can certainly help you from here. Why don't you come with me, Dr. MacGregor, and maybe you can help me stabilize the patient while Pat can go with Catrina to fill out our paperwork?"

As Damon followed Rose into the exam room, he looked back to see his dad walking with Cat, as if he had gotten the worst part of this deal. Cat led Pat to the registration area and got him started on the paperwork. "Pat, would you like a cup of coffee or water?" Cat offered.

"Coffee would be great. Thanks, Catrina." Pat's eyes were a softer color of blue, more like a cornflower blue than his son's, but they twinkled at Cat just the same.

"Please call me Cat. I go by Cat unless I'm in trouble." She smiled as she poured out coffee into a Styrofoam cup.

Pat looked up at her and crinkled his nose. "Hazel eyes, freckles on your nose, and a bit o' red in your hair. Don't suppose you have a bit of the Irish in you, lass?" Pat quizzed, laying his Irish accent a bit thick at the end.

Cat grinned, tilting her head toward him and squinting right back. "As a matter of fact, my mom's Irish, but my dad is Italian. So they compromised on the name. The story goes that my dad was making the case for my name to be Antonia Maria Carneri, but my mom had her heart set on an Irish name. Since she was very pregnant and very emotional, my dad couldn't handle the tears anymore, so he caved in."

Pat had a smug look on his face and replied, "Thought so. I've got a knack for picking the Irish out of almost anyone."

"Well, you certainly wouldn't have any trouble figuring out that your son was Irish. With all that wavy red hair, blue eyes, and pale skin, I'm surprised one of you isn't wearing a kilt," Cat remarked right back.

Pat chuckled. He recognized the spunk of an Irish lass, and he liked it. Perhaps there was a possibility that his son might find this lass to his liking and maybe finally settle down a bit and start making him a granddad again. Pat knew he had to have a bit of patience and not push his son too hard, but there was a moment when Damon had looked a little too long at her. Maybe there was something there after all.

After about thirty minutes, Damon came out, rolling down his shirt sleeves and sauntering over to where Pat and Cat were having a very animated conversation. Damon was almost a little jealous that his dad had got to spend more time with the pretty woman than he had gotten to do so far. With a tilt of his head, Damon interrupted them, "Well, well, Da, you do remember that you are a happily married man, father of six, and a grandfather. What would Ma say if she saw you flirting with a lovely young woman half your age?"

"Well, son, she'd probably say that it's good to see that I can still make a pretty girl smile, and if I can still flirt with a young woman, I can still flirt with the goddess herself anytime." Damon knew his dad could beat him in a game of wits. Damon bent his head down, shaking it, and put both his hands up to concede to the master of sass.

"And he wins again. I can never beat this guy." Damon walked over and punched his dad in the shoulder. Cat gave a full-out laugh, enjoying seeing the banter between the old and the young

MacGregors and really did feel special at being at the center of their verbal sparring. When Cat opened her eyes again, she noticed, for sure this time, that the younger MacGregor was seriously looking at her, and it was giving her the chills.

"Listen, I know that your organization works on donations. I'd like to make one in gratitude for what you'll be doing for that crane. Would it be okay to make one with my credit card?" Damon asked.

"Absolutely, Dr. MacGregor! I'll …"

"Please. Call me Damon. You helped me save that crane and have been shamelessly flirting with my dad; we're practically family now. Just call me Damon." There were those deep blue eyes again. Cat had to snap out of it and take care of business. Rose was coming out of the exam room and didn't look pleased with the little friendly group in the reception area.

"Okay, Damon. If you'd like to donate with a credit card, here is a tablet just fill out the information on the screen, and when you're prompted, slide your card with the magnet strip toward you. Let me know if you have any problems or questions. I'm happy to help." Cat's smile quickly left her face when Rose approached.

"Dr. O'Brien, Dr. MacGregor wants to donate to us. Isn't that wonderful?"

"Yes. Yes, it is. Dr. MacGregor, I know there are a lot of worthy organizations out there that you can support, but I don't think any of them will be as grateful as ours. Anytime you want to stop by and visit or if you'd like to volunteer, we'd be honored to have you here." Rose was laying it on thick, and it was starting to turn Cat's stomach. Had she eaten breakfast? She couldn't even remember. Now she was just praying that her stomach wouldn't make any noises while the adorable Dr. MacGregor was here and smiling at her. "Was he talking to her? Was Rose? Oh shit," Cat thought, "I'm not paying attention again!" She shook her head and started hearing words once again and tried frantically to keep up with the conversation and not look like she was out of it.

"Cat, can you look at this to make sure I did everything okay?"

"Sure can." With that, Cat walked around the registration desk to get closer to the tablet and to Damon. When she reached for the tablet, she accidentally brushed against his arm, and their fingers touched when he transferred the tablet to her for review. The connection was electric! He gave her shivers every time he touched her. That had never happened with any other man she was attracted to. Not even Jansen and she was with him for two years! She looked down immediately to refocus and to try and say something intelligent and look like she knew what she was doing. "Yes, Dr. MacGregor, everything looks great. We really appreciate your $500 donation! That will go a long way to help us buy things from our wish list." She refused to look up now because she needed to keep control of her emotions. She could feel the heat from Rose's eyes burning a hole in the back of her skull. She was going to pay for this, but Cat couldn't help it. It was clear she felt something for this man, and he was showing signs that he was interested in her too.

"Damon. Please just call me Damon. And you're welcome. You all do great and important work here. I'm glad you were here for us and this bird. I know horses. I don't know anything about birds, so you have saved a life this morning and I appreciate it." And he looked straight into her eyes when he said it.

"Well, Damon, thank you for your generous donation. You and your dad did a great job transporting the crane here, and I know that Dr. O'Brien will have no trouble getting it back on track to be released."

"Yes, Damon, as Catrina offered, we can't thank you enough for your generous gift and for bringing the crane to us when you did. She probably wouldn't have made it very long without her wing working. It was in bad shape, but I think she'll make it. Damon and Pat, thank you both. You did good work." With that, Rose extended her hand for formal handshakes to the men, and it was clear that it was time for them to go. They accepted her offer, turned around, and started out the door.

Then, just as some of the other staff were coming in through the opened door, Cat saw Damon spin around, reach into his pocket, and stretch out his strong, large hand to hers. "Would it be okay if I asked you to call me at work to let me know how the crane is doing and when you're releasing her? If I could, I'd like to be there." With that, Damon carefully put his business card in the palm of Cat's hand and lingered there just a moment longer than he needed to.

With a dry mouth, Cat focused hard at trying to say something kind of, sort of, coherent, "I'd be happy to." Damon flashed her one of those brilliant smiles that lit up his face, and, hey, wait a minute, did he have dimples?

The rest of the day went by in a blur. Rose was friendly to everyone else yet seemed to be on a warpath with Cat. Fortunately, her interaction with Damon earlier that day left Cat quite unfazed by Rose's contempt. By the time 4:00 p.m. came around, she was energized to grab her gear and go home.

It had been a little cooler and damp that morning, but the afternoon sun was beating down as Cat exited the building. She took off her cardigan and drove home in her pale pink cami and tan work pants. God, she couldn't wait to get home and get into some shorts. Maybe, after dinner, she and Mia could drive to Ottawa Lake and go swimming? It sounded like a plan.

By the time the thirty-minute drive was over, and she pulled into her driveway, she had calmed down a great deal. Cat even started thinking that that day's meeting with Dr. Mc … um, Damon, was just a nice business connection. What would a hunky veterinarian want to do with a simple grant writer? Nothing. She had just imagined all the sparks that she felt and his eyes staring at her. But she certainly hadn't imagined those eyes and those dimples. Wow.

She really did want to reach out and touch his face. She was so glad that she hadn't, especially in front of Rose. It would have led to an assassination—hers.

Cat didn't realize she was just sitting in her car when Mrs. Romansky came up to her dressed in her floppy gardening hat, white and pink gardening gloves, a pink pullover top, tan pants, and boat shoes. "Hello, Catrina. Are you all right?"

Cat shook her head a bit and turned to see her landlady with a very concerned look on her face. "I'm fine, Mrs. Romansky. Sorry to worry you. I was just thinking about something that happened at work today, and I guess I just lost track of what I was doing." Cat got out of the car, picked up her lunch bag, cardigan, and her purse, and started toward the back entrance. "Your flowers look beautiful today!" she called back, knowing that Mrs. Romansky's favorite pastime, besides watching *Wheel of Fortune*, was tending her flowers.

By the time she reached her landing, Cat could hear the tinkling of Mia's tags behind the door. She was grateful that with the day's heat, she'd thought ahead to close the windows and put on the air conditioner and fans to keep Mia cool in the flat. "Hello, baby girl! Did you miss me?" Hearing Cat's voice and seeing the door open, Mia's sleek black body shivered with excitement, and she had a bright green bouncy ball in her mouth as if to show it off. Cat reached down and gave Mia a back scratch before she went through her evening routine of feeding her dinner, topping off her water, and then taking her down the back steps for her after-work potty break. Once those three things were done, Mia was a little calmer and willing to let Cat get out of her work clothes and have a little dinner before they played together.

Due to the heat, Cat didn't feel all that much like making a meal, so she sliced up a beefsteak tomato on a plate and pulled out a fresh mozzarella roll that was already sliced. She placed a slice of cheese on each of the three tomato slices and then went over to her kitchen table where there was a little pot of fresh basil that was waiting for her to pull three leaves off their stems to make a caprice salad. On another plate, she sliced up a honey crisp apple and took out three squeaky cheese curds to go with that and, finally, a cranberry and walnut roll from the bakery in East Troy. She cracked open a cold water bottle from the fridge and sat down at the table to get some nourishment and start processing her day. Mia knew that when Cat sat down to eat, she wasn't allowed in the kitchen, so she picked up her green ball and walked back into the dining room to lie in waiting until dishes were cleared, and then she knew it was playtime in earnest.

With dinner cleared away, Cat put her hair up in a ponytail, threw on her blue swimsuit and boy shorts, grabbed two towels, a tennis ball, and Mia's leash and put them all in her beach bag to go to the lake. "Mia, let's go for a ride!" At that, the calm dog jumped up and scrambled down the stairs to wait by the back door of the SUV. Cat put the back windows down halfway to let Mia stick her nose outside while they drove the ten minutes to the state park.

The beauty of living in Mukwonago is that in thirty minutes or less you could get to Milwaukee, Illinois, or the Kettle Moraine Forest and state parks, trails, etc. She drove the windy roads through the forest that provided some shade in the heat. When she got to the park, the ranger saw her annual sticker on the left side of the window and waved her through. To the right of the ranger station was the campground where Cat's mom would take her and her younger brother, Ryan, camping on weekends when their dad had to work. To the left was access to state trails, the swimming beach, and the boat launch. Motorboats were not allowed on the lake, but people could bring their canoes and kayaks to paddle around the area. The boat launch was also the only place on the lake where dogs could swim. Cat found a spot to park, and because it was early in the week, the lot was empty. She put Mia in a heal so that she didn't have to use the leash and brought the beach bag to a nearby picnic table to set up their stuff. They both got to the water, and Mia was ecstatic with anticipation. She loved the water as much as she loved playing fetch with tennis balls. Put them both together, and she was a force to be reckoned with. Even though it was the peak of summer, there was still a coolness to the water that was very refreshing to Cat. She submerged till waist level and started the routine of throwing the ball into the open water and having Mia retrieve it. And so they played, again and again. After about an hour of this activity, Cat called Mia in, and they sat at the picnic table to catch their breath, have something to drink, and start the drying off process. Cat thought this might be a good time to talk to Mia about her day and see if she could come to any understanding about what she saw, how she felt, and what she should do next.

Cat spread out a large plaid blanket over the grass near the picnic table and started to lie down on her belly while Mia grabbed her tennis ball and lay right next to her with her tail wagging. "Miss Mia, I don't know what I'm going to do. I don't even know if I know how to tell you what happened today, but you are the keeper of all my secrets, so I must tell you. Don't I, girl?" With that, Cat propped herself onto her side and scratched Mia's back. Mia took this to mean that her belly was going to get a belly rub and proceeded to roll over and spread-eagled herself, letting her tennis ball drop to the blanket. Her bright white teeth showed in a grin while her pink tongue hung out of the side of her mouth.

"I got to work today, and this gorgeous guy and his dad brought a crane in with a broken wing. He was tall, with wavy red hair and the most amazing blue eyes! I couldn't stop staring at them." Cat had stopped scratching Mia's belly as she recalled her first meeting with Damon. Mia put her right front paw on Cat's arm to remind her she needed to continue with the belly rubs. "Oh, sorry, Sweetie. See what I mean? I got so distracted at work, and now I'm getting distracted just telling you about him!" Cat rolled her eyes back and started the belly rubs again.

After sharing all the little details of her day and her chance meeting, she looked Mia straight in her eyes and asked, "What should I do, Mia? I just got out of a really long relationship with an ugly break-up. Work is getting more and more difficult to manage with Rose's attitude toward me. I mean, if she were gone, I would love going to work every day. Everyone else is wonderful and she treats them pretty well, but there is something about me that just gets under her skin and I can't seem to make her happy no matter what I do. It's a decent salary and it's giving me great experience. I'm paying off all my bills on time and my rent. It's only been two years and I don't want to have to start looking for another job so soon after I started this one. But it feels like she's gunning for me. Like she wants me to leave or she will fire me. What should I do, Mia? What should I do?" Mia cocked her head, rolled over, and gave Cat a big sloppy kiss. Cat had been so serious that she was startled by Mia's action and started to laugh. "Maybe you're right. Just forget about it and enjoy the evening with my best friend." With that, they each took a short snooze in the shade, and when the mosquitoes started to come out, Cat packed up the blanket and the rest of their gear into the beach bag while Mia walked beside her carrying her prized tennis ball in her mouth. Nothing had been decided and yet Cat felt better for venting. Maybe Mia was right; just take it one day at a time for now and enjoy the good moments when they come.

By the time they got home, clouds started to roll in, and the wind picked up. Just as she put the SUV into the garage, large drops of rain started to fall from the sky. She and Mia quick-stepped to the back door and got into the stairway before the deluge let loose. Mia took her tennis ball and lay on her bed while Cat prepared a bath and started getting clothes out for the next day. She then arranged the fixings for a packed lunch. Hmm, tomorrow looks like a food shopping day, and good news! The farmer's market would be in Field Park in the afternoon! Fresh produce, squeaky cheese, and kettle corn. Sweet!

Cat shed her damp clothes and took the ponytail holder out of her hair while walking across the hall to check her running bath-water. Perfectly warm, and the bubbles from the foaming Epsom salts popped to her touch. She gingerly crept into the clawfoot tub and sighed as the warm water and bubbles sluiced over her skin. She closed her eyes and rested for a minute before beginning her routine of lathering up and then letting the water out so she could kneel down and wash her hair over the drain.

With her eyes closed, Cat's mind began to wander back to that gorgeous young vet. She thought about how it would feel to bring her fingers to his temples and draw her fingers through his hair. Then she imagined his smile and those dimples. The way his beard and mustache perfectly framed his full pink lips and white teeth. She started to think about how it would feel to bring her face close to his and touch her lips to his. What would they taste like? Would he open his mouth and let her feel the intimate way his tongue would push past her teeth and into her mouth to intertwine with hers? Would his ice blue eyes watch her as they kissed, or would he close them and get lost in the moment? Where would his hands be? She decided that they would be on her hips and slowly bring her body closer to his, so her breasts would be pressed against his chest. His hands would wriggle underneath her shirt and glide up her back to her bra clasp and expertly unsnap it with one hand. Then they would follow the curve of her rib cage and the palms of his hands would rest lightly under her heaving breasts while his thumbs would begin making a circular motion around her nipples. Her nipples would respond immediately to his touch and grow taut and achy, wanting more from him. Just then, her phone began to ring. The ringtone brought her out of her heady daydream and back to reality. "Shit! It's Mom!" Cat clumsily got out of the tub, drenching the mat on the floor while making waves in the tub.

As quickly as she could, she ran to her room where her phone was charging and picked up. Breathlessly she answered, "Hello?"

"Hi, Sweetie, it's Mom."

"Yeah, I figured. I got that ringtone for both of us, remember?"

"I keep forgetting. Of course, you knew it was me. I'm not keeping you from anything, am I?"

"No, Mom. I'm just getting ready for tomorrow. Why? What's up?"

"Well, I know how crazy it is for all of us to get together sometimes, so I thought I'd let you know that I got all of us our state fair tickets. I know it's a month away, but I was thinking that maybe you and Ryan would be able to give me a couple of dates that work for you two and we could plan our annual family trip to the fair."

"How about if I text you some dates? You caught me in the bathtub, so I am not able to get you those dates right now."

"Ooh! So sorry, Munchkin. I didn't know. Yeah, just text me those dates, and I'll get back to you on the final plan."

"Sounds perfect, Mom. Thanks for setting this up. Can't wait." "I know, right! So excited about the fair! Will you be my date for the *Kids From Wisconsin*?"

"Wouldn't miss them for the world. Love you, Mom!"

"Love you too, Cat." With that, they hung up, and Cat started the process of finishing up her nightly routine.

Feeling refreshed and ready for the next day, Cat looked at her color-coded calendar and texted her available dates to her mom.

In the Carneri family, there were certain things that were absolute: Christmas Eve, which included taking the first candy cane off the Christmas tree and piling in the family car to go and see Christmas lights before opening presents, and the state fair. The story that Cat's mom, Claire, would share with newbies to the family was that when she was fourteen, her parents divorced, and her mom moved the family to Milwaukee to be closer to her own family for support. Without much money, her mom found a way to take them to the fair for the first time, and it was magical. Claire had never seen anything like it before. It was like its own little city with street signs and vendor booths selling everything from beer and corn on the cob to woks and hammocks. The people-watching was tremendous! And the food … everything you could imagine was deep-fried or on a stick! What was even better was that there were ways to get into the fair and to eat and drink for free. The entertainment was included except for the main stage and the rides, but they always had a coupon or a deal that could help them have a few rides at least.

Since that year when Claire was fourteen, she hadn't missed a state fair since. Even if it was only for a few hours, she found a way to make it there. The closest call to not getting to go was when Ryan was born. He was born in summer, during fair time. Because of jaundice, he had to be under a pediatric nurse's care until he was cleared, the last day of the fair. Claire and Anthony packed up their young family. Cat was eighteen months old and Ryan was only one week old when their family made it to the fair on that very last day. Ryan had only been the size of a football, but the family tradition was born. It didn't matter how busy they all would get, everyone found at least four hours that they could carve out of their schedule in the first two weeks of August to go to the fair together. Cat was the only member of the family who had missed a fair or two, but that was because she went to school in Montana and had summer internships. Now that she was back in Wisconsin, she made it a point to make this time to be with her family. Who knew? Maybe a family get-together would be just what she needed to get her head screwed on straight again and stop making up romantic dreams about men she didn't even know.

After Cat had gotten into her sleep tank top and boy shorts, she looked out the window and saw that the rain had slowed down a bit. A good time to wake up Mia and get her outside for one last potty break before bed. When she opened the door to the backyard, she felt a cool breeze hit her face, which she had not felt when she had arrived home just a few hours before. Relieved that the humidity was going away, she smiled and called Mia back into the house before the mosquitoes noticed she was there.

Mia crawled up the back steps and snuggled down into her bed. Cat reached down to scratch her between the ears and was rewarded with a doggy kiss before Mia laid her head on her front paws to go to sleep. Cat checked her alarm and made sure that everything was ready for the next day before she climbed into her bed and under her cotton sheets. Even though it was summer, Cat always needed at least a light sheet on to feel safe and snuggly enough to go to sleep. Tomorrow would be a new day, and everything would be back to normal. Hopefully.

Chapter Four

Damon found it hard to concentrate at work. He found that he was antsy when he got home. Couldn't figure out what he wanted for dinner and didn't want to go and eat at the family house because then he would see his dad who would grill him about the beautiful grant writer that he couldn't stop thinking about. It was stupid really; there were a lot of women out there with nice smiles and great hair. But she was different somehow. Her eyes just locked into his, and he couldn't stop looking at all the different colors that were in them. Flecks of green, brown, and gold were everywhere! When he finally pulled his focus from her eyes, he noticed her hair. How thick it was, how she had it back in one of those ponytail holder thingies, and it seemed to hold another set of fascinating colors for him to focus on. Browns, golds, reds, it was like all his favorite autumn colors in one beautiful place. He started to imagine how it would feel to pull out the ponytail holder and run his fingers through her hair. Maybe it would feel like silk strands falling around his hands. Like silk ties that could be used to tie her soft hands to bedposts so that he could leisurely touch and kiss all the fascinating parts of her body that he couldn't stop obsessing about.

Damon decided to take one of the horses for a run and see if a bit of exercise would get him back on track. It's not that he didn't like women. He loved them. But since Paige, he had never felt like he couldn't stop thinking about any one of them. This girl, though, it just wasn't her soft curves and freckles on her nose; it was the way that she bantered with his dad. It was the way she didn't freak out when they brought the bird in. How she stayed calm and found a way to calm them down as well. It was the whole damn package.

Damon changed out of his work clothes and boots and put on his riding gear. It was hot out, so he needed to get into short sleeves, worn-out jeans, and his riding boots. Damon walked down to the stables and found his Western-style saddle, a riding pad, and bridle and walked on over to the most spirited horse on the farm, Butters.

Butters was a silly name for a gelding, but when his dad bought the horse for a steal, it was from a silly woman who thought riding horses would be more glamorous than it was. Butters was named for the beautiful color of its mane and tail. That creamy white that left you wondering if it was white with a hint of yellow or yellow with a hint of white in it. He was a Palomino with caramel-colored hair over the rest of his muscular body. He was a gorgeous horse and also very proud. He'd cost that woman a pretty penny, but she had been going through a nasty divorce by the time she found his dad and was willing to take a hefty cut in her losses to get rid of him. All horses have a unique personality. Added to that, some are strong. Others are fast. However, Butters excelled in all three categories, so it was always a good idea to have your wits about you when you were around him because the minute you lost focus, Butters would do something to knock your block off.

Nevertheless, Butters was exactly what the doctor ordered that night. Damon needed to get his mind off that woman. What was her name again? Catrina? No, she preferred Cat, he recalled as he smiled to himself. Damn, she was on his mind again.

Once Butters had his hooves cleaned and his gear on, Damon led him to the outdoor area to warm him up a bit. After one or two walking laps around the arena, Damon started to work with Butters on some of the skills he had learned when he was a show horse—walking backward, sidestepping, walking over obstacles, etc. When Damon felt that Butters was warmed up enough, he jumped off the horse and led him out of the arena and onto one of the horse trails through the rolling hills of the Kettle Moraine.

They started on the trail, and Butters tried to take control of the situation by stopping and reaching over to nibble on some fresh foliage. Damon wouldn't have any of it and made the split decision to run Butters in the pasture to show him who's boss and maybe run off a little of his own adrenaline built up over the last twelve hours. It was an incredible rush for Damon, and it was an incredible view for anyone who would be watching the two strong males locked together in a dance of strength and speed. Butters at full gallop was as smooth as a bullet train with his mane and tail coursing in the breeze they created together. The gelding's flanks were rippling with each stride, and the veins in his neck pulsed with every stretch of the lanky muscles in his neck. Damon matched Butters with intensity and drive. The breeze swept through his auburn hair to make it look like the flames of red-hot fire. His arms and neck tightened so that his veins were popping out with every hoof landing. Damon's eyes squinted in an intense focus that looked as if he were running through hell with the devil on his heels.

After the intense ride through the pasture, Damon slowed the pace a bit and let Butters trot to the creek where just a few hours before he had found the injured crane. Butters took the direction well, and they both slowed their breathing and relaxed their muscles while they followed the meandering creek toward the hills. At the foot of the hills, Damon found a path back to the main trail again and guided Butters onto the wooded path for a more relaxed ride.

With the rhythm of the horse's feet clopping along the softened dirt path, Damon got into a little bit of a transcendent state. Though his eyes were open, he really wasn't seeing the world around him. Instead, the rocking rhythm brought him back to thinking about her. He wanted to know more about Cat. Did she have someone, or was she single? What kind of music did she like? What kind of food did she like to eat? Did she come from a big family or was she an only child? Did she get along with her parents? Did she find him just as interesting as he found her? Would she go out on a date with him? Let him hold her hand? Kiss her? Ask her out again? Just then Butters reared up onto his hind legs and shocked Damon out of his stupor. Luckily, Damon was an experienced rider, and while he did lose his balance for a moment, he could right himself and get both feet back into their stirrups while being able to hold onto the reins with both hands. "Butters, what the shit??" The spirited horse looked back at Damon as if to say, You better keep your wits about you today. I just won this battle.

The two males spent a few more minutes out in the woods until the mosquitoes made it difficult to enjoy the ride much longer. After Damon guided Butters into the stables, he got off the horse, took off the bridle, and put the on the harness before clipping the guides onto the halter to begin the chore of cooling down and cleaning up the horse. Knowing that a bag of fresh bunch of hay was tied up in the stall, Butters was impatiently waiting for this routine to end so he could eat, drink, and be alone again. Damon felt the horse's intentions and verbalized them to confirm he knew what the horse was thinking. "I know you want to get to your food and get a nice cool drink. The quicker you let me brush you down and clean out your hooves, the sooner you get to eat and drink, buddy. By the way, thanks for a great ride tonight. I really needed it. Didn't appreciate you trying to get me off your back, though, but you did help get me back on track again." With that, Damon reached over into the bushel basket of apples his parents always left in the barn as a treat for the horses. Damon picked one and cut it into half as a treat for Butters. "You did good, Butters. Thanks."

Butters looked into Damon's eyes and then nudged his hand to get to that sweet, juicy apple. After the snack was over, Damon unclipped the guides and brought Butters to his stall and carefully removed the bridle before closing and locking the stable door. Butters immediately bent his neck down to get to the fresh pale of cool water that Damon had placed in his stall. After a few deep drinks, the horse raised his head and walked over to the stall door to put his nose through the bars. Damon reached out and stroked Butters' caramel-colored nose, and both males looked straight into each other's eyes. This time, it wasn't a test of wills. This time the look conveyed that they respected each other and had each other's back.

Back at his house, Damon reached down to pull off his boots and leave them on the rubber mat in the laundry room/mudroom. Stripping down to his boxer shorts, he threw the sweaty clothes into the washing machine along with the rest of the colored clothes that needed to be cleaned. After starting the laundry, he reached into the refrigerator and pulled out a frosty bottle of beer, used the bottle opener magnet on his refrigerator to open the bottle, and proceeded to take a very long and thirsty drink. By the time he put the bottle down, two-thirds of it was gone. He looked at his cell phone on the kitchen counter, and the red light was flashing. He had a voice message. After thinking about it for a moment, Damon decided he just wasn't in the mood to talk to anyone else today. He was hot, sweaty, and exhausted. Once he drank the rest of his beer, he set the empty glass bottle into the sink and walked upstairs to take a long shower.

Damon let the hot "rapid pulse" from his showerhead beat the tiredness out of his achy muscles while the steam rid his mind of all thoughts of her. His muscles were aching after such a hard ride. But instead of forgetting that long-legged woman with the soft curves and sexy smile, he started to think about what it would be like to have her join him in the shower and what it would feel like to have her nimble fingers work suds up his entire body. How it would feel for him to take the slippery soap in his hands, lather up, and begin the slow process of lathering up her perfectly round breasts, making her nipples hard, then reaching around the back and grabbing her heart-shaped ass before lifting her up so that those long, luscious legs would wrap around him and … "Damn!" Now he had a hard-on that hurt like hell and no woman in the shower to take care of it. Since the hot water was just making everything worse, Damon turned on the cold water instead. "Fuck!!!" That did the trick. Now he just had to rinse off as fast as he could before his prick shriveled up and died.

After toweling off, Damon was in a worse mood than he was when he had come home. Maybe it was hunger? At the thought of food, his stomach reacted with a growl that could be heard out of the confines of the bathroom. He put on a clean pair of boxers and ran his fingers through his hair; then he walked back downstairs to see if there were any leftovers that could make him a decent meal. A look in the frig revealed two brats, sauerkraut, and sliced potatoes and onions leftover from a cookout at the family house. Good enough. Putting the brats and the potatoes and onions onto a plate, he microwaved them while he cracked open another bottle of beer and got the brat buns sliced and ready to go. Once dinner was ready, he brought the beer and plate over to the leather recliner and turned on the television. He looked through the sports channels, and then he found a baseball game and started watching that until his phone went off. Looking at the display, he knew it was his mom. If he didn't answer it, she'd just continue to ring. "Hey, Mom. What's up?"

"Damon, your dad told me about that crane you found this morning. I know that I had seen a pair of them on our property a week ago, and I'm concerned about how the other one is doing without its mate. Tomorrow I'm having your dad go back down to the crick to make sure there isn't a nest with a baby or another injured bird on our hands. Could you call the sanctuary or stop by to check on the one with the broken wing? You know how I get when I know an animal has been hurt."

Damon did know his mom. She'd hound him until she was certain that the bird was doing okay and in a safe place. While he didn't want to get that close again to Cat, he knew his mom would never let up until he did go there in person and check on that bird. She was Irish and Catholic. She could nag God himself until he'd think about leaving heaven just for some peace and quiet. "Yeah, sure, Mom. I'll cut out of work early tomorrow and see how it's doing. Okay?"

"Sounds perfect, baby. Thank you. Now I can have a good night's sleep. Love you, baby."

"Love you too, Mom."

When Heather MacGregor hung up the phone, she looked straight into her husband's eyes and smiled. "It's done. He'll stop by tomorrow afternoon to check on the bird."

"You are one devious person, Mrs. MacGregor. I'm so glad I married you instead of scorning you." With that, Pat kissed his wife's smiling lips.

"Of course, I could get him to see her again. I'm his mom. I can get any man in this family to do what I want and when I want them to do it. It's my gift." With that, Heather lifted her right eyebrow, and the once smug smile turned into a sensuous smile that had strong meaning behind it.

"Yes, you can, luv, and I know exactly what you want me to do to you right now." Pat took the hand of his lovely bride of forty years and led her to their master bedroom so that he could show her exactly how much he loved her.

The next day wasn't as bright and sunny as the day before, but the humidity was still enough to make Damon keep the windows up and put on the air-conditioning in his truck. He blared country music on the radio as he weaved through traffic to get to work. He was in a foul funk, and the horns honking at him just added to his mad mood. It was hump day, so once this day was over, he only had to get through the next two days and then he could maybe get away for the weekend. Camping, maybe? Fishing?

By the time he got to work, he was focused on just getting through the day so that he could get the visit to the wildlife sanctuary over with. While he thought he was being effective and time-efficient, his co-workers noticed a huge change in his attitude. When he was questioned, he laid into them until they left cowering. At 1:00 p.m., his best buddy and partner, Pete Rossi, pulled him aside and said, "Dude, what's up with you? You're growling at everyone, and you made little Mary cry a bit."

"Mary always cries, unless she's talking about *Dancing With the Stars*."

"Seriously, what's going on? You are definitely off your game today. You always come in here with a smile and a joke. You are the happy-go-lucky guy and the one who calms the horses down when no one else can. Now they are even sensing your agitation." Pete's dark eyes looked into Damon's blue ones and saw something that made sense. "It's a woman, isn't it? Did you get dumped? Did she turn you down?"

"No, it's nothing like that. It's that I just met her yesterday, and I can't stop thinking about her. You know about that crane I dropped off at the sanctuary?" Pete nodded his dark curly head. "Well, she works there. As a grant writer. She just took me by surprise, is all. I haven't thought about a woman like this since …"

"Since Paige."

"Yes! And it's pissing me off! Now my mom wants me to stop by there again today after work, so I can check on the damn bird because, you know how she is, she has to make sure it's doing okay otherwise she can't sleep." Damon was pacing and running his hands through his hair as he was talking.

Pete nodded his head in silence because he knew about Paige and what it had done to his friend. After a work outing to a basketball game, they ended up walking to a nearby sports bar and grill for a few beers, and that's when Damon opened up about his whole messy break-up, how it messed him up, and now his philosophy of dating only, no relationships. "Look, I get it. But Paige was a long time ago, and not all girls are like Paige. Look at my Angie. She's as sweet as they come, and as soon as I saw her, I knew I was hooked. You know I was a player back in the day, but once Angie came into my life, I couldn't stop thinking about her. I couldn't wait to marry her, so I didn't have to worry about any other guy making a move. Now she's having a baby, and I can't stop thinking about being a dad. It's crazy, but I love my life. Look, just take it one step at a time. Get the hell out of here because you are scaring the shit out of our staff and the horses are edgy when you're around. Go to the sanctuary, check on the damn bird, and ask her out for a cup of coffee. That's it."

"What if she's dating someone else?"

"Then go to the bar, and I'll meet you there for a beer and we can shoot the shit."

Damon looked at his friend and saw the concern in his eyes. "What if she's not?" he said quietly.

"If she's not dating someone else, then ask her if she'd like to meet over a cup of coffee. Who knows? Maybe you've built her up in your mind, and after an hour in the coffee shop, you'll find out she annoys the hell out of you.

"And if she isn't annoying? If I find her completely fascinating?" Damon looked like a lost puppy at his friend, his best friend.

"Then you ask her out on a date. A real date. During coffee, find out what her interests are, where she likes to go, and then ask her out. You've done this many times before, with lots of women. You know the drill."

"Pete."

"Yeah."

"She's not like any of the women I've dated before." "I know, buddy, I know."

After he finished writing up the notes on his patients, Damon handed off the transcriptions to one of the vet techs, shed his white lab coat, and walked out the door. The drive to the wildlife sanctuary was a long one. He kept replaying the scene of what he would say to Cat once he walked in the door. Would he play it cool and aloof? Would he take a page from Pete's playbook and stun her with a corny pickup line? Tell a joke? Why didn't anything sound right? And why was it so much easier with the other women he asked out? Simple, she made him feel something. While he didn't know what just yet, she did make him feel again, and that scared the shit out of him.

With that realization, he noticed he was already pulling into the parking lot. He looked at the time, and it was 3:00 p.m. Damon looked into the rearview mirror, ran his fingers through his hair, and checked his face to make sure he didn't have any leftover crumbs or anything stuck in his beard. Climbing out of his truck, he double-checked that his shirt was buttoned correctly, and his pants were zipped up—nothing more embarrassing than having a serious conversation with someone and your zipper was down the whole time. Not that that had ever happened to Damon before … When it seemed, he couldn't waste any more time outside, he took a deep breath and walked toward the door to the lobby.

Once through the door, the air-conditioning hit him and took his breath away, again. After a brief pause to get his confidence back, he took two long strides to the reception desk. A nice-looking young blonde receptionist looked up at him and her jaw fell open. Damon smiled; even scared shitless, he still had it. She finally got her wits about her and asked, "Can I help you?"

"Yes, I'm Dr. MacGregor, and I was wondering if Cat was working today? She helped me and my dad with a crane that broke its wing on our property." The young blonde blinked a few times, and that seemed to get her to break the trance she had been in since Damon walked in. Just then, Cat walked up to the reception desk wearing jade green glasses and her hair up in a messy bun with tendril curls falling all around her face. Damon noticed that today's shirt color was also green under a cream-colored short-sleeved cardigan and a matching cream-colored pencil skirt with nude pumps. She reminded him of a sexy librarian. All she needed to do was to drop a pencil and slowly reach down to pick it up with her backside facing him, so he could enjoy the view of her heart-shaped ass.

"Shelli, I'm going to be putting letterhead in the printer, okay? I've got to get the thank-you letters out for the last few days' worth of donors for Rose's signature before she leaves on vacation." Oblivious to Damon, she did him the favor of turning around and bending over to place the letterhead into one of the lower trays of the machine. Damon automatically switched his focus to the curvy backside in front of him and found that he was tilting his head to get a better view.

When the letters were printed, Cat stood up, turned around, and found him with his head still cocked, a crooked smile across his face. "Can I help you?" she asked, annoyed to find a man staring at her behind. Damon snapped out of it, stood straight up, and looked straight into those eyes that had mesmerized him the last time he was here.

"Hello, Cat, I'm just checking in to see how the crane is doing. I promised my mom and dad that I would stop by after work."

It was now Cat's turn to be surprised because once he stood straight up, she stopped breathing, and her eyes grew wider as she slowly raised her head to look into those amazing blue eyes again.

"The crane. The crane." Come on, Cat! Think! He's trying to have a conversation with you. Answer him before he thinks that you are mute. "Oh yes! The crane! Dr. O'Brien did a great job of splinting the broken wing and cleaning her up. Today we've been able to get her to eat and drink a bit, which will help with the healing process. Her pain also seems to be managed, so it was good that you got her in when you did. Thank you." As she looked into those pools of crystal-clear blue, she remembered that one of the letters she had was his thank you for his donation. "Oh! If you could wait just a moment more, I'll have Rose, I mean Dr. O'Brien, sign your thank-you letter for your gift, and then I can give it to you before you leave."

"Glad to hear about the crane, and yes, I can wait around for a few moments." With that, Cat scrambled out of the reception pod and down one of the hallways and out of sight. Shelli smiled at Damon, sat up a bit straighter, and offered him a seat in the waiting room. After what seemed like an eternity, Cat came back with the letter and walked right up to him, so he could catch a whiff of her scent, vanilla with a hint of lavender. Mmmm.

"Here you go, Dr. MacGregor. Thanks again for your generosity. We really appreciate it." Cat held out her hand with an envelope, which he accepted, and then kept her hand out for a handshake, which he gratefully obliged. Anything to touch her again and see if those sparks were still there or a figment of his imagination. Just as he touched his fingertips to the palm of her hand, he felt all tingly as if his hand and arm were going to sleep. Cat looked down at their locked hands as if she felt something too.

"Please, call me Damon. You were kind enough to open the center for us before it was supposed to. The least I can do is thank you for your help. Would it be okay to treat you to a cup of coffee for your trouble? Do you have plans after work today?"

Cat was struck dumb. Was he asking her out? What should she say? What did she want to say? "Coffee? Umm, I don't drink coffee." She saw his smile fall off his face. Shit! She was doing this wrong. How could she fix this? "What I mean to say is, there is this cute coffee shop in town. I don't drink coffee, but they serve tea and I do drink tea. Would that be okay?"

Damon's smile went back on his face, bigger than it was before. Yes! "Perfect. What time do you get off? I can meet you there when it works best for you. My workday is over, and I'm not on call tonight."

Cat looked at the digital readout on the desk phone. "I'm off in thirty minutes. Why don't you head on out now and I can meet you there? There are several fun stores you can browse not too far from the coffee shop, like The WeatherVane Gift Shop."

"Sounds like a plan. Here's my cell number on my business card in case you're running late." Damon reached into his pocket and pulled out a card and handed it to her. This time, Cat gently took it, careful not to touch his hand, he noticed. Then he looked up and over at Shelli, who seemed to be gawking at them. He nodded his head. "Nice to meet you, Shelli." Turning around, Damon planned each footfall and silently talked himself through opening the door. Once outside, he let out his breath in relief. He felt like he had just passed his medical boards! Hopping inside his truck, he googled coffee shops in Oconomowoc, and headed on out toward their rendezvous location. For the first time in twenty-four hours, Damon felt excited, almost happy.

In just a few short minutes, taking Highway 67 to Wisconsin Avenue, he found the rustic chic storefront. Lovingly restored cream city brick and exposed beams framed the quaint establishment. Local art adorned the walls while black iron-framed gray wooden tables and chairs were strategically placed throughout the space. Damon looked at his phone for the time and noticed she'd be leaving work in about ten minutes. Since he had a few spare moments and didn't want to get antsy waiting for her, he took Cat's advice and drove to Oconomowoc where he found a local bookstore, Books & Company. He hadn't browsed a book shop in ages. Suddenly, he got that happy feeling again, the excitement brought about by the possibility of finding a new book and bringing it home. In the front window was a book he had heard about and was even made into a movie a few years ago, *A Walk in the Woods*, by Bill Bryson. It sounded like it would be a perfect summer read. He reached for his wallet and paid for his purchase, noticing that he still had a minute or two before she would be showing up at the coffee shop.

As he was leaving the bookstore, Damon saw Cat slide out of the driver's side door of her SUV her skirt riding up to mid-thigh. Once her feet hit the ground, her luscious legs were again respectfully covered. Cat took a clip or pin out of her hair and shook it so that all the curls bounced out of their confinement and landed softly on her shoulders, each one highlighting different colors in the autumn spectrum. He was in awe of how naturally beautiful she was and how oblivious she seemed to be of her beauty. After shutting the door to the SUV, Cat looked around and caught Damon's eyes. Her whole face lit up when she smiled and her nose crinkled a bit. She moved off the street and onto the sidewalk to meet up with him. "I see you found the place okay."

"Yeah, and thanks for recommending that gift shop. I found a book that I've wanted to read."

"Really? That's great. What book is it? I am always interested in reading new books."

"*A Walk in the Woods* by Bill Bryson."

"I love that book! My parents own the movie. It's a bit different from the book, but it's a family classic."

Damon smiled. This might be easier than he thought. With that, Damon walked up to the door and held the door open for Cat. She strolled up to the register, and he followed behind her. "I'll have a medium chai tea with skim milk, please."

"I'll have a medium latte, please." He paid for their drinks and waited on the other side of the bar to bring them over to the table that Cat found near the front windows.

"Thanks," she said as she took the cup from his hand. Sipping it carefully, she put it down and looked at him for a moment. "You know, you didn't have to do this. It's my job to help out when new animals come, as well as take donations."

"I figured. It's just … ."

"It's just what?"

Damon looked at his hands when he started to answer her, "It's just that I wanted to see you again." As he finished, he slowly looked up at her to see what kind of reaction he was getting. Her eyes got as big as saucers, and her mouth was open into a small "o." "Is that okay?"

"Oh. Yes. I'm glad you did." Cat's eyes changed now from a look of shock to a happier look that included a very soft smile. "If I'm honest, I was thinking about, I don't know, seeing if I could hand-deliver the thank-you letter so I could see you again." She looked sheepishly up over her glasses. "I just wish you'd picked a day when I wasn't wearing my glasses. This morning my eyes were acting wonky and wouldn't let my contacts go in."

"I don't mind your glasses at all. In fact, I noticed right away that your top matched the frames. You look really good in green. If you don't mind me saying so."

Cat blushed. "Thanks, I guess." She looked back into his face and thought she'd better get all the facts right out into the open. No need to get involved with someone and then find out there are skeletons in the closet or worse you aren't the only relationship he's having. "Damon, are you seeing anyone at the moment?"

"Ah, straight shooter. I'm relieved. I don't like playing games with my family, friends, or anyone I am seeing, which, as it happens, is no one at the moment. You?"

"Nope. I just got out of a two-year relationship that ended on a very sour note. Ergo why I am now, as you say, a straight shooter."

Damon nodded to himself. So, she got hurt by a player. Idiot. She's not the type of woman a man could fool around with. She's the type you keep. "Sorry. We aren't all that way. I had a serious relationship, once. Eight years ago. It ended badly, and I promised myself that honesty was the best policy. So, no, I am not in a relationship. My last date was a week ago, and I don't plan on calling her back."

"I'm glad," Cat said as she smiled sheepishly. "What do you think of this place and your latte?"

"I like how they marry the raw wood with the black metal. It's similar to how I designed and built my home, although the art isn't quite my style." Damon smiled back.

"So, you designed and built your house? Wow! That's impressive. My dad and brother are passionate about woodworking and making furniture from scratch, but they didn't build a whole house. Where do you live?"

"On a horse farm in the town of Erin. My parents own the farm, and I built my house on their land." Damon took a moment to assess her reaction to the fact that he lived so near his parents—a little surprised, but it didn't look like she would bolt any time soon. Wonder how she would react when she realized he had five brothers and sisters. "What about you? Do you live out here?"

"Not really. I was born in Wauwatosa, but since I was about two years old, my family and I have lived in Mukwonago. My parents still live in the same house in the town, and I rent an upper flat of a bungalow in the village. Not too far away and yet not too close either. My brother still lives with Mom and Dad, but he's saving up for a place of his own. Do you have any brothers and sisters?"

"Here it comes," Damon thought. Better just get it all out in the open now and see how freaked out she'll get. "Yes. I'm the middle of six kids. The oldest three live off the farm and on their own. The youngest two, the twins, still live with my parents in the family house. They help out around the farm when they're not in school." Damon looked for signs to assess how she was feeling about all this open and honest conversation. So far it looked like she was genuinely interested in what he had to say and was taking it all in.

"So, working with horses must be in your blood. But why acupuncture? That is such a niche; not many vets practice that kind of medicine. What got you interested in that?"

Boy, she's good. Really good. Get it all out in the open and then decide if his skeletons were worth the time and energy. Okay, here it goes. "Remember when I told you I had a relationship eight years ago? Well, that break-up messed me up pretty bad, and I couldn't get myself out of the funk. My mom was really worried about me, so she told me about how acupuncture works for anxiety and depression in many people and being a guy, the selling point was that I didn't have to talk about my feelings to anyone. I was tired of moping around all the time, and I wanted to get better. I just didn't know how to do it, so I said yes. My mom found this nurse through family friends. It sounded legit and worth a try. After the first treatment, it was like the dark and dreary sky just opened up, and the most amazing sunrise was breaking through the clouds. The best part was that I didn't have to talk to someone I didn't know about feelings that were so personal. I couldn't even tell them to people who cared about me." Damon took a deep breath and looked for signs from Cat as to how she was taking all this in. This was turning into a very heavy coffee date. The funny thing was, though, he didn't mind sharing this stuff with her. It was like he was compelled to share himself with this woman.

Cat leaned back in her chair, took a deep sip of her chai tea, and stared at him for a moment. Carefully, she placed her cup on the table and leaned forward on her forearms. "Unbelievable."

"What is? That I live so close to my family? That I don't like to talk about my feelings? Or that I tried acupuncture?"

"No. Not those things. It's just … it's just that I use acupuncture myself. Do you happen to remember the name of the nurse that you went to eight years ago?"

Damon had to think a little bit. "I think her name is Cathy. She could speak with a Chinese accent. It was crazy!"

Cat shook her head. "Unbelievable. Her name is Cathy Dejewski. She was my acupuncturist too until she retired." This time Damon sat back in his chair, cocked his head, and squinted his eyes.

"Are you kidding me?" Was she making fun of him or was this an amazing coincidence?

"Totally serious. I don't kid about acupuncture. It saved my life. When I was younger, I had migraines regularly, and nothing could touch them. Then, one day at the office, my mom heard from a co-worker how their daughter's migraines were improving after acupuncture. So, she brought me home the information. We talked about it and thought it was worth a shot. We started going to Cathy with a 'what have I got to lose' attitude. I left after the first appointment scared shitless about what had just happened. Cathy told my mom to just pay attention to how I feel and call her with an update in a couple of weeks. She said that if nothing improved, I didn't have to go back. Well, I went a whole month without a migraine, and I didn't miss out on any school. We both decided that I should continue with them on a monthly basis through the school year and then test out summer break. Turns out I was such an A-type personality during the school year, I would get so anxious it would manifest into a migraine when the stress was too much."

"So, you went in to see if it could help your migraines, and it helped with your anxiety also?"

"Yeah. I felt like I could be happy again. With the pain gone, the anxiety, from 'what's waiting for me around the corner' dissipated. I had hope for the first time in a long time. As I had more treatments, the self-assurance came back. It gave me the confidence I needed to go off to school in another state, away from my friends and family, so I could learn how to do what I love to do, which is work with animals." Cat took a deep breath and stared into Damon's eyes. Wow, she could look right through to his heart with those eyes. Instead of getting ready to bolt out of there as he likely would have with another woman, Damon wanted more. Then he heard a stomach growl. Was it his? Or hers?

"Cat, it sounds like one of us, okay, maybe both of us, is really hungry. Want to go a grab a bite to eat?" Cat looked down at her watch and then at him.

"Oh, man! I didn't realize it's this late. I'm sorry, but I've got a dog, and if I don't get home right now, she's going to go to the bathroom where she knows she shouldn't, and she'll start eating stuff she knows she's not supposed to eat. Another time maybe?"

Good. At least it wasn't a "no." "I totally get it. Fur babies come first. How about this weekend? Are you doing anything on Saturday?"

"Saturday's out. My family goes to the state fair every year, and that's the only day we all are available. What about Sunday?"

"Sunday's no good for me. Church in the morning and family dinner right after. Though I like spending time with you, I think it's a bit too soon to have you meet the family over church and family dinner."

Cat laughed. "Yeah, that's getting too deep, too soon. How about Friday night? Waukesha has Friday Night Live that starts at 6:30 p.m. We could meet in the bank parking lot and walk around to listen to all the free music. There's plenty of places to get something to eat or drink."

"That actually sounds pretty great. I like live music and food. Does it get as crowded as the music festival downtown? I'm not a huge fan of drunken crowds."

"No. I prefer Friday Night Live because you can walk around without hitting people or getting beer spilled all over your clothes. Plus, there's a lot of families, and people bring their dogs out for a nice walk. This way you can meet my 'fur baby,' Mia, and she can let me know if there's a third date in our future."

"Well, then I sure hope I do pass the test with Mia. To make sure, I'll line my pockets with meat treats," Damon replied with a smirk.

"That's cheating, you know."

"I'm a vet. I know lots of tricks to get animals to like me." With that, Damon stood up and took both their empty cups and put them in the dirty dish bin near the door. He held the door open for Cat and then followed her to her SUV.

When Cat reached her door, she turned around and almost ran right into his chest. She looked up at Damon and said, "I was very nervous about spending time with you alone. But now I feel very comfortable with you. It's crazy that I told you so much about me when we only just met over coffee, I mean tea." Cat smiled up at him. "Mia and I'll see you Friday night at 6:30 p.m. at the bank. Thanks again for the tea."

Damon, a bit more relaxed and a little perplexed, responded, "I can't believe I just blurted out so much of my personal life to you, but I couldn't help myself. Just like how I had to come out here to see you again. I promise I'm not a stalker. Never have been. But I'm really glad you were willing to have tea with me tonight. I'm looking forward to Friday night. Have a good night, Cat."

"Night, Damon. See you Friday."

Damon stepped onto the curb and watched Cat back up into traffic and drive away. In his own truck, he kept replaying the coffee date over and over in his head. When he got home and walked past the hall mirror, he noticed he was smiling. She brought back his smile. Nice. When he walked over to the refrigerator, his cell phone went off, and looking at the screen, he saw it was Pete. "Hello, Pete."

"How'd it go, buddy?"

"Great, actually."

"Sweet! What happened?"

"I got there, and she was still working in this outfit that looked like one of those of sexy librarians we would dream about but never saw."

"Oh, man! Did you ask her out?"

"Yeah, she met me for coffee, I mean tea, and I just got home.

I'm starving! Who knew talking to a girl makes you hungry?"

"Dude, you didn't eat all day. You just yelled your head off. Sounds like she was just the medicine you needed to get your happy-go-lucky attitude back. Way to go, Ginger! When do you see her again?"

"Friday night. She invited me to Friday Night Live in Waukesha, and she's bringing her dog to make sure that I pass the dog test."

"Smart woman. Get that litmus test done early on, in case the dog hates the guy and she has to give up either the guy or the dog. Listen, Angie is calling me to dinner, so I gotta go. Congrats, bro! See you tomorrow morning." With that, Pete hung up.

Damon grabbed the steak that he'd left marinated in Italian salad dressing overnight. He went out onto his deck to light the gas grill and pulled out a potato and onion to start slicing a pile to put in the middle of heavy-duty aluminum foil with salt, pepper, and butter. He folded up the sides of the heavy-duty foil to make a pocket and brought the steak and the pocket of fixings over to the grill to start cooking. Then Damon went back into the kitchen to throw together a quick green salad with Lighthouse French dressing on the side. Back in the refrigerator, he found a lone bottle of beer, cracked it open, and took a long cool drink before going back out onto the deck to turn over the meat and check on the potatoes.

After thirty minutes, Damon had his dinner ready and sat down to eat. He flipped on TV to see what kind of no-brainer television was available. Great! *How I Met Your Mother* was on. A few episodes later, Damon got up to stretch and put the dirty dishes away to start his evening routine of getting ready for the next day before bed. When he got to the bathroom to start his shower, he looked in the bathroom mirror and saw that he was still smiling a bit. Wow. She really made an impression on him with just one date. Wonder what would happen after the second one?

With his clothes laid out for the next day and his shower finished, Damon climbed into bed and fell asleep like a rock.

Chapter Five

When Friday came, the day seemed to go by in a flash for Cat. With Rose off on her vacation, Cat worked through lunch so she could leave a little earlier and get home to freshen up a bit before meeting Damon at the bank. By 3:10 p.m., Cat had cleared off her desk and was on her way home. No surprise, when she arrived in the driveway, Mrs. Romansky was working in her garden.

"Catrina, is everything okay? You're home early." Today, her landlady was wearing a blue T-shirt with a pale-yellow short-sleeved buttoned-down overshirt and tan walking shorts.

"Everything is just fine, Mrs. Romansky. It's just I have a date tonight, and I wanted to have a few minutes to freshen up. I'm taking Mia with me, you know, to make sure she approves."

"And if she doesn't?"

"Well, then, we pack up and go home. We girls need to stick together!" Cat put her hands on her hips and nodded her head. Mrs. Romansky gave her a chuckle and went back to work on her flowers. "Oh, hey, what time do you want me to stop over tomorrow to pay rent?"

"How about noon? I've got some fresh zucchini from the garden. We can have some zucchini bread and lemonade while 'we girls' review the date and decide if he's a keeper." With that, she gave Cat a wink, chuckled a bit, and went back to her garden.

"Sounds like a plan. See you tomorrow!" With that, Cat bounded up the stairs. Upstairs, Mia was going bonkers when Cat opened the door. "Ready to go outside, girl? We have to make it quick because we have a date tonight. You need to give me your honest opinion to make sure that he's worth having around. Okay?" Mia just looked up with her whole body in wiggle mode and gave Cat a great big wet kiss.

After Mia was taken care of, Cat went to the bathroom to freshen up. She sprayed her hair with a little curl refresher, picked out a silver Celtic knot clip to hold her hair away from her face but keep the curls bouncing off her tan shoulders and back. She lightly powdered her face and applied new jade green eyeliner, pale-pink blusher, and her favorite shade of bronze lip balm. Keeping her white T-shirt bra on with the spaghetti straps, she took a floral-patterned flowing sundress off its hanger and slipped it on over her head, shimmied it down over her hips and smoothed it to her knees. Cat found her favorite silver hoop earrings and her silver necklace with a lowercase "c" made with Celtic knotwork. Her parents had brought it back from their anniversary trip to Ireland. On her right ring finger, she placed another present from that trip, her silver Celtic knot ring. Looking down at Mia, she said, "With all this Irish jewelry on me, I'm bound to get lucky with this guy tonight, right?" Mia just lifted up her ears, cocked her head, and panted in a smile. "Well, not sex lucky, too soon. Like he may be a keeper lucky." Cat bent down to scratch Mia between her ears, and Mia rewarded her with a sloppy kiss on her cheek. "Hey, girl! I just put makeup on. Don't go licking it all off right away. We've got to make a good impression."

Cat looked at the time, 5:45 p.m. Better get the finishing touches together. Next, she spritzed a little perfume on her wrists and rubbed them together. Reaching down she put on her tan strappy sandal flats that crisscrossed over the top of her feet and crossed again around back to buckle on the side. Next, she grabbed a simple tan purse with a long strap so she could wear it across her body. She put her keys, wallet, an extra in the back pocket while Mia's leash and a few plastic bags and a bottle of water were in the front. "Come on, girl, it's time for our date. Let's go for a ride!" Mia may not have understood the date part, but she definitely knew what 'let's go for a ride' meant. The young lab scrambled down the back steps and jumped up and down by the SUV door. When they were all set in the SUV, Cat rolled down a window for Mia to stick her head out.

"Have a great time, girls! See you tomorrow!" Mrs. Romansky waved one of her gloved hands and smiled at her two tenants. Not tenants, friends. She got just as much joy out of having them around the house as they seemed to have living there. There are all kinds of families in this world; some are born, and some are made. Mrs. Romansky loved her ready-made family and couldn't wait to get into the kitchen to start baking that zucchini bread she had promised for tomorrow's visit.

Cat found an empty spot near the edge of the parking lot, so she thought it was a good time to get Mia out on her leash in case she needed to go potty before Damon arrived. Nothing could kill a good mood like carrying around a poop bag on a date. On the grass, Mia was deep in sniffing mode and forgot for a few moments what she needed to do. "Come on, Mia, go potty before our date gets here. We need to make a good first impression. Right now, I need you to focus because there's grass and a nearby garbage can. It can't get any more perfect for you to do your dooty duty." Mia seemed to understand and went to work. "Good girl," Cat said. As she was cleaning up and tying the used bag in a knot, she heard a familiar voice.

"Hey there!"

Cat stood straight up still holding the stinky bag, which was now swinging back and forth in her hand. "Hi," she replied self-consciously.

Damon was wearing a Hawaiian-styled shirt with the colors of a sunset and shadows of palm trees rising from its lower hem. His cargo shorts had a plethora of pockets, and he was wearing what Cat's dad would call his "Jesus shoes," leather sandals. In his hands, he had a small bouquet of brightly colored cottage flowers and a bag of dog treats in the other. He noticed Cat's hands. "Looks like both our hands are full. How about I let you take care of your bag? I'll stand on Mia's leash and wait for you to get back before formal introductions begin." With that, he smiled that bright open smile that lit up his face and brought those adorable dimples out of hiding.

"Great idea." Cat dropped the leash near Damon's foot so he could step on it while she walked over to the garbage can. When she returned, with a little less dignity than she started the evening with, she continued, "Well, that shoots down any intention I had for a positive first impression. I should have just shown up in muddy overalls and hay in my hair."

Damon's smile faded as a more intense look came across his face. "No. You're perfect." He paused as he looked from her pale pink painted toes, sliding up over her freshly shaved tan legs, a little longer look as he focused on her breasts, and then finally locked onto her hazel eyes. "Cat, you make an awesome first impression. You look so incredibly beautiful tonight." As he continued to stare, Mia started to get antsy. "Hello, little girl. I didn't forget about you. Just a minute though, I have to do something first." Damon reached out to Cat with the bouquet of flowers and let his fingers linger a little bit while she accepted them.

"Thank you for the compliment. You clean up pretty good yourself." Cat smiled and then looked down at the bouquet. "They're beautiful! Are these zinnias?"

"Yeah. My mom has a great garden. She says all good Irish women have a green thumb. I asked her permission to take a bunch for our date. I wanted to make a good first impression, too." This time, Damon looked a bit sheepish. Cat smiled, just imagining what the scene might have looked like when a grown man would be asking his mommy for permission to take flowers from her garden.

"Is it okay that I brought bribes for the other lady I'm taking out tonight?" Damon cocked his head and raised an eyebrow at Cat, looking for approval to give Mia some treats.

Cat nodded her head and began the formal introduction. "Mia, this is my new friend, Damon. Damon, this is my dog and very best girlfriend, Mia." At that, Damon bent down into a catcher's crouch to be eye to eye with Mia. Slowly he put his left hand out, palm up, just before her nose so she could smell him at her own pace. She sniffed that hand and then licked his palm. Her body got so excited to meet another person that she sprang up from her sitting position to a full-on tail wagging position and scooted closer to him so that he could pet her. As she got closer, her keen sense of smell recognized that there was something yummy in his other hand and started nosing into that hand to see what wonderful surprise was in store. Damon chuckled and opened up his closed fist to show her the heart-shaped treat that was just for her. Mia snatched it like a frog would snatch a fly with its tongue.

Introductions completed and Mia approved, it was time to start this date in earnest. "Let's walk toward the bridge. The music's on the other side of the Fox River," Cat recommended, and all three strolled toward the crowd and the electric guitar playing a rift at a nearby tavern. "Every Friday night in June, July, and August, they close down several downtown Waukesha streets and set up stages all over so that you can walk around and check out all different types of music. You want old-time rock and roll? Go to the stage over by the H.O.G. Want a brass band? They usually play over by the theater. Dancing music? Several places for that. Old men singing hair band rock? That's by the cigar bar." They found a similar walking rhythm, so they were side by side with Mia on Cat's left.

"Wow. Does it cost anything?"

"Not unless you want something to eat or drink or you want to go shopping. The local businesses sponsor the stages in the hopes that getting the pedestrian traffic at night will boost foot traffic into their stores." Just then Cat stopped in front of a pretty big crowd. The band was about six members strong and all wearing tie-dye shirts. Though they all had silver hair, and a few were sitting on stools, their music and harmonies were energizing. Cat looked up to see Damon's reaction, and he seemed fascinated to take it all in.

The band was singing a 1960s song, "Windy," originally sung by The Association. Damon watched as the group started to move to the beat, and soon people were breaking up into couples to dance.

Then Cat's favorite person showed up on the outskirts of the dancers to start shuffling to the beat.

"They're really good!" Damon said over the music.

Cat nodded and pointed to the petite older man wearing a cream-colored button-down shirt over light-tan pants. The silver hairs still left on his head were plastered down in a comb-over, and his smile was showing underneath his bushy silver mustache. He seemed to be singing along with the song while he shuffled, but it didn't look like he knew the words very well. Cat patted Damon on his forearm and spoke over the music while she pointed. "See that older guy over there in the white?" Damon bent down to hear her better and looked in the direction she pointed. Once he nodded, she continued, "He's here every single Friday night. I think he comes alone because he's always dancing by himself at every band I stop to listen to. Most nights, he finds someone who is willing to dance with him a little bit. He's my favorite person to watch because he always enjoys himself, regardless of the type of music. He can't seem to stop moving!"

Damon nodded in agreement and then noticed how Cat's hand had returned to his forearm and just stayed there. He was no longer watching the band or the dancers. He was watching her out of the corner of his eye. Cat was so enthralled by the scene before her and trying to be the perfect tour guide that she almost didn't see Damon's stare, but when she did, he smiled right at her, moved her hand from his forearm to his hand, and closed his hand around hers. Cat hadn't realized it at the time, but throughout that whole movement, she ceased breathing. She stopped hearing the music and watching the dancers. All she saw was that familiar twinkle in his eyes and dimples appearing when he realized that she was squeezing his hand in return to let him know that she wanted to hold it. Next thing Cat knew, the music stopped, and everyone was clapping.

The lead singer got off his stool for a moment to introduce the next song. "For all you lovebirds out there, here's one of our favorites." He sat back on his stool, and the band started to play as he crooned out the words to a Righteous Brothers' ballad. Just then, Cat felt the tension on her right hand start to change as Damon led her out onto the impromptu dance floor on the street. Mia, of course, followed along, excited that they were on the move again. Cat followed without a sound, and when Damon found his perfect spot, they stopped. He took the bouquet of flowers out of Cat's left hand and handed them to an elderly woman sitting in her walker chair. "For you, pretty lady," he said, kissing her gnarled hands.

She blushed, and a tear started to form in the corner of her clouded grey eyes. She whispered, "Thank you," and brought the flowers up to her nose to smell them, as if reminiscing of a time when she'd been given flowers on a first date.

The shock Cat felt when Damon took the flowers from her wore off and was quickly replaced with a warmth that she hadn't felt in a very long time. But that warmth didn't last long. Once Damon took a few short steps into the middle of the dancing bodies, he stopped, turned toward her, moved his left hand down to her waist, and drew her to him while his right hand held hers and Mia's leash near his chest. The next thing she knew, they started to sway to the melody. As the singer crooned, Cat closed her eyes, breathing in his musky scent. Out of nowhere, she thought to herself, "I'm going to marry this man." Suddenly, the tense knots she had previously felt in her stomach melted away, and in their place grew a slow stirring sultriness beginning in her heart and rippling throughout her body. Damon must have felt her relax because he used his left hand to draw her even closer; Cat relented.

At the ballad's end, they still lingered in their embrace for a few moments longer than everyone else. The music changed to something upbeat. Cat opened her eyes and heard Damon talking to her, "I guess the song's over." She shook herself out of the trance she had been in and looked up into his eyes and saw something in them that wasn't there before. Could it be that he felt something as strong as she had? Did she say anything out loud? Before she could get a clear answer, Damon held her hand and guided her out of the dance area. "So, what else is around here?" Damon inquired as they strolled out into the middle of the street.

"Let's take a right over here and see if the old-guy hair band is playing tonight." Sure enough, there were five guys her parents' age singing "Once Bitten, Twice Shy" by Great White, and they banged their heads and made their guitars sway to the beat. Cat smiled and found an opening underneath a tree with some grass so that Mia had a cool place for her paws to get off the asphalt. As the band played, Cat got lost in the moment and started singing the words to the song while headbanging with the band. Damon looked over at her and started to laugh.

"How do you know this song?" he asked.

"My mom. She and my aunt would do hair band rock and roll karaoke when we would all get together camping or for dinner. They used to go to Def Leppard concerts every year, and the next morning my mom would ask me to put pain relieving cream all over her back and neck because she strained every muscle by dancing and head-banging all night long. She looks and acts like a mom, but she's got a wild streak about her. She's the musician in the family and taught my brother and me to sing harmony and dance." Cat looked up to see what reaction she was getting.

"She sounds like someone I have to meet. I wonder if she could beat me in rock and roll trivia. "

"I don't know about you, but she's a force to reckon with when it comes to music. Every summer she came to visit me in Montana, I'd take her into downtown on Thursday nights to listen to the music, and if she liked the beat, she'd drag me onto the dance floor. Then we'd go to the store to pick up a bag of Epsom salts and a tube of pain relieving cream. She always stayed at The Howlers Inn so she could use the Western Room's jacuzzi tub to soak her sore muscles."

"I wish I had seen that." The old-guy hair band was taking a break, so they started to stroll to another street that had Latin music playing and dancers teaching Latin moves to the audience. The next stop was in front of an artist in a black-and-glitter fedora who was painting to rock and roll music. Tonight's portrait looked like a cityscape with skyscrapers and Lake Michigan emerging in the background. As they walked toward the artist, a man on a bike with a parrot in a cage pedaled past. Damon, fascinated by what he saw, kept his eyes peeled on the spectacle and stepped right on Mia's front paw. "Yipe!"

"Oh damn! I mean, I'm so sorry, Mia," he apologized as he bent down to feel her paw and receive "apology-accepted kisses" from his fur baby date.

When they stopped to watch the artist, Cat inquired, "What about your mom? What is she like?"

Damon smiled and started, "Well, she's the glue that keeps my family together. My dad might have a louder voice and stronger muscles, but she rules the roost. She had to keep all six of us in line, the farm going, and help Dad not only with the chores but also the lessons. Still she found time to garden; as you could tell, she's a miracle worker with flowers and vegetables. She could make cucumbers grow out of rocks. That's why Sundays are family days. If you are anywhere near the farm on Sunday morning, you will go to church. Doesn't matter if you were out partying until all hours of the morning, you will be up and ready to leave the house at 9:30 a.m. for 10:00 a.m. service. No excuses. As for music, she loves all kinds of music, but I can't see her as a headbanger like your mom. Lots of the time we listened to Celtic music. She's a huge fan of Celtic Thunder and Celtic Woman. And she can cook. You can give her a potato, an onion, and leftover hamburger, and she'll figure out a three-course meal that can feed all eight of us for dinner." As Damon spoke, Cat paid attention to how his voice and demeanor changed. She could tell that he really loved his mom and thought very highly of her. "Speaking of cooking, aren't you getting a little hungry?"

Cat's stomach growled at the thought of food and looked at her watch. They'd been there for an hour. It was past the time when she usually has dinner. "That sounds really good right now. How do you feel about burgers?"

"Seriously? What kind of man would I be not to want a good burger? Lead the way, madame. My stomach will follow you." Cat noticed that Damon hadn't let go of her hand since they stopped dancing. She enjoyed how it felt to have hers nestled in his. She dodged and weaved through the crowds to get them back to the parking lot.

"I'm going to take you to this little burger joint nearby. Follow me, but if we get separated, it's on Sunset Drive. I'll grab us a table outside so Mia can join us."

"Sounds great. I've got a gray truck. I'll pull up right behind you, and you can lead me to burger heaven." He smiled at Cat, crouched down to ruffle Mia behind the ears, and gave her another heart-shaped treat. "You were such a good girl, Mia, and you're a pretty decent dancer for a dog." After she gobbled up the treat, Mia licked his palm and sniffed around for some more.

Once they climbed into the SUV, Cat asked Mia, "So, what do you think? Is he a keeper?" To that, Mia licked Cat on the side of her face before she stuck her head out of the window. Cat laughed and wiped the slobber off her cheek in enough time to see a grey truck pull up behind her. When Damon waved out of the window, she led them the few short miles to her favorite burger restaurant in Waukesha.

Cat found a parking spot near one of the picnic tables. She pulled the water bottle out of her purse and tied Mia up to the bench. "Here you go, girl," she said and started pouring water out so Mia could lap up cold water streaming out of the bottle. She looked up when Damon closed the door to the truck and walked over. "Would you mind if I gave you my order and some money so I can keep Mia outside?"

"This is my treat. I asked you out on a date, and my mom would skin me alive if she knew that we went Dutch. She can be a real bear if any one of her kids doesn't show they have manners. I'll be happy to take your order and bring the food and drinks out here if you give me a recommendation on what I should order."

"Fair enough. I don't want you to get skinned alive. I'll have the burger and a diet soda. You'll want to try the cheeseburger, an order of fries, and a chocolate shake."

"What's so special about their cheeseburger?" "They use fried cheese curds."

"Cheese curds on a burger?"

"Mm-hmm. Only true Wisconsin men can handle such a monster burger. Let's see if you can."

"Sounds like a challenge. I'm on it." Damon grinned, winking, and turned around to get their order.

A little while later, Damon returned to the picnic table bogged down with drinks and food. "Okay, let's see if this burger was worth the wait and being away from two such pretty ladies for so long." Mia wagged her tail and started chewing on some ice that Cat scooped out of her drink. Damon opened his mouth as wide as he could and took a big bite. Cat waited to see his reaction before she bit into hers.

"Well? What do you think?"

"That was pretty damn good. I'm impressed. But sometime, I'll have to take you to my favorite restaurant out by me. They've got great burgers there too and awesome ambiance." Then he raised the burger back to his mouth and took another large bite. "Who knew? Cheese curds on a burger."

Cat took a moment to bite into hers and was happy she'd kept her meals and snacks on the light side that day so she could enjoy this treat without the guilt. When Mia saw that attention was on the food and no longer on her, she lay down under the table and rested her head on her front paws. They pretty much ate in silence except for a few offers to sample each other's burgers. After Cat couldn't eat another bite and her soda was gone, she leaned away from the table and said, "I'm stuffed."

"What, no dessert? I saw that they had butter pecan custard as their flavor of the day."

"Honestly, I don't think I could fit another bite of anything into my mouth right now. I forgot how big those burgers are."

"Umm, didn't the sign that says, 'Big Burgers and Custard' give you a clue?"

"Funny. I was so hungry I forgot how filling they are."

"Want to go somewhere to walk it off?" Damon looked at Cat, who had a sense that he didn't want the date to end just yet. If she was being honest, she didn't want it to end yet, either.

"I'd like that. There's a park on the Fox River. We can park near the kids' playground and then walk along the river for a while. How does that sound?"

"Perfect. I'll follow you." Damon got up, took all the garbage off the table, and was just about to move away from the table when Cat put her hand on his forearm.

"Thank you for dinner and thank your mom for raising a decent man with manners."

Damon smiled at her, nodded his head, and replied, "My pleasure. I'll be sure to let her know. It'll give me brownie points for the next time I get into trouble with her."

They piled into their respective vehicles, and Cat led the way to their next destination. With it being 8:30 p.m., the park was relatively quiet. The sun was still out for a little while longer, staving off the mosquitoes that would become a nuisance at dusk. After parking, Cat led them past the playground and onto the walking path near the river. Mia noticed the water and kept looking up at Cat to see if this was a place where she could go swimming. "No, Mia. Sorry, no swimming tonight. We're just walking, baby girl."

Damon was looking straight ahead when he reached for Cat's hand again. She felt as if their hands always belonged together. It was such a natural feeling now that she didn't know how it was that they didn't always hold hands when they saw each other. Much of the walk was silent, as they found new confidence in themselves and comfort as a couple. Cat took this time to take in all the little details of the night because she already knew that he was something special. No matter how long this lasted, he would always be someone important to her. Instead of worrying about how long this one would last, Cat relished being present in the moment. She felt the slight breeze go through her hair, which cooled her skin. She smelled the sweet aroma of freshly cut grass. She heard the soft footfalls of their sandals on the paved walkway. She felt her heart practically jumping for joy as they continued holding hands together while the sun slowly dipped down past the full green trees in the distance.

Once they got to the bridge, they stopped for a moment and looked at a family of ducks swimming past. Cat didn't understand how she knew, but she had a vague awareness that something was different before she felt Damon turn toward her. He took his hand out of hers to push away a loose curl that had broken free of her clip. He stared into her eyes as he said, "I know that you've just gotten out of a long relationship. I know that we've just met. I also know that I haven't wanted to take a girl out more than one or two times before I let them go. But since I met you, I can't stop thinking about you. You are so beautiful, and you smell like a warm, summer breeze, but that's not all. I want to know more about you, your family, what makes you laugh, anything that can get me more time to spend with you." He paused because he saw how Cat's eyes became as wide as saucers.

"Oh shit. Am I scaring you?" He cupped her face gently as his eyes took on a sense of panic while they scanned her face for some sign of what she was thinking.

"No. I'm not scared of you. Yes, I am scared a little bit because I'm feeling the same way. I already feel different about you than any other guy I've ever dated. I swore I'd take time off being with someone and just focus on me for a while. But as soon as you walked through the center with the crane, I stopped thinking and breathing. I don't know what this all means, but I do know I want to see you again." Cat searched his electric blue eyes for a sign of what he was thinking, but she didn't need to wait much longer. Damon dipped his head toward her mouth, and she instinctively tilted hers to meet his. When their lips touched, she felt a sultry surge flowing through her body. She bent her body so that it was pressed hard up against his, as she took her free hand to run it through his wavy hair. Cat thought she heard him sigh as she slightly scraped her nails against his scalp. Knowing that she affected him that way, she opened her mouth to take him fully into hers and show him how much she wanted to be with him. At first, she felt his shock at her bold move. Then he matched her in intensity, and his hands moved from her face down to her hips, pushing her closer to the hardness that was growing in the V of his cargo shorts.

Neither of them wanted to stop. They were so engrossed in what they were learning about each other's responses. Unfortunately, Mia was getting antsy again and wanted to start walking. Her tugging and whining got their attention. Cat slowly pulled away and sucked on his bottom lip as she left the heated space that she had occupied a few short seconds ago. "I guess we need to start walking back. Mia has lost her patience with us."

Damon had lost all frame of thought and was frozen in place until he felt Cat place her hand back into his, pulling him along to join Mia and her for the walk back to their trucks. Cat was smirking a bit, feeling a bit proud that if he were wearing them, she had clearly knocked his socks off. Good. Something for him to think about tonight.

When they finally arrived back at the parking lot, Damon crouched down again to Mia's level. "Well, little one, it looks like we're going to be seeing a lot more of each other from now on. Just so you know, I won't let you take me away from kissing Cat again. You and I are going to have to come to some kind of understanding moving forward." Mia knew he was talking just to her and took it to mean that she should give him one of her famous big sloppy kisses.

Cat opened the back door and the windows before motioning Mia to jump into the SUV. Turning to shut the back door, she started to say, "Damon, I really had a … oomph!" Just then, she felt his hands around her waist, turning her toward him. He stared into her shocked hazel eyes with very intense blue ones.

"That was some kiss you gave me back there, Cat. I just want to return the favor." With that, Damon took both of his hands to her face, brushed back the rogue curls, and crushed her mouth with his. This was a feverish kiss. One that let her know that there was more passion within him just aching to come out. His tongue pushed through her lips and opened her mouth to get to her tongue and give her a small taste of what was in store for their future. Cat lost her ability to control the situation and lost herself in the moment, following him and teasing him with every movement. While his hands were on her face, hers were free to go around his waist and rest on his muscular ass and squeeze hard to let him know what she wanted—to be with him. Just as she was losing herself in the moment, Damon abruptly stopped and pulled away to gently kiss the lips that were swollen from the passionate lovemaking they had just encountered.

"Touché," she whispered, and he grinned.

"Cat, I don't want this to become a game between us. Honestly, it was more that I didn't want to stop kissing you when we did, and I wanted to get back that intensity because I haven't felt that in a very long time. Hell, I'm not sure I ever have. You're stirring up something inside me, and I just met you. I don't understand what's happening. But I do know I want to see you again and really soon." Damon continued to hold her head and search her golden-flecked eyes for some sense of what she was thinking.

"I promise I don't play games, and I loathe people who do. I feel this penetrating connection with you. I tried to set up a wall to slow down my emotions, but every time you touch me, it's so potent that I end up losing myself and the wall just crumbles around my heart. It still is tender from my last boyfriend. I know you can't promise me that you won't break my heart because that's a piecrust promise. But can you promise that you'll be honest with me? That if there comes a time when you are bored with this or you want to date someone new, you'll let me know first? I won't be cheated on again." The gold in Cat's eyes started to glisten as she held back tears that wanted to leak out in remembrance of what Jansen had put her through just a few short months ago.

Damon looked her straight in the eyes and vowed, "I promise. No games. Honesty always. No cheating. Can you make me the same deal?"

As a single tear dropped from the corner of her eye onto his thumb, she whispered, "I promise. No games. Honesty always. No cheating." Cat smiled, reaching up and lightly brushing her lips over his to seal her commitment to him.

When they pulled away, Damon asked, "I know we both have plans this weekend, but what about next Saturday or Sunday?"

"I think I'm free on Saturday. What do you have in mind?" "Can you get a dog sitter?"

"I can work on it. Why?"

"I'd like to take you to a medieval fair. Best people-watching in the area. Have you ever been there?"

"Maybe my parents took me when I was little, but it's been a really long time. Don't people dress up in costumes?"

Damon performed an overexaggerated bow. "Yes, they do, milady. I happen to have such fair wear to don on this occasion. What about you?"

Cat looked quizzically at him. "Umm, I don't believe I have anything that would look remotely renaissance. Does that mean I can't go with you?"

"Heavens no, milady! I will procure you appropriate fair wear. Will you let me do you the honor of paying the renter's fee for your costume?"

Cat laughed. "It would be my honor to have you procure an appropriate costume so that I may accompany you to the fair." Cat curtsied and tried to curtail a giggle as well. Then she looked up at him in all seriousness. "Can I be a lady pirate? I've always wanted to dress up as Captain Hook in *Peter Pan.*"

It was Damon's turn to laugh then. "I will search inside every shop in the village to make your wish come true, milady." Then Damon reached for Cat's hand and gently kissed her knuckles. "Text me your address so that I can pick you up on Saturday around 9:00 a.m. The gates open at ten."

"I can't wait!" She gave him a great big smile and then turned to get into her SUV. Damon stayed still and waved to her until she drove out of the parking lot. With a big sigh and a big smile, he walked over to his pickup truck and headed home. He had to find a way to keep busy for the next week until he saw her again. That was going to be a challenge.

Chapter Six

Saturday morning, Damon woke up with more energy than he'd felt in a long time. He started a pot of coffee and scrambled up some eggs with cheddar cheese and ranch dressing with a side of bacon and toast and his mom's rhubarb strawberry jam slathered on top. The breakfast of champions.

He sat down at his kitchen table and kept going over the date in his mind—how her hair blew in the breeze and sometimes tickled his shoulder, breathing in her scent of lavender and vanilla, the comfortable way they held hands throughout the evening, and the electric current that ran through him every time they kissed. Holy shit! That kiss blew his mind. Now he had to wait until next Saturday before he could see her again. How was he going to keep his mind occupied?

Today he'd help Da with chores around the farm. Tomorrow was church and the family dinner. Maybe he should call Pete to see if he wanted to play a little one-on-one game of hoops, go fishing or maybe paintball. Maybe it wouldn't be a bad idea to give Cat a call midweek just to make sure that the date was still on. Everything sounded like it was a go on her end, but they were both caught up in the moment. Never hurt to check in and make sure they were on the same page.

After cleaning up breakfast, he threw on a ratty T-shirt, ripped jeans, and mud-encrusted work boots before putting on his favorite camo baseball cap. Pouring the rest of the coffee into a silver travel mug, he was off to find his dad and start the day's work.

He didn't have to look very far; his dad was working on a part of the fencing that was nearest Damon's house. The four-wheeler was hauling a trailer full of supplies and tools to fix some of the fencing that had pulled away from the timber post. "Morning, Da. Need some help?"

His dad was dressed similarly, but he was faring a few more wrinkles and a whole head of silver mixed in with his red hair, so it wasn't as shocking as Damon's tended to be. His pale, blue eyes squinted under the brim of his hat to get a look at Damon making his way to the fence. "Morning, son. I can always use an extra pair of hands. Grab those snippers on the trailer and help me get this fence back on the post."

Damon enjoyed working with his dad. The work went fast; they seemed to know what each other was thinking or needing without words. That was perfect for Damon because he wasn't sure he was ready to talk about Cat just yet. Occasionally they stopped to drink some of their coffee or to look at the work they'd just finished, and then they would get back on the four-wheeler to do the next chore that was on the list.

Today's sun was shining in between billowy white clouds; it meant that there was a nice breeze coming over the hills and providing moments of heat relief for the two men who were now chopping up a dead oak tree that was leaning a little too close to the barn. Once dry, it would be nice firewood, but right now Pat was using the chainsaw to break it up into manageable chunks while Damon swung an 8 lb. mall to split the wood and put the freshly cut quarters onto the trailer for hauling back behind the main house to stack under the firewood shelters they had built a few years earlier.

Manual labor was just what the doctor ordered. Damon was so focused on the work to be done, and matching his dad's efforts, that the morning was just slipping away. When he looked up to see the sun shining straight down through the grove of oak trees near the fallen tree, his stomach began to growl, loud enough for his dad to hear it. With a chuckle, Pat said, "Sounds like it's time for some lunch. Why don't you finish stacking that wood and I'll meet you back at the house for some of your mom's ham and cheesy potatoes, leftovers from last night."

"I love Mom's cheesy potatoes! I'm in!" With that, Damon started to double time stacking the wood onto the trailer. Within fifteen minutes or so, he was washing up in the laundry room after kicking off his work boots before he dared step into his mom's kitchen. He loved this room because so many family memories could be traced back to it. Through the years, he and his siblings had helped with remodeling projects to keep it up to date, but it still held that same old homey feel that kept him from moving too far away.

Now the kitchen was a denim blue with white cabinets and appliances. Over the oak kitchen table was a blue and white gingham tablecloth. In the middle was an antique silver kettle with a spout and wooden handle. His mom always had an arrangement of fresh flowers from her garden in the kettle, and today's arrangement held large balls of pink hydrangeas and a variety of blue delphinium. Pat was already sitting at the table with Heather who had her hair up in a clip, wearing a sleeveless cotton shirt, the color of cotton candy, and jean shorts. "Afternoon, baby! I have the ham and potatoes on the island; just go ahead and nuke them. I also made fresh lemonade. It's in the frig. Help yourself." To that invitation, Damon's stomach growled again.

While Damon was piling potatoes and ham high on his plate, he missed the eye signals his parents were sharing across the table from each other. It was clear they could see a change in his demeanor. Heather mouthed the word "Well?" to Pat, who just shrugged his shoulders. She returned the favor with an "I'm disappointed in you" look and nod of her head. Heather realized that she would have to take matters into her own hands to find out what was going on. As the many years of successful parenting had taught her, she'd wait until he sat down and took a mouthful of food before starting the inquisition. She'd invested thirty years in this child, she wanted to make sure that her investment was going to pay dividends soon … in the form of grandchildren.

Damon brought his overflowing plate and glass of cold lemonade to the table and sat next to his mom. With many years of manners drilled into him, he looked at her and gave her a peck on the cheek and his famous smile. "Thanks for lunch, Mom," he said before he dug in. On cue, with his first bite just barely passing his lips, Heather began.

"You're welcome, baby. So, how was your date last night?" Damon stopped chewing mid-bite and began choking on half-chewed food. He was grateful for good manners now because he needed to formulate a response and could use chewing time to figure out a plan. When he looked up from his plate, his Da had a smirk and was shrugging his shoulders to let him know that he was sorry, but not really.

"It was really nice." Taking another big bite, he waited for the rest of the interrogation to start. He needed all the extra time he could to make sure he wasn't saying too much but saying just enough to appease his mom. It was a strategy akin to battle planning or a chess match. If he gave her something to ponder for a bit, he would be able to keep the really important things to himself for a while as he tried to figure out what was going on with him and Cat moving forward.

"Where did you go again?"

"We met at Friday Night Live in downtown Waukesha. Then over to Murf's for burgers and custard." Another big bite. Shit, he was already halfway through his lunch plate and she had just started. Poor strategic move, eating large bites. Next strategy, smaller bites eaten more slowly.

"What's her name again? What does she look like?"

"Her name is Catrina Carneri. She's about your height, 5 feet 8 inches or 5 feet 9 inches or so, and she's got naturally curly brown hair." He didn't want to get into details of how her cheek nestled softly into his shoulder when they danced. Or how she always smelled of vanilla and lavender to him. Or how each curl seemed to take on its own hue of browns: chestnut, sandy, chocolate, golden, on and on. Or how her eyes glistened when she looked up at him so he could see countless flecks of gold, green, and brown in her eyes.

"How did you two meet again?" This time he looked at his dad to help him out. He needed time to reformulate a defensive plan.

"I thought I told you, she works at the wildlife rehabilitation sanctuary where we took the crane. She's the one that let us into the place. You asked Damon to check on the bird a few days ago, and she gave him the update." Pat felt good that he had found his place of neutrality in this battle. He needed to show support for his son yet prove allegiance to his wife with whom he intended on spending the rest of his life, as long as she allowed him the privilege. It was a tricky game, but Irishmen have a long tradition of being strong negotiators. In the battle between love and family, he needed all his wits about him to keep his loving wife appeased while showing support to his kids. That was of course if she was in charge of the situation. If the tables were turned and he needed to take charge, he knew that Heather would always have his back and provide support to the child or children needing parental control.

Heather nodded and looked up at the ceiling for a moment. "That's right. I forgot. Thanks for reminding me, love." Pat smiled sheepishly as he played his role to perfection. "I don't think I've ever been to either. What was it like? Did anyone else join you two?"

Damon paused as he tried to design an answer that didn't give too much away but would satisfy his mom. Mia! He would talk about her dog. Mom always loved having animals around. She'd love it. "Actually, I think you and Da would love it there. It's like a mini downtown music festival except it's free and not as crowded, and lots of people bring their dogs with them." Damon knew he was winning this round. "As a matter of fact, Cat brought her dog, Mia, with her. She told me that if Mia approved of me, then the date was still on. If she didn't, she'd leave me high and dry in the parking lot." Damon saw his mother's eyes go from serious to playful and even heard her chuckle a bit.

"Smart girl. Wait a second, I thought you said her name was Catrina?" Shit, Mom didn't miss a thing; she was paying attention to the details.

"Sorry, her name is Catrina, but she prefers to be called Cat." "Is she Italian?"

"Um, I think she said her dad is, but her mom is Irish. That's where the curly hair comes from." His mom nodded to confirm her approval of the Irish connection.

"Sorry, baby, go on."

"So, yeah, we met in the parking lot. I got to meet Mia, who is her two-year-old black lab. I brought treats and asked for permission to give her some. From then on, I had Mia eating out of my hand, literally." He saw both parents smile and engage in eye contact to show their approval of his methods. "The first band played music from the 1960s, and lots of people were dancing in the streets. Then we saw a brass jazz band and some guys about your age playing heavy metal. By that time my stomach was growling, so I followed her to the restaurant and I treated her to burgers. We ate outside so Mia could join us, and that was about it." Good. Done. See her break holes into this.

Heather paused before she spoke. "Sounds like a perfect evening, but I don't think you're telling us the whole truth here. Seeing only bands and then having burgers doesn't get you through the whole night, considering how late you came home. Anything else that is suitable for your parent's ears?"

Damon choked. She was good. Really good. He had to give her something. He realized that she was now looking to see if Cat was the kind of woman who would sleep with a first date or if she was a potential keeper. He needed to figure out a way to tell her she was definitely the latter of the two, without giving too much away. It was only two dates in, and he didn't want to ruin their third date with disapproval from his mom. But he also was thirty and needed to be able to be seen as an adult and respected as one by his parents or this living situation would not work out. "You're right. We decided to take a walk in a park by the Fox River after dinner to walk off the burgers." Now he looked at her straight in the eyes with confidence and seriousness. "I was a complete gentleman, I promise. She's someone I want to take the time to get to know better. When I think of her, I see there is the potential of a promise."

What he saw in his mother's eyes was something he hadn't seen before. The concern washed away, and a warmth washed over her. He felt her soft hands clasp his forearm, and he swore he saw tears welling in her eyes. "Thank you, Damon. That's all I needed to know." She kissed him on his cheek, rose, and cleared the lunch dishes.

At that moment, Damon knew he had won the battle, yet there was something else he felt but couldn't quite put his finger on. At that moment, their relationship changed. She respected him as a man and wouldn't probe any further. He felt the relief of a champion winning a difficult competition but at the same time the loss of something else. His mother no longer thought of him as a boy that needed to be nurtured at her bosom. She now recognized him as a man.

Before he could ponder what had happened any further, two red hair mopped teens trampled through the door and gave him a warm welcome, "Dweeb."

"Dork."

"Afternoon, you two lazy butts. What've you been up to while I've been bustin' my hump fixing fences and hauling wood for Da?"

"We were working for a living. Didn't you see all those cars in the parking lot? We've had riding lessons all morning, and we're famished!" Ian spoke as he and Cathy, his twin sister, sat down at the family table. Whereas Damon's build was strong and husky with muscles everywhere, Ian's build was long and lanky. There was no fat on those bones, and he had to wear a belt to keep his pants up, but he was no weakling. His long arms and legs were filled with roped muscle that, when put into motion, rippled with tension to provide the strength necessary to throw a bale of hay into the barn or wrangle a high-strung horse.

Before Heather could present that day's lunch options, Ian was already grabbing the gear necessary to enjoy a plentiful platter of provisions that would keep him satisfied until dinner a few hours from now. "Thanks, Mom!" He prattled off as he sat down next to his dad and shoveled food into his mouth as if he'd never eaten before.

Cathy was a bit more patient, but it was clear that she was just as hungry as her twin brother as seen by the portion sizes on her plate. "Thanks, Mom." Cathy was taller than most of her friends and lanky as well. Where Ian was an expert at calming horses with his steady strength, Cathy had the perfect personality for working with clients. She was patient and soft-spoken, but persistent. Those horses were her babies, and every time someone climbed on the back of her precious mares, she spent a great deal of time making sure that the riders were respectful and studied in how to manage their horses. She had a long mane of auburn hair that she often just pulled back into a ponytail. Her blue eyes were softer than Damon's, more like the color of a robin's egg. She also had fair skin, but even at the ripe old age of nineteen, she sported a few freckles over her nose and cheeks.

Ian and Cathy oftentimes bantered with pet names like Dork, Dweeb, and some that were too offensive to be uttered in front of their parents, but they worked well together. Ian's talent to talk sense to the horses and Cathy's talent of matching individual personalities of the riders with the horses kept the horse farm running smoothly and profitably. Both were students at UW-Madison, Ian a major in agribusiness while Cathy majored in equine science. It was clear that of all six of the MacGregor children, Ian and Cathy were grooming themselves to take over the horse farm when Pat and Heather retired.

With a new set of kids to keep his parents company, Damon saw his opportunity to move along. "Thanks again for lunch, Mom. Da, I've got some of my own chores I need to catch up on. Is it okay if I call it a day and see you guys at church tomorrow?"

Pat nodded and replied, "No problem. You helped me a great deal this morning. Thanks, kiddo. See you tomorrow."

"See you tomorrow, baby," Heather chimed in. It was clear that they were ready to start a new interrogation, but this time he wasn't the focus.

Damon got back to his home, kicked off his work boots, and clapped them together to get most of the morning's dirt and mud off them before he put them on the rubber mat in the laundry room. He shed his dirt-encrusted, sweaty clothes right there on the floor and walked buck naked up the stairs to his bathroom where he turned on the showerhead at full force to scrub all the dirt and grime off his body. Then after he was scrubbed clean, he dried off the dripping parts and started up his bathwater and shook a whole handful of Epsom salts into the heated stream of water filling up the basin. When it was about half full, Damon eased his sore body into the steamy, bubbly water to soak. He didn't care about the chemistry behind the reason that a four-dollar bag of Epsom salts, when added to a tub of hot water, could ease his muscles better than any muscle relaxer. He just enjoyed the heck out of how it seemed to unlock the knots that developed and released the tension collecting in his knees, shoulders, back, and neck.

He tried not to think about anything in particular, but his mind kept going back to how Cat had looked at him after their goodbye kiss and his mom—how she had looked at him after he told her that Cat held the potential of a promise. Women were intuitive, that was a certainty. The female minds of humans and animals were bafflingly similar. Before a male would even know what's going on, the female could feel it and react before the action actually happened. Women fascinated him.

When the water cooled down, he opened the drain and began to prep for the rest of his day. He texted Pete earlier to see if they could have some bro-bonding time that afternoon. After drying off in the bathroom, he moved over to his bedroom to pick out his favorite T-shirt, a Dropkick Murphy's concert tee he had picked up at the Irish Fest a few years back and slid on some jean shorts. Looking at his phone, he saw a text message from Pete. "Angie wants you to come over for dinner. Bro-bonding after. Deal?"

"Deal. Time?"

"5:00 p.m."

"Got it. Should I bring anything?"

"Better not. She's in a nesting phase. She wants to do it all tonight.

Bring u. Pub pool after." "K."

Damon looked at his phone for the time. 3:00 p.m. He had an hour to kill before jumping in the truck to go to Pete and Angie's home in Waukesha. He picked up a book he'd been itching to finish, *Indian Creek Chronicles* by Pete Fromm. Damon was intrigued about the premise of the memoir, a young man fascinated about mountain man life agrees to watch over a salmon spawning site in the Bitterroot Valley located in southwestern Montana over the winter. He sat down on one of his overstuffed chairs and set the timer on his phone. Damon knew two things: 1) he would get so engrossed while reading that he lost track of time and 2) never come late to a pregnant woman's invitation to dinner.

Before he knew it, his alarm was going off and he'd already read three chapters. Looking around the house, he realized that everything was in order, and he had a little bit of time to put together a bouquet of fresh flowers from his mom's garden, with her permission, of course. He texted her and, knowing she wouldn't say no, jumped in the truck toward the main house. It so happened his mother was already in the garden, and she had a beautiful bouquet of poppies, cosmos, and dusty miller that she was trying to tie together with a ribbon. As soon as she saw him, she smiled and directed him. "Here, hold this right here. I've got a pretty red ribbon that will pick up the color in the poppies." He did as he was told, while she worked like a pro and put together a perky multi-looped bow before cutting off the ends at an angle for that finishing touch.

Damon bent low enough that he could kiss his mother's cheek under her sunhat. "Thanks, Mom. You're the best." Heather shivered and giggled a bit.

"You're welcome. By the way, you need to cut that fuzz off your face. It tickles." Although knowing the answer would be no, she had to get her two cents in. He had already turned around and was practically in the truck with a brief wave of goodbye.

Thirty minutes later, Damon arrived in the driveway of a mission-style two-story home in the Town of Waukesha. Its dark gray exterior was trimmed with bright white borders around all the windows, and a bright yellow door welcomed visitors. The front porch was highlighted by the stained wooden railing and beams that created a focal point over the door. Grabbing the bouquet that he lay carefully on the seat next to him, he jumped out of the truck just as the door opened to show his best friend. As Damon got closer to the door, wafts of garlic, basil, and oregano streamed through the opening and into his nose. "Mmm. Angie's cooking Italian tonight."

"All day she's been going strong. She made her noni's marinara sauce and my mom's gnocchi. I hope you're hungry. She made enough to feed all of Waukesha." Pete's eyes rolled as he finished, but it was clear that Angie was everything to him. He was wearing a bright red polo shirt and khaki shorts as he opened the door so that Damon could sneak by him and into their American-Italian home.

Both Pete and Angie's parents had come from Italy, but they hadn't met until college. Pete had been dating around a lot, and his mother was very concerned about the quality of his love interests. She happened to know Angie's parents through the Italian fesitvals in downtown Milwaukee, and the two families devised a plan to get the two youngsters together on a semi-blind date at a festival where Angie was a part of a traditional dance troupe that danced every day during the weekend festival. Pete's parents made a big deal of the entire family going down to the festival grounds to see this dance troupe, eat pasta, and watch the fireworks. Pete went because he knew of those times his mother would not take no for an answer, and this was one of those times. So, he canceled his date with—he didn't even remember her name now—and went, convinced he wouldn't have a good time.

His mother introduced him to Angie's parents at the stage, where Angie's parents happened to be saving seats for him and his family. Thinking he wouldn't be that interested in the entertainment, Pete started people-watching in the crowd. Then the music started, and the dancers came out in traditional red and white costumes. Coming out in pairs, from the sides of the stage, each set seemed to skip toward the middle of the stage with big bright smiles for the crowd. When the last couple came out, Pete had to take a second look. The woman looked sensual, exotic. She wore a red skirt with a white lace apron tucked underneath a bright red corset that lifted her well-endowed bosom, which was covered in a white cotton blouse with a lace collar. As he gazed up her long elegant neck, he was taken by her lush red lips and big dark eyes. Then he saw her ebony hair swept up into a wreath of flowers and ribbons, and he was a goner. He couldn't stop looking at her as she performed the intricate dance moves, and he swore that a few times she caught his eyes on purpose.

After the dance ended, Pete was the first to get up and give a standing ovation for the troupe. What he didn't see was that both mothers looked behind his back and nodded. They knew that their work was almost done. Now it was a matter of seeing Angie's reaction to Pete. Angie stopped down between performances to hug and kiss her family and to be introduced to Pete. She got caught in his dark brown eyes, long black eyelashes, and thick curly hair; she was twitterpated. Angie agreed to meet up with Pete to walk around the festival grounds after her last performance, which was in two hours.

When the time came that she was available for their "date," Pete was even more infatuated with her. Angie's hair was long and shiny like black patent shoes. She parted it down the middle, so it framed her oval face and tan skin. She wore a simple little white cotton top with pearl buttons down the front and spaghetti straps and a denim mini skirt showing off her long tan legs and leather sandals. In her ears were golden hoops that gave her the look of a gypsy woman. If she were to tell him of his future at that moment, he already knew. He wanted Angie to be his one and only for the rest of their lives.

At the end of the festival, there was a huge fireworks show. They sat on one of the break wall rocks separating the festival grounds from Lake Michigan and shared their first kiss. While it hadn't been all vino and roses through the years, they had broken up a few times along the way, they were both stubborn Italians and refused to give up.

When Damon walked into the foyer, he heard the familiar voice of his best friend's wife, albeit a little more out of breath these days. "Damon! God, it's been ages. I've missed you." Angie came at him with her arms flung wide and a large smile across her glistening face. Her hair was up in a messy bun and a little flour was dusted on her cheek. She was wearing a light blue maternity tank top and maternity jean shorts. She was wearing tennis shoes in the home, which was otherwise taboo. After their hug, she pulled away and saw the bouquet of flowers with the red bow. "Oh my! Are these for me?"

"You are the most beautiful woman I know."

"Liar! But, hey, these days, I'll take any compliment I can get from a handsome man. Now that I'm as big as a house." With that, Angie reached down and patted her impossibly round belly. By this time, Pete had joined the couple; he bent down to kiss her stomach and then kissed her lips.

"See, I told you, you are the most beautiful woman in the world. Pregnancy looks good on you, baby."

"Both of you are liars, but you're my liars." Angie smiled and kissed both of them. After kissing Damon, she scrunched her face. "Ugh, you may be handsome, but you have to do something with that beard. It itches." Angie turned around to go back to the kitchen; she found a lovely pottery vase to put the flowers in and placed it as a centerpiece on their oak and black iron kitchen table. Pete reached into one of the kitchen cupboards to collect the bright green Fiestaware plates and bowls to set the table. A bottle of Chianti was sitting in the middle of the table airing, and Pete brought out a bottle of sparkling red grape juice to set by Angie's plate.

Damon followed Angie's direction to sit down at the table, and he poured the Chianti for Pete and himself and then poured Angie's sparkling grape juice. Pete brought over the large ceramic pasta bowl filled with steaming dumplings of gnocchi, bathed in an aromatic marinara sauce. Angie brought over a tossed salad and a set of oil and vinegar carafes. Pete went back to grab the garlic bread fresh from the oven.

Once everyone was seated, Angie lifted her glass and encouraged them to follow suit. "To loving family, good friends, and nutritious food. Salute!" They clinked their glasses together to signify the beginning of the meal. Damon's stomach had forgotten that he had just eaten a few hours ago because an embarrassing growl was heard in the silent pause when everyone was filling their plates.

"Excuse me," he impishly said. Angie saw it as a sign that her meal would be appreciated and smiled. Pete just laughed because all boys, of any age, laugh at burps, farts, and stomach noises. The evening was going famously. Though none of them could remember how long it had been since they'd done something together, it was as though no time had passed. Friends this close tended to act more like family than sometimes families did. Because Pete and Damon were as close as brothers, once Angie came along, Damon felt she was like another sister. He valued her opinion and wouldhelp his friends if they ever needed him, no questions asked. And he knew that they would do the same for him, no questions asked.

After stuffing himself and seeing that everyone else was equally satiated, Damon offered to clear the table, although Angie would take it as a personal offense if he did the dishes. Angie looked at the clock over the sink. "Boys, it's time that I have a little time to myself tonight. After dishes, I plan on putting in a chick flick and am putting my feet up for the rest of the night. You two can go and rekindle your bromance for a few hours. But if you are drinking a lot, call me and I'll pick you up. I don't need to get a phone call from the cops telling me that my husband and friend are wrapped around a tree or are in jail. Understood?" They both looked at her and nodded and then each took a cheek to kiss her goodbye.

Hopping into Damon's truck, they drove the few miles down the road to the H.O.G. in downtown Waukesha. Damon found a parking space around the corner, and they entered the establishment where a young trio was singing and playing Irish tunes on the small front stage. They ordered two beers, expertly poured, and headed toward the back where the pool table was located to start their game. As soon as Damon chalked his pool cue and lined up the cue ball for his first shot, Pete asked, "Dude, how'd it go last night? Angie's been picking my brain trying to get every detail out of me, and I don't have anything to share. You've got to give me something so I can get her off my back!"

Damon chuckled because he could picture the scene exactly as it played out. "Okay, okay. The last thing I need is a guilt trip from a pregnant woman and her husband. I'll give it, but I thought this was our night. You know, drink a beer, shoot pool, shoot the shit, and then go home. I didn't think you got into this lovey-dovey stuff on bro-night."

"Look, you know as well as I do that Angie sees any unmarried adult male as a potential client for her 'matchmaker' instincts. You know that her mom and my mom were in cahoots to get us together, and look how good it turned out. Angie feels she has the same intuitive gift and wants to try it out on you. She loves you, you know."

"I know. I love her, too. She doesn't have to look out for me. I'm a big boy and I can take care of myself."

"So? Get to the dirt, man! What happened? What's she like? Are you going to see her again?"

"Chill out. I promised I'd talk, and I will. Just let me take my shot." Damon bent over his pool cue to line up his next shot and scratched. Pete reached in to get the cue ball and line it up for his shot while Damon took a sip of his beer and sat one cheek down on a black vinyl and wooden barstool. "We went to Friday Night Live down here, and she brought her dog, Mia. Told me that if the dog liked me, then we could continue on the date, and if not, she would leave me high and dry in the parking lot."

This time Pete chuckled. "Dude, that's harsh. Smart on her part, but harsh. Go on," he replied as he bent over to take his next shot into the corner pocket.

Damon regaled the rest of the night, leaving out the butterflies, fireworks, and electricity that he felt every time he looked at or touched her. It was his turn to shoot, and as he lined up his shot, he glanced over at Pete through the corner of his eye. This shot he made, and then another, but he was getting antsy waiting for Pete to say something. Finally, he missed one. "Well?" he said with exasperation.

Pete paused a bit longer. He was standing up with his hands folded on his pool cue and his chin resting on them. "Well," he paused again. "Dude, you're in deep. Any clue how she feels about you?"

It was time for Damon to pause. How much was too much information? "I'm pretty confident she feels the same way." Then because the seriousness of the conversation was making him uncomfortable and unbro-like, he said, "Her dog sure loves me, though." Damon's brilliant smile grew wide as he put both of his fists on his waist and laughed aloud.

"Dick. That's a no-brainer. You love animals and they love you. You're the fucking pied piper of Erin, Wisconsin, for Christ's sake! You know I can't take that to Angie. She'd filet me for giving her such lame stuff. Can you at least tell me what she looks like? Do you have any photos? Anything I can bring back with me as proof that she's the real deal? Otherwise, you might be looking at a list of blind dates that you will be required to accept." Pete lifted his right eyebrow and took a long cool drink from his glass. The ball was now back in Damon's court.

Damon put his hands on his cue stick and looked straight into Pete's eyes. He couldn't bullshit a bullshitter, and he'd never lie to his friend. Still, he was trying to figure it all out in his own mind; how could he explain it to anyone else? He didn't know the words he should use to express how he felt, and most importantly, he sure as hell didn't want to end up dating another Paige. Get all goo-goo over a girl and then have her shit all over him again. His heart couldn't take it. "Okay, okay. First off, you can tell Angie that she's half Italian, on her dad's side. Her last name is Carneri. I know she lives near her parents in Mukwonago but that she and Mia live in her own apartment. You know where she works and what she does. Isn't that enough?"

Pete could see his friend was struggling, but he wasn't about to give up. He knew something important was brewing underneath Damon's cool exterior. "You know it's not. Spill."

Damon sat on the barstool, put one elbow on the sticky wooden table, and rested his chin between his thumb and pointer finger. He sighed. "Okay, okay. She looks like the most beautiful Irish goddess you've ever seen. She has curls that pick up every possible color of the sun; she has eyes that every time I look into them a different color is reflected. She has luscious curves that I can't seem to stop thinking about how much I want to touch them—skin on skin. And she smells like lavender and vanilla. I know it's only been two dates, but it's more than her looks. It's how she was willing to let me go out of her life if her dog wouldn't accept me, even if I was Mr. Right. She lives near her parents but has her own life. She writes grants to help animals. These things tell me that she's loyal, that family is important to her, and she's compassionate. There's real potential with her, and when we kissed, it was like a Goddamn explosion. I stopped breathing at some point, and I stopped thinking about anything except how I wanted to put babies in her belly." Damon paused to search Pete's eyes for some sense of what he was thinking. "Bat-shit crazy, right?"

Pete reached over and put both of his hands onto Damon's shoulders, looked deep into those troubled blue eyes, and said the only thing he could say, "Not bat-shit crazy, Man. She's your Angie." With that, Damon's head dropped, and Pete felt him take a deep breath.

"I'm scared, bro. What if I fuck it up? What if she fucks me up? I can't come back from that again."

"If she's anything like you say she is, she won't fuck you up. Not on purpose. I can't promise that it will all be beer and sex all night every night, but if she's worth it, you'll find a way to make it work. Look at me and Angie. She's put up with a ton of my shit over the years, and she's kicked me out a few times. I wasn't a good man when we started going out, coming over to her place on a date night already stinkin' drunk or letting old flames flirt with me when we were out. The last time she broke up with me was six months before we got married. You know, you were there. I was a basket case. I got a little too drunk and let that Donna chick at the bar drive me back to my apartment. She was dressed for sin and thought she could get a late-night bootie call from me so when she was reaching into my front pocket for my keys and Angie opened my door and saw her tits in my face and her hands down my pants ... well, I deserved everything I got that night.

"What love did for me was to wake me up. Did I want to be a drunk and sleep with every piece of ass that wiggled in front of me? Or did I want something that made me feel like a man? Something I could be proud of and build on. My mom slapped me across the face and wouldn't talk to me for a month. My dad came over, sat me down, and told me, 'Son, what is it you want out of life? A piece of ass or a bosom that will nurse your babies? Do you want to sit at the bar and drink beer until you pass out or do you want to pour a glass of wine for you and one for your wife after a long hard day and be proud of the life you've crafted for yourself? Do you want to be a boy who needs immediate satisfaction all the time and is alone because he is selfish, or do you want to be a man who sees the big picture and is willing to take the long road full of sacrifices and detours to get there with his soulmate? Grow up!' Then he also smacked me across the face.

"You picked me up after my parents and Angie left me in shambles. You didn't ask questions and you didn't lecture me. You were there for me, and I promise, I'll be there for you, too, if you need me. No questions asked. But if I see you are being a dick and screwing up something special, I will tell you. I will be honest with you. I promise."

Damon looked up into his friend's eyes and remembered what a screw-up Pete had been and how long it took to get back into his parents' and Angie's good graces. Though it took a bit longer for her parents to accept him, he did ask Angie's dad for his permission to date and then marry his daughter to show his respect and humility to them and to Angie. When Angie said "yes" but that she wanted a small, private wedding, he was surprised. All Italian weddings were showcases. Each family tried to outdo the last wedding. Everyone in the Italian community was always invited. Their mothers would be so upset to miss out on being the center of the Italian universe for a day, but Damon recalled that when Pete asked him to be his best man, he said, "Angie wants us to have a simple ceremony because she doesn't want the meaning of what we're about to do to get lost in all the pageantry. Once we make it to twenty-five years, then she wants the mother of all bashes. But besides our families and the priest, you're the only other person invited to attend the wedding."

Damon remembered how honored he was to be invited and the privilege he felt when he was asked to be Pete's best man over his own brothers. It was then that he knew he also loved Angie and that she loved him too. Not in a romantic way, but in a family way. They both loved Pete and would work together to help him build his legacy as a successful man, a family man. Coming back into the present, he reached out with his right hand, grasped Pete's, pulled him into a manly hug, and said quietly, but sincerely, "Thanks, bro, for having my back," and Pete responded by pulling the hug in tighter.

After that serious moment, they silently toasted each other and played one final round of pool to work off the beers and to bring some levity back into their bro-night. Damon pulled into Pete and Angie's driveway at about 11:00 p.m. The lights were already off in the house, but a porch light stayed on. Before Pete got out of the truck, he looked over at his friend and said, "You're a good man, Damon. If any woman tries to treat you like Paige did, you can bet that both Angie and I will rip her to pieces. Figuratively, of course." Pete paused, stepped out of the cab, and turned around to look back at Damon with his arm holding the door. "Unless Angie is still pregnant, then I can't promise there won't be blood." They both laughed heartily while Pete shut the door and walked into his home. Their home, Damon corrected himself. Pete was coming into his own as a successful man, a family man.

Chapter Seven

Since Friday night, Cat's head had been spinning. After spending a few hours at the state fair with her family, she was still antsy. She tried to keep busy by cleaning the apartment, washing her SUV, and doing some food shopping. She even called her friend, Aurelie, to go to the gym and try out a hot yoga class that she'd heard about. "Something's up. You never invite me to go to the gym. What the hell is hot yoga anyway? It sounds gross! Tell you what, let's meet at the high school on Sunday afternoon and play some tennis. That way you can tell me what's going on and we can still get a workout."

"Fine. See you at 1:00 p.m.?"

"Sure thing, Kitty Cat."

"You know I hate that nickname. Can't you find something else?"

"When you can spell my name correctly, I will. As it is, I have to suffer through text messages and birthday cards with my name spelled 'O-a-r L-e-e.' We've been friends since kindergarten. Haven't you figured it out by now?"

Cat smiled; she loved teasing Aurelie about her name because it got her so crazy, and the honest answer was, it was a bitch to try to remember how to spell. "Hey, we've only been friends for twenty years. I'll work on it for the next twenty, deal?"

"Deal. Oh, and by the way, my sister saw you with a hunky man at Friday Night Live. You're on my list for not telling me about him. What kind of friend are you when I have to get the juicy gossip through my sister? I have a rep to protect as your best friend, you know."

Cat knew it was coming but wanted to put it off until they were face-to-face. "That's why I wanted to get together with you this weekend. You have to help me deconstruct the date, so I know what steps I have to take next. You know I'm not that great with guys or making new friends for that matter. I can't lose you; you're the only true friend I've got. I wouldn't keep this from you, I swear."

"Hmm, I'll let it slide as I was working double shifts at the store to help out with summer vacations. Pretty pumped I got Sunday and Monday off in a row. I will pencil you in for all of Sunday. We've got a lot to do, my friend. Be prepared to work hard."

"All right, all right already! See you on the courts!" Cat hung up and smiled. Aurelie was right; she was her best friend, and Cat needed to tell her what was going on. She looked down at Mia, who was napping with her favorite chew toy tucked under her chin. Perfect time to prep some meals for the week since Sunday would be devoted to girlfriend stuff. As she began cutting up vegetables and writing meal names and cooking instructions on baggies, she reminisced about the first time she had met Aurelie.

Aurelie came from a larger family than Cat's. She was the youngest of four and the shyest. When it was time for her to go to preschool, she wailed and threw a tantrum because she didn't want to leave her mom and was petrified of new people. Her family had emigrated from Quebec, Canada. Her parents were high school sweethearts and married shortly after graduation. Her dad became a famous oncologist and was recruited to work for a prestigious cancer center in Madison. While Madison is a welcoming city for international students, faculty, and staff, Mrs. Beres was concerned about raising their family in a city. They looked everywhere, and while many may consider Mukwonago's hour-long distance from Madison a long distance to travel to work daily, she fell in love with the small-town atmosphere and the easy access to the Kettle Moraine forest: its hiking trails, camping, and fishing. Besides,

Dr. Beres traveled frequently for work, so it was what was best for the family that concerned her as she was the parent raising them. Mrs. Beres was a strict and formal woman but loved her family fiercely. School was a priority and chores were a must. There were two rules in the Beres home that were drilled into Aurelie and her siblings from the moment they could walk: 1) Doing well in school is your job; therefore, studying is a priority. 2) It is a privilege to live in my house; therefore, you will keep your room clean, your bathroom spotless, and will accept chores without complaint as it is understood that chores are the equivalent of rent payment. Should any Beres child refuse to complete a chore or do it poorly, rent would be charged.

Within the Beres family, the children were well disciplined and loved. No surprise, they also did very well in school and went on to work at prestigious companies, or in the medical field, or as dentists. Aurelie was not a problem child, but she didn't fit into the Beres family mold. She broke the mold. While they all looked similarly beautiful, long and slender bodies with shiny black hair and pristine skin and teeth, Aurelie seemed to have a wildness about her. No matter how many times her mother brushed her hair and carefully plated her hair into two perfectly matched braids, Aurelie's hair was often in disarray with, quite possibly, a stick or two wedged in her strands. And while everyone in the family woke up before their alarms, excited about the day ahead, Aurelie felt waking up with the alarm was optional, which meant she was often late to school. Despite the battle of wills between Aurelie and her mother, Mrs. Beres assured Aurelie that she was loved unconditionally. Aurelie looked up to her brother and sisters and put her mother on a pedestal. She tried to fit in with the rest of the family, but with each failed attempt, she was found crying on her mother's lap, trying to explain her side of the story through tears and hiccups. It should come as no surprise that her favorite bedtime story was Hans Christian Anderson's *The Ugly Duckling*. Mrs. Beres would be heard softly speaking to her youngest, "Shh, shh, mon cherie. You will be the most successful of my children because you have the biggest heart and are not afraid of failure. I promise you."

As the years went on, Aurelie looked forward to summer vacations around the globe with their parents and short weekend jaunts camping, hiking, and canoeing in the state parks and rivers throughout Wisconsin. When it was time for preschool, even though Aurelie was familiar with the alphabet, numbers, and colors, she was very shy with anyone who wasn't her family. Mrs. Beres would not budge on this. She explained how important it was to learn how to be with other people and how interesting it would be to learn about other children and what they like to do. Aurelie wouldn't have any of it. No one would be as interesting as her family! Mrs. Beres was at her wit's end when she and her husband finally came up with a plan. Instead of paying rent via chores, which Aurelie was not successful at, they devised a game of sorts that for every friend Aurelie made at school, she could choose to be released from a chore each week. Because Aurelie loved games and wanted to be rid of some of her chores, even if it were only for a week, she was very agreeable to rules of the game, and with a new sense of confidence and focus, little Aurelie would scan her preschool class for potential friends each week, and that's how Cat came to know her first school friend.

It was during recess, and Aurelie had just come outside to play when she saw Cat hovering around the swings because she was too afraid to ask for a turn. Aurelie walked straight up to Cat, stuck out her hand for a handshake, and smiled, "Hello! My name is Aurelie Beres. You and I are now friends. What's your name?" Cat was astonished and intrigued by this bold and brass behavior. Something inside her told her it would be worth her while to shake this little girl's hand and become her friend.

"Hi, I'm Catrina Carneri, but I like to be called Cat. I'd like to be your friend."

"Cat? As in kitty cat?"

"Yes."

"That's weird. But that's okay. I'll just call you Kitty Cat since you're little. When we get older, then I'll call you Cat. Deal?"

"Um, no. I don't like Kitty Cat. Just Cat." "Okay."

A new friendship was born. Soon, Aurelie had made friends with the entire class and was moving into making friends from other grades. With her shyness all but a memory, her parents felt that their plan was a huge success. Aurelie was very successful in preschool and grade school, but when things became more logical like math, science, and grammar (which she honestly felt was very illogical and her English grades reflected that mentality), she started to regress. She was never going to be as smart as her parents or siblings. Middle school was very difficult for her, and she was starting to drift into crowds of kids who preferred to do things that her parents did not approve of. Cat was doing well in those classes, but still pretty low on the friend-o-meter, so she was very concerned about losing her only real friend.

Cat set up study sessions for them and helped Aurelie take practice tests. After a while, Aurelie's parents got involved with the school and tested her for learning disabilities. Eventually, they figured out she had a form of dyslexia that was making it difficult for her in school. They invested in tutoring specialists and focused all their free time in helping Aurelie find a way to manage her dyslexia without giving up. Cat pitched in where she could, and the Bereses were very grateful. It was then that they realized that perhaps having lots of friends may not be as important as having a small number of true friends.

It was also during this time that Aurelie's passion for art, especially music, was found. It turned out that she was exceptional in listening to a musical piece and picking out the notes that were being played or sung. She had a beautiful soprano voice that was perfectly on pitch. Her music teacher worked with her tutors and parents to come up with a study plan that incorporated music, which seemed to help improve Aurelie's other subjects.

Aurelie's penchant for music led to acceptance into a university music program in Milwaukee and eventually becoming a high school band teacher. While her family could assist her with making a living, she worked at a department store during the day and played in a band on summer break. When she finally had a moment to herself, she tried to connect with Cat. She didn't have a man in her life; she had several. Hopelessly devoted to five or six at the moment.

Her model-like looks, her vibrant and free personality, and her music made her very popular with the boys. She knew what real love looked like; all she had to do was see her parents together. Forty years strong and still one could see the passion they held for each other when they had a moment alone. That's what she wanted, and she wouldn't settle for less. Still, at her age, her parents were already married six years and were young parents living on their own. She wouldn't consider this part of her life a failure just yet. She always seemed to be the late bloomer in her family, and she was just fine with that.

As for Cat, however, this hunky man sounded promising. She couldn't wait to hear all about it on Sunday.

Around 1:15 p.m. on Sunday, Cat was bouncing tennis balls off the practice wall when she heard a familiar voice belting out Katy Perry's "Roar" to blaring music coming out of a tan sedan. Out stepped Aurelie in a perfectly matched racerback neon green tank with a black and neon green tennis skirt. Her shoulder-length black hair was held back in a simple ponytail, and a neon green bandana was tied across her forehead.

"Bandanas went out in the 1980s with Olivia Newton-John and Pat Benatar," Cat commented.

"Oh, and you're such a fashionista yourself, Kitty Cat. What're you wearing today? A ripped and paint-stained gray T-shirt and gray sweatpants cut-offs? Classy. By the way, your crazy hair could use a bandana today. It's starting to frizz out," Aurelie replied with one eyebrow lifted up, waiting for the next comeback.

"I dressed to play tennis, not to make a play, bitch."

"Let's get this show on the road, then, potty mouth. I dress for success and for the possible hot guy that may be watching us play. You know I like to keep my options open."

"No shit. Are you up to ten guys now?"

"Noooo. Five or six at the moment. Come on. You seemed warmed up with your arms and your lips. Let's see what you've got."

One of the nice things about their friendship was that they liked many of the same things. In high school, they both made the tennis team and even played doubles together a few times. While not the tennis stars of the team, they both won enough games to earn their varsity letters before their senior year. With Aurelie now the band teacher at the high school they graduated from, it was a nice throwback and an easy rhythm for both of them to get into.

After a few practice hits, the game started for real. It was evenly matched as each woman knew the strengths and weaknesses of her opponent. During water breaks, Aurelie quizzed Cat on the first meeting and two consecutive dates with Damon. These breaks were for taking in information. After the game, there would be plenty of time to get into the meat of the situation.

An hour and a half later, Aurelie won three games to two with several going into tiebreakers. Both sweaty and out of breath, they agreed to go back to Cat's place to get on swimsuits and spend the rest of the afternoon on the beach at Ottawa Lake. When they got to the little bungalow, Mrs. Romansky was sitting outside with a glass of iced tea reading the Sunday paper. Today, she was dressed in her church clothes, a pale-yellow cotton top with a boat collar and short sleeves over a flowy white skirt and white sandals. She saw the two cars coming into the driveway and smiled when she recognized the two young women. "Hello, ladies! If you've got a moment, I have snickerdoodles coming out of the oven in a few minutes. Want to be my official taste testers?"

Even though Aurelie was lean and lanky, she had the metabolism of a roadrunner. She could eat everything and anything and not gain an ounce. She didn't even have to blink an eye. "Sounds fabulous, Mrs. Romansky. Thanks for the offer!"

Cat, on the other hand, was mentally checking off how many calories she had already eaten today and how many she burned off. If she just stuck to one, she'd be okay. "Smells delicious! I think I can have one too. Can we take them on the road? We're going to the beach."

"Perfect. You girls go on up now and get ready for the beach. I'll pack up a nice snack for you both. Don't worry about being back for Mia's dinner. I don't have any dinner plans tonight. I'll be happy to feed and let her out, and she can keep me company while you girls enjoy yourselves." That's why Cat loved living with Mrs. Romansky. She was so easygoing and willing to help out with Mia when necessary. Plus, her baking was amazing—too good, actually.

The two young women went up the stairs, gave the required amount of love and attention to the other lady in the flat, and then each took a bedroom to change into swimsuits. Aurelie's car was a bit of a catastrophe, but when she needed something outside of the plan, it seemed to magically appear somewhere in her car or trunk. She just happened to have yet to unpack a bag full of clothes that she had bought on clearance with her employee discount that week. One of those items was a string bikini in metallic hot pink. With her bronze skin tone and dark features, the suit would just pop on her, and she knew that the boys would come running. She threw a T-shirt into an empty bag she found on the floor of the car and shimmied on a pair of jean shorts she had also found in the catastrophic, yet magical car.

Cat put on her lime green halter and boy shorts swimwear and threw on an oversized T-shirt. She found her beige and gold beach bag and threw in a couple of towels, two bottles of water, and sunscreen. She lent a pair of flip-flops to Aurelie, and they both headed down the stairs. At the bottom, they found Mrs. Romansky with a paper sack filled with cookies and fresh fruit. Each girl gave her a kiss on the cheek and a warm hug to thank her for their treats and for watching Mia. Aurelie opened her car door and started throwing piles of junk out of the passenger seat and into the back seat to make room for Cat. "You've got to clean out this car, Aurelie! It could have creatures living in it!" Cat carefully sat down and strapped in, afraid to touch something that would touch her right back.

"Hey, I've made progress. My parents finally got me to clean my room and bathroom. I need one space that I can have as my messy place. This car is it. You wanna drive?" The truth was Cat didn't. She just wanted to chill out today and not think about anything like crazy drivers.

"Sorry. My bad. You can drive." With that, Aurelie stepped on the gas, and they sped off toward the Kettle Moraine Forest and Ottawa Lake. Driving through the forest felt like driving in northern Wisconsin. Tall pine trees lined the windy roads, and when the wind rustled through them, their scent wafted into the car. The girls were singing Bon Jovi at the top of their lungs with their ponytails swaying in the breeze.

Because it was a Sunday afternoon, the beach wasn't as busy as it had been earlier in the weekend. Most people were packing up to go home. Ottawa Lake was a great camping spot for out-of-towners and townies who just wanted a break from home life for a few days. Aurelie's mom would take the kids tent-camping here on weekends when her dad was away on a business trip. Each kid had their own responsibility for putting up the campsite and taking it down. They could get the whole car unpacked and a fire going in the fire pit in twenty minutes flat. Though she didn't make a lot of money, Aurelie felt that paying for the state park sticker every year was worth every penny to enjoy for small jaunts like a day at the beach or a weekend camping with friends.

They found a spot on the grass right before the sand beach. It had an empty picnic table next to it, and it wasn't that far from the flushing toilets and changing station. After spreading out their towels and disrobing, they walked into the tepid lake water to get used to the cooler temperature. Aurelie took out her hair tie and put it on her wrist and dove right in. Cat wanted to take more of a slow and steady pace to get used to the water, but Aurelie wouldn't have any of it. She broke through the water and started splashing her friend until Cat dove under to escape the assault. They swam to a quiet spot near one of the buoys and began to tread water. "Well?" Cat questioned her friend.

"Well," Aurelie paused.

"You're killing me! What do you think? What should I do?" Cat quizzed her friend.

"Let me finish," Aurelie responded in her teacher tone, which made Cat shut her lips sheepishly.

"Well, based on everything you just told me and what I know about men, he's really into you. I know you're gaga over him already. So why do you need me?"

"Because … you know the only real relationship I had just ended a few months ago, and he turned out to be an awful person and it was very hard on me. Aur, I need you because I don't trust my instincts. I'm not that confident that I made the right decision in expressing my feelings for him so soon."

"Cat, Jansen is a dirtbag. I don't care how much money his family has; it doesn't buy class and it doesn't buy character. He was a partier in high school, a stoner through college, and now he's got a sweet ride going by working at his daddy's company that he's being groomed to run someday. Plus, he's just plain creepy. You got lucky." Cat's stare looked like it would reach out and slap Aurelie across the face. "Just a minute. Listen. You got lucky that he cheated on you now. I know you, remember? You'd probably keep moseying along because you equate comfort with happiness and agree to marry the fleabag and live in a big, overpriced house on Beaver or North Lake and then find out his prick was in between the legs of every cougar on the lake." Cat looked past the buoy toward the edge of the water where a family of Canadian geese was swimming.

"Cat, you know I'm right. It hurts like hell now, but it would have been even worse if you married the creep. Since I see you are still mulling it over, I've got something to confess." Cat's head swiveled toward her friend with a keen sense of curiosity and focus. "Cat, Jansen made a play for me a while back." Cat's eyes went as large as softballs and her mouth opened into an "O." "Yeah, I didn't tell you because you seemed to want to make this work. Nothing happened, I promise. Okay, I grabbed his nads in my hand and squeezed hard to show him what kind of 'handjob' I had for him. He squealed like a baby pig and practically ran away from me. It was at one of the parties at his family's lake house. He left me alone and gave me a wide berth after that.

"The point is, he isn't and never was worth your effort. This Damon dude may be the real deal. He's a vet; he understands the value of acupuncture, so he'll be supportive of you in that way. He's a family man because he lives on his family's farm, and Mia adores him. Oh, and the fact that he makes you feel like all gushy inside. Look, I may not know what the real thing feels like just yet, but I do know it exists and what it's supposed to look like. My parents are a great example of it. Maybe ask my mom the story about how she knew that my dad was the one?

"I may not know how you are feeling, but I can sure as hell help you with your next steps." Cat's eyes went back to normal but with more warmth and feeling. "I promise I'll be there for you no matter what," she added to break up the seriousness of the conversation. "And if he tries to feel me up, I'll grab his nads and yank them until he squeals like a baby pig." Both girls laughed wholeheartedly at that and swam back to the beach that was pretty much empty by now.

They lay down on their towels, and Aurelie broke open the snack bag while Cat grabbed two drinks of water. "Damn! That woman can bake. These are so yummy. I can taste the cinnamon, and it just melted in my mouth. I need another one!" With that, Aurelie forced her hand back into the bag for cookie number two. Cat slapped it, and she pulled it back in shock.

"Hold on! I get to have a cookie before you eat them all. I've already counted on these calories for today. You may not have to work at your gorgeous figure, but I work very hard for mine. Let me have just one Goddamn cookie before they're gone." Cat reached back into the bag, pulled out a pale-yellow morsel dusted with cinnamon on the top, and bit into it. Her eyes immediately closed, and she moaned, "Oh God, they're still warm." Her eyes closed, she slowly nibbled away at the rest of the snickerdoodle until she only had crumbs left on her fingers, which she meticulously licked off. Aurelie just watched in awe.

"Damn, girl! You almost had an orgasm over a cookie. How long has it been for you?"

Cat's eyes burst open, and she glared at her supposed friend. "You know how long, idiot. Besides, you're supposed to enjoy your food, savor it." As she said the last part, she lifted her head up in the air with a sort of pompous flare.

"Two months. You're on the edge of using a housewife's battery-powered special friend ..." Cat slapped Aurelie on the arm in shock and then started to laugh. "Seriously, though, if this guy is as good as you say he is and makes you feel like that, how long are you going to wait before you sleep with him?"

"I didn't think about it like that. Should I have a time-tabled strategy for sleeping with him? Is that how I should do it? I just thought it would come naturally, you know, romantic-like."

"Well, it sounded like if you two were in your apartment instead of a park, you'd be fucking his brains out on the first date."

"It was the second date, remember? And I wouldn't be fucking his brains out. I want it to be special, romantic. Not just perfunctory, like animals do it. I want it to mean something, you know?"

"Oh right, my mistake, sorry. Would the term 'bonking' be more appropriate here, professor?" Cat laughed. She knew that Aurelie was much more experienced than she was and was making a little fun at her expense. But they were getting into important territory.

Had she gone too far and too fast with Jansen? Jansen was a skilled lover, and he always made sure she was satiated as much as his feral needs were met. But Aurelie had a point. Was she making too much of it, the meaning of it, or should it just be natural? First date or fifth or one hundredth? Did it matter when?

"Seriously, I know you, Kitty Cat." "Stop calling me that, Oar."

"Okay, that's just mean. I'll try again. Seriously, Cat." "Go on."

"Okay, you've got a date set up for next Saturday at the medieval fair, but no interactions confirmed in between, correct?"

"Correct."

"I think tonight you should text him to see if he has a moment to say 'hi,' ask him how his weekend went. Then reiterate how much fun you had on Friday night and how much you're looking forward to Saturday. I'll see if I can have off on Friday night and Saturday morning so we can have a sleepover, and I can help do your hair and makeup, so you look like a sexy pirate and see what kind of reaction he gives you."

Cat smiled and kissed her friend quickly on the mouth to show her thanks. "Be careful there, wench. Girl on girl gets guys hot." Cat laughed some more and gave Aurelie a peck on each cheek and her forehead. "Oh baby, you need to get laid. You're getting me all tingly." At this, they both ended up lying on their backs and laughing until they had tears rolling down their cheeks. "You said he commented on how you smelled like vanilla and lavender, correct?"

"Yeah, why?" Cat rolled on her side and propped her head on her hand, intrigued at where this was going.

"My mom has some fantastic perfume from France that Dad bought her on one of his trips. It's got a musky, spicy smell to it. I think a pirate needs to smell the part, don't you?"

"You mean like dirt, sweat, and dead fish?" Cat couldn't stop giggling at this last part. Just then, Aurelie reached over and pushed her down on her back, though Cat still giggled.

"No, you idiot. Like a sexy pirate. All spicy and musky; maybe drink some spiced rum or whiskey. Wear those gold hoops of yours, and I have some thigh-high black boots that I wear on stage sometimes. I'll bring those over for you, and we'll do manis and pedis. You need a bright red polish. You got any of that?"

"Yup."

"We'll do your hair in waves or curls. It has to be down. But your corset needs to fluff your girls up as high as they can go without playing peek-a-boo. Yeah, this is going to be good. Real good. This will show us what kind of man he really is. You're taking two separate cars?"

"No. He asked me to text him my address so he could pick me up. Is that bad? Should I ask to meet him there?"

Aurelie thought for a moment. "That can be the reason for the phone call tonight. Confirm he got your text and offer that you can meet him there so he isn't driving so far out of the way. If he accepts your offer to take two separate cars, you can be assured of your continued abstinence for another week and that he's just not that into you. Unless you get him so hot and bothered he comes at you like a horse in heat behind the smithies' forge. But if he confirms he's picking you up, you can find out how much he's into you and then save the romantic sex session for another day. If, on the other hand, his eyes go wandering to all the other scantily dressed wenches at the fair, I think you'll know the answer to the question you haven't asked me yet."

"What's that?" "Is he worth it?"

Lying on the beach towel, she turned her head to look at her friend. "Is he?"

Aurelie turned her head in return. "We'll find out." With that, both women rolled over on their stomachs and let the heat of the sun dry their backsides while they took a light nap. When they woke, it was because Aurelie's stomach growled.

"Seriously? Didn't you eat like six cookies?" Cat grumbled at her friend.

"Ah, if I remember correctly, you slapped my hand going for the sixth cookie, so I had five, thank you very much. I need real food now. You hungry? We can grab a slice of pizza at ZaZing! and then get going home. I've got some practice I need to do for the band. We're playing next weekend at a church festival."

"Where?"

"Waterford."

"That's my parents' church! When?"

"Saturday. I think we go on at 8:00 p.m. and play till 10:00 before the main band goes on."

"Well, if everything goes well at the fair, maybe we can come and see you in the band and you can meet him in person. Then you can call me on Sunday and tell me what you think."

"Well, if everything goes right, he may be the one picking up the phone on Sunday morning after a night of hot crazy sex with a lady pirate." Cat rounded up her towel into a rat's tail and slapped her friend on the backside with a loud "crack!"

"You slut!" Cat yelled. With that, they both got up and packed up their beach gear to take back to Aurelie's sedan.

"Have to be one to know one!" Aurelie called back as she reached her car. After putting on their tees and shorts, they climbed into the car and drove the five miles into North Prairie for a slice of pizza and a soda to finish up their girlfriends' date. Lots of giggles and burps later, Aurelie drove back to the bungalow to drop off Cat for the night.

Cat reached in the back for her bag and stuck her head through the opening of the passenger window. "I really needed this today, Aurelie. Thanks, you're the best."

"Anytime, Kitty Cat. Anytime." Aurelie threw her car into reverse and started down the driveway before the inevitable was heard.

"Don't call me that!" she heard Cat yelling at the moving car. She put on the radio and started singing Duran Duran at the top of her lungs as she listened to a 1980s radio station.

Cat got up the steps and saw a familiar furry face smiling back at her. "Hello, Mia. Miss me?" With that, Mia got up to grab her favorite stuffed animal and dropped it at Cat's feet. Cat scratched her dog behind the ears and went to clean up after a long day outdoors. Once she had put the dirty clothes away in the hamper and took a quick bath to get off the sunscreen, sand, and lake water, she got into a simple white tank and boxer shorts to get ready for bed. She looked at her phone and the time. 9:00 p.m. Not too early and not too late. Better make the call before she lost her nerve. Oh yeah, first the text. "Hey, when would be a good time for a quick phone call?"

"Now's a good time," Damon texted back.

Cat took a deep breath and dialed. Two rings later, he answered, "Hello?"

"Hi."

"I'm glad you called."

"You are? I mean ..." She looked at her notepad with the talking points she had written down from her day at the beach. "Umm, I wanted to thank you again for such a good time on Friday night. I hope you enjoyed it."

"Yeah, I really did. I'm looking forward to the medieval fair on Saturday. I hope you don't expect me to wear tights."

Cat laughed. "No, I thought a big, brawny Irish lad, who is a medieval fair connoisseur, would have a kilt lying around somewhere."

Damon laughed. "You're right. I do happen to have one or two lying around for Saturday. Have you thought about your costume? Do you still want to dress like a pirate?"

"Would it be okay? I've always wanted to dress up as Captain Hook."

"Hmm. A highlander and a pirate. Let me think about that." Damon paused. Cat struggled not to let out a giggle. "I think that could be arranged, milady."

Smiling to herself, Cat breathed a sigh of relief. The word "arranged" clicked. Now she recalled the main reason for the call. The relationship litmus test that Aurelie suggested.

"Umm, also there's something else I wanted to talk to you about. I just found out my best friend's band is playing at a church festival in Waterford at 8:00 p.m. Wondering if it would be easier for you if we drove separately and then I could hit the band after our date? Or do you still wanted to ride together and then maybe hit the band afterward?" Cat's heart was thumping so loudly she was afraid he could hear it over the phone.

"A gentleman always picks up his date. Seeing a band after the medieval fair sounds perfect! What's the name of the band? What kind of music do they play?"

"The Hot Rockin' Horns. They play a variety of music and have a fantastic horn and rhythm section. My friend, Aurelie, is the lead singer."

"I'm really glad you called." She smiled and got all warm and gushy inside.

"Me too. And Damon?" "Yeah?"

"I'm really looking forward to seeing you again."

There was a pause. "Me too." Cat hung up with a smile on her face. She couldn't wait for Saturday.

The week went by in a fantastic blur. With Dr. O'Brien on her second week of vacation, the office was humming along at a constant pace. Cat confirmed the fall gala invitations were printed and ready to go out in the mail at the required eight weeks before the event. Things were moving along like clockwork in the planning of the upcoming event, and the grants were coming in nicely. Just this week she was notified of two grants; $10,000 and $5,000!

At home, she made plans for Mia to have a sleepover at her parents' house from Friday night to Sunday after church. Since she was feeling a little anxious about Saturday, she went through her wardrobe to pick out an outfit that would work for before and after the medieval fair. As she would be in a dress with high-heeled boots all day and walking, she wanted something more casual and easier for dancing. Cat found a pair of aqua capris and a neon yellow cotton button-down shirt under which she could put a white cami. Looking through her shoes, she found a pair of flat leather sandals that would show off her newly painted red toes and be a heck of a lot more comfortable for dancing, if he liked dancing. God, she hoped that Friday Night Live wasn't just a fluke.

Friday night came and Aurelie told her to grab a pizza and some ice cream for dessert. Aurelie arrived about 6:00 p.m. and broke open the pizza box on the kitchen table, then grabbed paper plates out of the pantry while Cat opened a bottle of Italian red table wine and poured two glasses. A nice breeze was coming in through the windows, so they chose to eat on the back porch in a couple of lawn chairs Cat had placed out there. After a bit of catch-up from the week, it was time to get the sleepover on!

Aurelie grabbed the bottle of a fire engine red nail polish and started with Cat's toes and then went on to her fingers. Cat chose a bottle of mocha polish for Aurelie's fingers and toes. Music playing on the radio, the girls giggled, sang, and just had a fun time primping for the next day. Afterward, they put in *Mamma Mia*, the movie, and they sang and danced to all the musical numbers.

On Saturday morning, they got up to an alarm to make sure they'd have plenty of time to get Cat ready before Damon came to pick her up at 9:00 a.m. After a quick breakfast of Greek yogurt, fresh fruit, and granola, Cat took a quick bath and used unscented lotion over her freshly shaved legs and her arms. After drying off, she put on her capris and the white cami while Aurelie set up a beauty parlor station in the dining room. She powdered Cat's face first, then moved to a dramatic vermilion blush, and ended with smoky eyes, leaving out the mascara that she knew Cat couldn't wear because it made her eyes itchy and watery. On her lips, Aurelie smoothed on a bright red lipstick and packed it into Cat's little black purse. Next, she moved to hair. Cat had washed her hair the night before and used a light mousse to keep it from frizzing overnight. This morning, Aurelie used a curl enhancer spray to perk up the locks from the evening before. Once they sprung into place, Aurelie used her fingers to finger comb them into place and used a small curling iron to tighten up a few stragglers. She found a simple white satin ribbon that she tied into place behind her right ear and let the strands hang down near Cat's left shoulder. Cat reached over to put her gold hoops in her ears, and Aurelie moved to put a dab of the French spice perfume behind each ear, right above her cleavage, and a dab on each wrist and motioned to Cat to rub them together. "Perfect," she said as she was inspecting her masterpiece. "If he doesn't want to have sex with you after today, I just might."

"You and I are straight, remember?"

"True. But seriously, go look in your mirror. You are gorgeous and it's only eight thirty. Shit! Eight thirty! I gotta get out of here otherwise he'll smell something fishy going on." With a quick peck on the cheek and a sweep of the apartment to make sure all of her things were in her bag, Aurelie hastily made the second bed and waved as she grabbed a diet soda out of the frig on her way out the back door.

Cat waved back and mouthed, "Thanks!" making sure the door closed all the way before she took a look in the mirror.\

"I'll be damned!" If she had been a conceited person, she would have expected what she saw. Instead, she was surprised; wasn't even sure it was her, but she pinched her arm and it hurt. It was her, but a more vibrant version of herself, imagining what she would look like in the pirate costume.

When her calendar reminder went off on her phone, she also heard a knock on the door. She yelled through the kitchen window,

"Come on up!" She listened as the corresponding footsteps followed suit. As his shape shadowed through the curtain over the window in the door, she turned the knob and smiled. He was already dressed in his kilt and leather high boots on his feet. The woolen fabric was black and red plaid, a perfect complement to what she had in store. "Hi," she almost whispered. "Come on in. I'm just getting my things together, and we can go."

Damon's smile seized. His eyes traveled slowly from the top of her curly head to the tip of her newly painted toes. They landed back at her freshly made-up face and the smile grew. "Wow! You look incredible! I can't imagine what you'll look like in costume. You are so beautiful." At that moment, she reached up on her tippy toes and lightly brushed his pink lips with her red ones. Then he sniffed her neck; it was erotic and exciting, but then he pulled away. "Whoa, you smell amazing. Different, though, not lavender and vanilla. What is it?"

"Thank you, I borrowed some perfume from my friend, which matched better being a pirate." Cat backed up to have a good look as well. "Wow! I really like this highlander look on you. Maybe if I'm good today, you'll consider wearing it on our next date?" She cocked her head and smiled a flirtatious smile back at him. She was starting to get into a rhythm of coquettish confidence that she didn't know she had, and yet it was coming through her as if instinctive. She noticed that Damon couldn't take his eyes off her. She grabbed her things and joined him on the stairs. After turning around to lock up the apartment, he gently took her bags out of her hand and proceeded to the truck and loaded them into the back seat.

"Well, since today we have a theme going, I thought I would bring out appropriate music for the ride there. How do you feel about Celtic Thunder?"

"Oh my God! My mom took me to their concert on my eighteenth birthday. We were second-row center. It was awesome!"

Damon reached into the middle console and brought out, "The Best of Celtic Thunder," and slipped the disc into the player. Once the drums started playing and the flute's notes soared, Cat exclaimed,

"'Ireland's Call,' I love this one!" before singing along. Throughout the one-hour drive, he was amazed at how many of the songs she knew the words to. She even knew a few he'd forgotten. But they both belted them out and held hands during the more tender ballads. Finally, they reached their destination and were directed to a parking spot on the grass. Damon hopped out first and went around the front to open Cat's door and offered to escort her into the fair.

Since they got there at opening, it was busy, but they got a decent spot and were able to get their tickets and entrance into the gate fairly quickly. Cat accepted a copy of the day's schedule and took Damon's hand to go through the crowd at a strong pace, as if he was on a mission. He knew exactly where the costume rental vendor was and wasn't about to lose another moment to see Cat in her costume. Once they arrived at the light blue and white building, the lady vendor told him it would be a few minutes and pointed out a few of the vendors he might like to visit while he waited. Luckily, they also offered lockers that Cat could put her clothes and bags into once she dressed. After changing into her new outfit and adjusting her corset to show just the right amount of cleavage, she went to the boots and zipped them up. Next, the vendor procured a perfect pirate's hat with white and red plumage, which she carefully placed on Cat's head so that the large black brim was slanted over her left eye, and the side that was plastered up with a black lace bow and gold medallion had the plumage flowing down the backside of the hat. Cat found her little black purse and refreshed her lipstick before looking at the whole ensemble in the mirror. After a careful assessment of herself in full pirate regalia, Cat smiled a wicked smile and walked out.

At first, he didn't recognize her. He was still people-watching a bit, completely intrigued by all the elaborate costumes and some that just didn't fit in. Then he eyed the most mystical creature he'd ever seen. Thigh-high black boots that barely hit the front of a waterfall of black lacy fabric that was cinched at the waist under a red corset laced with black leather laces, barely holding in round globes of pink flesh that he had to use all his strength not to reach out to and hold in his hands and kiss with his mouth. Her breasts raised the white cotton fabric that barely covered them and shimmied off her shoulders. When he didn't think he could take it anymore, he looked up to find those smoldering eyes that he'd begun to recognize and found them dancing in excitement. Then he saw the hat. He swore he didn't want to see anything upset the mane of copper curls he loved so much, but that hat was the sexiest thing he'd ever seen on a woman! What he wouldn't do to have her just wear the hat and boots and nothing else. Holy hell, he was in for a very long day and night.

Once Damon took everything in, Cat smiled a truly catlike smile. She got the reaction she was looking for. He was a goner. Damon couldn't move a muscle and his mouth was wide open. When Cat got to the point of reaching him through the crowd, he grabbed her, a bit too rough, but he was doing everything he could to control himself. He held her face in his hands and crushed his mouth onto hers, forcing her lips to open wide and welcome his tongue into her mouth. He was filled with passion and wild abandon, and she had to hold on to her hat as her head bent to take his whole mouth into hers. Finally, with his aggression calmed, he gently finished the kiss with a brief brush of his lips on hers. She still wanted to be in control today and continue playing the part of the flirtatious pirate, so she reached up with her mouth, sucked in his lower lip, and bit it just a little harder than a nip and slowly let it out.

When the embrace was done, Damon's breath was coming heavy and he was flushed. His skin was almost the color of his flaming red hair. "Holy shit, Cat. I didn't mean to do that to you. I don't know what came over me, and it isn't even noon yet!"

Cat smiled and looked deep into the storm of his blue eyes, "So, you like the hat?"

"Damn! I mean I love the hat, the boots, and whatever it is you are not wearing. You are the sexiest woman I have ever met. I can't believe you're with me."

"Well, the boots aren't mine, I borrowed them from my friend, Aurelie. But the rest of the outfit you paid for. I'm glad you like it." Then she looked down to see that he had really liked it, and he noticed.

"Shit. I'm so embarrassed. I think I need to find a shop with a sporran and a large cup of ice." This time she roared with laughter, knowing how powerful it felt to be able to make a man feel for her in that way. She laced her arm through his as they meandered toward the Celtic vendor just down the street. With a sporran purchased and appropriately fit on the front of his kilt, it was time to take a look at the schedule to see which of the many possible entertainment venues they wanted to watch. Cat recommended they plan for the joust and final joust and then work backward.

Since Damon knew more about the entertainment, eating, and libations, he recommended they pick out two more shows and then just drift around the grounds until the jousts. The first stage they stopped at was a musical group. Cat was thoroughly impressed and started whooping it up until she heard Damon and the rest of the crowd yell, "Hazzah!" The rest of the day when either of them saw or heard something they liked, they belted out a hearty "Hazzah!"

After the show, it was time to eat. Damon had to have a turkey leg while Cat ordered a bowl of sautéed mushrooms. They each washed it down with a foamy mug of beer and went in search of the next show, which was a commedia dell'arte; an audience participation comedy routine. Damon kept quiet about the theme of this particular show—how new Musketeers of the Guard flirt with young maidens, in other words, romance. The masked actors invited the participation of men in the audience to learn how to adore women.

Cat conjured up the confidence to raise her hand and volunteer Damon, excited to participate in the farce. When they found her in the crowd, one of the masked comedic actors approached Cat and decided to engage her in a bit of medieval fair conversation.

"Come hither, sir, and kind lady, may we ask your names?"

Recalling Aurelie's advice to "play the part" and be a courageous flirt, Cat went all in. "'Tis Catrina, queen pirate of the seas." Their eyes twinkled, and the rest of the crowd was captivated by the conversation; however, Damon was getting a little miffed that the Musketeers were flirting as well. Cat, who didn't know the outcome of the show, was very pleased with herself on how it was going so far and was just enjoying the moment, anticipating how it would end.

"Queen Catrina, we are but your humble servants and wish to take these volunteers and turn them into the young lovers you so deserve and desire." The blonde masked Musketeer bowed low in an exaggerated gesture. Damon jealously noticed how his masked eyes glanced over Cat's heaving bosom.

"It is my wish that you do so."

The dark-haired Musketeer then asked, "Queen Catrina, is there a token of your personage that we may receive as an incentive for these fine volunteers to become generous lovers?"

Cat reached into her top and pulled out a white handkerchief that the dark-haired Musketeer delicately took from her hand, which he then kissed. Damon looked astonished at first and then pissed. Cat laughed and whispered to him, "Don't worry, I promise, I like men in kilts better than men in masks." At that, he lifted an eyebrow and walked up to the stage alongside eleven other "volunteers." Cat and the rest of the crowd roared as the Musketeers of the Guard took the men through the phases of the romantic, exaggerated gestures that attract young maidens. The audience would clap and yell "Hazzah!" at the end of each phase, and then when their training was completed, the Musketeers of the Guard presented each man with a long-stemmed red rose, then go back to their seats, and embrace their women with the love and passion that they so desired.

Damon had learned his romantic gestures. When he embraced Cat, he pulled off her hat, dipped her so that her hair was practically touching the bench, took the rose out of his mouth, and smothered her in a smoldering, ravenous kiss that took her breath away. Next, he brought her upright and pulled away slightly, to see she was still in a daze. He placed her hat back on her head, handed her the rose, smiled, and said, "You're welcome." He guided her other arm through his and walked her out of the audience to a round of applause and "Hazzahs!"

The rest of the afternoon went quickly, and Cat was just as fascinated with the vendors as she was with the people in costume, intrigued to figure out which were actors, and which were guests like them. They walked to the grandstand, and Cat let Damon take the lead as he wanted to sit in the best place to see the next show, a jousting exhibition.

Cat sat next to him and enjoyed the jesters who were selling jerky and champion flags to the stands before the joust began. Soon they heard the horns sound that the queen was in the arena and the joust was about to begin. Cat was like a kid in a candy shop and so was Damon. He seemed to be in his element at the fair and he could see why. She shed all her responsibilities at the gates and reveled in the make-believe world where pirates and queens could join together with a Celtic warlord and, wait, was that a stormtrooper next to them? And a stormtrooper could cheer for their favorite champion.

Cat got excited to see the horses gallop past them in all their pageantry and armor and was pleased to see, at first glance, that they were healthy and well taken care of. She was exhilarated by the exhibition and wondered how it was that she'd lived so close all these years and had never been here before. Damon helped Cat get out of the stands as they went looking for another tasty treat.

Cat asked for a chocolate-covered frozen banana on a stick. He watched in fascination at the erotic way she nibbled off each piece of broken chocolate and slowly guided the banana through her mouth to take small bites until it was all gone. He wished she'd ask for a second one so that he could watch the scene all over. Thank God, he'd bought the sporran because he knew his kilt was tenting again.

Though Cat knew she was playing with fire, she was having a hell of a lot of fun doing it. Between the teasing and flirting and kissing, she'd been paying attention. Purposefully walking away from him from time to time to see if he would be looking at other women the way he was pining over her. It never happened. Aurelie was right. He wasn't a womanizer, and he sought her out when she went too far. Not in the controlling way that some guys act, like their girlfriend is their piece of property, but in the way that he wanted to be with her. It was nice to feel like she was someone's special girlfriend. Wait a second, did she just say girlfriend? Was it too soon to think about being serious like that? Although she wouldn't sleep with someone unless they were monogamous. Truth be told, she would never be the type of person who could sleep around, and she'd never knowingly be with someone who did.

Throughout the day, Damon found ways to reach out and touch her—holding her hand, a kiss on her neck, sitting close so that her bare leg touched his. It was fulfilling and sexy. It made her feel like a woman, more so than she'd felt in a long time.

They meandered toward the costume rental vendor where Cat disappeared after another long, lingering kiss from Damon. "I want to say a fond farewell to my pirate queen. I hope to see you again soon. Very soon." She may have stumbled a little as she was released from his embrace and shook her head briefly to clear it to focus on what she was supposed to be doing at that moment. Once she saw the lockers, she remembered and went to work on transforming from Catrina the pirate queen to Cat, just plain Cat. But she no longer felt plain. She felt transformed internally as well as externally. As she replaced the thigh-high boots with leather sandals, the sexy almost lingerie dress with capris and a top, and the pirate hat with a white satin ribbon, she felt different from before. Damon was making her feel different. Perhaps she had it all along, but he was bringing it out in her. She was learning how to be a woman, and she really liked how it felt. After freshening up her makeup, she collected her things and walked outside. Damon was already in a pair of jean shorts and was carrying his kilt. She tried not to laugh, but he still had on his boots.

"Interesting look. Where did you hide your shorts? I didn't see you bring them in." Damon blushed a bit.

"Well, I chickened out a bit and wore them under the kilt. My tennis shoes and socks are in the back seat of the truck." Cat howled and gave him a solid kiss on his lips, leaving a bit of red lipstick on his mouth.

"Love it. Actually, I think only a manly man can pull off that look, and you, sir, take the cake."

They got to the truck and were out of the parking lot by 6:30 p.m. Plenty of time to get to the church festival. Instead of music this time, they reminisced about their favorite sights and goings-on at the fair. Cat was pumped to make this a regular summertime event. When they reached the church, Cat guided him to some parking across the street and made their way into the beer tent to find Aurelie before her band's set started.

Tonight, Aurelie had kept her hair down on her left and a series of three short cornrows on the side with red, white, and blue hair extensions braided into each. She wore a white buttoned-down shirt, red bow tie, and suspenders attached to skin-tight black pants. Completing the ensemble, she wore platform black patent heels. She had on bright red lipstick and made cat's eyes with black eyeliner and mascara. She was a force to be reckoned with, and she had the talent to match. She saw Cat and Damon coming in through the side of the tent and made a beeline toward them. Aurelie gave Cat a great big hug and whispered in her ear, "You aren't kidding! He's adorable!"

Cat hugged her back and whispered in reply, "He only had eyes for me at the fair." Aurelie broke away to look into her friend's eyes and gave her a great big smile. Next, she looked straight into Damon's chest and then readjusted to lift her head to meet his eyes. "Aurelie, this is Damon. Damon this is my best friend, Aurelie. She's the lead singer of the Hot Rockin' Horns."

Damon shook Aurelie's hand and said, "I hear you're really good.

I'm looking forward to hearing you sing and play." "Thanks, do you sing or play an instrument?"

"Well, I did do some singing in high school and college, but I only dabble on the acoustic guitar occasionally."

"Bass, baritone, or tenor?" "Bass."

"Good to know." With that, she gave Cat a kiss on the cheek and ran back to do a soundcheck with the band.

"What'd she mean by that?" Damon questioned.

"I have no idea. Listen, I could use some real food. They have a pretty decent chicken dinner here. Are you interested? My treat."

"I am interested, but this is a date; it is my treat. Find us a place to sit, and I'll be back with two beers and plates." There were a couple of seats still left in the center section of the picnic tables, and Cat grabbed them. A few moments later, Damon returned with the food and drinks. He pulled the utensils and napkins from the pockets in his shorts. She gave him a quick kiss of thanks and dug in. Soon the Hot Rockin' Horns were introduced, and Aurelie conducted the band into a fun and peppy swing dance number so that a few of the older couples drifted toward the stage to dance the jitterbug or any number of other big band dance moves.

Next was something from the 1960s, which had a few younger couples and singles joining in. Aurelie did a fantastic Frankie Valli impression as she sang "Sherry." Then she started to introduce their next number from the 1970s. "Ladies and gentlemen. I have a wonderful surprise for all of you; a special guest will join me for this next number, Mr. Damon MacGregor!" Damon was baffled but was willing to shake it off. He knew he was being tested and loved a challenge. The 1970s wasn't his favorite kind of music, but he could fake it if he couldn't make it. "Well, Damon, I understand you have a strong bass voice, so I'm gonna give you the guy's part in this one, and I'll sing the girl's. It's sort of a duet that has special meaning to my friend over there, Cat. We're gonna sing 'Paradise by the Dashboard Light' by Meatloaf for you beautiful people! Enjoy!" With that, she winked at Damon, and he shook his head. She may have thought it was in defeat, but Damon whipped out a pair of sunglasses from his pocket, brushed his hands through his hair, and started shaking like he was having a seizure, but in fact, he was getting into character. He belted out his lines with pitch precision and so much energy that the crowd gathered closer and closer to the stage. Once he finished a line, Aurelie went right back at him and challenged him to out sing her.

Cat just watched in awe at the two of them who did not even realize how great they sounded together, and their showmanship matched like a glove. The band was gathering speed for the final bridge in the song, and the crowd went wild when Damon belted it out as if inspired by Meatloaf himself. Aurelie, not to be outdone, gave the last part of the song everything she had. Cat noticed that the crowd was surging now with energy, the kind only seen at rave parties, and noticed that they were drawing a crowd from the other areas of the festival into the tent. When the song was done, they got a standing ovation. Aurelie reached over to Damon and gave him a giant bear hug, and he kissed her hand like a gentleman. He took off his glasses and bowed to the audience, catching Cat's eyes and winking. Aurelie announced him once again to the audience, "Again, Mr. Damon MacGregor, everybody! Wow!"

Cat was on her feet, clapping and whooping it up as much as or even more than the crowd around her. When Damon reached her, he lifted her up, swung her around, and gave her a great big smooch. "I had no idea you could sing like that!" Cat exclaimed.

Damon replied, looking deep into her darkened hazel eyes, "If music be the food of love, play on."

Cat blinked several times and shook her head. "Wow. Did you just make that up?"

Damon snickered while shaking his head no. "Actually, it's from one of the plays I read in college. It's Shakespeare. I thought it might impress you." He gave her one of his potent smiles, dimples and all. Then he spoke to her in her ear, "So, did I pass the test?"

Cat laughed, nodded yes, and kissed him right back. "Good call. I'm impressed."

The next two hours were spent in the beer tent singing and dancing to the music. Aurelie was in her element, and it seemed that that night the band was at its best. When the song "The Rose" originally sung by Bette Midler was announced, Cat led Damon to the dance floor. He pressed against her, took her right hand into his left, and held them tight against his chest. His other hand pressed against her waist. Cat rested her cheek on his shoulder, and at that moment, something hit her like a lightning bolt. "I love this man. I will marry him." She should have been petrified, but instead, it gave her warmth and confidence that this was the real thing she'd been waiting for. When the song ended, Damon still held her close as if there was no one else in the entire world but the two of them.

Too soon for her, he slowly pulled away and kissed her lightly on the mouth. "I better get you home. I have church and family dinner tomorrow. Better be on time or my mom will skin me alive."

Though she was sad that the day was ending, she honestly had nothing to complain about. The ride back to her apartment was silent, yet perfect. She felt contentment with him she'd never felt before. As they got closer to the village, she wondered if she should invite him in. They hadn't talked about exclusivity yet but didn't want this sexual energy to leave either. When he pulled into her driveway, Cat took a deep breath and asked, "Would you like to come up for a little while?"

Damon paused, stared straight into her eyes, and replied, "I'd love to." He went around to open her door and take her bags for her while she fumbled for her keys and unlocked her door. When they got to the top door, her hands were shaking so bad that she kept missing the lock. Shockingly, she felt his whiskers on the nape of her neck as he was kissing and licking her there. Her sexual energy was now off the charts, and she was afraid she'd fuck his brains out right there in the stairwell instead of making it a few more steps into her kitchen. Her wobbly legs brought her into the room. She felt his hot breath on the back of her neck as she set the keys and her purse on her kitchen table.

Damon turned Cat around and savagely attacked her mouth, running his hands up and down her back with an urge like he was trying to push her into him. Cat responded by moving her hands underneath his white shirt until she got to his shoulders and scratched his back with all her nails slowly all the way down to the waist of his jean shorts. It was clear that she had his attention; he moaned in her mouth, and his shaft was hard pressed against her thigh.

Damon returned the favor by going straight for the cami and lifting both shirts over her head with an expertise that left her breathless. In the course of the shirts going over her head, her white satin ribbon broke free, and her curls were in a wild frenzy that made her look even more animalistic and sensual to Damon. He was struggling, unsuccessfully, to find some semblance of control. However, there was something innate about wanting to be with her, to be inside her. It was the strongest need he'd ever felt before. It felt like destiny, as if she was his mate for life, and he needed to be with her sooner rather than later so that no other man would ever come close to her again. His need was primal.

This time it was Cat's breath that hitched a bit as he paused to look at her two perfectly rounded breasts heaving in a white lace underwire push-up strapless bra with a light pink bow in the center. He bent down and gently kissed each of them with his hands expertly holding them on their undersides. This time it was Cat who moaned. When he had thoroughly kissed both breasts, he lifted his head and stared straight into her smoldering eyes as he swiftly unclasped the bra and let it slip effortlessly to the ground in the growing pile of clothes.

Cat's blood was boiling, and she wasn't thinking anymore. She was being moved by a force she'd never felt before, a need that begged to be satiated. Now it was her turn. She moved closer to place slow, lingering kisses on his neck and chest while unbuttoning his shirt. She kept up the relentlessly slow pace until she had complete access to each of his nipples, which she scraped her teeth with to make them stand at attention. Cat slid her tongue down to his navel and paused, looking up at him for a reaction. She didn't wait too long. This time he shook his head in an attempt to clear the fog she'd just put him in and lifted her up so he could return the favor. With Cat standing again, he lowered his head to wholeheartedly take turns putting each of her breasts in his mouth, as his hands moved under her capris, then under her panties to the soft round buttocks that he'd been itching to get his hands onto for weeks now.

Cat responded by pulling away, which at first, he thought was a sign for him to stop. Then he saw her unbutton her capris and then guide her white lace panties with matching pink bow off her hips to show him her womanly body. His mouth went dry, and his erection went hard against his zipper. Damon responded by dropping his shorts and boxer shorts to join their menagerie of clothes. As they both stood there naked, fascinated by the comeliness of each other's heaving bodies, they experienced an extrasensory perception that this was going to mean much more than just sex. It would be the acceptance of each other as their mate for life. Cat mustered her confidence, closed the gap between the two of them, put her arms around his neck, and with a slight jump wrapped her legs around Damon's hips. He responded by lifting her buttocks with his rugged hands while he ravaged her mouth.

Instinctively, Damon walked through the kitchen and dining room to the door opening into Cat's bedroom. He gently lay her on her bed all the while nipping, licking, and mastering her mouth until she couldn't think anymore. She had so many nerve endings going off at the same time all over her skin she didn't want the feeling to end yet couldn't wait for the next sensory explosion to start. Cat wanted to be with him so urgently that she opened her legs to welcome his muscular torso on top of hers to complete their lovemaking. Damon instinctively understood and followed her lead. He gently lifted his body above hers, not missing an opportunity to kiss her on every surface his mouth could find. Then he lay down on her with his manhood hard pressed against her womanly mound. This was it. This was the culmination of all their flirtatious jests, hopes, and dreams. He paused and he looked into her eyes and saw a mixture of lust and love that he'd never seen before. He did this to her. She wanted him. All of him. She wanted him now. But that pause gave him time to think.

"Fuck!"

"Yes!"

Damon shook his head and stilled his body even as Cat's was moving to a rhythm they had both started just moments ago. "I didn't bring anything. I didn't think it was even a possibility tonight." He pushed himself off her and lay down beside her with his arm across his forehead. Cat's mind struggled with this new information. She had finally gotten to the point of not thinking about her next move, but just let her body guide her, and it felt so freeing and powerful. Now she was breathing heavily and feeling all achy inside. Didn't he want her? She looked over and saw all the signs that, yes, he most definitely did want her. But what did he just say? What did he mean? Oh … Fuck …

"I don't have anything here either …"

"I'm so sorry. I should've never let it get this far. Do you hate me?"

"No, I didn't think it would happen so quickly either. I thoughtit was just going to be a day of flirtations to see if you were really interested."

"I'm really interested."

Cat giggled. "I can tell."

Damon rolled over to look at her. "Cat, you are the sexiest, most gorgeous woman I have ever met. You're smart, caring, and funny. I don't want to screw this up. If we go through with this tonight and, believe me, I want to, we can never take this back. We might be biting off more than we can chew because we weren't smart."

Cat rolled over on her side and stared into his eyes. "I know what you mean. You make me feel like a real woman. I've never felt this way before. But I've never slept with a guy that I wasn't in a monogamous relationship with. I'm not sure I could live with myself if I broke that code."

Damon reached over and played with a loose curl that was in front of those amazing eyes of hers. "Cat, I don't want to make you do something you don't want to do. But if I'm honest, I want to make love to you sooner rather than later. But not just for the sake of sex. I feel like there is something inside of me that is missing unless I'm with you. Tonight, during all this, I felt something even more. Like I needed to be inside you to complete me. I don't want to be with anyone else. I want to be with you. We can wait as long as you need to, but in all honesty, I stopped looking or thinking of other women the moment I met you. I'm in this for the long haul, if you'll let me."

With Damon's confession, Cat's eyes glistened in tears, and she kissed him gently on the mouth. When the kiss was over, Damon felt the salt from the tear that lingered on their lips. "I don't want to be with anyone else either. I choose you." It was Damon's turn to feel his heart tug and his breath hitch. She wanted him and only him. That admission made it even more important that he leave right now before something happened they couldn't stop. He made love to her mouth after her confession to show her how he truly was beginning to feel about her. Afterward, he got up and went to the kitchen to begin to dress for the long, very long, ride home.

"When can I see you again?" he asked as he was trying to concentrate on getting his shorts on correctly and find his truck keys.

When he looked up, his heart fell, again. This time, she was standing in the opening of the kitchen wrapped in a sheet with her hair in a wild entanglement of curls. God, he wanted to just drop every- thing and kiss every inch of her and make love to her until the sun came up. It was taking every bit of control he had to keep his mind focused on doing the right thing.

"Do you think you can get a little time off work for a long weekend?" That sexy coquettish look was back, and it was breaking his heart.

"I think I can do it. I haven't taken much time off since Christmas. What do you have in mind?"

"Well, I have a friend in Lake Tomahawk who has a cabin she lets me stay in for weekends up north. I know she's out of town next weekend, so we'd have the lake all to ourselves." Cat lingered on that last part so that it was clear what she had in mind, lest Damon forgot what almost happened here.

"I'll definitely make this happen. What time should I pick you up on Friday? What should I pack?"

Cat smiled.

"Okay, first on the list, condoms. Got it. Anything else?"

"Well, I usually like to get going about 1:00 p.m. so that we can have dinner up there and miss the Madison traffic. If you can get off on Monday and Tuesday as well, then we can spend Monday night in Lake Tomahawk to eat homemade pie and watch some snowshoe baseball. How about if I text you a packing list so you don't forget anything?"

"Condoms, condoms, and more condoms. Got it." He smiled and noticed she was smiling too, but her eyes still held an intensity he hadn't ever seen before. "Yeah, I can make that work. Will Mia be joining us?"

"Good question. I can ask my parents to watch her for me. I'll have to let them know why I'm taking a long weekend, though." With that, Damon saw a little worry wash over that sexy face of hers.

"Is your dad old-fashioned?"

"Umm, to say the least. Add to it that he's Italian and I'm his only daughter."

"Got it. How about this? Why don't you let me know which night would be a good night to come over and meet your parents? I can talk to him and let them meet me before I, you know, take a long romantic weekend with their only daughter."

"Actually, that's not a bad idea. No other boyfriend has ever asked to meet my parents, and some were scared right off the porch. Maybe if you meet them and let them know that you want to date me, it may ease your torture a little bit."

"Sounds like a plan then. Text me the packing list and the night I'm meeting your parents, and I'll remember to go to the store and get condoms." Damon walked over her pile of clothes and closer to the Irish goddess he saw before him. He took her face in both of his hands and planted a strong but sensual kiss on her full lips. When he pulled away, she looked at him in the eyes very seriously. "I know, condoms." She smiled and watched him leave down the back stairs and waited to hear the roar of the truck before she went back into bed to try and sleep off the whirlwind of emotions and sensations that were inside her body.

Chapter Eight

After Saturday night's fiasco, Damon took the coldest shower he could possibly stand and kept replaying the day in his mind.

He had the most magical time he could ever have imagined, and it almost killed him to leave her, but if he hadn't, they would have gone through with it and regretted every moment until they were sure one way or the other that she wasn't pregnant. What would that have done to their budding relationship? As painful as it was to leave in the condition in which he had, with her looking at him the way she had, Damon knew it was the best for everybody; if his body would only concede instead of fighting him on it.

On Sunday morning, Pete texted to see when they could connect so he could get the lowdown on the date. Unfortunately, Damon was in church with the family and couldn't text and pray at the same time; his mother would have his hide. He'd wait until after Sunday dinner with the family to get a hold of Pete. Sunday dinner was a pot roast his mom threw in the slow cooker along with baby carrots, red baby potatoes, and baby pearl onions. "What's with the baby theme?" Damon thought to himself. He'd taken control of the situation, why did his food have to remind him of what could have happened? He swore that on Monday after work he would be visiting every drug store in the county to make sure he was always covered from here on out.

His parents seemed happier than usual, and his brothers and sisters, who tended to get on his nerves, happened to be getting along rather well. Damon didn't want to brood, but he wasn't in the mood for the whole family. Actually, he felt like being alone and wanted to start packing for the long weekend ahead with Cat. Which reminded him, he needed to give them the heads-up that he wasn't going to be around next weekend. He should probably plan for an explanation that wouldn't invite even more questions.

"Hey, Mom and Da, I thought you should know that I won't be home next weekend." He looked up sheepishly, waiting for the interrogation to begin.

"Oh, where are you going?" Heather asked.

"Catrina, I mean Cat invited me up to a family friend's place in Lake Tomahawk for a weekend of fishing, and on Monday night, they have snowshoe baseball." Damon was waiting for the volley of questions from his parents to begin.

"Snowshoe baseball, huh? I heard that's a blast to watch. Hopefully, you'll have good weather up there. Will you take some videos or photos of the game? I've always wanted to see that," Pat responded.

"Do you need us to do anything for you while you're gone?" Heather inquired. Damon was shocked but wasn't going to look a gift horse in the mouth.

"Umm, yeah. It'd be great if you could water the flowers on the porch and put the mail on the kitchen table."

"Easy, peasy. Consider it done." His mom smiled at him and winked. When did she ever wink? Something was up, but he wasn't sure what was going on. Just then his phone went off again. He looked down and it was Pete.

"Thanks for dinner, Mom, and for helping me out next weekend." He got out of his seat, took his dirty dishes to the sink, and kissed her cheek as he left the rest of the family to their normal chaotic chit chatter, waving to the brood as he left.

Back at his place, he sat in one of the rockers out on the front porch. He decided he needed to call Pete instead of texting. After only one ring, Pete picked up. "Spill, bro."

"Nice to hear your voice, too."

"Yeah, yeah, yeah. Get to the good stuff. I've been dying over here. Angie is now into this crying phase. Everything makes her tear up. I love her and all, but I'm going out of my mind already. I need something to cheer me up, and nothing will do that better than hearing about all the sex that you're having and I'm not. I can live vicariously through you." Damon laughed one of his boisterous laughs.

"Dude, listen, I don't kiss and tell. You know that. But if I did, I think you'd be smoking a cigarette right after the story."

"Damn, it was that hot? Tell me what she looked like. What happened? You're killing me!!"

"Well, you know those sexy Halloween costumes you see online?" "Yeah?"

"Even better."

"Shit! What was she wearing?"

"A sexy pirate costume with those thigh-high black boots and a short skirt."

"Oh, man. I can picture it. Angie's got to come out of this crying jag soon or my balls are going to burst."

"Pete, man, once she has the baby, she can't have sex for like six weeks, man. Don't forget she'll have to nurse the baby, too. Who knows when you'll get a chance to have conjugal visits with her breasts again?" Damon was smiling and trying not to laugh as he heard his friend's groaning on the other end.

"You are a very mean person, Damon MacGregor. I still love you like a brother, man, but, dude, you're pissing me off. Seriously, did you guys have sex?"

"First of all, it's none of your business. Second of all …" "Yeah?"

"I forgot to pick up a few things before our date."

"No fucking way!"

"Correct." Damon could hear Pete trying to control his laughter and then losing it into rolling bawdy howls. "That's enough. If you don't stop laughing at me, I'm hanging up right now."

"Okay, okay. I'm done. I promise. When are you seeing her again?"

"Well, she's invited me up to a friend's lake house up north for the Labor Day weekend. I'm wondering if you could cover my patients on Friday afternoon and Tuesday so I can go."

"That's not a problem. I'm saving all my vacation time for family leave when the baby gets here. Plus, just because I have blue balls doesn't mean we both have to suffer."

"Dude, mine were as blue as the color of a blue raspberry slushy after I left her apartment."

"Man, I sympathize. Better get to the drug store soon so that next weekend isn't a lost cause."

"I know. I have a packing list started, and condoms are on the first three lines."

"Oh shit, Angie's crying again. I'd better go and see what it is this time. Last time it was a card commercial."

"I feel for you, brother." "Thanks."

The rest of Sunday went like a blur as Damon started packing and checking his patient schedule for the next two weeks to make sure that Pete could handle the load. Then he texted Cat to find out if he could meet her parents sometime before Friday so he could hopefully make a good impression with her dad, who sounded like he was a hard man to please. He needed to do something that would show her father that he wouldn't be the kind of guy to just use her and leave her. He also needed to do something nice for Cat's mom. That should be easy enough. His mom's wildflower garden held a variety of flowers that any woman would be jealous to have. But what to do about her dad?

He remembered that Cat said her dad loved working with wood. Maybe there would be a piece or two from the tree they took down that could be used in one of his projects. Damon left the porch, took a 4-wheeler to the place where he'd been working just a few days before, and found a beautiful piece with the bark still on the outside and the rings were a dark umber with a light beige surrounding each ring. The tree was hickory, so once it was polyurethaned, the contrast would be intensely beautiful. He loaded up the piece, which was about four feet long and three feet wide, onto the rack on the back and headed back to his truck to place it in the truck bed.

After a full day of planning and chores, Damon stepped into his shower and just let the pressure of the hot water jets clear his mind and relax the tense muscles in his neck and shoulders. Drying off, he put on his boxer shorts and checked his phone for messages, finding a text message from Cat.

"Thinking of you tonight. Looking forward to this weekend."

Damon texted back, "I couldn't stop thinking of you all day. I've already packed and made a list for things to pick up. Can we go see your parents before Friday? I want to meet them."

"I'm going there on Wednesday with Mia to drop her off. Wanna come with us?"

"Perfect. I'll stop by your place after work."

Wednesday came and Heather showed up at the clinic with a large bunch of flowers from her garden tied in a blue gingham ribbon. They were a combination of delphinium, snapdragons, gerbera daisies, and coneflowers. Damon kissed her on the cheek, and he mouthed, "Thank you," to which she smiled and mouthed back, "Good luck."

When his last client of the day canceled, he finished up his paperwork and flew out of there like a bat out of hell. With a combination of nervous energy and excitement at seeing Cat again, he couldn't sit still. He grabbed his mother's bouquet and put them in a beaker he found and soaked a sponge to put in the bottom for the stems to rest on so they wouldn't wilt during the drive to Mukwonago. In his locker, he found a deodorant stick and freshened up a bit before he got into his truck. The thirty-minute drive to Mukwonago seemed like forever; the traffic was thick and, of course, there was construction to deal with, but he did get to Cat's around 5:30 p.m. No sooner was he in her driveway than she was down with Mia and a tote with Mia's food, toys, etc.

He jumped out of the truck to help her load up the dog supplies in the back and let Mia sit in the back seat of the cab. Once that was all situated, he grabbed Cat, lowered his head, and opened his mouth over hers to let her know how much he'd been missing her these past few days. The sigh that came out of her and the way her arms were linked behind his neck and her fingers were ruffling through his mane of red hair made it very clear she'd been missing him too. After a few uninterrupted moments, Mia started barking in the back seat. She knew they were going on a ride, and she was showing her impatience. Damon pulled away and waited until Cat jumped into the cab before he shut her door.

With expertise, Cat directed Damon to her childhood home and into the driveway. Damon smiled; he could see her mother's touch in all the blooms and variegated greens that meandered in the front of the home and her father's masterful carpentry in the variety of arbors that Damon could see adorned the front lawn and a side rose garden. It was clear that both of her parents were skilled and passionate about their hobbies; they'd built a home of love, the kind of home he'd grown up in. Maybe this initial meeting wouldn't be so bad after all? "We better hurry it up. Mom is making dinner, and I told her we'd be here about 6:00 p.m. If I know her, if we are not in our seats by 5:59 p.m., she'll freak and say we're late."

"No problem. We still have about five minutes to spare." Damon raised Cat's hand and gently kissed her knuckles. Cat smiled and used her other hand to caress his cheek and then scratch his beard. While Cat got out of the truck and then let Mia out, Damon went to the trunk to get Mia's things to bring them into the house.

Claire met them at the garage door with a smile and held it open for them. She had her hair up in a clip that let some tendrils waterfall down around her face and onto her neck. Her hazel eyes smiled at seeing the two of them. She was wearing a maxi dress with a black V-neck sleeveless top and a multi-colored skirt. "Come on in, everybody!" Mia pushed herself past the three of them, which made Claire giggle. "Okay, little one, make yourself at home." Then she gave Cat a quick kiss on the cheek as she passed by. "Hello, Munchkin, it's good to see you." She caught the eye of Damon and the smile grew a bit larger. "Hello, Damon, I'm Claire. Come on in and put that stuff in the corner by the patio doors. Anthony is on the deck grilling brats and burgers for dinner." Damon nodded and found the corner she described.

After putting the dog's stuff in place, he went back out past the women to get the flowers. He didn't want to screw this up by starting a conversation without his conversation starter. When he came back in, he handed Claire the bouquet and saw her smile widen, and as she took a big whiff of the flowers' fragrance, he explained, "Mrs. Carneri, thank you for letting me join your family for dinner. These are flowers from my mother's garden. I thought you might like them as a centerpiece for dinner."

"They're lovely, Damon. Thank you! And please, call me Claire. Mrs. Carneri makes me think that I'm in school or you're talking to my mother-in-law."

"Will do, Claire. Thank you for inviting me to dinner." As he followed her and Cat outside, they passed by the kitchen table, which had the makings of a gun-cleaning project spread out over the newspaper. He noted that the gun was a shotgun, so he started formulating the conversation with her father, Mr. Anthony Carneri. When he arrived on the deck, he looked out into the lush 1.5 acres that the Carneri home sat on. A wildflower garden the size of a city lot was in the back, and several mature trees were located throughout the lawn. The deck was painted a terracotta color that was a lovely contrast to the Tuscan tan siding of the home. Again, the deck and the patio furniture of Adirondack chairs and a picnic table set were evidence of a man's eye for quality workmanship and usefulness. On the right of the deck was a set of drum-like cookers, a grill, and a smoker. Anthony had his back to his guests as he was flipping burgers and spearing brats onto a platter he was holding in his other hand. Damon smiled when he read the back of the black and white T-shirt: Dads Against Daughters Dating

So, her dad had set the stage for a duel. Damon loved a challenge but wanted to be careful to be respectful as he beat him at his own game.

"Dad, why are you wearing that shirt tonight? It's embarrassing." Cat rolled her eyes at her father's back. He turned around so he could see his daughter, which he very clearly wanted to do since as soon as their eyes locked, his pale blue eyes twinkled and his mouth, which was surrounded in a salt and pepper goatee, grinned.

"What? You bought me this shirt. I thought it was a nice gesture to wear something you bought me as a present."

"I was sixteen at the time, and it was a joke. I give you permission to retire the shirt, Dad. Tonight even."

The smile turned into a soft grin as he set the platter down on the wooden bench/buffet, where the rest of the dishes were set aside for a buffet-style dinner. There were fresh-baked brat and hamburger buns, a plate of a variety of sliced cheeses, and another with onions, tomatoes, and lettuce leaves. Assorted condiments were next to a relish dish of baby pickles, black olives, and pepperoncini. A glass bowl filled with fresh spinach and strawberries and a side shaker jar of poppy seed dressing were next to a bowl of cut-up fresh fruit, and the pièce de résistance was a homemade apple pie with a crumble crust that was still warm from the oven. On the opposite side of the patio doors was a cooler filled with beer, water, and soda.

Anthony brushed his hands off on his jean shorts and reached out his hand to shake Damon's. Damon grabbed his hand with a strong grip, a solid stare, and a smile on his lips. "Mr. Carneri, thank you very much for inviting me to dinner tonight. It smells fantastic."

Anthony kept a solid grip on Damon's hand and squinted his pale blue eyes a bit. "You're welcome. Glad to have any of Cat's friends over for dinner. As you can see, we have plenty. There's beer in the cooler behind you."

Damon noticed the release of pressure on his hand and let it drift to his side. Here's test number two. If he doesn't accept the beer, he may be judged as less of a man. If he accepts the beer, he may be judged as someone who may take too many risks, like driving drunk with his daughter. Figuring out the answer to the first test was easy. He had addressed Anthony as Mr. Carneri and wasn't corrected. Therefore, the answer to test question one was to continue to address him as Mr. Carneri or sir until otherwise corrected. The answer to test question number two wasn't as easy but could be navigated. "Thank you, sir, but I'd prefer a diet soda or water if I could. I'm driving and I don't drink and drive."

"There's water and soda in the cooler as well. Help yourself. It's just that Cat mentioned when you went out on Saturday you had been drinking beer, so I wanted to make sure we had some for you."

Test question number three right out of the gate.

"True, but we walked around for four to five hours at the fair and then we danced for another two at the festival. I switched to water an hour or so before I drove anywhere." Anthony nodded, directing Damon to the plates, and as Damon was filling his plate, he thought it was time to take the initiative. "Sir, I saw your shotgun on the kitchen table. Nice gun. Reminds me of the one I shot my first turkey with a few years back." Eyes still set down to look at the food he was piling on his plate, he did see Anthony stop cold as he was putting black olives onto his.

"I'm getting it ready for target practice with our son later this week. Which shotgun do you have?"

"Oh, it's a 12-gauge, semi-automatic inertia driven with a 2 and ¾ chamber. Where do you go target shooting?" Damon knew he had him and worked very hard not to leak a smile as they both left the buffet and headed toward the table.

"There's a shooting range in Eagle."

At that moment, everyone was seated and now holding hands. Damon had to sit across from Cat, so he was holding Anthony's and Claire's hands with his head bowed while Claire led the prayer. He was perfectly comfortable saying grace as that was a requirement at his family dinner table every Sunday; the rest of the week was just too crazy with people zig-zagging in and out of the kitchen, but on Sundays, when everyone was together, Damon's mother insisted they at least pray at that meal.

The food was tasty, and Damon was grateful that his stomach hadn't growled with all the amazing aromas filling his nostrils. After some small talk and Cat clearing away the larger plates, Claire brought the apple pie to the table and Cat came back with the dessert plates and forks. Damon closed his eyes as he took in the smells of baked apples and cinnamon. Although he was satisfied, he couldn't wait for a sample of the sweet delicacy in front of him. He dug in and savored the first bite as the crumble crust and baked apples melted in his mouth. "Claire, this is a damn fine apple pie!"

Claire and Cat laughed and explained that a family friend had said the same thing many years ago, so the title of the recipe was "Damn Fine Apple Pie." Damon laughed his full laugh, and even Anthony cracked a smile.

When dessert was finished, he offered to help Claire and Cat clean up the dishes, which was quickly rejected. No time like the present to get to the next test. He looked straight into Anthony's eyes and said, "Sir, I'd like to ask you an important question." Anthony nodded and took a long swig out of his bottle of Corona.

"I want to ask for your permission to exclusively date your daughter." Anthony put the glass bottle down with intention and sat back in his seat for a moment.

"Damon, she's twenty-six years old. She's dated lots of guys before you, and she's never asked for it before. You don't need my permission to date her now." Anthony's eyes looked square into Damon's and cocked his head.

"True, I know that she's dated other guys, and I've dated other girls for whom I never asked permission to date. However, your daughter is different." Damon knew he had him. Now he had to keep him. Damon put his elbows on the table and leaned in. Anthony laid back even further.

"Go on."

"Well, when I first met Cat at the rehab center, I was dumbstruck. She was so calm and empathetic toward the crane that I was impressed. Then she smiled, and it took my breath away. Sir, I had to see her again to find out if it was just a fluke or something else. We went out for coffee, and it felt like I could talk to her for hours. I didn't want to go. You already know this, but it's worth repeating. Cat's an intelligent, caring, funny, and fascinating woman who also happens to be the most beautiful woman I've ever met."

At this confession, Anthony shifted in his seat to sit up and move his arms onto the table and looked up at Damon.

"I want to ask you for permission to exclusively date your daughter because I believe, in my heart, that she and I have a future together. I know how important you and Claire are in her life, and your opinion matters a great deal to her. I get that she's independent, but it's clear to me that she is also very loyal to her family, just like I am to mine. Because I don't ever want to be the reason to pull you two apart, I want to show my respect for your role in Cat's life and hope that you approve of the possibility of her future with me." Damon stopped talking, but his heart didn't stop racing. He hoped that he shared equal amounts of respect for Anthony and adoration for his daughter without sounding like a sappy mess. He needed to sound like a man who could also love his daughter the way she deserved to be loved.

Anthony set his chin on his folded hands and sighed. "Damon, I appreciate your request and everything you've said about Cat and what she means to this family and to you. Again, she doesn't need my permission to date a man, but I am grateful that you've asked for it nonetheless. It shows me you have integrity and that you value family." Anthony paused and Damon stopped breathing. "You have my permission to date my daughter. But if at any time, you feel that you no longer want to date her exclusively, be respectful of Cat and tell her in person before you start dating anyone else. She's fiercely independent and a strong woman, but she also has a tender heart. Be honest with her and with yourself."

Damon began to breathe again and leaned forward. "I will promise you that I will always be honest with your daughter and treat her with respect."

Anthony lifted his head off his hands and reached over with his left hand to touch Damon's right arm. "That's all I can ask. Thank you, Damon, and you can call me Mr. Carneri." Anthony winked and grinned. Damon shook his head and laughed his bawdy laugh.

"Mr. Carneri, sir, I have something in the back of my truck for you. I thought you might like it because you do such beautiful work with wood. I figured you might have some use for it. If not, no big deal, we'll just add it to our burn pile." With that, Damon led Anthony through the house, past the women finishing the dishes—winking at Cat—to the back of his truck. He reached into the tailgate and gently laid a piece of hickory into Anthony's hands.

Anthony accepted the recently milled hardwood as if it were the finest piece of silk in the entire world. He bent his head down to smell the fragrance of freshly sawed hickory with an audible, "Ahh."

"I think I might have a project in the works that this would be perfect for. Thank you, Damon." Anthony took the slab of hardwood and carefully navigated it through the garage and into the basement. Damon shut the tailgate of the truck and saw a familiar black body wiggling with excitement and a tennis ball in her mouth.

Damon bent down to give Mia attention and led her to the backyard, where he threw the ball into a patch of tall grasses near the end of the property so she could play hide and seek with her favorite toy. Once dishes were done and Anthony was back from placing his present in a preferred spot down in the magical basement, the four adults and one exhausted puppy sat for a few more moments in the Adirondack chairs. When the mosquitoes started to come out, Damon and Cat said their goodbyes and retreated to her place. With work coming early again Thursday morning, and no protection … again, Damon felt it was best if he stayed in the cab of the truck and declined a nightcap in her apartment.

Cat reached for his face and pulled it toward her and warmly kissed him goodbye. Just as she left the cab, she turned around with a quizzical look on her face. "I forgot to ask how it went with my dad. What did you guys talk about out there?"

"Well, I asked his permission to exclusively date his daughter. He gave me permission and offered that I call him Mr. Carneri moving forward."

Cat smiled. "Oh, is that it?"

"Well, he told me that you didn't need to get his permission to date, but that he saw I valued the role that family plays in your life. He also asked that I be honest with you throughout the relationship."

"What did you say to that?"

"I promised I would always be honest with you. Unconditionally." Cat stared into his eyes.

"Unconditionally?"

"Well, I should have an amendment that if you're binging on chocolate or wearing something ugly, I have the right to bend the 'honesty' rule a bit so I don't get slaughtered." Cat smiled again and laughed.

"I accept your amendment. On a serious note, though, I'm really looking forward to this weekend. The property is going to be empty except for us, and the weather is supposed to be gorgeous. What time do you think you'll be here to pick me up?"

"Pete's taking my afternoon patient load. I'll pack up the truck tomorrow night after work, so I think I can be here by 12:30 p.m. at the latest."

"Perfect. I plan on leaving work by 11:00 a.m. so I can get all my stuff together and ready for your truck by then." Cat turned to walk away and then stopped to turn around again. "Hey, Damon?"

"Yeah?"

"Thanks again for talking to my dad. I know he's a bit old-fashioned, but I know that it meant a lot to him that you asked. It meant a lot to me."

Damon leaned further toward the passenger side as Cat was leaning into the window. "You're worth it, you know. See you Friday."

"See you Friday."

Damon watched as Cat walked away and into the back door. He waited until he saw the kitchen light switch on, and then he eased his way out of the driveway and onto the street. He was really looking forward to Friday. He thought he better hit the drug store he saw on the way into town.

Chapter Nine

Friday morning was a blur for Cat. Dr. O'Brien's vacation was ending, and the staff at the center was managing like a well-oiled machine. For Cat, reservations were coming in nicely. The gala seemed like it would be a sell-out this year. She pulled a comparison report on sponsorships and noted that the amount of money in sponsorships was up 10 percent from the past year. On the auction side of the event, items were coming in daily. Today, in fact, they had acquired a pedal tavern and a suite package for a Packer home game against the Bears.

Organizing her desk and putting the fundraising reports in Dr. O'Brien's incoming basket, Cat gathered her personal items to go home. She was hoping to sneak out of the office without an inquiry from Shelli, so she peered around the hallway to make sure she left when Shelli was on the phone or assisting clients. Good! A couple had come in with an opossum; Shelli would be busy for the next few minutes. Cat waved to the vet techs and Shelli as she flew out the door. Once she got to her SUV, she opened the sunroof and turned on the radio, almost at full blast to accompany her on the thirty-minute trip home.

Cat was closing the doors to the garage when she heard Mrs.

Romansky outside. "Afternoon, Catrina!"

"Hey, Mrs. Romansky. Off to the senior center to play cards?"
"No, not today. My grandkids are coming to visit. I'll try to keep

those little monsters from making too much of a ruckus for you."

"Don't worry about me or Mia. We're going away for the weekend. Mia's at my folks while I go up north with a special friend."

"Oh …" As the awareness of what Cat meant by "special friend" hit her, a smile grew on Mrs. Romansky's face.

"Oh, in that case, I just made a few coffee cakes, so let me go inside and wrap one up to take with you. That way you don't have to worry about making breakfast while you're up there," she said with a wink.

Cat blushed. "Thank you. I've got to go up and get my stuff together. He should be here in half an hour or so. Will you still be home so I can introduce you?"

"I sure can be. I'd better get inside to freshen up if a man's gonna be calling on us." Mrs. Romansky fluffed her curls and put her nose up in the air and batted her eyelashes. Cat laughed and took a large step over to her landlady to give her a hug and a kiss on the cheek.

Upstairs, she organized all the dry goods in her laundry basket and put the ice she'd been making all week into the coolers along with the beverages and the items needing refrigeration. From the second bedroom, she grabbed the duffel bag that held her clothes and toiletries. A backpack held odds and ends like books, cards, suntan lotion, bug spray, and an umbrella.

Just as she changed into a red tank top and jean shorts and swept up her curls into a ponytail holder, she heard the truck pull into the driveway. She went out on the back porch and yelled down, "Hey there! The door's open. Do you mind coming up to help me bring this stuff downstairs?"

"No problem. Let me open up the tailgate and I'll be right on up." Damon was wearing a white T-shirt and jean shorts with black basketball shoes. He was sporting a red baseball cap and black sunglasses.

Cat buckled her leather sandals and put her backpack on while lifting the laundry basket up to her hips. Damon took the steps two at a time and reached down to take the basket from her while he kissed her hello. "Mmm. I've been thinking about that all day. Here let me take that from you."

"Is that all you thought about?" Cat asked with a little flirtatious pout.

"Absolutely not, but I figured I shouldn't scare you off when we've got to spend four to five hours in the truck together."

Cat smiled at his confession and replied, "I'm glad. I couldn't stop thinking about being with you this weekend, either. It was hard to concentrate on work." She looked up to see his smile grow on his face. "I've got this, but if you could help me with the coolers that'd be great. The food cooler is the green one. It can go in the back of the truck, but the blue one has sodas and waters for the trip up north. We can keep that in the cab along with this." She nodded to the laundry basket. "I've packed us snacks for the road in here."

"Cool. I'll get to work then. The sooner we're packed up, the sooner we can get on the road."

"And the sooner we can get to the lake and the cabin," Cat finished with smoldering eyes.

Damon audibly gulped. "If you keep making innuendos like that, we'll never get up there."

Cat laughed. "Good point. I promise I'll be a good girl for the rest of the trip."

This time Damon's eyes smoldered. "I'm looking forward to you being a very bad girl for the rest of the weekend."

Cat's eyes went wide and almost dropped the laundry basket. "I'd better get this downstairs before I lose my grip." When she walked past Damon, he didn't move, so she had to brush past him and felt the hard reality of what lay in store for her when they arrived in Lake Tomahawk.

After a few trips to get everything into the truck, Mrs. Romansky showed up with a Rubbermaid container filled with a fresh coffee cake that she promised to Cat earlier. "Here you go, Cat. My famous coffee cake for your breakfast treat." She handed the container that was still slightly warm to Cat, while her eyes roamed over the larger-than-life red-haired man towering over Cat in his red and black outfit to accentuate his own coloring.

"Thank you, Mrs. Romansky. It smells amazing! Mrs. Romansky, I'd like to introduce you to my special friend, Damon MacGregor.

Damon, this is Mrs. Romansky, my landlady and baker of amazing cookies and the coffee cake we get to take with us."

Damon reached out to shake Mrs. Romansky's hand, and with a twinkle in his eye and a smile on his lips, he responded, "It is very nice to meet you, Mrs. Romansky, and I have to correct Cat here. I'm her boyfriend." Both women's eyes opened wide and mouths turned into "Os."

"Oh really?" she inquired.

"Yes, I received Mr. Carneri's approval to date his daughter on Wednesday; it's official. We're dating." Damon stretched his other arm and wrapped it around Cat's waist to make his point.

"I see. That is a big deal. Well, congratulations. I've known Anthony for many years now; getting his approval is no easy feat."

"I appreciate that and thank you for the coffee cake. It smells amazing. I only hope we can hold off on eating it while we're driving up north." Mrs. Romansky smiled and blushed a little.

"Speaking of driving, we'd better get going if we want to make it up there for dinner. Mrs. Romansky, thanks again for the coffee cake! Have a great time with your grandkids this weekend." Cat kissed her gently on the cheek and then jumped up into the cab of the truck. Damon followed suit and kissed her on the other cheek and stepped into the driver's side. They both waved as they eased out of the driveway and onto the road.

During their drive, they took turns talking about work and their families and belting out songs on the radio. Cat switched empty water bottles and soda cans with ice-cold ones and provided pretzels, chips, and trail mix when the munchies hit. Once they got up to the Wausau area, Cat tuned in the radio to The Big Cheese. Soon Lita Ford was heard through the speakers belting out "Kiss Me Deadly." Damon was singing the lyrics he knew as Cat was rocking out next to him. "Wait a second," Damon asked curiously. "Did he just say, 'The Big Cheese?'"

Cat smiled, "Yep, my favorite station up here. Plays all those great 1980s songs that you can only find on streaming radio." Damon laughed wholeheartedly and began singing to the next song, Alice Cooper's "School's Out for Summer." Cat opened her window all the way down and took a deep breath.

"What are you doing?" Damon asked. "Roll your window down."

"Why?"

"Just do it." So, Damon did just that and glanced over at her. "Now take a deep breath," Cat demonstrated, and Damon followed suit.

"Wow, you can really smell the pine trees around here," "That's the up-north smell. Every time I get to this point in the drive, I open my window and take a deep breath. It calms me, and I forget all the stupid little things that are stressing me back home or at work." Damon took another breath.

"Yeah, I can see what you mean." He glanced over at her and smiled. She pulled his right arm toward her and held it.

"We've only got about an hour to an hour and a half left. Do you need a break?"

"Nah, I can manage. I want to see this lake that you keep talking about. No one else but the loons will be up there?"

"That's right. And the weather is supposed to be clear all weekend." "Sweet. Can't wait to go fishing all weekend long." Damon slanted a sly smile toward Cat. She replied by digging her nails into his skin a little too hard. "Ouch!"

"Brat." With that, Damon brought her hand up to kiss it and ended their teasing. Holding hands the rest of the way, Cat would point out different landmarks that led to their final destination. Around Tomahawk, the four-lane highway merged into a two-lane road with periodic passing lanes. She pointed out the sign that said they only had twenty-four more miles on this road before turning onto the highway leading to Lake Tom, as the locals called it. The road meandered, rose, and dipped, lulling Damon's anticipation into quiet contentment. He felt peaceful as his eyes darted to glance at a family-run motel or the rusty railroad bridge that they drove under before the next turn.

The road less traveled was what he thought of as they toured this lazy country road—thick with pine trees and their sickly, sweet sap aroma wafting into the cab of the truck. Periodically, the trees would thin and royal blue waters in a variety of sizes and shapes would peek through the blanket of green. Cat pointed out the hairpin turns so that he could slow way down and not skid on the pockets of gravel that must have been kicked up by cars that took the curves too fast. When they got to the camp for wounded warriors, he felt good that there was this piece of God's country that could be offered to those who gave themselves up for their freedom.

Zigzagging past several lakes, the road began to straighten out, and periodic homes started to show through the wilderness. Several had "Garage Sale" signs peppering the road to point to a "Huge Sale" going on down a gravel driveway. Showing the way out of the wilderness and into the semblance of a town, there was a lone Stop sign ahead. A few simple homes and storefronts popped out of obscurity. This was Lake Tomahawk, Wisconsin, a sleepy little north woods town that came alive on the weekends and during the summer months. There would be time to venture into this little hamlet, but Damon's body was getting achy from sitting in the truck for four-plus hours and he was getting restless.

Cat directed him through town, where he viewed a variety of log homes and cabins dotting the landscape. Damon could feel her anticipation as they got closer to their destination.

Damon felt he was going back in time as soon as he made the turn onto the rutted gravel drive. A rusted gate lay open as if it couldn't remember its purpose anymore. A deteriorated sign was lying in a pile of leaves off to the left with many of its letters missing so that its purpose and message no longer made sense. While he paid attention to the potholes that regularly cropped up in the driveway, he was amazed at the variety of trees that shaded them from the sun. Then there was a break. Damon almost stopped driving as he tried to take in the vision that was before him. A vegetable patch with eight feet high chicken-wire fencing surrounding it welcomed them out of the thick forest. From the garden was a two-acre patch of wild grass lawn that seemed to have been freshly mowed up to the line of the forest surrounding the property from three sides. On the far side of the grassy lot, abutting the tree line was an old-fashioned outhouse, and a few steps past it was a wooded path that led to who-knows-where. Then, as if it had always been there, there was a simple bungalow home with a porch overhang, and a mishmash of patio furniture invited visitors to the porch and asked them to stay awhile.

The two-story bungalow reminded Damon of the older homes in Milwaukee and West Allis, not quite what he was expecting as a lake cabin. It looked like it was cared for with what was available at the time, a mixture of colors, textures, and building supplies. Though it was a bit of a mess, he had an immediate warmth flow through him when they drove past its covered porch. There were homemade wooden flower boxes that held a variety of begonias and other flowers that he just couldn't make out. The sandy drive turned in front of a small floral garden patch appearing under a grove of pines with a sampling of different colored bowling balls adorning the space. In the front of the home, there was a continuation of the lawn, and large trees periodically dotted the scape down to the shoreline of what Cat told him was Loon Lake. On the right side of the home, there was a much larger flower garden again sheltered by an eight-foot chicken wire fencing and handcrafted wooden garden gate. On the other side of the driveway was a small tinker's shed; which at some point in its history had been a one-car garage with attached living quarters and a summer kitchen. Today, the garage had its door open all the time, and a plethora of rusted tools and saws hung from nails off the walls while a brand-new push mower and riding mower were kept dry on the dirt floor. To the left of the shed, the driveway led into the woods that would lead to the guest cabin they'd be staying in for the duration of their romantic getaway.

Cat couldn't bring herself to take in what Damon's initial reaction was as she was reminiscing about the person she missed most in this world and who couldn't be here to greet her anymore, Uncle Marshall. Once Damon got a hold of himself, he looked over to see

Cat looking solemn and misty-eyed. He grabbed for her hand and squeezed. She reacted by squeezing back and slowly moving her head toward his so that he could see she was tearing up. He used his other hand to wipe away the teardrop that wouldn't stay put. "Sorry, it's just that every time I come here, I still believe that he'll be sitting on an old metal stool working on some crazy project like stripping the copper out of old appliances from the thrift store in town so he could sell it."

"Who?"

"Marshall Luther. Ryan and I called him Uncle Marshall. He and his wife are good friends of my parents. His grandfather bought this land as a young wealthy entrepreneur and built all the buildings you'll see. When Uncle Marshall came across some hard times, he moved his family up here permanently and was always here to greet us when we arrived. His hair would be all messy, wearing a dirty and holey T-shirt with rubber clogs on his feet, busy as a beaver just tinkering away. Then when he'd see us, he'd smile and give out the best bear hugs to us kids. I think he had a thing for my mom, though, because he always tried to get a kiss from her." Cat smiled at that memory. "Then he would say to me and my brother, 'What's the only rule up here?' and we'd say back, 'kids rule!!' and he would have this gravelly chuckle like a Santa that had smoked three packs of unfiltered cigarettes for twenty years. He was dirty, smelly, swore a blue streak, and could drink anyone under the table…"

"But you loved him a lot. What happened to him?" Cat nodded her head and sighed. "Cancer."

"I'm sorry."

"So am I. This place just doesn't feel the same without him, but I can't seem to stay away either. He always called himself the old curmudgeon of the woods. We just called him Uncle Marshall." After a few silent moments, Cat perked up and showed Damon the path to the other cabin.

When they got there, Damon smiled again. It seemed that the owners had the same issue with this cabin as the other one. The cabin was adorned with white trimmed windows and wooden screen door, but the siding was in need of a fresh coat of paint. Someone had built a sandbox on the side of the cabin, and several old-fashioned metal kitchen tools were in various levels of being buried. Cat went into excitement mode and hopped out of the cab and practically ran to the barn red outhouse fifty feet away. "I'll be back!" Damon thought that looked like a good idea, eyeballed a tree that looked just as good as any other, and started measuring it when he heard her opening up the tailgate.

"Ummm, that's the tree where Uncle Marshall's ashes were buried." "Shit. I'm sorry."

"No, it's piss. If you want to shit, you'll have to use the shitter I just came from."

Damon reached Cat in just a few strides and lightly tapped her on her butt. "Smartass."

"Yes, and so's the rest of my body," Cat said and smiled. Damon reached around her to give her the kiss he'd been aching for. Cat put her arms around his neck and warmly took his tongue in her mouth in a long ritual of finding each other again. She pulled away when her insides starting synapsing again. As much as she had been waiting for this weekend, she wanted their first time to happen more romantically than just jumping each other's bones in the back of a pickup truck.

Each of them took bags and entered the cabin that was going to be their home away from home for the next few days. Damon took in the oak floorboards and ancient needlepoint and rag rugs that adorned the floor. To his right was a miniature kitchen with black-enamel countertops, pine cupboards, a red water pump over the sink, and a pint-sized white refrigerator and stove set. The great room was no larger than a small bedroom at home but lined with windows on all three walls and a myriad of furniture that was an eclectic mix of handcrafted wooden tables with 1970s upholstered chairs and a couch. Whitewashed camp chairs and a pine bench surrounded the pine polyurethaned kitchen table. But it was the hearth of the fireplace that had his attention now. It was a three-inch-thick wooden shelf hand-chiseled and painted to represent several indigenous scenes from this neck of the woods: Indian heads, peace pipes, and the infamous hodag, a mythical creature located in the Rhinelander area that has fine green fur, the head of a frog, the face of an elephant, stout legs, a spiky, dinosaur-like back, and a long tail. Placed on top of this shelf was a single totem of a winged creature that was painted in a way to tell a story about its life. Its beak and round belly contrasted so that the creature looked almost like a cross between an eagle and a koala bear that had stepped into a paint shop and rolled around. Damon was fascinated.

The pine push doors to the two bedrooms were closed. Cat motioned that they were going to be sleeping in the far bedroom that featured a mission-style hickory bed frame hosting a queen-sized mattress under a handmade quilt of silhouette loons in a sunset sky. A grandfather clock was stationed at the foot of the bed with barely any space to put down anything else. On the left wall were an antique ebony-colored dresser and matching mirror. Next to the bed was a handcrafted simple table holding a miniature jewelry box with a candle and lighter on top. Cat placed her duffel bag on top of the dresser and went back outside to grab another load. Damon followed suit.

In just a few short minutes, the truck was unloaded, and the couple began organizing their supplies for the weekend. Cat was placing food items into the frig while Damon opened the crank windows to let in some air. When it looked like everything was in its place, Cat said, "I know we just got here, but it's tradition to go to the Shamrock for their Friday night fish fry, and if you think you can handle it, you can try their OMG burger."

Damon, who was in their bedroom, peeked out of the doorway, holding three bags in his hands. "You promised me a romantic getaway. I went shopping!" He held out the shopping bags from three different stores. Cat went into hysterics.

"Well, I can check those off my packing list now. I know I promised, but I need sustenance first. Then you can show me what you bought."

"Fine." Damon put down the bags in defeat and pulled Cat into his arms. "What's an Oh My God burger anyway?"

Cat pecked him on his nose. "I can't tell you. You have to experience it."

They jumped back into the truck, and Damon slowly wove the truck around the makeshift circular drive back toward the main house that led to the highway. In just a few short moments, they were back in town and parking in the public parking lot behind the soft-serve ice cream stand. The Shamrock was bustling with activity as patrons were shuffling in and out of the establishment. The bar area was full at capacity with patrons enjoying their favorite ice-cold beverage while a hostess in a black Shamrock T-shirt was taking names. A table for two had just opened up, so Cat and Damon followed the hostess to their table. The Shamrock had three distinct rooms. The front room was the bar area with big-screen televisions hanging from the ceilings and beer posters adorning the walls. The second room was slightly smaller and had to deal with the continuous activity from the kitchen. Black vinyl and metal chairs were filled with both townies and vacationers anticipating their deep-fried vittles coming through the swinging door. The third room was a bit larger and had local artist paintings decorating the walls. Damon noted that the painting above their table was of the bridge they had passed under earlier.

When the waitress came around, Damon ordered a beer on tap and Cat ordered a hard cider. Damon was people-watching and loved the fact that it looked like a combination of a bar and diner all in one place. Returning with their drinks, the waitress took their orders. "I'll have the fish fry and French fries, please," said Cat. "And he'll have the Oh My God burger with fries."

Damon looked at the menu again. "What's an Oh My God burger? It's not on the menu?"

The waitress looked at him and smiled. "It's four all-beef patties on a brioche bun with lettuce, tomatoes, pickles, cheddar cheese, and onion rings."

Damon's eyes grew wide, and he smiled. "I hope I'm up to the challenge."

"When Ryan comes up with the family, he always orders it and can finish it before the waitress finishes putting everyone's plates down."

The young waitress smiled and said, "That's impressive. I've had people order it but not finish it before," as she turned around to take their orders back to the kitchen.

Damon, sitting across from Cat, took her hands into his and smiled. "I like this place. Not too fancy and not too dingy. I'm not even sticking to the floors!"

Cat chuckled. "If you must know, I'm not a stickler for fancy places. I like places with good food and great character. I love this place because it has both. Someone took one of the old brick buildings in town and turned it into a fancy restaurant. I guess it gets good business from the vacationers from Illinois, but when I'm up here, I don't want to get dressed up, you know? I just want to relax and have a good time."

"Well, I know now where to take you for our first anniversary."
"Where?"

"My house to grill out burgers and drink ice cold beer from my cooler." And he kissed her knuckles.

"It's a date then."

"Definitely." Shortly after, the waitress came back with her hands full of platters of steaming food. The oversized burger was placed in front of Damon, and his eyes glazed over. "Oh My God!" he exclaimed.

In unison, the waitress and Cat replied, "Exactly."

Cat couldn't control her laughter as she watched Damon try to figure out an angle with which he could fit his mouth around the sandwich. People at tables nearby were peering around each other to get a look at him. When he finally finished the final bite, Damon looked as though he would burst. Cat had left one of the three pieces of fish on her plate and a few of her fries. "Ready for dessert?"

Damon looked at her as if to say, "Are you joking?"

"Okay, okay, tomorrow we'll eat something not so intense so we can have dessert." Damon paid the bill, and they waddled out of the Shamrock and almost into a guy who looked like he had drunk the bar dry—but was continuing his party onto the street.

The sun was starting to set, and the gloaming set in. The fiery colors in the sky were magnified through the variegated greens of the trees. Whether it was the fact that they were settling from their large meals or contemplating their next moves, both Damon and Cat were quiet on the trip back. Damon parked the truck snug against the cabin so there was a pathway left between the woodpile in the center island created by the dirt driveway.

"Come on and get into your trunks. I want to take you to the beach before it gets too dark." They got into the cabin and took turns getting into their swimsuits, and Damon made sure to stash a few condoms into his trunks. Wrapped in her towel and black flip-flops on her feet, Cat took the lead, jibber-jabbering with little vignettes from her past about earlier trips to Loon Lake. She felt the waves of anticipation, so she prattled on like a teenager just to keep herself from getting more nervous. Damon didn't seem to mind, though, and periodically asked questions to clarify parts of the stories she told.

Cat led them onto the wooded pathway beyond the main house and up the high ground so that he could see the drop-off toward the lake. Once in a while, they had to maneuver past a fallen tree, but as soon as they had crested, they started their descent. From the soft, squishy wooden path, the bright white of the sandy beach came up to meet them just as the tree line separated to showcase a pristine white sandy beach. The color of sapphire, the water was still—like glass. The sun was resting on the treetops across the lake. A simple square raft with a yellow plastic slide was anchored just past the shallow bay that lapped against the sand. A large metal mailbox was placed where the trees and water met. It held body shampoos as well as bug spray and suntan lotions should guests need it.

Damon dropped his towel and ran splashing into the water with a big dive finale. He emerged from the spray with a yelp as the heat from his skin met with the cool waters. After he shook the droplets from his face, he motioned for Cat to join him. Cat stared straight at him and slowly, lingering, dropped her towel to the ground. Next, she pulled the hair tie out of her curls and shook them free, continuing her longing stare at Damon. She didn't know how she could be this brazen, but her body and intuition were taking over, and she didn't want it to stop.

Damon's face was stunned. He was breathless as she continued her striptease routine on the beach, well out of his reach. Next, she lifted her hair with one hand while the other untied the loose knot holding the emerald green bikini straps in place. When the straps dropped down, the flimsy triangles of fabric concealing her voluptuous breasts followed suit. As soon as the night air hit her nipples, they strained into tight peaks while the milky white skin rose in a series of goosebumps. Cat reached behind her and unsnapped the back strap so that her womanly figure was only hidden by the shimmering green fabric that was between her legs. She remedied the situation by using her fingers to glide the skimpy panties down past her moistening mound, over her hips, and past her round buttocks. After she stepped out of them, she looked into Damon's eyes to find a hunger that excited her and scared her a bit. Once Damon felt he had his faculties under some control, he walked through the water to the point where she could see the tent of fabric that was growing between his legs and knew her striptease had the intended effect she was looking for.

Damon reached down, pushed off his bright red swim trunks, and flicked them onto the raft. His shaft was long and thick and at an intense level of excitement. Cat walked toward him and shivered a moment as she tried to acclimate to the temperature of the water. When she was barely a fingertip's length away from him, Damon reached out to grab her, slamming her body against his. She put her arms around his neck while her legs wrapped around his hips so that her ache to have him inside her would be momentarily appeased.

Teeth gnashed, fingernails scraped, moaning ensued as mouths licked, sucked, and ravaged every part of each other's bodies above water. Damon carefully laid Cat on the cool flat surface of the raft as he gently suckled each of her heaving breasts lovingly while discreetly rolling on a condom. He heard her moan softly and felt her body moving in a rhythm that invited him into her. He lifted his head to stare into her stormy eyes as he slowly guided his body to join hers, as it was meant to be.

Cat let out a breath that was almost like a calling as Damon entered her. The fire that had been brewing all of these weeks when she touched him ignited into a passionate inferno that she could no longer control. She practically wept as she was swept up into the emotional and physical roller coaster following each of his movements to enter her more fully and bring them both to a climax of their physical and emotional love.

As if the heavens opened up for them, the sunset and the moon shone on their glistening and heaving bodies as they came together in mutual release. Cat lost all sense of being except for what she was feeling. It was animalistic as much as she rode the waves of lust, passion, and love as each feeling crested over her. At the moment of her own climax, Damon had his in synchronicity with hers. It was a powerful feeling to be able to bring a man to his knees yet have him lose control in unison with her; she knew that she never had and never would have this connection with anyone else. Damon was her one and only.

Damon collapsed, breathing deeply next to her with his arms encircling her waist. She lifted herself onto her side and softly kissed his lips. Looking straight into his eyes, she took up the courage she'd been savoring. "I love you, Damon MacGregor. I will always love you." She knew in her head that he didn't have to say anything back. She committed to him because her body compelled her to do so. Still, her breath stopped as she waited for some response from him.

Damon reached up with both of his hands and clasped her face to bring it closer to his. His azure eyes sparkled with intensity as he replied, "I love you, Catrina Carneri. I will marry you and make you my wife, I promise."

Cat moved her body so that she was over his. Straddling his hips between her thighs, she maneuvered so that he could feel her wanting him all over again. His body's response was urgent and intense. This declaration of love between them became an urgent need to consummate their intimate bond as Mother Nature stood witness to their unspoken marriage vows.

After making love on the raft, Damon and Cat swam in the moonlight, holding on tightly, kissing into oblivion. Cat hooked her ankles around Damon's waist and lay back, letting the rippling water rush over her breasts and soaking in the night air. Damon watched her intensely, taking in the sensual sight of her pink nipples rising up out of the water and then sinking just under the water's surface. He couldn't take it any longer, so Damon scooped up Cat, bringing her up to a standing position once again; he bent his head over her breasts so he could slowly and methodically suckle each one individually. Cat, lost in the moment, ruffled through his hair and arched her back and neck so she could get closer to him. His whiskers were scratching her already tender peaks as she pulled his mouth away from them and back to her mouth, which she opened and welcomed him inside her once again.

Not knowing how much time had gone past, their worn bodies were showing signs of fatigue. The newly anointed lovers grasped hands, wrapping their tenderly loved, caressed skin in oversized fluffy towels, and began the journey back to the cabin where they would fall into bed with a newfound awareness of each other. Climbing under the sheets, Cat lay on her back, waiting for her lover to join her in their bed. Damon followed suit and knelt at the foot of the bed while he spread her tender thighs so he could kiss them and her wetness until she came again in strong panting breaths. He was pleased he could offer her so much pleasure. After her fits subsided, Damon lay next to his love, kissed her on her temple, and reiterated the words he had said when they first consummated their passion, "I love you, Catrina Carneri. Always." And he fell into a sound sleep as she rolled into his arms.

Cat slept soundly, but the next morning her stomach was growling intensely, and she needed to feed it now. As she had grabbed the closest thing she could find, Cat was now wearing Damon's white T-shirt while her sleep-sexy head of curls was focused on the hot sizzling strips of meat cooking on the griddle. Damon didn't think anything could wake him from the deep slumber that enveloped him until that unique and savory aroma hit his nostrils. "Bacon." Damon couldn't believe that he would react so quickly and with such need as he watched her, in his shirt, flipping the bacon strips and bent over slightly to adjust the flame. He couldn't take it anymore; he had to have her again. Now.

Cat was unaware of his actions until he was upon her. So focused on food, she knew he had woken up, but not what was on his mind at this moment. As she bent over one last time to adjust the flame, she felt the back of the shirt lift up. Her breath hitched a moment as she felt his hands spread her legs farther apart and bring her rosy cheeks farther back. Just as she was aware of what was happening, Damon bit her neck and moved her so that she could bend over the end of the kitchen table while he entered her from behind. Cat's surprise melted into oblivion as this new set of senses went off throughout her body, and she found the rocking rhythm that had Damon crying out her name as they shared mutual release. Holy shit! She'd never had sex from behind before and damn if she didn't find it incredibly erotic how he didn't even talk to her but reached out and took what he wanted from her, no, what he needed from her. Well, two could play at that game.

"Morning, Cat," Damon mumbled into her hair and kissed the love bite he had made earlier.

"Good morning to you, too," Cat replied as she turned around and adjusted the T-shirt. "I guess I shouldn't have packed so much. I just needed to wear a ratty old T-shirt to get you hot and horny in the morning."

"You are incredibly sexy in that T-shirt. Knowing its mine and what we've just done with you wearing it. I honestly don't know if I can ever wear it again without getting a hard-on." Cat giggled and walked back to the bacon to take them off the burner and placed them onto a platter lined with paper towels to soak up the grease.

Using the grease left on the griddle, she began frying up eggs to serve with the bacon and a fresh coffee cake that was already sliced and on the table next to softened butter. When the eggs were cooked, Cat slid them off onto their plates and brought them to the kitchen table. Damon found the juice glasses and poured them each some orange juice.

"This is the best breakfast I've ever had," Damon exclaimed as he finished off his sixth strip of bacon and used a slice of bread to soak up the yolk from his third egg.

"I don't think I've ever seen anyone eat as much as you just did for breakfast."

"Seriously, woman, you have worn me out. I need to feed often to meet your sexual demands." Damon looked at Cat with innocent doe eyes as she rolled hers.

"Oh please. My sexual demands. What about you? I was just innocently cooking bacon, and you 'wham, bam, thank you, ma'amed' me out of nowhere." Once she finished, she saw the concern in his eyes. "Oh no, it didn't feel like that at all. I'm sorry. I was shocked because I wasn't expecting it, and I'd never done that before."

"Did I scare you? I'm so sorry!"

"No, no. Not like that. It was a shock, but then it was very exhilarating like I was caught doing something naughty." Cat's eyes narrowed and went dark. "Actually, I kind of like being a bit naughty once in a while. Stay here. Close your eyes."

Damon did as he was told. He could hear a commotion coming from the bedroom, and then he felt her brush past him and to the refrigerator. "Now, I want you to hold out your hand and follow me." Damon followed her orders and was feeling a bit nervous and excited all rolled into one. "Stand here and take off your boxer shorts." Which he did. "Mmm, I'm feeling like a little something sweet for dessert. Open your eyes."

Damon opened his eyes. What he saw in front of him was Cat in a purple lace push-up bra with a satin bow sitting in the cleavage and a matching purple lace thong that accentuated her heart-shaped ass that he always wanted to grab. When his eyes left the sexy lingerie, he noticed she was holding a can of whipped cream in one hand and pushed him down onto the couch with the other. As she stood there shaking the can, his excitement grew and was very eager to participate in whatever activity she had planned. Cat reached across him to grab a pillow, and as she did so, Damon reached out to grab her. Sternly, she slapped his hand and said, "No. No touching. This is my dessert. You have to wait." He was getting harder just thinking about her next move when she maneuvered the pillow between his legs, spread them, and proceeded to spray whipped cream over his hardness. First, she used her hand and then licked off the cream. Then she bent her head down and used her tongue to clean the whipped cream off lick by lick. Damon was in a frenzy. A super-hot woman in sexy lingerie was in his lap, and he couldn't do anything about it. He couldn't control his actions anymore and he needed relief. Damon took his hands to her shoulders to bring her up to eye level. Cat saw the desperation in his eyes, shimmied off the thong so that her rear was in his face as she jiggled it to become clear of the purple lace between her thighs. When he groaned as if he was in pain, she turned around, stepped over his lap, and impaled herself onto his rock-hard shaft. They moved in a frenzy as he licked the cream off her face. It didn't take long for their climax, but they were both sticky and sweaty from the morning's activities and needed to wash up.

The morning was turning out to be just as beautiful as the day before. The sun was rising over the lake as they took their naked, glistening bodies to the beach. Taking turns diving into the water, they massaged body soap into each other's scalps and caressed it over their bodies. It was an erotic experience and a very romantic one as well. When they had been thoroughly cleaned, Cat unhooked the raft from its anchor and set them adrift into the middle of the lake. There was something natural and yet erotic about lying naked in the middle of the lake with the one you love.

They took cat naps while they lay on their backs and then on their stomachs. Between naps, they couldn't keep their hands off each other and gently caressed those body parts they had been constantly loving throughout the past twelve-plus hours.

After drying off, they dove back into the lake to swim the raft back to shore and hook it up on its mooring. They talked like school children, all giddy and giggling up the wooded pathway back to their love nest. Once the breakfast dishes were cleaned up, they snuggled back into bed for a long nap. "I think that since we are a couple now, we need to establish a few things that couples do," Cat said as she spooned against Damon's back.

"Yeah, like what? Like pet names? Or a song?"

She kissed his back and hugged him a bit closer. "Yeah, something like that. What about if I call you schmoopsie?" She could feel the giggle coming on strong, and she tried really hard not to have it heard.

"Schmoopsie. What the hell is a schmoopsie?" Damon rolled over, a cross look on his face.

"You know, like from 'Monster's Inc.' You could be my schmoopsie. Look, I'm canoodling with schmoopsie!" Then Cat started snorting to add to the giggles she'd been working so hard to control earlier.

"I think we need to think about this a little bit harder. How about we sleep on it?" Damon kissed the tip of her nose while Cat wrapped her arm around his vast chest and wrapped her leg over his.

"Sounds like a plan, schmoopsie."

"Yeah, I'm not sure I will ever want you to call me that again."

Later, Cat heard Damon get up and try to carefully get out of bed. She rolled over until she heard him rummaging through his duffel bag and put on some clothes. After a long yawning stretch, she got out of the bed, straightened the sheets, and pulled her hair back into a ponytail with the ponytail holder she had on the nightstand and chose a white tank top with her jean shorts. When she got to the kitchen area, she saw that Damon was wearing a blue T-shirt and his jean shorts as he was putting together peanut butter and banana sandwiches. She moved in behind him and kissed his back while her arms hugged his chest. "Hello, sleepy, wanna sandwich?" Damon offered.

"I am kinda hungry. Not sure about the banana and peanut butter sandwich though." She moved around him to get to the refrigerator and brought out string cheese and an apple.

"Suit yourself," Damon said as he took a large bite out of his. "So, what do you want to do today?"

"Well, I thought you might like to go into Minocqua for a little bit, and we could pick up something to grill for dinner. Or there's the Wisconsin River where we can rent tubes and float down it for a few hours, or we can just stay here. There are hiking paths, apaddleboard, and a rowboat. If you want to fish, there's awesome bass in this lake."

After taking another large bite and washing it down with a diet soda, Damon looked out at the lake. "Well, if I catch us some fish, we don't have to go into town at all. I can clean it and grill it for dinner."

"Perfect. Is it okay if I just sit in the boat with you and read a book? I know how you guys are about being quiet, so the fish don't get scared."

With a serious face, he said, "It's absolutely true. One wrong move and you could be facing an empty net. If you promise to be quiet, I'll let you stay in the boat."

Smiling, she replied, "I just found that book we talked about on our first date. I'd love to read it again. I'm all set. Follow me to the basement and I can help you get the boat ready. "

"Great! I'll get my pole and tackle box out of the back of the truck and meet you down there." He kissed her lightly on the mouth, and Cat could smell the peanut butter on his breath.

Down in the basement, she opened the door to the musty-smelling sand-bottom storage area. Piles of items were everywhere. There seemed to be no semblance of organization, but it was fascinating to see in any event. She pointed to the life vests piled in a corner, and they found two cushions to take with them. Standing up on another wall were a variety of oars, wooden and plastic in a variety of lengths. Damon picked out a pair as if he knew what he was looking for and carried them out.

The sun shone brightly when it wasn't hiding behind a bright white billowy cloud. A slight breeze moved the water into shallow ripples that made the water bugs dance. When all the items were loaded in the boat, Cat helped push off the boat and then stepped into the bow of the boat to sit down. Damon gave it another strong heave and stepped in, careful not to fall onto Cat.

Damon rowed the boat with ease. Cat closed her eyes and enjoyed the slow smooth movement of the boat cutting through the water.

When he came to a bay near a clump of trees that were hanging over the shore, Damon carefully put down the oars and went to his tackle box for the spinner lure that was his favorite for catching bass. Cat took this opportunity to reach for her book and started reading.

So much had changed in the past three weeks. Cat felt contentment, safe, like a strong, sensual woman. She wasn't stressing about work or why she wasn't good enough to keep a man from cheating. She felt like she belonged with Damon; she didn't have to change who she was or wanted to be to suit him. She could be herself, sometimes a book nerd, sometimes a pirate wench, sometimes a passionate lover. She felt loved.

Soon, Damon was in a bustle of activity as he worked his magic to secure the bass on his line that was jumping, running, and diving to get off the hook. But Damon's skill was a strong match, and he refused to give up. Finally, he asked Cat to get the net and pointed to where he wanted her to hold it as he reeled in a seventeen-inch smallmouth bass. Cat was happy for him but not too thrilled to hold the net. As soon as he gave her the okay, she relinquished it to him and watched in awe as he swiftly took the hook out of its mouth and then inserted a stringer through its gills. "Want to touch it?"

"Oh no. That's okay. We have an understanding. They allow me to swim in their lake, and I don't catch them for dinner."

"But we're going to eat it for dinner?"

"You caught it, not me. There's a difference."

Damon nodded and replied, "Ahh," as he placed the fish and stringer over the side of the boat, swished his hands in the water, and then proceeded to get his rod and lure ready for the next round. After he had one other nice-sized bass, Damon called it a day and began the journey of rowing back to the cabin. Cat helped bring the boat onto shore and took up the cushions and oars, letting Damon manage the fish and his gear. She found some old newspapers in one of the red firestarter containers and brought it out to the glass picnic table and spread them out for Damon's chore of cleaning the fish. She even found a plastic bag and a fillet knife as well.

Keeping herself occupied as the fileting was happening on the porch, she started slicing up sweet bell peppers, onions, and potatoes and put them into grill packets along with Italian spices, salt, pepper, and butter. She brought out a white wine from the refrigerator and found two wine glasses from the storage cubby above the fireplace hearth. After filling the two glasses, she set the table for dinner, slicing up a few more pieces of the cranberry walnut bread. Though she had offered that that night they could go out for ice cream, she felt that they may want to just be alone instead. Cat found a few apples and began peeling them and slicing them into thin wedges. Melting some of the butter on the stove, she poured it onto the bottom of an 8x8 square pan and sprinkled cinnamon and sugar over it. Then she began layering the apple slices, making sure to overlay each layer. When the apple slices were laid, she sprinkled a little more cinnamon and sugar on top. Next, she took a small cereal bowl to add 1/4 cup flour to 1 tsp. cinnamon, ½ tsp. nutmeg, and 3 tbsp. butter. Using a fork, she mixed the ingredients together and sprinkled it on top of the apples. When the stove hit 350 degrees, she guessed, Cat slid in the baked apple cobbler and set her cell phone timer for thirty minutes.

By the time she was done with everything, Damon had finished cleaning and washing the fish so he came in to wash his hands and grab some seasonings that he could use on the grill. He saw the wine on the table and took a drink. "Mmm, that's really good. What is it?"

"It's from a vineyard near my dad's family home in Italy. I can only find it online, so Mom and I split a case whenever they have a sale going on." Cat took a sip and watched as Damon's nose started going crazy like a bunny rabbit.

"What smells so good in here?"

"I made an apple cobbler for dessert. It's baking in the oven."

His right eyebrow went up. "I thought you wanted to go out for dessert tonight?"

A bit sheepish, Cat replied, "Well, you wanted to stay here all day, so, I thought, you might want to stay here all night as well."Damon took another drink of his wine and walked over to where Cat was standing by the kitchen table. He gently put his arm around her and pulled her into him for a lingering kiss.

"Good call." Damon broke away before things got intense and he wouldn't be able to keep his mind on the food that was cooking on the grill. After fifteen to twenty minutes, Damon pulled the pockets of vegetables and the fish off the grill and brought them in as Cat pulled the bubbling apple dessert out of the oven and placed it onto the stovetop. When Damon sat down, he noticed that she'd lit candles for the table and around the cabin for light and had started a fire in the fireplace. He refilled their wine glasses and served their dinner.

Before they dug into their meal, Damon held up his wineglass and Cat followed suit. "A toast to us. May we always enjoy fine wine, delicious food, and good company together. May we always remember this weekend as the beginning of a long and happy life together. I love you, Cat. Always." And he bent over the kitchen table to kiss her to seal his promise of hope.

Cat put the first forkful of steaming fish and vegetables in her mouth and moaned, "This is so good! Oh my God, you can cook for me any time!" just as she put another forkful in her mouth. The rest of the dinner was spent talking about their favorite meals and telling tales of family dinners gone wrong. When they couldn't fit anymore into their bellies, they sat back and sipped wine until they knew it was now or never to clean up the kitchen. Cat set the tea kettle and coffee pot on burners to heat the water while Damon cleared the plates and organized the leftovers for the refrigerator. They worked together as if they'd spent years perfecting their team effort. Once the water was ready, Damon took the position of washing the dishes so that Cat could dry them and put them away.

"As kids, my mom would teach me and Ryan songs in the round or in harmony so we could sing while we did chores like dishes."

"Really? So did my mom. My favorite was 'Row, row, row your boat" because we made it a contest to see who would screw up the round first. Wanna try it? I have a pretty strong record."

"I'm sure you do, but I don't think I've ever been beat, either." Damon started the song in his deep baritone voice while Cat chimed in with her soprano. When he sped up, she matched him until they were practically screeching and giggling at their horrific sound.

After the dishes were done and the table washed and cleared, Cat excused herself to the outhouse for a moment. When she came back, Damon had moved the couch back against the kitchen table, added more wood to the fire, and made a makeshift bed in front of the fireplace by spreading out a sleeping bag on the floor with a sheet cover and the bed pillows. He had also moved their wine glasses to a small table next to the red brick hearth with the wine bottle and the pan of apple cobbler and two forks. He even found a moment to put on black silk boxer shorts.

Cat smiled when she saw the scene created for her. "I'm impressed." "Thank you. I felt that since you had your dessert earlier today,

I deserved to have mine tonight."

"If you can wait just a minute, your dessert would like to freshen up a bit before you start sampling it. By the way, I really like the silk boxer shorts; they're very sexy on you." When she walked by, Cat took her left hand and ran it across the front of them and felt a jerk as she grazed his front. When she got into the bedroom, she pulled out the ponytail holder and shook her curls loose again. She rummaged through her duffel bag and found the perfect outfit. She slid on the black lace thong and then pulled on the matching silk baby-doll top with a jeweled clasp between her breasts.

When she walked out of the room, Damon's eyes widened and then scanned her from the top of her head to the tip of her toes. His mouth went dry and his rod hardened. He walked over to her, and his hand reached out to lightly touch each piece of fabric. When he got to the silk triangles covering her breasts, he used his finger and his thumb to grab each nipple and rub them until they were taut with anticipation. He kissed the bare skin left between the two strips and used his tongue to lick her nipples through the silk. When her breath hitched, he stood straight up and stared into her eyes as his right hand reached over her lace panty and used his middle finger to place pressure onto her erogenous zone. Cat moaned but didn't break eye contact; instead, she spread her legs and wished he would do more.

Damon released his hand from her wet mound and dragged it down so that his pointer finger was able to inch its way in between her bare thighs. He dragged it from her front to the back and then squeezed each round globe until she moaned again. When he bent down to taste her, he couldn't stop himself from giving her a love bite on each cheek and then using his middle finger to find her pleasure spot one more time. He used his hand expertly to tease her into a frenzy as he nibbled on her neck. He wanted her to beg him because she clearly had every intention to seduce him with all these seductive outfits, and she was definitely getting his attention.

Cat was losing herself to the feelings of urgency and passion he was igniting in her with his hand on her erogenous organ, teasing it until she couldn't hold back anymore and screamed his name; she shivered from the explosion that happened throughout her body. Damon pushed down his boxer shorts and ripped off her thong to expose her to his need. He guided her onto him as her back was to him. He put his hands on her breasts and teased her nipples as he set the rhythm they would ride together to climax. She screamed even louder the second time and lay back onto his chest as she was gathering her breath.

As they recovered from their frenzied lovemaking, Cat guided them down to the makeshift bed in front of the fire. Damon lay on his back while Cat laid her head on his chest and lightly played with the ginger curls on his chest. Damon had one hand under his head and the other was caressing Cat's back through her silk negligée. "This has been the best Labor Day weekend of my life," he declared.

Cat grinned and lifted her head to look into his soft blue eyes. "Ditto."

"You were right; this place is magical. There's something about it that I can't put my finger on, but it's captivating."

"I know, right? For me, I love all the old rusty, dusty stuff all over the place, and then, out of nowhere, you find a first edition Dr. Seuss book, which is right next to a ratty scrapbook that's lying on top of family photos of a bride and groom cutting a six-foot-tall wedding cake. There's also this scent. Not just the trees, but the old musty smell of the cabins that also mix with a bit of fire smoke and propane. It sounds like it should smell awful, but to me, it smells wonderful. I get all excited when I open the door and see all the old things that I grew up with and one or two new things that people left behind. It feels like family."

Damon was intensely watching Cat as she clearly went back in time in her mind to share her memories with him. He could see what she was seeing, and he had already smelled what she smelled when they opened the cabin. "For me, it looks like it's been loved."

Cat looked at him quizzically. "What makes you say that?" "Well, you remember the kid's book, *The Velveteen Rabbit*?"

Cat nodded and waited for Damon to go on. "To me, I see worn furniture, floorboards, and books. It looks like a lot of hands and bodies have been here to enjoy a warm fire or a comfortable corner to read a book. In *The Velveteen Rabbit*, he knew he was loved by how much he was worn out at the end of the book. It was bittersweet, but it taught me a valuable lesson. Only have things that you will use and only love those who want to spend time with you and won't handle you with kid gloves."

Cat's eyes smiled. "You were a very smart little boy to get all of that out of a book."

"Actually, my mom would read that book to me every night and remind me of the moral to the story. Growing up in a large family, there isn't a lot of money or space for everyone to always have their own things and new things. I think part of the lesson was how to make things last so that all of us kids could use the clothes or play with the toys. It helped us take care of and appreciate things more because if we lost it or broke it, there was no guarantee it would get replaced."

"Your mom's smart," Cat replied as she laid her head back down on his chest.

"Yes, she is, but also very practical. You'd like her and she'd like you."

"Well, I don't know about that." "Why?"

"Because your dad was flirting with me at the center, and he even said he had a bit of a crush on me. She might be mad jealous," she said as she grinned.

"My dad flirted with you? He's more than twice your age!"

Cat patted his chest. "Don't worry. It was all in fun. It was clear he was trying to test me out to see if I would be a good fit for you."

"Oh. Well, he's a smart guy." "Well, am I?"

"Are you what?" "A good fit?"

Damon gently moved her off his chest and lay on his side with his arm propping up his head. His other arm traced the silhouette of Cat's side in the firelight. "Mmm. Perfect fit," he confirmed and then leaned in to gently kiss her in a slow lingering embrace.

All through the night, they took turns learning more about one another through romantic caresses, thoughtful conversation, and lovemaking. When they finally fell asleep, the fire's flames were dying into burning embers that kept the dampness of the cool night air out of the room.

When Cat finally awoke on Sunday morning, she heard eggs cracking in the kitchen while rain pitter-pattered off the windows. "Morning, sunshine!" Damon called to her.

"M … m … morning. Sounds like it's raining." Cat tried to wipe the sleepiness out of her eyes while she yawned.

"It is. I just checked the weather, and it looks like it's going to be raining all day long. I think this is a great day to see how good you are at board games. I'm pretty competitive you know." Damon stopped focusing on the French toast he was cooking and turned his head to wink at her.

"If you must know, after an ice-cold diet soda and some of those yummy-smelling French toasts, I will be kicking your butt from here 'til Tuesday in all games." Cat stood up and put her hands on her hips. Then she had a queer look on her face. "But first I've got to find some boots and a raincoat. I've got to piss like a racehorse!" Damon belted out a good strong laugh as Cat flitted around like a life-sized hummingbird trying to quickly find what she required to stay dry when she visited the little girls' room outside.

When she returned, Damon had already placed steaming platters of crispy sausage links and golden French toast triangles in the middle of the table. A carafe of orange juice and another of hot coffee joined the collage of items that he'd gathered for a sumptuous lumberjack breakfast. Cat sat down and began piling the vittles on her plate and dousing them in syrup. She poured some orange juice into a green Tupperware juice cup and breathed a welcome sigh when she heard the familiar "Pop!" of the soda can top break the seal and set the bubbles dancing to ignite her caffeine frenzy. She took a long drag on the soda can and began to relax. "Thank you for all of this, and especially for the diet soda. Boy, do I need it after that marathon session last night."

Damon grinned like the Cheshire cat in Lewis Carroll's *Alice in Wonderland.* He took her confession as a huge compliment that stroked his ego. "You're welcome."

Cat looked at him quizzically, and then when it sunk in, she rolled her eyes and said, "Oh please. I was the one who made your mouth drop down to the floor. I knocked your socks off and set the pace for the night, old man."

"Perhaps, but who was up first to make breakfast?"

"Good point." Cat knew that they were just teasing each other and didn't want this to get into a pissing match, so she relented.

"I'd say we both wore each other out equally. Now, if you want to compete, my friend, I'd suggest you help me clear these dishes and get ready for a game of Battleship."

Damon chuckled, nodded his head, and helped her clean up the table as she put on the water to get the dishes started. Damon freshened up the makeshift bed on the floor and joined Cat back into the kitchen for the cleaning of the dishes. Since the weather wasn't letting up, they changed into baggy sweats and took their seats for an exhilarating game of Battleship that included personal sound effects. Damon shook his head in defeat as Cat found the last hole in his destroyer. "What do I win? What do I win?" Cat was jumping up and down, doing her own special victory dance.

"What do you want?" His eyebrows went up as he asked, intrigued about what she might say. Cat walked over to him and whispered in his ear what she wanted. He shook his head. "I thought you were tired."

"Not anymore. Come on now. Give me my winnings!" She moved to the bedroom and patted the bed next to her for another round of lovemaking, where she dictated exactly what she wanted him to do to her, and where, until they were both panting and screaming in ecstasy. Afterward, they crawled under the sheets and slept intertwined until another bout of lightning and thunder shook the cabin to its core, waking them up in a start.

The rest of the day was a replay of the morning. They took turns beating each other at board games and card games, and then the winner would set the tone for the sex sessions that came next, which then led to either a feast from the kitchen or a nap. When the rain slowed down and the sun began showing its face again, they ventured outside with rain boots and jackets on to get some fresh air.

Cat got them each a bowl and told Damon that they were going for a walk on trails where the wild blackberries would be ripe and ready for picking. When the rain subsided, it brought in a cool front that felt refreshing after several days in the upper eighties and lower nineties. Cat chatted about the different types of trees and plants that she had learned about during nature walks she and

Ryan had taken with Marshall many years ago. She could almost feel him guide her toward the next patch of sun-ripened berries as they got to the beaver's dam.

"Is that a dam?" Damon looked like a kid in a candy shop.

"Yup. This dam has been here for years. My mom tells a story about a time when she came up here alone with us. Uncle Marshall agreed to watch us while she and our dog went for a walk. The dog walked on top of the dam and made it across. She tried to follow him and sunk hip deep into the goo and couldn't get out. She tried screaming and yelling, but nobody came. She was getting very afraid because every time she tried to move, she just sank deeper into the muck. Finally, she found a long stick and asked her dog to play tug of war, which he did and was able to pull her out. She carefully made her way back the way she came and arrived at the main house all covered in mud. That was the first time I'd ever seen my mom take a fully clothed body bath in the lake. Uncle Marshall thought it would be a good time for everyone to take a bath, so he stripped Ryan and me down to our diapers, and he went in his holey underwear and joined my mom. We all had a blast throwing wet washcloths at each other's faces. When one would hit Uncle Marshall, he'd scream really loud and then dunk down under the water. It made us laugh so hard we'd pee in our diapers until they were saturated and practically falling off. But we had such a good time playing that game that we didn't want to stop."

"Well, I don't know about you, but considering it's been raining all day and the dam looks like it's still pretty mucky, I think we should turn around unless there's another way around it," Damon suggested. Cat looked around.

"Hmm. The last time I was able to walk the whole lake, there was a drought and the lake wasn't nearly as high as it is now so we could walk in front of the dam. I'd say we turn around. By the time we get back, it'll be a good time to start dinner. I can make a cobbler from the blackberries we picked unless you ate them all."

"Oh, well, I didn't eat them all, but I'd better stop so you have some left to bake. Because when the rain lets up, I can grill out. Did you pack any meat for tonight?"

"Actually, I was thinking we could take a quick drive into Lake Tom and grab some steaks from the butcher and a pint of vanilla from his wife's ice cream shop. Then you can see where we'll be going tomorrow night for the snowshoe baseball game."

"Sounds perfect. All this talk about food is getting my stomach growling. Let's get going!"

Damon and Cat turned around just in time to see the loons flying overhead and land on the lake. The small group turned out to be a mated pair and a youngling. They stopped for a moment to take in the sight. With the sun trying to shine behind one of the larger gray clouds, the golden rays set the sky and the lake on fire. After such a dark and gray day, it took Cat's breath away to see all this color exploding from the sky. "Breathtaking," she said as much to herself as she did to Damon. He moved his bucket of berries to his left hand so that he could hold hers in his right. He shifted a bit so that he could turn her to him and warmly kiss her until she needed to catch her breath.

"I'm going to remember this weekend for as long as I live. I can't thank you enough for bringing me up here, Cat. I can see why this place means so much to you. Even though it rained all day, I honestly didn't mind it. I can't wait to see what tomorrow brings, and I know I'm going to be sad to leave here on Tuesday." Cat squeezed his hand and started walking down the path and back to the cabin.

They put their berries into a colander, rinsed them under cold water, and set the colander on a towel to let them drip dry until they came back. Hopping into the truck, they drove carefully down the long sand and dirt roads leading up to Loon Lake Road, trying to miss as many potholes as possible. When they got to the road into town, Cat pointed out a young hawk that flew over them with his meal of a mouse in his talons. The hawk perched on a young pine tree and watched the young couple for a moment before he spread his wings and flew away. "Damn, I have to start remembering to get my phone out to take some photos of this stuff. Unbelievable how close he was and then he just looked at us like we were invading his turf!" Damon exclaimed.

After a short drive into town, they parked on the gravel after the butcher's shop and his wife's ice cream shop. They walked up the wooden stairs onto the covered porch and then opened the spring-loaded screen door into the meat market. A man in his forties wearing a butcher's white paper hat and a bloodstained white apron was behind the counter and greeted them. Damon ordered two porterhouse steaks, while Cat perused the freshly baked loaves of bread, a variety of canned items, and homemade jams. She chose a fresh potato loaf with white flour dusted on top along and a jar of strawberry jam. After the butcher wrapped the thick slabs of meat and rang up their order, they moseyed next door into his wife's establishment.

The owner had her auburn hair up in a clip and had a few young staff helping another family with their ice cream order while Damon browsed the eclectic gathering of Lake Tomahawk graphic T-shirts right next to a set of antique china that happened to be right next to a recipe book for "rednecks." A few scattered ice cream parlor furniture sets were available for patrons to sit and enjoy their tasty treats indoors or on the front porch. There were those with wooden seats and black wire legs and backs bent in the shape of hearts. Then there were those that looked like the 1950s soda shop table and chair sets. Those were framed in chrome with shiny plastic red cushions and vintage red napkin holders. "This place is great!" Damon expressed.

"I know, right? Takes you back to another time, doesn't it?" "My grandma had a kitchen set just like this one, except that it had a few rips in it by the time we came around," he mentioned as he put his hand on one of the red and silver chairs.

When they collected their ice cream, Damon held the door open for Cat to mosey out of the shop and head toward the truck. "One of the reasons I like coming up here so much is that it's a different pace of life. Everything back home is so hectic. Getting up at the crack of dawn to take care of Mia, get ready for work, then the workday, come home and take care of Mia, get ready for the next day, and go to bed before it starts all over again."

"Are you tired of taking care of your dog?"

"No, that's not it. I don't know. I mean, I do good work and it feels good when a grant comes in or we have a successful event, but once a check comes in, Rose is always looking for the next big thing. Nothing ever seems good enough for her. It gets disheartening." Damon held the door open for Cat to climb in, and they drove back to the cabin while Cat continued sharing.

"I went to college thinking that I would actually get to work with the animals. Then I had all this debt and I was homesick, so I looked for the closest thing I could that would meet my immediate needs. Rose seemed like a great person to work for. She's a gifted veterinarian, and she's got a lot of important connections. I thought that the grant work would be temporary and that she'd take me under her wing to learn more about rehabilitating the animals."

"Why don't you ask her?"

"I have. A lot of times in the beginning and it always comes back to the fact that she can get a vet tech to do the work with the animals, but what the center really needs is a talented fundraiser. Without the funds, the work wouldn't be there, and the animals wouldn't have a place to go."

"So, she makes you feel guilty but important."

"Well, guilty, yes. Important, I guess I used to think I was valuable to her. Now, I'm not so sure. It seems that nothing I do makes her happy anymore. This vacation she took was a breath of fresh air for me. I could do my work without looking over my shoulder all the time. The event next month is really coming together, and all the reports show that we are ahead of last year's numbers. She should be pleased, but I'm fearful that she will still find something to be disappointed about," Cat continued as they got out of the truck and brought their bags into the kitchen to get dinner ready.

Damon went out onto the deck and started the grill while Cat put away the ice cream and started making the blackberry cobbler she was so looking forward to having with the fresh vanilla ice cream they had just picked up. Damon came back and started seasoning the steaks with a spice rub seasoning and a little extra virgin olive oil.

After the cobbler was put into the oven, Cat began making the salad while Damon found a merlot to uncork and pour them each a glass. As she was tossing the baby spinach and then cutting up fresh strawberries and red onions, she went on, "I want to enjoy going to work every day, but most days, I walk in there with a knot in my stomach that doesn't leave until I walk out that door at four. It's sad, isn't it?"

"Yeah, it is." Damon sipped on his wine as he looked at the coals to see if they were ready for cooking. "We've got a few minutes more on the coals. Come outside with me. What do you want to do? Have you looked at other places?"

Cat washed her hands and picked up her glass to follow Damon out onto the porch during the gloaming. She chose a gray metal patio chair with plastic weaving for the seat and back. She sat back and sighed. "I have, but I make a pretty decent salary and benefits. The opportunities around here don't offer benefits. They'd take me in an instant, but as a volunteer, and they help rehabilitate people, not animals. For me to work with animals the way I want to, I probably have to move to like Kentucky, Wyoming, Texas, or somewhere like that. To get benefits, I'd have to work with the park service as a government employee. If you've noticed, there aren't any national parks in Wisconsin. I'd have to leave my family again and be willing to travel a lot. I'm not sure I'm ready to do that again."

Damon looked into her eyes and then reached out to hold her hands. "I guess I was lucky that after I did my stint in Florida, I found what I was looking for practically down the road from home. I often wonder what my life would be like if I would have stayed in Florida. Would my parents be able to keep the farm going without my help? Would Pete and I still be best friends living so far away from one another? Hell, I love working with that guy. I can't imagine not working with him. He loves the gory stuff, finding out what's wrong and going in to fix it. I really feel good when I can listen to the animals and feel what's bothering them. This week, for instance, I had this pregnant mare who was miserable. I listened to her huffing and felt down each of her flanks, her back, and her belly, and when I came to her left hip, she almost bit me. So, I got out my needles and talked softly to her and figured out that the foal was lying in a way that it was pinching a nerve in her back end. Once she was relaxed enough, I could work the foal a little to shift where it was lying, and she walked out of there practically batting her eyes at me. The owner was grateful not to have to give her any medication and not to stress out the foal any longer.

"See, that's what I mean. I never get to touch the animals to make them feel better. I used to be able to have such a strong intuition with the horses we worked with and some of the other animals in my classes. Now, I can write about them, but I don't know if I can fix them like I used to. I miss that."

Damon squeezed her hand and then checked on the coals. "It's time for the steaks to go on. I'll be back."

Cat looked out onto the lake and felt almost melancholic. Then she shook her head and started talking to herself. "What am I doing? Why am I feeling sorry for myself when I've got this hot guy who wants to be with me? I'm ruining it! Snap out of it, Carneri!"

"What'd you say?" Damon asked as he started laying the steaks next to the hot coals.

"Oh, nothing. Just a little self-talk to stop being such a Debbie Downer when we're having such a good time together." She got up, put her glass down, and wrapped her arms around his neck while she pressed her body against his and opened her mouth to accept him into hers. Damon responded quickly. His arms found their way around her waist, and his hands squeezed her ass and pressed her closer to him.

"You're trying to distract me when I'm trying to be a good boyfriend and listen to your problems. I can't be supportive and horny at the same time, Cat. My body doesn't work that way." He pulled away slightly to look into her hazel eyes where the gold flecks were picking up the sun's rays and sparkling a bit more brightly than usual.

"You are doing a great job, Damon. I just don't want to ruin this amazing romantic weekend with a bunch of whining. Honestly, I'm doing very well for myself. I enjoy the other people that I work with. I love my little apartment and Mia is a lovebug; who wouldn't want to come home to her every day? And now we have this." She brushed his lips with hers lightly and felt his whiskers tickle her nose. "I can't believe how lucky I am to have you in my life. I can't wait to see what happens next." She closed in, put her head on his chest, and squeezed him in a big bear hug.

"Well, what happens next is we get to eat damn good steaks for dinner, and I'm already drooling over the aroma from the oven. When can we dig into the cobbler?" Cat giggled and let go. Damon grabbed the platter and stacked the sizzling steaks onto it while Cat went inside to get the salad and the fresh bread with fixings.

After stuffing themselves with savory meat and tangy salad, Cat got up to spoon up mouthwatering blackberry cobbler with a buttery crumble crust and a scoop of melting vanilla ice cream for each of them. Damon attacked it like he'd been starved instead of stuffed.

"Oh my God! This is so good!" he mumbled as he stuffed more into his face, leaving crumbs and ice cream dripping from his whiskers. Cat laughed at him and then put her plate down to lick the remnants off his face. She could feel the beginnings of a moan coming from his chest and leave his moist lips. Cat was amazed that such a little gesture was getting him aroused, which was getting her insides all tingly again. "Now for my real dessert," Damon spoke gruffly while leading her through the cabin door and to the kitchen table.

Damon quickly swept off the semblance of kitchenware off the table and then lifted Cat up onto it. He pulled her shirt over her head and unsnapped her bra with the flick of his thumb and finger. Cat gasped at his efficiency and his focus. He wanted her now, and she couldn't move a muscle. She was excited and a little bit scared at what was going to happen next. The last time this table was involved in their lovemaking, he made her experience something she'd never done before. She could feel her heart beginning to race as he unbuttoned and unzipped her jean shorts and slid them to the floor with her panties. There she was, naked and breathing heavy as she sat on the edge of the kitchen table, not sure what was coming next.

"Lie back and close your eyes. No peeking," Damon demanded. She did as she was told, feeling very vulnerable but yet also feeling the excitement of what he would be doing next. In such a short period of time, Damon had built trust with Cat. His commitment to honesty was vital to her willingness to believe he wouldn't hurt her and her willingness to try new things with him. A man who had been hurt by love before wouldn't want to make another feel that broken. Besides, she knew that if horses trusted him to put needles into their skin, he wasn't about to purposefully or maliciously hurt her.

With her eyes closed but her heart open, she anticipated his first move. "Interesting," she thought as she heard the refrigerator door open and close. Then she held her breath as she felt his presence right in front of her womanhood. Next, she shivered as she felt a coolness drop on top of her hips and then the drips of the melting ice cream running down on either side and then another cold sensation on top of her freshly shaved nether region and dripping down between her legs. The slowness of the liquid gliding down the hotness between her legs was gathering intensity of pleasure, and she felt as if she could cum without him even touching her.

Damon must have sensed that she was beginning to climax on her own accord and refused to let that happen. He dipped down and casually began licking off the remnants of the melting sweetness over each hip and down to each cheek. Then he glided his tongue over her quivering stomach to suck the liquid out of her belly button, which made her moan and start moving, which made the melting ice cream drip into new places. Cat was losing all sense of reality and began following her instincts. Her hand reached up and felt for the hair on his head. She grabbed it and pushed his head to meet her growing need. When she felt his whiskers prickling her tender skin, she winced a little until she felt his warm, moist tongue licking her slowly at first. But as she was pushing his head down, he realized that she needed him to join her in her frenzy and he couldn't hold out much longer himself. He picked up the pace to match her breathing, which now had turned into a series of guttural and high-pitched moans. She was lifting her hips to meet his mouth, which was ravaging her until she couldn't control herself any longer and let loose in a loud fury. Her hips bucked to complete the climax he had brought her to.

Damon lost all control. He didn't care about the performance and watching her in passion. He needed to be inside her now. He practically ripped off his own clothes, and as her climax was dying down, he pulled her so that her "V" was nearly off the table. He wrapped her legs around his neck and plunged into her, which made her scream out in another wave of pleasure. No time for slowness now. Damon was caught up in the animalistic urges he was feeling to make her his. No other man would ever make her feel this way again. She was his and he was hers. United in their possession of each other, they reached primal intensity and groaned in unison as Damon exploded into Cat, and she came like a woman possessed.

When the moment had passed, Damon lay down on top of Cat, panting. She ran her fingers through his unruly locks and kissed the top of his head. "I didn't know vanilla ice cream had that effect on you. Can't wait to find out about the other thirty flavors." He began to laugh huskily.

"Cat, you've gotta know, it wasn't the ice cream. Although I'd be willing to test your theory." He lifted up his head and sucked on each nipple before he lifted himself off and felt their sticky skin pulling away from each other with a bit of pain that also felt like a bit of relief.

"Why don't we go clean up down at the lake? I don't feel like putting on clothes right now, and I'm kinda stuck to the table."

Damon mumbled, "Sorry," as he took her hands and gently lifted her back off the table.

After a loving kiss and warm hug, they pulled apart again so Cat could grab towels and sandals for their trip down to the beach. They walked hand in hand silently down the wooded path until they reached the cool sand that had been pockmarked from the rains before. The stars were out, and the moon was rising so they had illumination over the bay they would be swimming in.

Damon swept Cat off her feet, literally, and carried her into the lake while small waves broke against the sand. Cat closed her eyes and let her head fall back just enjoying the feeling of being protected and comforted simultaneously. When Damon reached the raft, he gently set her down so she could stand in the waist-deep water next to him. Looking down at her, he confessed, "You know, Cat, I thought I knew what love felt like before. I thought I knew what making love to a woman felt like. But I was just a dumb ass. I knew nothing. You," he spoke in all sincerity, as he reached up to push curls away from her face. "This. I honestly know what it means to really love a woman now. Cat, you have changed me in all sorts of little and big ways already. I know we have a long way to go to know what all this is leading to, but I know what I'm feeling is real. Don't get scared when I tell you this, but I am seeing a future with you. The home, the yard, dogs, kids, horses, the whole thing. I haven't thought about that at all for a very long time. Thank you for bringing me here, it's so magical—I'm not going to want to leave in two days."

Cat's heart grew, and she took a deep breath as she listened to his words, but more importantly, she felt the positive energy he was exuding. She reached out to brush his cheek with the back of her hand. The heartfelt confession he shared was so powerful for her. It connected them on a new level, bringing them closer than just sex alone could ever do. Cat felt the shift, from being infatuated, being lusty, to being loved. "You know, maybe God has a bigger plan for me, for us. As much as I complained about my job earlier today, if I hadn't been working there that morning you brought the crane in, we may never have met. Not knowing you or being with you would have been a tragedy that I wouldn't have fully known. I'd be just living my life without purpose or meaning. Who knows how long it would take for the hopefulness I feel to turn to hopelessness? I'm changing my mind about my job. I'm glad I work there and help animals the way I do. Without that job, you and I wouldn't exist."

Damon bent down and hungrily took her mouth and searched for her tongue with his until they were intertwined. Cat's hunger for him grew again. This time, without inhibition, she turned around and coyly looked over her shoulder as she was holding on to the edge of the raft and pressed her heart-shaped ass toward his growing loins. Damon didn't think twice. He wanted her any way she would have him and gladly spread her willing cheeks to accept him once again. When he penetrated her, Cat pushed her backside toward him, closing in the gap between them and encircling his member. Damon needed no further clues as to what was on her mind and took one hand and wrapped it into her curls and gently pulled her head back so he could bite her neck with every thrust he made into her willing woman's mound. His thrusts quickened, and her grinding pressed on until they captured rapture, screaming out into the night and rustling the feathers of several loons and other night birds in the shadows.

After a brief reprieve, the couple lovingly applied lavender body shampoo to all the places they had been touching each other for the past several days and nights. Diving under the cool water, Cat felt refreshed, shaking out the pools of water that settled into her ears. Damon followed suit, except that his body displaced much more water than hers as he submerged, and the raft began to quake from the waves that rocked it from its sleepy existence. The day's rainfall had turned the night air into a bit of a chill; therefore, the young couple snuggled into their towels and walked the short hike back to their love nest in the woods.

Once back, Damon built a fire to help dry off the last bits of wetness that had settled on their skin. Cat went into the bedroom to brush through her curls with some detangler before they'd settle on being impossible later on. On her way back into the great room, she lay down the makeshift bed they'd enjoyed the night before, and on the arm of the sofa, she sat a bottle of essential oils for massage. Without words, she made Damon lie on his stomach and straddled his hips while her hands went to work massaging oil into his neck, shoulders, back, and arms. Damon's body relaxed with each pressure point Cat found and worked until the tight knots released. When she had finished with the upper body massage, she turned around to work on his muscular legs. Starting with his tight ass, she massaged it with her hands and then worked down each thigh, careful not to start another marathon lovemaking session. This sensation wasn't about sex; it was about teaching him that she could offer him a safe place to let go, just feel, just relax. In the short time they'd been together, she understood him to always be there for everyone else. Packing his days with work, the family farm, and his friends. She wanted Damon to understand that he didn't have to always be there for her; she could be there for him. Sometimes, it isn't those things that are physically strong that are the strongest; sometimes it's the meaningful things that are stronger.

By the time she was done, Damon was snoring on the ground with his head cushioned by the pillow he was hugging. Cat put a few more logs on the fire, wiped off her hands, and snuggled in next to him to close her eyes.

Monday morning came into view with the bright sun glistening off the water and a very annoying woodpecker working away at the dead birch tree right outside one of the front windows. Cat woke up first and put on a green tie-dyed T-shirt with her last pair of clean panties and bra. No frills on this set. She smiled as she remembered Damon's reaction to her myriad of lingerie she'd packed for this trip. Truth be told, she didn't need it. She'd have been just as successful seducing him if she were buck naked this whole trip. However, Aurelie would be very disappointed in her as she had worked very hard at helping purchase those unique and tantalizing outfits online. Thank God for online shopping! Cat would have been mortified picking out lingerie in a store.

It already felt like it would be a scorcher out there, so she rummaged through her bag to find a clip to set into her hair twist to keep those locks off her neck. Next, she walked carefully into the kitchen to assess what was left from her food stash to make a decent breakfast. She knew they'd be eating at the ballpark for dinner, so she didn't have to worry about that. Ah hah! She found enough eggs, milk, and bread for the beginnings of an eggie bake, a fan favorite when the whole family was out together camping or at the cabin. Cat cut up the leftover bread into cubes, then found that she still had several slices of bacon that hadn't been fried, so she cubed those up and threw them into a bowl with the milk, eggs, bread, some brown mustard, and lots of cheddar cheese. After mixing it all together, she sprayed a baking pan and poured the concoction into the pan and into the hot oven for an hour. Next, she started the teapot full of water and grabbed her chai tea tin to scoop some of the spicy goodness into her tea press awaiting hot water to steep. In the meantime, she grabbed cold water out of the cooler and tiptoed out of the cabin and onto the deck for a moment or two of stillness.

The warm breeze that rustled the green leaves on the trees and bent their bows had a calming effect on her. She closed her eyes and didn't realize it when Damon came up behind her and wrapped his muscular arms around her and squeezed while he nuzzled her neck. "Morning, beautiful," he spoke.

"Good morning, handsome."

"I haven't slept that soundly in a very long time. What did you put in that massage oil? Opium?"

Cat chuckled. "No, silly. I just so happen to be a talented masseuse. You were finally able to sleep because my capable hands were able to work the knots out of your body. The massage oil just helped me get a bit deeper than I could have gotten on my own. Plus, it made you smell nice."

"Damn, woman, I know you're talented, but I wasn't expecting this," he said as he kissed her on the nape.

"Mmm. I'd better check on the coffee and tea. We have a few more minutes before breakfast is ready. Want to sit out here or on the kitchen table?"

"Better sit out here. We still haven't cleaned up since dessert last night," Damon snickered.

"Good point. Can you set the table for breakfast out here, and I'll be back with some go-go juice for both of us?"

Damon begrudgingly let her go and followed her into the cabin, which had a montage of aromas combating each other. Smoky, spicy smells perfumed the area between the sofa and fireplace. Sticky sweetness hovered over the kitchen table, and strong coffee and bacon wafted from the kitchen. Damon found the plates and silverware to put outside and set aside the disinfectant wipes that he would use to clean the kitchen table later.

Cat was daydreaming while she served up the piping-hot coffee and tea. Damon grabbed her around the waist and sat her in his lap while they looked out on to the path that led to the boat launch. "God, Cat. I will never get bored of this view or of being with you out here. What are you thinking?"

"Honestly, it's going to sound a bit corny, but I was thinking about what it might be like to serve you coffee in our own place. You know like an old married couple."

Damon squeezed her a bit more. "It doesn't sound corny at all. I think that's what we all want. When Pete thought he'd lost Angie, he told me that what he missed the most was the lazy Sunday mornings drinking coffee and sitting with her reading the paper or watching television. I think what that means is that you wish to be truly happy and at peace."

Cat pondered what Damon just said: to be truly happy and at peace. Had she ever had that feeling before? Not as an adult, but certainly as a child. That's why this place was so special to her. So many memories of just being here. Nothing fancy. No all-inclusive vacations with midnight buffets and Vegas-style shows. Just enjoying nature and her family. Yes, she knew the feeling well; it just had been lying dormant for a while.

Cat's nose started sniffing the air and she motioned to get up. "Breakfast is ready."

"How do you know? I didn't hear a timer go off."

"I can smell it. Can't you?" Cat arrived in the kitchen and opened up the oven door to see a golden brown-crusted top with crevices filled with bubbling cheese. She carefully set it down on the top of the stove while she gingerly kicked the oven door shut. Finding a butcher knife in the butcher-block holder, she sliced the eggie bake into squares and found a spatula to insert for serving the breakfast delight.

Damon's nose was going into overtime until she set it down in front of him. He served her the first piece and then dug into his own. In just one bite, he'd managed to eat half of his slice. "Damn this is so good. Shit! It's really hot!" he exclaimed as he was blowing out of his mouth in an effort to cool it down a bit more.

"Of course, it's hot, silly. I literally just pulled it out of the oven." Cat finished her square and noticed that Damon was on his third; half the pan had been demolished. She thought about how portion size meant something completely different to the two of them. She then wondered what else she'd be learning about him? Where else were they different?

When Damon had had his fill, they cleaned up the dishes outside and brought them into the cabin for the morning clean-up. Cat set water on the stove to boil for dishes while Damon cleaned the kitchen table with the disinfectant wipes. Cat picked up the makeshift bed and put together the one in the bedroom. When the water was ready, they both pitched in, and Damon started singing salty Irish tunes that had Cat roaring in laughter. With all their morning chores done, they decided to finally venture into town so that Damon could see what a small north woods town was all about.

Climbing into the truck, Cat noticed he'd already become quite familiar with the route to Lake Tom; now she needed to direct him down Mid Lake Road to take the back way into Minocqua, away from all the crazy Illinois drivers. Minocqua is a very popular north woods town. It is nestled on an island, which is accessible by bridges. During the tourist season, every nook and cranny on the lake and in town is filled with visitors. Minocqua became a bustling tourist town once the railroads, catering to sportsmen and vacationers, saw the opportunity to exploit the vast waters and sandy shores for more lucrative opportunities. Today's Minocqua is filled with souvenir shops, candy- and taffy-making storefronts, jewelry, and rustic home décor businesses. It isn't uncommon for a person to run into a rusty old truck idling next to a shiny red sports car at one of the few stoplights in town.

Damon found a parking spot in one of the public parking areas on the island. They meandered through a variety of shops, laughing at some of the cheesy trinkets, surprised at the ostentatious prices of some of the clothes and jewelry in the boutiques. Damon's favorite shop was a thrift store run by a local church. Apparently, Labor Day weekend was a time when everything in the store was free so they could switch out the merchandise for the next season. He loaded himself down with a variety of books, a few shirts suitable for farm work, and a card game. They snacked on popcorn and ice cream while washing them down with ice-cold sodas.

When Cat looked at the time, she was surprised that they had spent four hours already downtown just shopping. Most guys would be bored and begging to go home. Instead, Damon sat on a park bench licking his melting ice cream cone while people-watching. She, in turn, was watching him lick his ice cream and remembering what he had been doing to her with it just the night before.

When their ice cream cones were all but a memory, they meandered through the streets until they found his truck waiting for them to come back. "We have a few hours before snowshoe baseball starts. What do you want to do next?" Cat questioned.

"Well, I haven't had the opportunity to fish in a few days, and if I'm lucky, we could have a fish dinner."

"Then it's a plan. I'm at a really good point in my book, so I can't wait to get back to it." They drove the rest of the way in silence but held hands. Cat's heart raced as she felt Damon's strong fingers caressing hers. Her deep-rooted sadness had all but left her memory. She felt contentment and hope once again. Perhaps happiness would be her new norm.

At the cottage, they changed into swim gear and sandals and then walked down to the rowboat where Damon had left his gear from the last time he had fished. Cat balanced herself to get into the boat with the least amount of rocking and sat at the bow while Damon pushed off and then hopped in, making the boat rock a bit more where mini waves pushed away from the silver sphere and disrupted a few lily pads near the shore. Damon expertly rowed the boat to the far shore and set his line and bait for his first cast. Cat reached over to kiss him quickly on his cheek while she settled in to enjoy the adventure her heroine was about to embark on in the book *Tiger's Curse,* by Colleen Houck. Cat understood the need for silence for fishing; her father and brother were passionate fishermen and reminded her and her mom that they couldn't keep talking because it scared the fish. Still, she loved how easy it was to talk to

Damon and to carry on a conversation with him about anything. He seemed to fit her perfectly.

The rest of the afternoon continued that trajectory, Cat finding something humorous, scary, or emotional in her book and would let out a little noise that seemed to echo all around the lake. Once when they were on the cottage side of the lake, something got a hold of his line, and he almost lost it. Damon strengthened his grip and held on for dear life. The fish on his line was going for a run and trying to lose the line under the boat. When that didn't work, it broke to the surface and writhed and jumped to rid itself of the barbed hooks that got it on the side of its mouth. "Cat! Grab the net!" Damon yelled as he braced his foot on the side of the boat for leverage, and he fought against his worthy opponent. When Damon motioned to her to get close to him, she carefully stepped toward him without rocking the boat. She got the net ready and watched the water, fascinated at the intricate dance that was taking place between fish and man. She got so entranced in the movements that she almost missed the cue that Damon gave her to bring the net flush to the water as he finally was able to use his brute force to get the largemouth bass into position with the net underneath it. Cat lifted the net out of the water and brought it into the boat to lie down at Damon's feet. The fish continued to flail, but Damon used his skilled hands to gently glide underneath the fish's slippery skin and grab it by the gills to get better control so he could wriggle the hook out of its mouth.

"Hot damn! This bad boy is a big one! It must be twenty-four inches long!" Damon was as giddy as a young boy hitting his first home run or sinking his first basket.

"He sure is! Looks like he could feed the two of us and then some." Cat grinned and shied away when the fish tried to do another flip out of Damon's hands and into the water. Damon caught it and began threading the stringer through its gills so he could get it back into the water while he rowed the boat back to the bay where it would be beached for the night. Cat took up the oars and the cushions to put them back in the basement while Damon grabbed his pole, gear, and the stringer to walk it all up to the deck, where Cat was already ahead and had spread newspapers down on the glass patio table and was coming back out with bowls of ice water to soak the filets. Damon set his gear down against the barn's red siding and leaned in for a kiss, but Cat shrunk away. "Not until you finish with cleaning the fish and washing off the fish guts."

Damon pouted. "That's it? I worked really hard to get you dinner." "After the game, we can celebrate," Cat said with a wicked smile.

"Okay." Damon continued to pout but went to work getting his filet knife out of its leather pouch and painstakingly gutting and cleaning the fish until all that was left was balled-up newspapers and pure white fish filets floating in ice-cold water.

Meanwhile, Cat set the kitchen table and made a large mixed-greens salad with fresh tomatoes, cucumber slices, and strips of red and yellow peppers. On the stove, she placed the cast iron skillet and waited for the fish to be coated in beaten egg, pancake mix, and paprika. Damon brought in the fish and snuck a kiss on Cat's nose while she got to work beating the egg and mixing in the paprika into the pancake mix pile she poured into a shallow bowl. Damon went to work scrubbing his hands, periodically sniffing them to see if the smell had gone away.

Cat fired up a burner on the stove and poured oil into the pan, waiting for it to begin to smoke. With the two fish filets ready to go, a light smoke began to waft over the pan, and Cat carefully laid the two filets into the blackened pan, careful to not get burned by the sizzling, popping liquid.

Damon pulled out two beers out of the frig and set one down by Cat's side. "Smells fantastic, Cat. I can't wait to have a taste. I'm starving!"

"Just a few more minutes on this side, and then I have to flip them for a few more. Wait a minute, how can you be hungry? We had a big breakfast and then snacked on popcorn and ice cream in town."

"Babe, you better get used to it. I'm always hungry. How do you think I keep this amazing bod in shape?" Cat howled and then looked out to the side to see Damon flexing his biceps and trying to kiss them.

When the breading had turned a warm golden brown, Cat lifted each filet carefully out of the hot oil and onto a paper towel to soak up the grease before setting them on the platter. Damon served Cat a heaving portion of salad and cut a slab of the cranberry walnut loaf and smothered it with butter, then placed it on her plate along with one of the steaming fish filets and then began putting together his plate. Before Cat could dig in, Damon lifted his bottle for a toast and held Cat's out to her in the other. She took the bottle from him as he looked deeply into her eyes and spoke, "I want to give thanks to God for bringing us together, for this incredible weekend, and for this delicious meal. I am so very blessed right now."

Cat smiled, lifted her bottle to clink with his, and leaned in for a sweet kiss before taking a long drag on her cold beer. "Nothing like an ice-cold beer with a hot fish fry!" she thought to herself and then dug into the flaky white meat for a taste. "Wow, this is hot, but it tastes so good!" she said out loud as she blew on the next piece that made it onto her fork. Damon didn't make time for a reply as he was busy stuffing the hot crispy goodness into his mouth before it cooled off.

Eating in silence, Cat felt the contentment of a woman who had found love and was at peace with the period of quiet. No need to nervously make small talk so that every moment was filled with mindless chatter. She knew from experience with watching her parents interact over the years that much of their time together was in tender quiet—they knew what each other would need and muscle memory would kick in, to hand over a screwdriver or pour an ice-cold glass of lemonade or serve up a piece of pie or pack up a campsite. One of her favorite moments from watching her parents ct was when it was family movie night. Anthony would let Claire get comfortable on the sofa and then take a pillow, prop it up between her leg and the back of the sofa so he could lay down while her fingers would lightly play with his silver-streaked hair. If Cat was being honest, that was exactly what she was hoping would happen with Damon and her moving forward. Those simple moments where they'd find their comfort with each other and without even thinking show how much they loved one another with love touches.

Cat hadn't realized she'd stopped eating and was staring out straight ahead. "Cat, you okay? Are you done eating?" Damon looked at her quizzically.

"What? Oh, no worries. I'm fine. Just thinking about my folks for a moment, and I just zoned out a bit." She took another bite of the fish and realized that she wasn't hungry anymore. She offered it to Damon, who took it and the rest of her plate. "Hey, buddy. You'd better leave room for pie."

"Don't worry about me. I always have room for pie," Damon replied with a little bit of a grin.

After dinner, they got up, but Damon stopped her from cleaning up. "You made such a delicious dinner, I'm gonna clean up. Why don't you freshen up and get ready for the game? I'll be right behind you."

"Deal!" Cat didn't mind doing dishes but was even happier letting that chore go to someone else. Besides, she'd ordered snowshoe baseball caps online a few weeks ago and wanted to root away in her duffel bag to get them out for their special date out. In the bedroom, she wriggled off the green bikini and long T-shirt and freshened up her deodorant and makeup. She found a T-shirt bra and a white short-sleeved T-shirt to go with her khaki capris and leather sandals. She brushed through her hair and whipped up a quick ponytail braid that she stuck out the back of the cap. Taking Damon's present in her hand, she yelled from the bedroom, "Close your eyes!"

"Last time you told me to do that, we ended having wild animal sex. Should I drop my swim trunks first?"

"No! Well, maybe later. I have a present for you, but I want it to be a surprise." She peeked out past the pine flip door and saw that his eyes were indeed closed as he held a dishtowel. She walked up to him, stood on her tippy toes, and placed the cap on top of his unwieldy red locks. He felt the top of his head and then opened his eyes to see Cat in her hat. She turned him to the small square mirror nailed to the upper china cupboard.

Damon bent down to see himself in the mirror and adjusted the hat to his liking. "This is so cool! Thanks!" He swirled around and planted a deep kiss on her freshly made-up lips. Damon bent over, and she held on to his neck while she enjoyed her thank you.

"Well, you are very welcome. I can't wait to see what I get in return for the next present."

"You got me another present? Let me see!" Damon practically dropped her, and his clear blue eyes went wide with wonder, darting around the cabin to see if he could pick it out.

"Honestly, I'm done with the presents for this trip, but now I know that I have to keep my wits about me if I want anything to be a surprise from you." She giggled. "You are the biggest kid I know."

"It's true. It's true. Sorry, I kinda lose it when someone tells me I'm getting a present. Some people hate surprises, but I don't. I think surprises are mostly for good, so why wouldn't I want one?"

"Why don't you go get dressed and I'll finish up in the kitchen? We should get going if we're going to be able to get a head start on that pie." Damon's eyes went wide as saucers as he realized that getting dressed was between him and pie. He gave Cat the damp dishtowel and made a beeline to the bedroom to switch into khaki camp shorts, his "Jesus shoes," as Cat called them, and a blue T-shirt.

With everything tidied up and the couple in fresh clothes, they piled into the truck and drove back to town, enjoying the windows down with a fresh breeze to provide some relief from the day's heat and humidity. After finding a spot behind the soft-serve ice cream shop, they walked across the street and directly to the pie line. About ten people ahead of them, Cat took the blanket she had brought from the truck to save two spaces on the bleachers while Damon impatiently waited in line and squirmed to see the pie sign.

As she returned to the line, Damon moved her beside him so he could watch as the young woman with the dry erase marker went over to the pie list to make some changes. "Don't erase strawberry rhubarb, don't erase strawberry rhubarb," Damon started to chant. He was practically jumping out of his drawers to see what she had erased and what she added. "Hallelujah! The pie stays!" Damon rejoiced. Cat just giggled at the spectacle he was making.

"Be careful not to get too attached there, buddy. Last time I was here I wanted banana cream pie, and just before I got up to the window, they'd sold the last piece. Best to pick out a second choice now, just in case," said a portly man with a chewed-up cigar dangling from his scruffy face.

"Thanks for the advice there, fella. I'll do just that." Cat started coughing to hide the roaring laughter that was trying to burst out. Damon held her shoulders and whispered, "Shhh," in her ear to try to keep her from losing it any further.

Finally, they reached the window where they could order pie. Damon practically dropped on top of the ledge to ask for his pie. "I'd like a slice of your strawberry rhubarb with a scoop of vanilla ice cream, please," Damon requested with the biggest grin he could finagle and batted his eyelashes at the lady with the blue hair and pin curls behind the counter. She blushed a bit as she found a slice and presented it to him with his requested ice cream scoop.

Cat ordered pecan pie with whipped cream, and together they walked toward the bleachers to their blanket to commence the savoring of their sweet pastries. "Well, what do you think?" Cat inquired as she took a bite of her pie.

"If I'm honest, it's not as good as my mom's, but it is hitting the spot. Hey, speaking of hitting, when's the game gonna start?"

Cat looked at her watch and saw that the game had about five more minutes before the national anthem would be belting out of the speakers on the nearby media tower. Only on her second bite, she peeked over and noticed that Damon had devoured his piece and was scraping the crumbs and cream drippings onto his fork to get every last delectable bite.

A tinny rendition of the national anthem played on what could only be discerned as an old turntable. Everyone in the crowd took off their hats and placed their hands on their hearts. An elderly male voice belted out the song while the crowd sang every word in unison. At the end of the anthem, the crooner yelled out, "Play Ball!" and the two teams on the field got into position.

Damon knew quite a bit about baseball, so he didn't have questions about how it was played but had a keen interest in the sawdust on the field, the "baseball," no mitts, and of course, the snowshoes. Cat thoroughly enjoyed watching Damon's fascination at the game, and she realized that watching snowshoe baseball with someone you love was far more fun than watching it alone with a crowd of strangers. When the melon was brought out to the pitcher's mound, Damon looked quizzically at the field and then at Cat, who shrugged her shoulders. The pitcher threw the pitch, and the batter swung and splattered the orange matter all over himself, the bat, and home plate. The crowd went wild, as did Damon. Though everyone knew it was coming, it was still a crowd-pleaser.

After the game, Damon chatted Cat's ear off about different things he'd seen and his favorite parts of the game. "God, that was a blast! Can't believe I've never seen that before. Cat, that sure was worth coming all the way up north to see. We've got to make this an annual tradition." Cat's heart grew so large she felt it nearly jump out of her chest. She curled her arm through his and set her head on his bicep until they reached the truck. Damon turned her to face him and gave her a hard, smacking kiss before he left to hop into the driver's side.

On the way back to the cabin, he continued to chatter like a squirrel bickering to its neighbor. Cat, however, began thinking about how much she'd been looking forward to taking him to the game and how quickly it was over. She sighed a bit, realizing that tomorrow morning they'd be packing up to go home and leaving their lover's hideaway until next season.

The sun had dipped below the trees, giving everything a warm glow on the lake. A pair of loons basked in one of the sun's rays that made it onto the lake. Once out of the truck, Cat meandered down to the lake by the boat beach to take it all in. She knew that there would be other times she'd be coming up here, and quite possibly with Damon, but they wouldn't be as special as this time had been for her. She sighed a moment and then felt a warm bear hug coming at her from behind. She fell into the embrace, leaning her head onto the massive chest behind her.

"I'm going to miss this place. I can see why this lake has so many special memories for you," Damon reflected, then kissed on top of her baseball cap.

Cat reached up with both arms and squeezed his biceps. "I know. Still, this time is one for the memory books. I'm kinda sad that our time here is almost up and we have to get back to the real world."

"I know, but wow! We've had an incredible time. Thank you, Cat. This has been one of those times where I know I'll remember every single detail." He turned her around, gently took off her baseball cap, tilted her head, and bent down to kiss her. When his lips touched hers, a spark went through him that brought him to press her further into his embrace. Her reaction was immediate. Cat wrapped her arms around his neck and pressed her body as close as she could. Her hands unwrapped and flicked his cap off his head so her fingers could entangle themselves into his unruly red crop. Then she used her fingernails to scrape his scalp, which sent him into a frenzy. Damon deepened the kiss, which, in turn, caught Cat a bit off guard, and she unwittingly moaned in response.

Feeling where this was going, Cat, pushed herself away so that she could get a grip on his T-shirt and pull it over his head. With his bare chest in front of her face, she closed in on his right nipple, gripping it with her front teeth and teasing it with her tongue. His moaning caught her attention, and she grinned. Next, she let her tongue guide her mouth to the other nipple, which received the same attention and a similar response. When each nipple was lovingly cared for, she used her tongue once again to glide down his six-pack abs, which quivered to her touch. Feeling more confident, she kneeled down and expertly used her hands to unlatch his shorts and push his boxers down to his ankles. She saw his reaction to her, and she smiled.

Damon's eyes closed immediately, and he put his hands into her hair as he fell into a meditative state with what she was doing to him. When he felt like he was about to fall over, he hated doing it but pulled her face away from his manhood and lifted her up. Cat, at first, felt that she might have been doing something wrong—she wasn't as experienced as he was, but then she realized by his next action that she was wrong. Dead wrong.

He pulled her up, and she saw the storm brewing in his eyes. But what he did next took her breath away. His hands moved from her face and gripped the V-neck opening of her T-shirt and ripped it into half, leaving her breathless and only in her white lace T-shirt bra and her capris. Next, he expertly used one hand to unclasp her bra and let both, the rest of the shirt and her bra, fall to the ground. The night breeze that was cooling down coupled with the heat of his touch had her nipples grow hard and stiff as little goosebumps appeared on their milky white skin. Damon didn't wait for an invitation but ravaged both breasts at the same time. Using his hands to push them together, he used his whiskers to tease one nipple while he devoured its sister.

Cat was going out of her mind and was losing her grasp of reality and her ability to stand. She could feel her inner animal instincts kicking in and her connection to intelligence flutter away into the breeze. She pushed his head away and saw his look of wonder and then understanding as she unbuttoned her own pants and slid them down along with her white lace panties around her ankles and kicked them off. Damon kneeled before her and then buried his head into her lady's mound and went to work licking, nipping, and sucking at her wet and inflamed folds. Her hands grabbed locks of his hair, and she spread her legs apart for his further access and her enjoyment. As the sun continued to dip behind the trees, as if it recognized their need for privacy, Cat saw stars behind her eyelids as his expert tongue went to work to show her places that have never been reached before. As she screamed in a peak of passion, she pushed his head further into her until the peak calmed down and her legs started to lose their ability to stand.

Damon guided her down onto the soft grass and guided his engorged shaft into her quivering core and began a rhythm that engaged her hips to join him. He stared into her eyes as if burning the image of their lovemaking into permanent memory. Cat matched him thrust for thrust and felt the surging wave hit her again as he released into her with a passion that shook the trees and made waves on the quiet water. As quickly as they came, Damon gently fell on top of Cat, breathing heavily into her neck. "God, woman, what do you do to me? I wanted to make love to you slowly tonight. Our last night, and instead I took you down in the dirt and ripped your shirt. Damn, I'm so sorry about that. I'll buy you a new one as soon as we get back home."

Cat chuckled, trying to catch a breath with the large beast of a man lying on her chest. "Damon, don't you dare apologize. I wanted you, wanted this. When you tore my shirt, I got all tingly inside. I wasn't sure I was doing it right and was a bit nervous. Then when you ripped my shirt, I kinda got all proud of myself—what I did to you made you do that to me. I felt like a sexy woman. I've never felt like that before."

Damon lifted himself off her, holding his head up with his arm as he continued to lie down on his side next to her. "What do you mean, you've never felt like a sexy woman? You exude sexy all over the place. I can't stop thinking about making love to you, in all kinds of places: in my bed, in your bed, on a desk at work, in the back of my truck, in a fitting room at the store, in the moonlight, sunlight, bathtub. I have to focus on not tearing your clothes off every time I see you."

Cat's eyebrows wrinkled together as she was trying to take it all in. "Wow, I had no clue I had that effect on you. Or on anyone for that matter. When I was with Jansen, it was more methodical. This is what you should do. This is what you are supposed to say. This is how it feels."

Damon looked deeply into her eyes and asked, "Tell me. Did you enjoy sleeping with him? Was it fun?"

Cat thought about his questions. "Well, he wasn't my first, but my first was also his first. We didn't know what we were doing, and it wasn't that great. Jansen was shortly after that and he was experienced, so I let him lead me. It was better than my first, but nowhere near how it feels when I'm with you. If I'm honest, I'm not sure I ever had an orgasm with Jansen."

This time it was Damon's turn to knit his eyebrows together. "What are you talking about? How do you not know if you've had one or not? Isn't it obvious for a woman?"

Cat tried to put into words what she felt. "I'll try to explain it. With you, I see fireworks, an explosion of colors. My entire body reacts from my toes to the inside of my eyelids. There's an emotional release. When I was with him that never happened. I would get all hot and bothered but it felt like it was … technical. First this. Then that. If I'm honest, it was about his teaching me about physical pleasure. Emotional pleasure? Never."

Damon stared at her and then responded, "Jansen is an idiot. You know I've been with other women before you, and I always made sure the pleasure went both ways. Having said that, pleasing you is a priority for me. You get me all riled up just knowing how I can make you feel. I can't wait to be inside you, but I enjoy getting to know you first and foremost. Sex with you isn't a game for me; it's a journey."

Cat's eyes started to glaze over, and she could feel the start of a tear leaving her eye and rolling down her cheek. Damon noticed too, so he leaned over and kissed it away. "I may not be the world's authority on love, Cat, but I've learned a few things watching my parents for thirty-plus years and Pete with Angie. Love will hurt you; it may even crush you. But it will also pick you up and make you whole again. Love gives you that mustard seed of hope when everything is out of control and going wrong. Once you find that person who loves you back, you realize you were never whole before. Even though you give a piece of your soul to that one person, you become better and stronger than you were before. If they should leave you, that piece of your soul doesn't come back to you; it stays with them, and you feel an emptiness that is as void as a black hole."

Cat furrowed her brow. "Wait a second; is that how you felt when you caught Paige cheating on you with the professor? Did you love her that much?"

"Paige hurt like crazy, but it was a child's love. She never gave me what I gave her. She was a taker, a manipulator. But she did teach me a great deal about how to please a woman. In that way, she was an excellent teacher." Cat started to frown, not liking where this was going. "But Paige couldn't teach me about love because she never could love anyone above herself. She saw me as a means to an end and nothing more. It took me a very long time to understand that. During that dark time, I watched my parents interact a lot and I had Pete. When Pete screwed up with Angie and she broke it off, I saw what it did to him. Even though he deserved every bit of anguish he received, I could tell he truly loved her. In her leaving him, Angie gave him a gift. She gifted him the opportunity to rise up and be the man he was meant to be, with her."

Cat shifted her body from lying down on the grass into a sitting position, and Damon followed suit. "Well, I guess then should thank Paige for teaching you so well. I never thought sex was that great. Now I get what Aurelie has been trying to tell me. It's fucking fantastic—with the right partner." She reached out to grab Damon's face and pulled him into a possessive embrace. "But I better not see her, because as the daughter of an Irish woman and an Italian man, jealousy is a pretty strong emotion, and I'd hate to see what would happen if it reared its ugly head."

Damon chuckled but looked deeply into her liquid pools of gold. "There's no reason to be jealous of anyone, Cat. I am totally and emphatically in love with you. I don't know how it happened or why I did so quickly, but it's true. I now can see what Pete was talking about. Love changes everything. All I want to do from this point onward is to find ways to make you happy. That's it. My purpose in life from this moment on is to make you happy. What can I do to make you happy, Cat?"

"At this very moment?" "Yes."

"Take me to the beach so I can wash the dirt out of my hair and other places."

"Your wish is my command." Damon popped up and offered his hand to help Cat get up. She gathered up their clothes as Damon got to one of the rowboats and helped her in before he launched.

It was quiet tonight except for the ripples the oars and the boat's bow made as it cut through the water to take them to the swimming beach. Once there, Damon got out first, beached the boat, and helped Cat get out. When she slipped a bit, he caught her and gave her a deep kiss that melted her heart and her legs, which responded by wobbling. Damon grabbed her by her buttocks and lifted her so she could wrap her thighs around his hips. She responded quickly by running her fingers through his wavy locks and pressing her body closer to his, feeling his hairs tickling her belly and elsewhere.

Damon walked them out to the raft and gently lay Cat on top, spread her legs, and entered her as the moonlight shown through her hair and sparkled over her skin. Cat's eyes closed as she fell into the rhythm and relished in the rapture. Both of them moaned and cried out at the climax as Damon released and laid his head on her heaving breasts. Cat lightly scratched his backside and played with the loose curls that had tightened due to the perspiration gathering at his temples. "I don't think I'll ever get tired of feeling this way," Cat expressed.

"Me either. But I should probably get you cleaned up as I promised." Reluctantly, Damon peeled himself off of his lover and waded over to the large mailbox to get lavender body wash. He poured some in his hand and motioned for Cat to follow him into the deeper water so she could dive under and wet down her hair. Placing the bottle on the raft, Damon then rubbed his hands together to start a lather that he used when Cat returned with her backside to him. He gently massaged her scalp and worked in all of her shoulder-length hair into a lather. He motioned for her to flip over and he cradled her head with one hand while he cupped water over her hair to rinse out the soap. Cat let out a few mewls but let the sensual feelings of being pampered by her lover take over.

Next, Damon led Cat to the shallow water and squeezed another dollop of soap into the palm of his hand and rubbed them together to begin washing her front. Starting at her forehead, he carefully meandered his fingers away from her eyes, nose, and mouth, as he washed away the sand granules sticking to her face. Next, he trailed them down her neck, massaging her muscles as he went. From there, he made his way to her round breasts that were peaking in the cooler air. He massaged them in tandem as Cat closed her eyes and let her head sink back, another moan escaping her full lips. Further, Damon left her nipples in utter spasm when he pinched them as he left them to find his way down to her flat belly and below.

When he reached her mound and started to rub the area, Cat's head jerked up, and her eyes widened before they smoldered. "Keep your eyes open, Catrina. I want to watch you," Damon whispered. Usually, Cat would get annoyed when someone used her full name, but in this instant, it was utterly erotic, and she followed orders. Keeping her eyes peeled on his, Cat felt his fingers expertly move through her thighs as one of them found her womanly folds and masterfully began massaging her. When he found her special place, she gasped and started to close her eyes again. "Keep them open. I need to see what I can do to you." Cat opened them again to see the blue of his eyes become like steel, looking right through her to her heart. She took her arms and held on to his shoulders as her hips automatically began rocking against the friction that he was creating with the movements inside of her. When the feelings were at their climax, she dug her nails into his skin and screamed his name as she let the explosion wash over her. Damon let a naughty smile spread over his lips and his dimples deepened.

When he laid her on her back in the water, she thought he would expose her to more sensual excess. Instead, he lovingly cupped water and poured it over her skin and let it glide over her to draw the remaining lather into the lake. Guiding her to a standing position, he had her stand so that her back was to him, and he began the whole process over again, this time with her back. When he got to the place where her cheeks meet, he inserted another finger, and her hips thrust toward him. He withdrew it, and Cat backed up into him and methodically rubbed her backside onto his front side to share the lather he had created for her.

Cat had had enough of being the one the loving was done to. Now it was her turn to show him how much she wanted him, always. Though some of the lather stayed on his chest, she added a dab of soap on her hands, lathered them together, and began the same process with his face, neck, and chest—making sure she tweaked each of his nipples in turn. After he gasped at that, she moved down to his stomach and his semi-intrigued manhood. "Keep your eyes open, Damon MacGregor. I want to see how you react when I touch you." With her right hand, she methodically rubbed his shaft to erection and watched his face and his eyes come alive with eagerness. She increased the speed and felt the release as he groaned, and his head went back. It was Cat's turn to smile and then turn him around to wash his backside. After being all lathered up, Damon dove into the water and then shook off as a playful Labrador Retriever would after a play in the lake.

Damon swam up to Cat, took her right hand in his, and kissed her fingers. "Good God, woman. I will never look at your hands again without getting a hard-on."

Cat grinned. "Good. I feel the same way. Anytime I see your big hands, I start to shiver just thinking what you've done to me with those fingers in all different places."

"Fair's fair, Cat. Fair's fair." He kissed her fingers again. "Come on now, I've got to row us back before I don't have any light to guide us."

At the cabin, they took turns drying each other off, taking leisurely looks at all the hills and valleys, crooks and crevices, as if to memorize every single one. Then they went into the bedroom and lay together. With all the lovemaking they'd shared already, it was the pleasure of sharing a bed with one another that they sought. Having the liberty to sleep with and intertwine with their loved one was something that they each wanted without knowing they wanted it, initially. Damon kissed Cat gently on the top of her head as it lay on his curly-haired chest. "Good night, my love."

Cat kissed his chest and replied, "Good night, schmoopsie," and tried to conceal a giggle.

"Yeah, don't call me that." The giggle escaped her lips and echoed into the deep dark forest night.

Chapter Ten

"Dude, what are you humming over there?" Pete frustratingly asked.

"Huh?" Damon shook his head to try to focus on what his friend was asking from him. "Sorry, I didn't get that. What'd you say?"

"You didn't hear me talk because you're singing. Stop it. Now. I need to concentrate on getting these labs."

"Singing? Seriously? I don't think so."

"Um, yeah, you were. Now knock it off so I can focus." "Whatever, man. I think you're hearing things."

"Wait, now you're humming. Is it what I think it is? Is it a love song?" "Maybe."

"Damon, you've got it bad, dude."

Damon finished stocking his needles and other supplies while he hummed the classic song by Louis Armstrong. "Whatever, Pete. I had to endure months of you singing break-up songs over and over again until I wanted to break up with you, too." Pete laughed at the recollection.

"I was a sorry-assed loser at that time. Hell, I would have broken up with me, too." Pete finished his paperwork and checked a new text message from Angie on his phone. "Hey, looks like Angie isn't done hanging out with her mom and baby shopping. Wanna grab dinner? I'm craving burgers and beer. All Angie has been craving is pizza, and she gets sad if I try to pour a glass of wine or crack open a cold one when she can't have any. She gives me that pouty face, and I don't have the heart to drink in front of her. I need a man's meal. Interested?"

Damon smiled and turned around with his arms crossing over his chest. "Are you asking me out on a date?"

Pete shook his head and cracked a smile. "You're a shithead, MacGregor. I am in desperate need of grilled meat and a cold beer. Can you help a guy out?"

"Sounds like a date to me. Honestly, it sounds great. I was going to have leftovers anyhow and planned on cleaning the house."

Pete raised an eyebrow, and now he had his arms crossed. "What's the special occasion?"

"Cat is coming this weekend to meet my parents and see the place. I don't want her to think I live like a pig. I'm nervous enough to have my mom meet her." Damon took off his white coat and threw on a denim jacket and a beat-up baseball cap.

"Ahh, meeting the parents. This is big stuff, then. Sounds like you need to give me some details about what's going on, brother. I knew that the up north trip was good, but you've been stingy on the details. I think a beer or two may do the trick to loosen you up enough to give up the goods."

Damon smirked and hit his friend on the back. "Pete, you know I don't kiss and tell."

"Bullshit. You talk about your escapades all the time. That's why I was surprised you didn't dish when you came back. I need something to keep me from going crazy over which type of changing table we should use and what breast pump is the best choice."

"Aww, man, don't tell me that stuff. I don't need to know about Angie's choice of breast pump. That's gross!" Damon shivered and walked out of the clinic to his truck. "I'll see you at the H.O.G. as long as you don't bring up diapers and breast pumps."

Pete laughed heartily. "Dude, I'll be glad not to bring those up any more tonight or ever. See you there!"

"I don't know how you knew Angie was The One for you, Pete, but this weekend solidified Cat is The One for me."

"How's that?" Pete asked as he was adding ketchup to his burger. "I don't want to give away too many details, but you know how it felt with other women, right? It was the chase that was exciting, and then when it was all over, it was like, how fast can I get away from her?"

Pete laughed with his mouth full. "I remember. Go on." He took a swig of his beer.

"Well, with Cat, it was explosive and sweet and wild, and I didn't want it to end. I didn't want to stop holding her. There were times when I could see snippets of what our lives will look like together. We just couldn't get enough of each other. I was actually sad to say goodbye to her when I dropped her off. I was like a lovesick puppy and blurted out how I wanted to see her this weekend and have her meet my parents. Crazy, right?"

"Not so crazy. So, is it different than what it was like with Paige?" Pete asked carefully as he chomped on a fry.

"That's the crazy part. I thought I knew what love felt like with Paige. But it doesn't feel like that at all. I mean, Paige taught me how to make love to a woman. Not the 'wham, bam, thank you, ma'am' shit that all guys do in the beginning. She taught me how to make a woman feel right and the rewards of doing it right. Making love to Cat is a completely different animal. We made love all the time in all different kinds of ways. I didn't have to think about what I was doing; it was …" Damon paused and looked up at the ceiling as he tried to find the right words. "It was instinct. Like I was the key to her lock, and when I touched her, it unlocked all these sensations that I had never felt before, and I could tell it was all new to her, too, which made it all the more arousing."

Pete stopped eating for a second and looked at his best friend, trying to assess what he should say next. "Bro, I think you already know what the answers are to the questions you're asking me. I'll answer them anyway. Loving Angie isn't something I have to think about. It just is. I can be engaged in a conversation with someone, and the minute she enters the room, even if I can't see her, I can feel her, like an electric current running through me. There is nothing better than making love to my woman. If I could live my life without the responsibilities of paying a mortgage, bills, and all the other adulting I have to do, I would have no problem lying next to her twenty-four hours a day. I'm sure we'd get sick of each other at some point, but right now, with the baby coming, I don't have enough time in the day to lie with her and I miss being inside her. God knows how I'm going to handle the breastfeeding thing. She won't let me touch them now. They hurt too much. Dammit! They're so round and big, I just want to hold them and kiss them, and she screams that I'm hurting her if I just look in their direction." Pete looked at Damon, who was giving him one of those looks that say, "Really?"

"Sorry, dude, this is about you and your woman." Pete smiled and nodded. "Go on."

"Well, I don't know what else you want me to say." "Did you tell her you love her yet?"

"Yes." Damon sighed.

"Did you tell her you want to marry her and have babies with her?" "Maybe." Pete's eyebrows went up and he nodded his head.

"Well, I know it's been a short time that you've known her, but you've dated a lot. You got hurt really bad once. I think you're doing everything right, bro. Congrats, you've found yourself an Angie." Pete took his longneck and raised it to Damon's, and they toasted to Damon's Angie.

When Saturday rolled around, Damon was a hot mess. He cut himself trimming his beard, broke a juice glass on the kitchen floor, and somehow managed to trip up the stairs while carrying clean laundry in a basket that now was strewn all over the freshly washed floor. "Dammit!" By the time he cleaned up the laundry mess on the floor, he realized that he had sweat stains under his arms, and he needed to put on another clean shirt.

Once the laundry was put away, he rummaged through his closet and found another red and black plaid shirt and pulled a white undershirt from his drawer. After rubbing on some fresh deodorant, he changed his shirts, tucked them into his jeans, and ran his hands through his thick, wavy hair away from his face. He stopped dead when he heard the doorbell ring. Why was he so nervous? He had just seen her as naked as a jaybird for almost a week and she him. The doorbell rang again. "Shit." He shook his head to get a handle on the situation and went down the stairs in his stocking feet, finishing tucking the back of his shirt into his jeans.

At the door, his heart skipped a beat or two as he recognized her soft outline through the window. After he opened the door, his heart stopped a bit more as her dazzling smile lit up the great room and melted his bad mood. "Hi," Cat said softly as she smiled brightly. Today, she had her hair straightened and flowing around her shoulders. She was wearing a denim and flannel overshirt with a red T-shirt underneath. Her jeans fit snug around her waist, and she finished it off with a pair of working cowboy boots, perfect for a day at the farm.

"Hi yourself," Damon spoke out. He couldn't wait to get her into his arms, but he noticed a bit of a movement by her side and recognized her faithful companion, Mia, wagging her tail and smiling, waiting to be petted. "And hello to you, pretty girl. Wasn't expecting to see you today."

"Sorry about that," Cat said, and the smile left her face as a bit of concern showed in her hazel eyes. "My parents are away this weekend, and I couldn't find another dog sitter on short notice. I was hoping she wouldn't be too much of a problem on a farm."

"That shouldn't be a problem. I'm happy to show off my two best girls to everyone." And he bent down and scratched Mia behind her ears, then reached up and pulled Cat into an embrace and kissed her fully with one hand grabbing her hair and the other cradling her apple-bottom ass. "Mmm. God that felt good to kiss you again. I've missed you," Damon stated as he snuggled into her hair and landed soft kisses on her neck.

"Oh God, if you keep doing that, I'll never get to see the inside of your house, and everyone will get to see us 'getting it on,' on your porch." Cat's eyes rolled back into her head, and she closed her lids as she let the sensations warm her body all the way to her privates.

"As much as I want to take you up on that, I better get you two inside. I think even the horses would be telling tales if I took you down right here." With that, Damon reluctantly released Cat and let her into his home. "Would you two ladies like a tour?"

"Absolutely!" Cat's mouth fell open as he went from room to room and described the work that he and his family had done to complete his one-of-a-kind home. When they got up to the second floor and his bedroom, Cat reached down and felt the bed, then sat on its edge. "Oh, Damon. I can see why you love this place so. This house is perfect for you. You have a great sense of style, and I can feel the warmth that each piece you made brings to it to make it a home. You should be very proud."

Damon wanted to focus on what she was saying, but all he could concentrate on was that she was sitting on his bed, and he needed to be inside her and claim her in his space right now. He knew Mia would behave if he shut the door on her; he wasn't comfortable with the idea that she'd be in the room while they had sex. He could see a bit of surprise and then the "ah ha" moment when it registered in Cat's brain what he had in store for her.

Cat stood up and began a slow striptease, carefully unbuttoning her flannel shirt and shimmying down her jeans around her boots. Today she was wearing a dark blue and white lace panty and matching bra. Damn! She always matched them. How hot was that! Damon untucked his shirts and pulled them over his head. He was relieved to unbuckle his jeans and dropped his drawers along with his growing pile at the end of the bed. He was very excited to see her, and she came to him and reached out her hand to stroke him as she began to kiss and lick his chest.

Damon wanted to make this last, but it had been several days since their last coupling, and he couldn't wait much longer. He walked her back to his bed and guided her to lie down on her back while he spread her eager thighs and began showing her, in loving licks and nips, how much he missed her. She must have missed him just as much because it didn't take long at all for her moaning and squirming to turn into screams of passion and her hips to thrust up in wantonness, begging for him to enter her. Damon entered her wet, pulsing entrance and rode her until he was immersed in an electric current that ran from his head through his manhood, which showered its seed inside her. His thrusts continued, albeit slower and less intense until the pulsing subsided. When he caught his breath again, he saw her breasts heaving and begging for his touch. He gently suckled each taut nipple and then kissed his love gently on the lips. "Sorry. I couldn't wait."

"Don't you dare be sorry! I wanted to take you on the porch. You were a gentleman at least to have us rip our clothes off in your bedroom. I'm impressed you waited that long." Damon gently released himself from her and lay next to her fading sun-kissed skin. "Cat, I don't think I could ever think about this bed again without thinking of you lying like this, naked and smelling of sweet sex. I can't let you leave. You'll have to be my love slave."

"Mmm. That sounds tempting, but I have a dog on the other side of that door who doesn't understand why she's been left out. Hey, didn't I come here to meet your parents? What would they think if they came upstairs and I was lying on your bed buck naked?"

"They'd probably ask when they were going to be grandparents again." They both laughed at that and then realized that they hadn't used a condom this time. "Oh shit, I'm so sorry." Damon just acknowledged the fact that he forgot.

Cat looked quizzically at him and then sat up. He was trying to get a read on her but couldn't. He felt horrible. Not that he didn't want to make babies with her. Maybe that's why he didn't even think about getting the condoms from the drawer. Maybe his own biological clock was ticking and he wanted to start a family with her now. He knew he didn't like the idea of any other man spilling their seed inside her; that feeling, he acknowledged, was more territorial. She was his woman and he knew it sounded very macho, but he didn't care. It was an intense, strong need to make her his own, even if it was too early for her to accept it.

Damon looked at Cat more deeply. Now he was curious. She wasn't acting the way he envisioned her to act. She was actually pretty calm about it, but in a way that felt like she wasn't being totally honest with him about something. Cat looked back at him and seemed to recognize that he was looking for a response. "Oh,

I know you didn't mean it, Damon. Look, I wanted you, too. I saw this big comfy bed, and I couldn't wait to lie with you on it. I'm not mad. Honestly."

Now it was his turn to look quizzically back at her. "Why? I mean, I could have gotten you pregnant, and we've just started our relationship. It would be a huge mistake to have a baby now, wouldn't it?" If he were honest, he was starting to feel all warm inside about the possibility of being a father and watching her grow a baby inside her. But she wasn't on the same page yet, he was sure of it. Too soon. Still, she seemed to be searching for her words again. What was going on?

"Not possible," Cat said confidently and then looked a little scattered. "I wasn't going to say anything because it would just gross you out, but if you must know, I doubt you got me pregnant. I know this because I just finished having a short cycle yesterday. It's too close to the end of my period for my body to be ready to make a baby. Honestly, you don't have to worry about it. It's all good. I promise." Damon felt relief, but there was something about the way she was acting that didn't let him feel total relief. Cat seemed to sense his apprehension, and she slid off the bed and joined him standing on the plush throw rug on the floor. She clasped her hands in his and stared into his worried eyes. "I promise," she confirmed as she stood on her tiptoes to warmly kiss his mouth to seal her promise to him.

"All right, but from now on, condoms on or engines off. Deal?" Cat's eyes glistened a bit like she was holding back tears. Why would she want to cry? He questioned.

"Deal." And he pressed his full lips onto her pouty ones and drew her into a warm embrace.

Almost forgetting what had just transpired, he shook the lusty thoughts his lower extremities were shooting up to his brain and gently pulled away so they could get dressed and start the day. Damon took his two favorite girls and started the tour of the farm out by the paddocks where several of the horses were grazing on the last green grasses of the summer. Mia couldn't contain her excitement as she'd sprint ahead and then find something fascinating to sniff or uncover a tree branch that she could carry around like a trophy until she found something else to gain her attention. Cat, on the other hand, was very interested in what Damon had to say and asked a lot of questions about their training of the horses, the riding lessons, etc. When they got to the far paddock, she asked about the lone horse grazing in that section of the farm. Damon shook his head.

"That there's Butters. He's an ornery bastard. Thinks he's king of the hill. Scares the others and refuses to change his attitude. It's not my preference, but it keeps the peace to keep him segregated from the rest of the herd." As if he knew they were talking about him, the cream-and-white-colored gelding rose up on his hindquarters and let out a "neigh" and then shook his flowing mane when he landed on his front hooves before he went back to grazing.

"Oh, Damon, he's gorgeous!" Cat seemed infatuated with the prima donna horse and started walking toward the fencing for the paddock.

"Don't get your hopes up too high. He won't come near you. Hell, he barely listens to me. The last time I rode him he nearly cracked my head open when he reared up like that on the trail," Damon recalled. Then he saw something that he couldn't imagine. Butters had taken notice of Cat and was slowly making his way toward her. Cat pressed her body near the fence, and when he came within spitting distance, she reached out her right hand, opened her palm, and began talking softly to the fantastically proud Palomino.

Damon couldn't believe what he saw. The majestic beast came to her hand, sniffed it, and then nuzzled it. Cat called him in further, and he obliged, letting her pet his nose and neck and run her fingers through his mane. "I don't believe it!" Damon said, exasperated. "How are you doing this? He *never* lets anyone touch him without a fight."

"Do what?" Cat seemed to be focused in another realm and barely acknowledged his existence as she continued pampering the fiercely independent steed.

"How are you able to pet him like that? Haven't you heard anything I've said about his personality and why's he's so far out here? Why he isn't penned with the other horses?" Damon was practically pulling the hair out of his scalp in frustration.

"I don't know why. I just knew that he'd come to me and he'd let me pet him. I felt it. That's all."

"So, when you told me that you went to school to work with horses, you didn't tell me you were a horse whisperer." He meant it as a joke, but then he realized that's exactly how she was acting.

"A horse whisperer?" she asked and then paused. "I guess you could say that. Ever since I was a little girl, I always had a second sense about animals. My parents always had a dog in the house, and when I was fourteen, I asked for horse riding lessons. When I was on the horse for the first time, I felt free. Like I was meant to be there. As if I were connected to the horse in some way. Anyhow, that's when I knew I wanted to work with animals—especially horses."

"I'm impressed. He hasn't held still this long without a fight or a feeling that he was planning his next move."

"Damon, do you think I could ride him before I go home?" Cat stopped petting for a moment and looked sideways to get a sense of Damon's feelings on the subject.

After a short pause, Damon kicked the dirt a bit and looking down at the grass replied, "I guess so. But I've never seen you ride, so I need to know what kind of rider you are. Butters came from champion stock and isn't for the faint of heart."

Cat glared at him, and he realized he'd gone too far. "What kind of rider do you think I am? I have been riding horses for more than a decade, and I went to Montana to learn how to train them. How dare you infer that I am an inferior rider!" Her hazel eyes sparked, and the heat rose in her cheeks. Simultaneously, he thought he heard Butters laugh at him while he nudged Cat to continue stroking his neck.

"I'm … I'm sorry, Cat. I didn't mean to sound so condescending. I just don't want him to hurt you. I was pretty roughed up the last time, and I don't think I could handle it if he hurt you." Cat's ire calmed a few degrees, and her hazel-green eyes turned to a softer shade of gold.

"Look, I understand that you don't want me to get hurt, but I wouldn't have asked if I didn't feel confident that I could ride him. See? He wants me to touch him. I feel like he wants me to ride him."

Damon stared into her eyes and then looked at how she was interacting with the stately stallion. "Against my better judgment, I'll agree to it. But if I see one ounce of mischief in him, the deal's off and the riding is done. Got it?" He put his hands on his hips and spread his legs so that he looked like a giant Peter Pan to Cat, but she recognized he was attempting to show he was in charge, even though she and Butters knew better. Still, she was kind enough to show polite respect and accepted his offer.

Walking down to the stables, they held hands, and Mia continued with her adventures, on one occasion setting a field mouse scurrying away from her inquisitive nose. Once there, Damon pointed out the area where they hung the bridles, saddles, and helmets. He was adamant that she wore one, and Cat recognized this was non-negotiable.

She impressed him yet again when he glanced sideways and saw her expertly prepare her horse for a trail ride while he continued to prepare the horse he had selected for the afternoon ride, Shasta. Shasta was a seven-year-old Belgian draft horse with a white snout and white socks over her hooves. The rest of her broad body was a beautiful bronze with an auburn mane and tail. Her dark eyes were smitten on Damon, who happened to be whistling while he brushed her.

As soon as both horses were saddled and ready to go, Damon led them out of the stables and into one of the outdoor arenas where they could take a moment and warm up the horses with a brief walk. It also gave him the opportunity to view how Cat and Butters would work together and if they needed to cut the ride short.

To his surprise, Butters responded almost intuitively to Cat's subtle suggestions. He couldn't believe it. They were so in tune with each other that it was instinctive on both their parts. Cat rode flawlessly, and they changed direction, stopped/started, and trotted with such smooth transitions Damon thought he was watching a pair ice dancing.

On the trail, he relaxed a bit as he realized that Butters was just as infatuated with Cat as he was. Their effortless movements were intoxicating to watch. He recognized that a tinge of jealousy was rearing its ugly head when Cat would bend over and pat Butters on the neck, and he would respond with a satisfying whinny in return. Instead of looking at the trees beginning their fall transition into an extraordinary artistic compilation of colors, he watched the intoxicating sway of Cat's bottom as it rocked back and forth in sync with the movements of her horse's steps.

When the wooded trails opened up to a vast green meadow, he felt the couple ahead of him tense and go into a gallop to join the emerald green grasses and sapphire blue sky in an effort to become one with the space. Damon, not wanting to be left behind, urged

Shasta forward, and she responded quickly to his request. It was one of the most beautiful scenes he could remember in his lifetime. It was clear that Butters and Cat belonged together. Even if he and Cat didn't make it, although he shuddered at the thought of it, he could feel his purpose was to bring these two of God's creatures together in their lifetime. The synergy between them was intoxicating, and he almost forgot that he, too, was galloping and needed to focus on his own horse to make sure that everyone stayed safe.

Once the bonded pair reached the tree line, Cat slowed them down to a trot and then a walk, to cool Butters down for the return trip. On the way home, Damon's concerns were squelched, and he became content with the new pairing. During their quiet moments, his mind wandered to the possibilities of future memories of them riding together and enjoying picnic lunches by the creek, taking the whole family out for a ride in the summer and hooking up a sleigh to Shasta for a Christmas Eve sleigh ride. These daydreams became more like urges to Damon. He was having a very hard time not sharing these scenarios with Cat because he was afraid that he'd scare her off.

Back at the stables, they quietly went to work on their own horses, tying them up, putting away the riding gear, brushing their companions, and offering them apple slices as a thank-you for their hard work that afternoon. When everything was done, Cat followed Damon out to the pastures and walked Butters to the farthest one, where she said goodbye. Damon was amazed to see that Butters didn't seem to want to go back to his favorite haunt. Reluctantly, he left Cat and slowly walked into his paddock to rest. But this time, he kept looking back at her, as if he didn't want her to leave.

When Cat finally turned around and saw Damon waiting for her, she smiled and skipped toward him. "Oh God, Damon! I almost forgot what it felt like to ride again. I felt so free! No worries. And Butters—what an incredible horse you have. You are so blessed. He is magnificent; it was like he knew what I wanted him to do before I even asked him to do it. It was so easy to ride with him. Then when we got to the meadow, it was like, let's just see what we can do together, and he did! He really did! Man, that was exhilarating!"

Damon smiled at Cat prattling on and on about her experience. He could see her here, making a life here. Now he realized, even if she didn't quite yet, that she was feeling the same way. He reached for her hand, and they walked back to his home where they let Mia out to take a quick break before dinner. Damon's stomach growled, and Cat laughed. "I'm so sorry. I've kept you away from food way too long. Is there anything to snack on in your kitchen?"

Damon looked at his cell phone and saw it was already 4:30 p.m. "No time for that. Mom's probably fretting because we haven't come to see her yet for formal introductions and dinner's in thirty minutes. Should we feed Mia before we take the truck over?"

"That's probably a good idea. Should we leave her here then?" Damon looked at the concern in her eyes. She would do it if he asked her to, but she didn't like leaving Mia alone so much in a strange place.

"I don't think it's necessary. I mean, we've had animals all our lives. If it looks like my mom doesn't want her inside, we can always have her curl up in the cab of my truck." He saw her face switch from concern to relief in the matter of an instant. After a quick meal of kibble and fresh cold water, Mia was ready to go to their next big adventure. Climbing into the truck, Cat had an "aha" moment.

"Wait a second! I forgot my hostess gift to your family in the SUV. Just hang on a minute."

"A hostess gift? It's just a family dinner on the farm, not a cocktail party in my parent's penthouse." Damon felt a little frustrated. He didn't understand the need to bring a gift, and besides, it was more important to his mom that they should be on time. If they waited any longer, no present would be acceptable for being late. Cat climbed up into the cab again and held a bottle of Italian red.

"A bottle of wine from my family's town in Italy. An Italian wine that is not pretentious and yet thoughtful." Even though Cat sounded confident, she seemed a bit unsure of herself. Damon caught her free hand, held it up to his lips, and kissed her knuckles.

"Not pretentious at all. Very thoughtful." Cat looked sideways at him and seemed to let out a breath he hadn't realized she was holding. On the short drive to his parent's home, he mulled it over and realized that Cat saw this dinner as the next big step in their relationship. He had felt it was important, but because family dinners were always a part of his life, he hadn't realized how scary it might be for someone new to the event.

Cat let herself out of the truck's cab and opened the back door to let Mia out. Mia wanted to be more inquisitive but understood that she had to be on her best behavior and stuck to Cat's side. The three of them got to the front porch, and Damon opened the door to let his two best girls into the front hall. The door had barely shut behind them when Pat and Heather came out of nowhere to greet them. Mia recognized that she needed to continue to be on her best behavior and sat down where Cat stood.

Heather was wearing a light blue sweater that brought out her blue eyes, and she had clipped up the sides of her red and silver hair in the back, letting her bangs frame her face. Pat stood next to her, wearing a navy and black plaid flannel shirt over a white undershirt and a pair of softly faded jeans cinched with a black leather belt and large silver belt buckle with a horse's head engraved into the silver metal.

Ian and Cathy trailed behind and flanked their parents. Ian was wearing a concert T-shirt under a gray hooded sweatshirt while Cathy chose a pink thermal long sleeve peeking out of an oversized gray hooded sweater cover-up.

When it looked like Cat was a bit overwhelmed and Mia was about ready to burst if she couldn't lick someone soon, Pat stepped forward, reaching out his hand toward Cat. "Well, Cat, so good to see you again. Thanks for coming to dinner tonight. I've told Heather how helpful you were to us when we brought the injured crane to your clinic. The least we can do to thank you for getting it back on its feet again is to offer you a delicious home-cooked meal."

"Thanks, Mr. MacGregor. No need to thank me. I just helped with the paperwork. Dr. O'Brien and the rest of the clinical team did all the work. As a matter of fact, your crane will be released at our annual gala fundraiser next month. She's come a long way since you last saw her."

"Cat, this here's my mother, Heather." Damon put his hand on Cat's shoulder and guided her to his mother's outreached hand.

"Mrs. MacGregor, thank you for the invitation tonight. The food smells wonderful. I brought you a bottle of wine from my father's family's town in Italy. I hope you enjoy wine." Cat brought up the hand that was holding the bottle, and Heather accepted it wholeheartedly.

"Thank you, Cat. How generous of you. There was no need to bring a gift, but I look forward to tasting it with dinner." Then she bent down and put her empty hand down to let Mia sniff her hello. "This must be Mia. Damon has told us a lot about you, little one. He says you love belly scratches, is that true?" With that, Mia rolled over and let her tongue hang out of her mouth while enjoying the moment.

"I hope you don't mind that we brought Mia over. My dog sitter wasn't available, and I didn't want to leave her alone in Damon's house too long, when she's never been there before. "

"No trouble at all. Looks like she is very well behaved, and as long as she abides by the rule that she stays out of the kitchen when we are eating, we will get along just fine."

"That won't be a problem at all. She's not allowed in mine when I'm eating either."

When Heather stood up, she looked into Cat's eyes and smiled. "By the way, this calling me Mrs. MacGregor has got to stop. It makes me feel very old. Please call me Heather."

Cat smiled in relief and nodded. In the meantime, the two youngest MacGregors were getting a bit antsy waiting for their turn for introductions. Damon took the opportunity to introduce Ian and Cathy, and with introductions completed, they all went into the kitchen to help bring out bowls of steaming vegetables, platters of freshly cooked steaks, and baskets of warm rolls with a side of cinnamon apple butter. Cat was given the job of opening and pouring the bottle for the table.

Damon filled his plate with heaps of mashed potatoes, a slab of T-bone steak done medium rare, asparagus from his mother's garden, and a roll with butter. He noticed that Cat seemed to be contemplating what she should be putting on her plate and in considerably smaller portions than what he had done. He leaned over and whispered in her ear, "Is everything okay?"

Cat reacted a bit startled and responded, "Of course. Why?" "You never take this long or think this hard about what you are eating. Just making sure you feel all right." Then Damon grabbed his steak knife, sawed off a juicy pink section of his T-bone, and slid it into his mouth.

"Sorry, I guess I'm more nervous than I thought I'd be. Besides, I've never eaten a whole T-bone at once. Is it okay to cut a section off or do I need to take the whole steak? I don't want to seem ungrateful or wasteful." Damon stopped chewing and contemplated what she had just said and then reached over to the platter of meat and cut off a segment and placed it on her plate. Cat sighed and whispered under her breath, "Thanks." She then proceeded to fill her plate with mostly vegetables and took a roll without the butter.

The rest of the table was focused on the feast, except Heather. She looked through her downturned lashes to watch the interaction between her son and this new woman in his life. With her keen hearing, with which even in deep sleep she could identify baby cries in the middle of the night, she had heard every word and paid attention to the non-verbal communication. Before placing a spoonful of potatoes into her mouth, she gave a small grin, which her husband noticed. Pat noticed all the special touches his wife put into tonight's dinner and was pleased to see that she was accepting of Cat and the importance she was playing in their son's life.

"So, Cat, I heard that you work for a rehab clinic? What do you do there?" Cathy took a break from her meal to start a conversation. Damon was relieved that she was behaving like an adult and not asking silly questions or sharing embarrassing stories.

"Um, yeah. I'm a grant writer for the a wildlife rehabilitation sanctuary."

"Damon told me that you went to school for equine science.

Why aren't you working with horses?"

"Okay," Damon thought, "here come the hard questions." He felt a bit queasy but knew Cat had to handle it and would. "Well, life happened. I went to Montana to study and came home, stayed home because of a boyfriend at the time and I missed my family. Plus, I'm a good writer and I can help animals by raising money for our clinic to save more animals. But I have to admit I do miss riding horses."

Cathy seemed satisfied with the answer, but Damon felt the need to pipe in anyhow, "You should have seen her today. She rode Butters." He didn't have to look around the table to hear the complete silence that enveloped the group. The only sound came from Mia's quiet snores coming from the other room.

"Holy shit! You had her ride Butters? Does she have a death wish?" Ian exclaimed.

"Ian MacGregor! You watch your mouth when you are in my house." Heather's commanding voice rattled Ian into submission, and the rest of the table seemed to shrink a bit in their seats as well.

"Sorry, Mom. It's just that of all the horses at the farm, Damon has her ride the most difficult one. Just surprised, is all." Ian cowered but felt his explanation was accepted.

Cat decided it was time to expand on what Damon had offered. "It wasn't like that at all, Ian. Damon was showing me around the farm and the paddocks, and Butters took an interest in me. He came over, and we started to get to know each other. He let me pet him, and he seemed to enjoy me talking to him, so I asked if I could ride him." Then Cat went to work on her roll, taking it apart and eating bits of pieces with her fingers. Damon saw the look of concern on Pat's face and felt the need to speak up.

"Look, I could see she wanted to ride him, and y'all know that I was the last person who rode him, and he bucked me off something good. So, I set some rules, and she agreed to follow them. Turns out that he must have a crush on her because he was so gentle and rode so smooth with her that it seemed like they were meant to be together." Pat paid full attention to Damon's explanation and nodded in approval. Damon felt a sigh of relief leave his body and went on to take a second plateful of food.

"You must have some real skills to be able to manage that beast. He's as full of himself as he is strong and fast," Heather added to the conversation.

Cat thought about her answer for a moment. She felt as if she was taking a test and the way she answered Heather's question would mean the difference between family acceptance and family conflict. "The truth is, Heather, my mom told me that while I found it more challenging than most to make friends with kids my own age, I seemed to have a sixth sense when it came to animals. They seem to sense something about me and are curious about me. When I was fourteen, I asked my parents to let me take riding lessons. We didn't have a lot of money, but they knew it was important to me, so it was my job to research riding stables near us, and my mom took me to my first lesson. She was a bit trepidatious, at first, and I was as clumsy as an ox trying to follow the owner's example of how to get a horse ready for riding, but once I got on him," Heather became transfixed on Cat's face as it went from serious to ethereal, "it was like I found something that had been missing all my life until that moment. She told me afterward that she saw a glow around me and a smile that she had never seen before. It was at that moment she knew I had to continue to ride horses. They'd find a way to help me pay for lessons." She came out of her trance and looked over at Heather, whose eyes went all soft and misty. Then as quickly as their eyes connected, Heather looked down at her own plate and cleared her throat.

"Well then, you are welcome to ride any of our horses, Cat. If you can tame Butters, you will have no trouble managing any of the other horses. It would be a shame for someone who has such a strong connection with horses not to be able to ride them as your time permits. Damon?" Damon's back straightened, and the fork full of potatoes stopped midway to his mouth.

"Yes, ma'am?"

"Why did it take you this long to bring her around? She loves horses; she should have been able to enjoy them this summer."

He wanted to take her to the task but thought twice about it. Instead, he took the high road. "Mom, I promise to bring Cat around more often so she can ride whenever she has a free moment. Okay?"

Heather nodded and began clearing her place. Cat started to get up as well, and Heather shot her a look. "Cat, you're a guest in my home. No need to clear your own place. We can get that for you."

Cat felt this was one of those tests again. "I appreciate that, but my mom always taught me to help the host clean up. I'm sorry, but to stop you from being upset I would have to go against my mom, and I won't do that. She'll have my head if it ever gets to her that I sat by while someone else cleared my place." Cat finished getting all the way up and did what she intended to do. Heather let her, and the rest of the family just sat and watched the fragile truce that expressed itself in the silent task of clearing the table of dinner dishes and bringing them to the kitchen for cleaning.

Dessert was served on smaller plates with coffee, and the sense of the group was lighter and sillier than before. Cathy and Ian had started to regale Cat with stories from their childhood. Some were gross; at others she cracked a smile, and then there were those that had her eyes tear and a hard belly laugh exhale her lips. They retreated to the great room, and Mia woke up to the change in venue. She rubbed against Damon's leg but lay back down on Cat's feet when everyone settled down.

Damon put his arm around Cat's shoulders while they sat on the sectional, and the rest of the family found their usual spots to lounge in and rest after a very full meal and conversation. Cat was beginning to relax when Pat began to speak. "Cat, what's your intention with our son?" Cat's head bobbed off Damon's side and furrowed her eyebrows together. Pat tried to hide the smirk that ran across his face. He knew he had gotten her, and Heather was glaring at him, which made him prouder of himself.

Cat looked straight into his eyes and smiled. "I hope to marry him," she said and snuggled into Damon's side once again, smug as a cat basking in the summer sun. Damon kissed the top of her head and smiled triumphantly at his father. Damon couldn't have been prouder of her and couldn't wait until the day he would be sitting with her like this in their own home.

Ian looked smugly at his dad and said, "Guess she told you, huh, Da?"

Pat chuckled and responded, "I guess that's it then. Cat can come by and ride any of the horses at this farm. She's family." Cat looked up and smiled at Pat.

After a while, Damon made a motion that they were leaving, and Cat said goodbye to everyone, giving a quick peck on Pat's cheek. Mia saw they were leaving; she got up to stretch and followed them out of the main house, found a patch of grass to sniff, did her business, and then jumped into the truck.

Once they got back to Damon's place, he set a fire in the hearth and got them each a whiskey to sip. Mia found a soft spot on the throw rug to resume her evening nap, and Cat pulled a cream-colored Sherpa throw around her legs and then nestled into Damon when he snuggled with her on the couch.

"That was interesting," Damon ventured to say.

"Well, it could have been worse," Cat replied.

"How could it have been worse? My brother swore at the dinner table; he's lucky that he's still alive. Mom grilled you and then Da asked about your intentions."

Cat chuckled. "Damon, I think I had it a hell of a lot easier than you had at my house with my dad. Besides, I think they like me. I can come over anytime, with or without you, to ride your horses. I consider that a huge success." With that, she took her glass nestling whiskey and clinked it against Damon's. "Salute!"

After a sip, letting the amber-colored liquid sit on his tongue, Damon leaned down and kissed her with all the warmth and love he was experiencing in that instant. If he had a diamond ring on him, in that minute, he would ask her to marry him. But he didn't. He would remedy that soon.

Cat responded by pulling his head down and taking his tongue further into her mouth, reveling in the moment. She pretended that they were in their own home as a married couple and fell into their embrace as deep as she could while they were interwoven on the couch. Damon reacted immediately and, without breaking the kiss, put his glass and hers down on the side table, feeling her fingers feathering his hair and her nails scraping against his skull lightly. He didn't mean to, but a groan left his throat, and that got Cat all the more engaged. Cat's hands then moved from his head down his spine and under his shirts to cat-scratch his back, which turned off his thoughts and turned on his instinct mode.

Damon treasured making love with Cat and felt somewhat possessive about it happening in his own home. He wanted her all the time, but the feeling intensified when they were together in his home. His intention to be slow and methodical and adoring went out the door when her nails scraped his flexed muscles on his back and then found their way under his belted pants to squeeze his ass. No more Mr. Nice Guy. He needed to be inside her right now. Hard. Fast. He broke the kiss. Pulled off his shirts, unbuckled his pants, and dropped them to the floor. Next, he pulled her shirts over her head and watched as she unbuttoned her jeans. He thought he would explode over her as she shimmied her jeans down over her hips, buttocks, and thighs and kicked them off to join his on the floor.

Damon sat on the couch and guided his sexual nymph to straddle him. When both of her legs were on either side of his thighs and his rod was tightened and ready to work its magic inside her, Cat slowly lowered her pulsing, wet womanhood onto him, and he felt her muscles massaging his shaft as she moved her hips to an internal rhythm that she owned and he succumbed to. Damon placed his hands on her hips and worked them both into a lather as the rhythm increased in intensity and speed until he felt the explosion inside her as she threw her head back and screamed the cry of the Valkyrie while slowing down the rhythm as his shaft relaxed in its cocoon. Cat touched her forehead to his as her breath started to slow down with the rocking rhythm until it stopped. She shivered to his touch, but he knew now that she shivered right after because all of her nerve endings were at high alert.

Heads still touching at their foreheads, Cat began to speak. "You know, as we were just sitting here, and you began to kiss me, I pretended that this was our home, we were married, and we were making love on our couch. I couldn't wait to have you inside me, then. Are you mad? Am I scaring you?"

Damon laughed and felt a warm shudder in him. "Hell no. I was thinking that I should have pulled out a ring at dinner and asked you to marry me right there. I can't wait to make my life with you, Cat. Seems my body feels the same way. Every time I see you in my home, I just want to be inside you; it's almost possessive. Is that scary?"

"I feel the same way, Damon. It has never been this way for me before. Now that I know this is special; what we do to each other, I can't wait until we can have this all the time." This time, Cat landed a feather-light kiss on his lips, and he accepted it. Staying inside her, he took his arms underneath hers and held her tight to his chest.

"Hold on," he whispered as she linked her ankles around his waist and pulled her arms tighter around his neck. Damon pulled the throw down onto the floor and lay her back onto the super-soft fabric. He had grown again inside her and slowly began to move to his own rhythm while he placed warm, wet kisses down her neck and on each erect nipple. He watched her as she closed her eyes, arched her neck, and felt it as she matched him with the thrusts of her hips. While this time was slower and more romantic, it was no less intense. While he was concerned about possessing her, he realized that she felt she possessed him as she moved ever so slightly to increase the friction between their bodies and thus intensifying his experience. When he couldn't wait any longer, she too released her feelings, and they shook inside of each other.

"Mmm. That was lovely." Damon pulled out of her and almost felt disappointed that it was over, but then felt a whole new sensation as she lay on her side, and he spooned her from behind. They wrapped themselves in the throw, and Damon reached up to grab throw pillows to place under their heads. They lazily watched the flames from the fire turn into warm embers as they dozed off.

A few hours into the early morning, Damon felt Cat stirring and realized that there was a chill in the air. He grabbed their pile of clothes, took her hand, and guided her upstairs to his bed. He felt adamant about sleeping with her in his bed, correction—their bed. He desperately wanted her to sleep in this bed with him. He anxiously wanted her to live in this house. He wanted his life to become theirs.

Mia woke them both, a few hours later, with her whimpers to go outside. Cat threw on his flannel overshirt, and her curls were a mussed mess like a lion's mane around her sleepy eyes and kiss-swollen lips. She pulled on yesterday's socks from the clothes pile and shuffled down the stairs to the front door to let Mia out. Damon felt the cold and the emptiness that hit him when she left the bed. He threw on his jeans and followed her down the stairs. Hugging her from behind, he smelled her neck and hair. "Mmm. You smell like sex."

Cat giggled and said, "Well, I was ravished last night by this handsome horseman. I just couldn't resist. I feel like a slut."

Damon giggled this time. "Well, if you're a slut, then you're my slut."

Cat laughed, turned around, and slapped him lightly on his face. She kissed him hard on his lips and crinkled her nose when his whiskers tickled her nose. "Fine. If I'm a slut, then you're a man-whore."

"Fine. Then you're my slut and I'm your man-whore. Have me at your will." Cat laughed that full belly laugh that he so loved to hear and lightly slapped him again.

"I can't call you 'man-whore' in public. Can't I call you schmoopsie?" Damon shivered. "Hell no. I'd rather be called man-whore."

Mia showed up at the door, smiling and ready to be a part of the group hug that was going on. She'd left them alone for the better part of a day, but it was time for her to be shown some lovin' and some food.

Damon put on a fresh pot of coffee and started making scrambled eggs, bacon, and toast. Cat stood there and took in the scene. Her man was making her breakfast after a night of lovemaking. Damon felt her gaze on his back, so he turned around and smiled at her. Her smile back was wicked. He couldn't wait to consummate their new relationship in every room of this home. He turned off the burner and let Mia out onto the front porch. His pants weren't zipped, but he was feeling their uncomfortable tightness as he was growing while watching her put her hands on either side of the kitchen table, lift her bare ass in his direction, and gaze sensuously over her shoulder in his direction. In two steps, he was behind her and pulling out his erect shaft with one hand and spreading her round buttocks apart to slide into her. He groaned as their skin connected and felt her push back into him. "Oh God," he thought with the little brainpower he had; he needed to make her his and fast. Just at that moment, he expressed himself inside her and she screamed back her intentions, "Yes! Yes! Yes!!"

Chapter Eleven

W hat d'ya mean you didn't tell him?" Aurelie barely got out as she was hiking one of the steepest sections of the Scuppernong Trail located in the southern Kettle Moraine Forest.

"I couldn't tell him. I don't know. I guess I was afraid," Cat said, breathing heavily from her efforts up the gravel path that separated two sides of the deciduous forest ahead of them. Mia was bounding up ahead with her tail wagging as much as she was panting in the Indian summer heat of the day.

"Cat, you HAVE to tell him. Shit, girlfriend, you've met the parents, and you're already talking about marriage. At first, I thought I was going to freak out about the marriage stuff, but this is serious." Aurelie, sporting a brand-new pixie cut from their favorite hair salon, Inspire Hair Design, had a bead of sweat starting to run from her neck, down between her shoulder blades, and stop at her neon pink sports bra. Her bronze back was glistening as another bead developed and flowed from her bra down the middle of her muscular back to dip into the black and neon pink workout capris she chose for today's "workout with friends" date with Cat.

Cat wore a black cap with her hair pulled into a ponytail, which was now swinging from side to side. Her choice of top was an Under Armour neon orange tank with a racerback and black and neon orange workout capris. Her tank was blotched with patches of sweat that soaked through, and sweat from her forehead was constantly dripping into her eyes.

"I screwed up, okay?" Cat panted. "Look, can we stop for a water break now?"

"We're almost at the lookout. We'll stop there. But the grilling won't. Got it?"

"I know."

The Scuppernong is named after the Scuppernong River that winds through Waukesha County and leads to Ottawa State Park. It has several hiking trails ranging in length from two to five miles and ranging in difficulty. Aurelie and Cat chose the Red Trail for a shorter hike, but with the sun beating down on them, it was a bit more challenging than they expected. The trails meander through a cathedral of cascading pines and wildflower meadows and weave into a dense deciduous forest, where one can hear the scurrying of forest creatures, but the fauna is thick with variegated green leafy plants, making it difficult to see anything other than what is directly in front of you. In mid-to-late September, the foliage begins to change to brilliant yellows, rich oranges, and deep scarlets. The density begins to fall away as leaves float from their branches to dust the forest floor and create a multi-colored blanket for which to protect the roots of the trees and cover the tiny bodies of newly developed plants that need protection from the harsh Wisconsin winter ahead.

Aurelie, in the lead, veered right to take the trail that led to the overlook. Once there, the girls sat on the wooden bench, broke open their water bottles, Cat setting down a flexible bowl for Mia to drink from, and gulped down the cool liquid into their heated bodies. The overlook showed them blue skies with scattered white billowy clouds making shadows over the treetops seen from their ledge.

"All right, Cat, spill. Why didn't you tell him you can't get pregnant?"

Cat looked straight ahead, took another long drink from her water bottle, and then began, "I don't know. Maybe because I didn't think this would be a serious relationship. This was supposed to be the rebound, right? No need to get too heavy with the rebound guy." She stole a look over at her friend, who gave her a stern look that meant she needed to go on.

"Then, after we saw you and you told me that he's something special, I thought I'd better make sure this is the real deal before I say something serious like I can't have children. So, when we went up north, I knew we were going up there and sex would be part of the deal, but he was so focused on getting condoms and I wanted to play it safe, no need to get an STD as a going-away gift, you know?"

"Okay, condoms are important, especially in a new relationship when you don't know the last time they slept with someone else or how many someone elses they've been with. Go on," Aurelie said.

"Well, after up north, it did start getting pretty serious. He'd already met my parents; then he wanted me to meet his and, I don't know, we had a rhythm going." Cat had to stop because Aurelie was giggling. "Not the rhythm method, stupid, a rhythm of being together and condoms were a part of it. Until the last time."

Aurelie stared ahead, thinking. Then she smirked as she turned to look at her friend's face. "How many condoms?"

Cat took a swig from her water bottle. "A shit ton." "Seriously? Do tell!" Aurelie went from serious to seriously excited to get some dirt on the situation.

"I'm not going into detail, Aurelie, but let's just say, I don't think rabbits have anything on us."

"No shit! You've got to give me something. I'm dying here!" Cat laughed and turned toward her friend.

"I don't know what to say without sounding like a slut, but it's like he knows what gets to me and I understand what I do to him. It's different every time, yet it feels like the first time."

Aurelie stared at her best friend in awe. "I'm not sure I know what you're talking about, but I can imagine it."

"Really? I thought you'd know exactly what I'm talking about. You have had a lot more experience with guys than I ever have."

"Truth?"

"Truth."

"I have had sex with a lot of guys, but none of them made me feel the way you are describing. I get turned on; they get turned on. We have sex, which is mostly fun, and then one of us leaves. That's it."

"That's sad."

"Cat, I'm not looking for anything serious right now. I've got my teaching job, my band, and I don't have the time or the energy to devote to a relationship right now."

"Okay. But I still feel sad for you. You're the sister I've always wanted, and I want you to be happy. You deserve someone who makes you feel like I feel when I'm with Damon."

"Thanks, Cat, but it's just not in the cards right now. We need to get back to you."

Cat stared straight ahead again and said thoughtfully, "What if I tell him and he can't take it? He leaves?" Cat then turned her head, her eyes searching her best friend's eyes.

"Kitty Cat, if he leaves, then he wasn't The One. Never was." Aurelie reached out and held Cat's hand, squeezed it.

"It's just that when we were at his house, they had all these great stories about their family. All those kids getting into heaps of trouble, yet always having each other's back. I swear, at one time I thought I saw his mom stare at me when someone started talking about the grandkids. I mean, I just met them. What the hell?"

"Yet you're the one who blurted out that you intended to marry their son."

"I know." Cat lowered her head and then looked back out over the ledge. "I knew I was being tested, and I guess my Irish or Italian pride got the best of me to beat them at their own game." Cat turned her head and saw that her best friend was staring at her with all the compassion she had to give. "All right, I'll tell him after the gala. Work is taking over my life for the next few weeks until this puppy is under wraps. If that's okay with you."

Aurelie sighed, squeezed Cat's hand, and said, "It's okay with me." Cat let a little tear leave her eye and roll down her cheek. Aurelie caught it and looked deeply into Cat's glistening green-flecked eyes. "Cat?"

"Yeah?"

"He'll stay. He's The One."

Cat squeezed her friend's hand. "I hope so."

The girls finished their hike and then sat at one of the ancient picnic tables off the pine-studded parking lot to cool down while drinking the rest of their water. Mia lapped up the rest of hers and then lay down underneath the shaded space made by the table.

"How is work going by the way? You haven't mentioned the dragon lady at all today."

Cat laughed. "Yeah, she's still around. Loves to find the one thing I didn't get to or the comma that was misplaced. Thank God that we've sold out, and people are already bidding online. Can't wait for these two weeks to be over with."

"So, are you bringing Damon or are you going stag?"

"His clinic is one of the sponsors, and we're releasing the crane he and his dad brought in, so he's technically one of the donors."

"And your date …"

Cat blushed a little. "Yes, he's my date." "Have you found a dress yet?"

"I was going to wear the one I wore last year. It's classic, and it still has a lot of wear to it."

"Hell no! You wore that dress last year when you were with shithead. Don't jinx your night by wearing it with Damon. I will clear my schedule, and you and I are going shopping. Drink up, girl; we've got a lot of work to do." With that, they jumped off the picnic table and walked back to Cat's SUV. Mia jumped in the back while Cat opened the sunroof, and Aurelie cranked up the music.

After going back to Cat's flat and taking quick showers, the girls were ready for a day of shopping. Mia, on the other hand, was quite content at finding her dog bed and taking a nap. This time, they took Aurelie's car and flew down I-43 toward Milwaukee. "Look, you don't want something that everyone else will have," Aurelie commented.

"I can't afford what they're going to be wearing. I'm on a strict budget—and this new dress isn't in it."

"Okay, I can readjust our shopping schedule. What about that great place in Wind Lake where we used to get our homecoming and prom dresses? She had some really cute stuff, and we always found something in our price range."

"Oh yeah, let's start there. If we can't find anything there, we can try one of the malls."

Aurelie got off the expressway at Racine Avenue and traveled east to Hwy 36 and Wind Lake. On the corner of Loomis Rd and Hwy 36, there was a small square store offset by the teal and white paint job on the stucco façade. The consignment boutique was run by a wonderful middle-aged Hispanic woman named Roselyn. She wore her thick black hair behind her ears in a low twist. She was small of stature but large on personality. She made sure that every woman in that store felt like a princess when she shopped. Every crevice was filled with racks of dresses on the floor, racks of shoes on the wall, clutch purses with jeweled clasps were scattered around, and the jewelry was showcased in the glass display case holding the cash register.

There were two dressing rooms facing a vintage rose velour fainting couch stuffed with pillows, where guests could sit and watch the parade of gowns before them. Aurelie was on a mission and had her arms filled to the brim with possibilities, and Roselyn had hers full as well. There were several contenders, but the one that stole their hearts was a 1950s red taffeta. Its halter was crossed in front of the sweetheart neckline, which was fitted to an empire waist that flowed into an A-line, tea-length skirt. When Cat put it on, it fit like a glove. When she twirled, it took their breath away. Roselyn found the perfect black patent pumps that slid on her feet and brought that touch of missing elegance.

"Oh, Cat, you'll knock 'em dead in this thing. It is so perfect for you! Sexy but not slutty."

"But is it too sexy? This is a work function. I have to look presentable."

"How about 'flirtatious'?" Roselyn said.

"Flirtatious. That'll work. How should I wear my hair?"

Roselyn had the answer. She went over to her collection of jewelry and found a large silver comb with dozens of rhinestones on the edge. "Wear it up in a French twist and put this in it. With a pair of diamond studs, you will be stunning."

Shopping bags in hand, Cat quickly hugged Roselyn and paid her an amount that would have only covered the comb in any other store but paid for the whole ensemble instead. She hung the dress above the back window and put the bag on the floor. After hopping in, she looked over at Aurelie, who was belting out "Feel It Still" by Portugal the Man. "All this shopping has made me hungry. Where to next?"

"How about getting something to eat?"

"Mmm. That sounds perfect. I'm in the mood for an Italian beef sandwich."

"Wanna split a piece of their chocolate cake while we're at it?"

Cat looked at her friend up and down. "Aurelie, I do love you, but you're such a bitch sometimes. Everything you eat just melts away, but me, well that's another story. I will literally work my ass off for a week to be able to fit into that dress and still have room to breathe if I eat a piece of that cake."

Aurelie pouted. "That's not fair. I can't help it that I have the metabolism of a bunny and you have one of a sloth. It's genet- ics, babe."

"I know it's genetics, but I have to say 'no' to that scrumptious chocolate cake today and for the next two weeks."

The rest of the trip, the two besties belted out every song on the radio and reminisced about their silly high school antics and road trips. When they got inside the 1950s decorated restaurant, a teenage girl with braids took their orders. Cat loved the food here, but the atmosphere was something special.

They found an empty table in the middle of the dining area and began enjoying their Italian beef sandwiches, dripping in gravy and held together with a freshly baked French roll. Aurelie added hot peppers and mozzarella to hers and had a side of fries that she offered to share. They sipped on diet sodas and managed to continue their conversation in between bites. "Oh, man! I forgot how amazing these beef sandwiches taste. So glad they don't have one at home. I'd have to get a whole new wardrobe—two sizes larger!" Aurelie garbled as she continued to tackle her drippy, sloppy mess of a meal.

"Speaking of food, Mom is making homemade poutine for dinner tomorrow night. Wanna come over? Free food!" Aurelie's mom didn't often cook outside of the heart-healthy recipes she prided herself on making for her family, but once in a while, she threw together every possible combination of sweet, salty, and fattening food items you could imagine. Poutine is a dish of French fries and cheese curds dripping in brown gravy. Certainly not for the faint of heart, but worth every cholesterol, fat-filled bite, in Aurelie's opinion.

"Aww, man. I hate to miss it, but I'm going out with Damon tomorrow. We're going to do a day trip to Devil's Lake and hike around there a bit." Though Aurelie was disappointed, she understood.

"No worries. But hey, just want to let you know that they're really strict about public sex in the parks. Watch your back!"

Cat looked surprised and then laughed. "Funny. We don't always have to have sex when we're together. We do like to just hang out with one another too, you know."

"Yeah, but outdoor sex is hot. Just be careful, Kitty Cat. I don't want to have to bail you out of jail, again."

Cat looked up at her in surprise and then grinned. "That doesn't count. It wasn't a real jail. You put me in jail to raise money for the children's hospital."

The next day was another beautiful sunny day, and there was a nice breeze blowing. Cat braided her hair and put on one of her workout tanks; this one was gray with white polka dots. She threw on a darker shade of gray hooded sweatshirt over it, pulled up her gray workout pants and walking socks, and laced up her hiking boots. She walked over to the kitchen table, where she had her mini backpack open with Mia's flexible bowls, a sandwich bag of Mia's dog food, her leash, and a tennis ball in one section. The other had some sunblock, granola bars, her phone, and wallet. She put two bottles of water into the holders on either side and went back to get her cap, just in case.

She heard the truck roll up and waved out the kitchen window. "All packed, girl. Let's go on an adventure today." Mia perked up and barreled down the back staircase while Cat made sure the apartment was locked. When she reached the back door, Damon was already there to scoop her up into a long lingering kiss.

"I have missed you," he breathed into her neck. Cat squeezed him back.

"It's only been a few days, and we talk on the phone every night." Damon looked forlorn. "I missed you, too." The embrace relaxed, and they walked over to the truck.

"I've missed you too, Miss Mia. Look, I brought you a treat." At that word, Mia perked up and sat perfectly straight except for her tail moving a million miles a minute.

With everyone and everything packed into the truck, Damon backed out the driveway, put on for a little country music, and started down the road to hit Highway 83 toward the interstate. An easy two-hour drive to the park.

"You know, I haven't been able to eat at the kitchen table all week …" Cat looked over at Damon quizzically. "I keep picturing you and me and what we did on that kitchen table." Cat turned away and blushed. "And I can't even sleep in my bed without thinking of you being in there with me. I tried sleeping on the couch, but that made it worse." Damon took a side glance at her and saw her giggling. Cat felt mortified at first, then realized he was teasing her. If she had been a possessive woman, she would have been pleased with herself and the way that she marked his place as her territory.

"Well, it looks like your parents' house has plenty of room. You can try and sleep over there," she shot back. Damon looked stunned and then grinned.

"What would I tell them? Suddenly, at my age, I'm afraid of the dark?" At that, Cat laughed out loud and touched his arm. He made her feel all warm inside. She didn't have to guess at what he was feeling; he told her, showed her. She knew deep in her heart that she could trust him with hers, but she was afraid of how he would react or how his family would react when they learned that she couldn't bring children into their family. She was sure he loved her or thought he loved her enough to marry her. But could he love her enough knowing he would never be a father? Still, she had promised Aurelie and herself that she had to tell him why she wasn't so worried about the missed condom. If she wanted the man in her life to be worthy of her trust, she had to make sure she was just as honest with him. Cat just wished it wasn't so hard to be honest herself.

They got to the park around noon and decided to set up the picnic lunch that Damon had put together. He had got a chicken salad made with mayonnaise, walnuts, celery, and red grapes; fresh crusty country white mini baguettes that he had sliced; Rome apples; extra-sharp cheddar cheese slices; and iced bottles of hard apple cider. Cat set up Mia under the picnic table with her flexible bowl filled with water and started sampling the feast put in front of her. Damon opened up his pocket knife to the bottle opener and cracked open the ciders.

Cat was in heaven. A beautiful, breezy fall day; a delicious fall meal; and a handsome man to share it all with. She thought that they were going to concentrate on keeping the conversation light while they were eating, but Damon jumped right in. "Since you brought up marriage to my family, maybe we should talk about what we are looking for, planning for in a marriage? We've never really talked about the future much, just that we know we want to be together."

Cat almost choked on her bite of apple and cheddar. She quickly took a swig of the crisp cider to clear her throat as well as help her to get a little more relaxed for the inevitable conversation. "Okay. Why don't you start? I'm still choking on my food a bit," Cat replied.

"You okay?" Damon put his sandwich down and reached over to tap her back.

"I'll be fine. Just need a minute. I'm okay, really. You can start." Cat tried to deep breathe to get herself to relax.

"Well, I see a large church wedding at Holy Hill, since that's where my family goes. Then we could have a blowout of a party at that banquet hall that has gorgeous views of Lake Nagawicka, and we could have a band. Hey! How about your friend's band? They do a lot of variety. Some big band stuff for the older crowd and then some rock and roll and country tunes to round out the night."

Cat was a bit overwhelmed. "Hmm. Interesting. It has some possibilities."

"Why? What are you thinking?"

"Well, I always wanted a small, quiet wedding. Something outdoors so my dad and Ryan could make an archway to get married under. My mom is fantastic with flowers, so there would have to be lots of country garden-type flowers all over."

Damon furrowed his brows but nodded his head. "So we've got a little work to do to agree on the style of wedding. Not a problem. What about the honeymoon?"

"I've always wanted to take an RV and go camping at all the national parks. Thought it would be cool to get a few under my belt before settling down. You?"

"Hmm. I've always wanted to go to Ireland, England, and Scotland. Maybe we could combine the two? Camping in Ireland? Touring the national parks in England and Scotland? Or we could do some camping on the way to an airport out east and then fly to the Isles? The possibilities are endless."

Cat smiled, but behind her eyes, she was feeling trouble brewing. Maybe they were moving too fast. They weren't coming together on the wedding things; what would happen when she threw a wrench in the family plans?

"Next on the list. Where would we live?" Damon asked. "That's an easy one. At first, we could live in your house. You've

built a beautiful home, and I'd always be around horses. No-brainer." Cat felt confident that he would agree, but then he paused.

"What do you mean, 'at first'?" Damon asked curiously. "Well, you don't want to live close to your parents all your life, do you?

I mean, it's a great place to start our life together, but what if an opportunity comes for me and it means we have to leave Wisconsin? There's not a whole lot of options for me in Wisconsin. Most of them are in California, Texas, Kentucky, Tennessee, and Maryland."

Damon looked a bit troubled, or was it hurt? She wasn't sure what he was thinking, but she knew he hadn't got the answer he was looking for.

"Okay. I think that's one we do agree on, for now. No need to get too far ahead of ourselves. Now, the most critical question of all; how many children should we have? I think it's important not to have a middle child. You're one of two; I'm one of six. How about something in the middle? Like four?"

Cat's heart sank. This was more difficult than she thought. Not only couldn't she have one child on her own, but now she'd be disappointing him four times that. It was too much to bear. "New plan," she thought. Time for a distraction. "That's much farther out into the future than I've thought about. Besides, I thought we were going to hike around the lake before dark?"

Damon didn't seem to mind the change of conversation. "Wow, it's later than I thought. Sorry about that! Let's pack up and get on the trail. It's starting to get darker sooner these days." Cat smiled and packed up the food into their bags and containers while Damon organized it all back into the basket and cooler. He pulled out a bottle of water for himself, locked up the truck, and the threesome was on their way to enjoy a day's hike around one of Wisconsin's most popular outdoor destinations.

When they got to the trailhead, they decided on one of the shorter routes as they were concerned about the shortened amount of daylight left. The trail they determined was the best one for views of the lake and the geological formations was the 1.7 miles East Bluff Trail. This trail had some of the stone steps up to the 500-feet elevation, several opportunities to view the lake, and enjoy the shade offered by the wooded areas, and they still would see Elephant Cave and Elephant Rock along the way.

Cat felt her dread and anxiety melt away with every step. Exercise wasn't always her "go-to" coping strategy; it used to be ice cream, chocolate, and French fries. But with a great deal of focus, she found that more often these days, she went to sweating out the anxiety, fear, or anger than to eat it away. It felt so nice to just be together. On the steeper sections, Damon would let Cat lead so that he didn't leave her behind. On the easier passages, they often would hold hands and stand side by side. There were several vantage points where one or the other brought out their phone to take a selfie or a photo of the terrain in front of them.

Returning to the trailhead, they agreed it was best to grab something for dinner and then get on the road. They found a quaint local restaurant about three miles away in Baraboo, Wisconsin. They pulled up and found it had outdoor seating under a timber roof. Round thick tables covered in lacquer were partnered with branch-framed chairs. Inviting wood-carved bears welcomed customers, and Mia had to sniff them to make sure they were not a threat. Damon and Cat followed the hostess to a table in the far corner, and Mia took her spot underneath the table. Damon ordered them two tall glasses of diet soda and a pitcher of ice water to share with Mia.

"I can't believe how hungry I am. You packed a great lunch, and now I feel like I haven't eaten all day." At that, Cat's stomach growled loud enough that Mia growled back.

Damon's bright blue eyes glistened in the sunlight as his head fell back to let out one of his boisterous laughs. "I'm so glad that was your stomach and not mine. I've been hungry since the first set of stone stairs." Cat grinned back at him and then picked up her menu.

"I've never been here before, have you?" she inquired.

"Me? No. I just googled 'restaurants near Devil's Lake,' and it seemed like a good fit. I knew you didn't want to leave Mia in the truck in case she got too hot."

"You are always so thoughtful. Thank you," Cat said in a heartfelt way. She almost felt guilty enough to share her secret when another rumble from her stomach erupted.

"Okay, okay! Let's order quickly before you eat the table." Cat glared at him and then shook her head. She couldn't remember being this hungry in a long while. Perhaps two days straight of hiking was too much for her. Maybe she's that much out of shape.

When the waitress came back with their drinks in mason jars, Damon ordered the smoked beef brisket with homemade baked beans and French fries, and Cat asked for the pecan wood-smoked pork roast with garlic mashed potatoes and carrots. Damon asked for a side of rolls and butter, so Cat's stomach would calm down a bit.

"So, what's your week look like? Do you think we can get together before the weekend?" Damon asked.

"I'm sorry, but it's only ten days until the gala. I'll be lucky to get out on time any of those nights. Luckily, Mrs. Romansky has already offered to dog sit, if I need her to. She's such a great landlady." Damon looked a little put out, but then he seemed to push it out of the way and go on.

"We should probably talk about how the night is going to go. Do you want us to drive together? Separate? Do I need to do anything, prepare anything as a sponsor?" Cat was glad he didn't want to bring up their future again. She was hoping not to talk about work on an off-day, but she appreciated his interest.

"Yeah, we should go over the logistics a bit. I have to be there early to make sure the rooms are set up correctly and the volunteers know what they're supposed to do. I think it's best we take separate cars. I will have some setup to do on Friday night so that I don't have to be there too early, but I don't know what you're going to do while I'm running around making sure everyone's in their places with bright, shiny faces." Damon's dimples came out when he grinned at her for using that cheesy line his teachers used to use in grade school. Then the waitress came with the rolls and butter. Cat was going all warm and fuzzy looking at his dimples when she smelled the warm rolls and quickly grabbed the closest one to her and started tearing into it.

"Damn, woman! You almost bit my hand off." Damon's eyes went from smiling to curious.

"I'm sorry. I guess I'm hungrier than I thought." Cat took another bite of her pretzel roll and sighed as she devoured it. Not too long after the main meals were delivered, she dove into her pork roast and potatoes with a fervor.

They stayed quiet through dinner, only talking enough to make sure each other was enjoying their meal. As much as Cat had been starving before, she felt her stomach letting her know it had enough. She put down her fork and knife and leaned back in her chair. "Oh man, I am stuffed. I can't eat like this again until after the gala. I've got to fit into my dress."

Damon perked up. "Dress? What's it look like? Can I see it?" Cat realized he was very interested, and she thought it was curious that he was so interested in what she was wearing. "I bought it yesterday with Aurelie; she said I couldn't wear the same I wore last year. It was tacky. Why do you need to see it?"

Damon paused and then said, "Well, what if I want to dress to match? Or bring you flowers to match?"

Cat smiled. "That's very thoughtful of you, but please don't bring flowers. I have to make sure all the decorations and flowers at the event are Rose-approved. She is very particular about the whole thing. If mistakes are made, she feels it reflects poorly on her, and then she makes sure we know how she feels about that." Cat rolled her eyes and took a drink of her diet soda. He looked a little crestfallen, so she gave him a little smackerel. "Okay, okay. Stop your pouting. I'm wearing a red dress with black patent pumps. Better?"

"Can't wait to see you all glamor and glitz on Saturday night. Looking forward to it." This time, his stare wasn't pouty but sultry. Cat felt the stirrings of her nether regions react to his stare. Damn him. She really should get a better handle on how he made her feel. She couldn't go and attack him in a restaurant. They still had a two-hour drive home, and she had to get ready for work tomorrow. Damon seemed to sense her urgency to leave; he paid the check and got everyone on the road.

The car ride home was quieter than the ride to the park. Damon found a smooth jazz station, and Cat held his warm hand in hers and started to close her eyes to the rhythmic sound of Mia's soft snores in the backseat.

By the time they drove up the driveway, the sun had dipped, and the moon was rising along with the night sky stars. Cat let Mia take care of business while Damon brought up their bags. "Cat, do you want the rest of the picnic so you'll have lunch tomorrow?"

"That'd be a time saver. Thank you." She and Mia followed Damon up the stairs, and she began to put away their day-trip items. After she had put her lunch bag into the fridge for tomorrow, she felt Damon's arms go around her waist and his mustache tickle her neck.

"Do you mind if I take a bath before I go?" he said with a kiss that sent tingles down to her toes.

"Go right ahead."

Another kiss on the other side of her neck. "Will you join me?" Cat was almost comatose as she murmured back, "Mmm, hmm."

She made sure that Mia was taken care of for the night and then went into the bathroom to run the water in the claw-foot tub. She found some essential oils to scent the water and brought out fresh towels from the small armoire. When she turned around, he was already naked, and his hands worked the ponytail holder out of her hair and let her braid loose around her face. She stood in awe as he unzipped her hoodie and let it drop to the floor. She woke up enough to pull her tank and sports bra off over her head and shimmy her workout pants and socks down to the floor.

She guided him into the bathroom, where he motioned her to kneel with her head over the lip of the tub. She thought he was going to make love to her right there, but instead, he switched the water from the faucet to the hand-held sprayer and gently massaged her scalp with one hand while directing the spray to moisten all her curls with the other. He followed through with massaging shampoo and then conditioner into her hair, rinsing them out, and then carefully twisting the excess water out of her hair before handing her a towel. He was so close she could feel the heat of his skin near her, yet he held back. It was so sexy, the anticipation. She couldn't wait to reciprocate.

She led him to kneel in the same place so she could wash his hair with the same love and care he showed her. However, since he was so much larger than she, Cat brushed up against him as she stretched to reach for the shampoo and the hand spray. She swore she felt him quiver when their skin would connect, but he never breached the position he was in or took over her authoritarian position. It was if he had succumbed to her hand. When she was done, she handed him a dry towel that he used to dry the drips falling into his face and to shake the extra water out of his hair.

This time, he stepped into the tub and put his arm out to help her follow suit. He lay down with his back on the side and led her to sit with her back to him. He found a washcloth and lathered it with vanilla-scented soap before he pressed it to her back and began lightly scrubbing her skin in slow, methodical circles until he reached the point where her apple-bottom cheeks met the porcelain bottom of the tub. Damon dipped the cloth into the water, rinsed it out of all the soap, and then dipped it again so that it was at maximum capacity. He slowly twisted the cloth above her shoulders so that the excess water dripped down her back, taking with it soapy lines that reached the water's edge. When he was done with her back, he made her lie against his chest and performed the same flirtatious dance with the washcloth on her front side as he had done with her backside. However, this time, her nipples reacted immediately when the washcloth met them with the hot, soapy water. They relaxed their shape and color into bright red cherries, and then when the cloth was removed, they stood at attention for the shock of the cool air brushing against them again. When he had meticulously washed her whole body, Damon let her lie back on his chest and feel him inhale and exhale. He wrapped his long arms around hers in a protective, yet subtle way, and she was at peace.

They lay like that until the steaming hot water became more tepid, and then Cat returned the favor, treating him as if he were precious cargo and not a lumberjack of a man. She got out first and helped him onto the shag rug covering the tile floor. They continued caring for each other without a word, gently drying shoulders, stomachs, knees, calves, and feet. Afterward, Cat put a spot of body lotion into the palm of her hand and began rubbing it into his hot, dry skin. Damon followed her lead and made sure to cover every space from the nape of her neck to the tip of her toes.

Cat led him out into the hallway and across to her bedroom. No sooner had she pulled back the comforter and sheets than Damon flipped her onto her back and used his knees to gently open her thighs to offer her moist mound to him. Carefully lowering himself onto her, Damon's tip nudged its way into her steaming hot arousal, allowing Damon to thrust into her fully. Cat let out a gasp and held his gaze. No kissing or touching other than the coupling that they desired to fully experience together. When the rhythm began to increase, Cat could feel the tension rising and her hips readily met his as the passion began to intensify. She refused to close her eyes; she wanted to see him just one more time as he loved her this night. Cat felt her orgasm ready to crest just as Damon shook inside her and groaned his relief. Cat felt her body react to his and explode, but she held it inside of her, not wanting to release herself fully, her sadness coming through that he may not want to be with her like this after she told him her secret.

Damon kissed her warmly on her lips as she reached up to spread her fingers through his damp hair. "I love you," she whispered. "I will always love you," she confirmed as she kissed him right back.

He slid off her and then shifted to her backside, spooning her while nuzzling her hair. "I love you, Catrina Carneri. I always will." And he quietly began to fall asleep holding her in his arms.

"I hope so," she whispered back, unaware that his eyes opened at that moment.

Before the sun was up, Damon slid out of bed, found his clothes in the moonlight, and quietly crept down the back stairs. Cat felt the shift in the bed and heard the commotion, but was unwilling to leave the warm, flannel sheets and down comforter. She fell back asleep until her alarm went off, signaling the beginning of a crazy busy two weeks.

From the moment she arrived at work, Rose was her shadow. "How many people are attending?" "Let me see the seating chart."

"Did you finish my speech yet?" "Where's the program?" Cat was trying to keep it all together; however, she seemed less able to control her temper than in previous years. It didn't make sense. This was turning out to be the most successful gala fundraiser since she had started. They were going into it with a sold-out event and all the sponsorships were filled. Everything that came in that night would be pure profit.

Days were flying by and the event was the upcoming weekend. "Maybe it's because you're keeping something important from the man you love, and it's manifesting itself in other areas of your life," Aurelie suggested during a phone call.

"You're probably right. The event is in two days, and I haven't been able to see him since Devil's Lake. I had to cancel last weekend so I could catch up after that glitch with the mobile bidding program. It took me almost all weekend working with the vendor to get that figured out. I know he was disappointed, but I just couldn't be with him and still get done what needed to be done."

"Or you're avoiding him."

"Why would I do that?"

"Don't you dare play stupid with me, Kitty Cat. I spend eight to ten hours a day uncovering little white lies and great big ones from my students. I certainly don't need it from my friends." Aurelie's temper was felt over the phone.

"I'm sorry. I guess I am avoiding him. Avoiding the inevitable. It's been making me crazy, you know. One minute I am calm as a cucumber and the next I'm freaking out over table linens. Seriously. Who gives a damn about table linens?"

"Look, you know I love you and I support you, but I have to be honest here. If you don't tell him soon, I'll have to take a break from you, too. I can't stand seeing you this crazy, but you're doing it to yourself and to a really great guy. A guy who you told me you want to marry. I won't stand by and watch you screw with him. It isn't fair to him."

Cat started to tear up. "You're right. I'll tell him right after the gala. All that stress will be over, and I can focus on getting on with my life."

Saturday came around and Cat had everything under control. She took her time getting ready, straightening her hair so it was smooth and classic in its French twist, pulled together with the crystal-embellished comb, and wearing the pair of diamond studs her father and mother gave her for her eighteenth birthday. She stepped into the red dress and zipped up the back. It felt a little snug since the last time she had tried it on but not too uncomfortable. If anything, it enhanced her breasts in that sweetheart neckline. She slipped into the black patent pumps, grabbed her black patent clutch, kissed Mia, and locked the back door. She knocked on Mrs. Romansky's door to let her know she was leaving for the evening. "Catrina, you look like a Hollywood starlet!" Cat blushed, kissed her cheek, and drove off to the event.

Everything was moving along like clockwork. She helped the reception desk with a few missing nametags and switched out the batteries on a faulty microphone, but all things considered, it was going smoothly. Even Rose hadn't found anything to complain about in the last hour, and she wouldn't hear a peep from her during the event because she'd be hobnobbing with all the sponsors and major donors all evening. That'd be a relief.

She was looking over her checklist when a familiar hand touched her shoulder. "Hey there, pretty woman, may I offer you a drink?" She turned around, lifted her head up, and saw those incredibly azure eyes that sparkled when they smiled at her.

"I'd love one. A white wine, please." She could tell he wasn't paying attention as he held her an arm's length away and gazed at her from head to toe.

"My God, you get more gorgeous every time I see you, Cat. This dress is amazing on you." Cat blushed and looked him over as well, noticing that he was wearing a red bow tie and vest that matched her dress to a "T."

"Look at you, Mr. Handsome. I'm the luckiest woman at this event because I get to go home with you." The red on his face mirrored the red in his tie and his dimples deepened. She leaned forward to whisper in his ear, "And show you what I've got underneath this dress that's just for you …"

Damon's eyes got wide and the smile on his face grew. "I'd better get that white wine for you before I whisk you away from here to see for myself."

Cat laughed out loud, turned, and saw Rose glaring at her before she was drawn back into her conversation. Shaking off the cold feeling she got seeing Rose's face, she turned right into Jansen. His hair was a bit longer than the last time she saw him, but he always dressed well. He was wearing charcoal grey suit that matched his steel-gray eyes. "Cat, you are the most stunning woman in the room."

Cat's breath was taken away and her smile went with it. "Hello, Jansen. I was surprised to see you on the list. I didn't think fundraisers were your thing, wild drunken orgies, however …"

"Pettiness doesn't suit you, Cat, and neither does your new boyfriend. What's with that hair and beard? He looks like a ginger Santa Claus." Jansen chuckled at his own joke just as Damon joined them to hand Cat her wine.

"Thank you, Damon. Jansen James, this is Damon MacGregor. Dr. MacGregor and his clinic are one of the sponsors for tonight's event. He and his father brought in the crane that we're releasing later."

Damon's smiling eyes turned to ice in a matter of a second. He reached out his hand for a handshake that he was sure would break Jansen's hand if he hadn't controlled his strength and temper. "Jansen."

"Dr. MacGregor. I see you've gotten to know Catrina. Cat and I go way back. I know her well in case you need any pointers."

Damon's hold got a little tighter, and Jansen's knuckles were going white. "Oh, you mean how to get away with cheating on her and asking out her friends behind her back?" Jansen's look of surprise said it all; he was shocked that Cat had shared their history with Damon so soon. "Thanks, bud, but I'm not interested." Damon let go of Jansen's hand just as Mr. James came to join his son.

With salt and pepper hair and black eyes, Mr. James in a silver tuxedo continued to be a handsome man well into his sixties. "Catrina, is that you? Dear, you are breathtaking in that dress!" Then he looked at his struggling son and inquired, "Jansen, are you feeling okay?"

Jansen was quick to respond, "Yeah, Dad, I'm just going to get a drink." And he sulked away.

Mr. James hugged Cat, and she hugged him back. "Oh, Catrina, I do miss having you come around the house. You always were a bright spot. It's too bad Jansen didn't know a good thing while he had it. It looks like you're doing well." Then his gaze went to Damon, who had been standing a bit more protectively over Cat than before.

"It's good to see you too, Mr. James. May I introduce you to one of our newest sponsors, Dr. Damon MacGregor?" The two men shook hands and nodded in greeting. Cat looked at the time and excused herself to handle another situation brewing on the other side of the room.

Cat had to be flexible with her time and was floating around, mingling with all the guests and making sure the bidding was moving along as well as the program. When it was time to announce the releasing of the crane, Cat meandered over to Dr. O'Brien and queued her to get everyone's attention to walk out to the balcony and watch the release near the water's edge below. Damon moved in right behind her and lightly put his hands on her waist and whispered in her ear, "That was amazing. What a relief to see her fly away like that. Thank you. Thank you for everything." Cat leaned into him for a moment; then she caught movement out of the corner of her eye. Jansen was slamming down another drink and dropping the empty glass on the bar, ordering the bartender to get him another. When it was time to move the crowd to the dining area and to their assigned seats, Cat released Damon's hands so she could tell the announcer of the evening that the bidding was closed. Then she moved to the auction room to make sure that the volunteers there knew what to do.

When all of that was handled, she slid into her seat next to Damon in the front row, left side of the podium. She wanted to be near the speakers and the AV but not at the head table. She was grateful now that the Jameses were at Rose's table, where she was using all her charms to show just how grateful she was for their generous support. Jansen looked royally bored and continued drinking heavily throughout dinner. When dinner was over and dessert was served, it was time to play heads or tails, where guests put in ten dollars to guess if the MC's quarter would land on heads or tails—the last one standing won half of the pot and the rest was a donation. Jansen was one of the last ones standing, literally. He could barely stand and was sloppy at getting his hands atop his head. He was holding his liquor, but Cat was more concerned he would fall on the other contestants.

Next came the live auction, and boy, were the high bidders out for blood tonight. Cat was thrilled to see that all the auction items went for more than their value, and the one for a vacation for two to Cancun, Mexico, went for ten thousand! It was time for her to get up and make sure that the checkout process was going smoothly. She excused herself and went to find the volunteers who were handing out the invoices. She felt bad about leaving Damon so much, but she had no choice. This was her job, and she had to make sure that everything went smoothly. And it was, until …

It was the end of the night, and most of the guests were either in the checkout lines or were in the process of leaving. Cat was standing with her back to a wall and checking her phone for updates from the volunteers.

"Kitty Cat." Jansen put his right hand on the wall next to her head. She could smell the strong scent of brandy on his breath and felt a bit of spittle hit her face when he talked. "You're drunk, Jansen. Let me call you a ride." She had started dialing when he grabbed her phone and threw it across the floor. Cat gulped in, and her eyes went wide and then they went dark amber. Her anger for the past two weeks was at its peak, and he was about to feel it if he didn't move. However, she wasn't prepared to feel his hands on her wrists, squeezing them tightly.

"Kitty Cat, I don't need a Goddamned ride. I need you. I'm sorry, okay? I was stupid before. I've changed. I know you were the best thing that happened to me. Come home with me, and I'll show you how sorry I really am." With that, he laid his left hand on top of her breast.

Cat slapped his hand off, remembered the move to twist her other arm in the direction that released his continued grip and pushed him off her. "Get. Off. Me," she delivered. "You don't deserve me. You never did. You are a drunk and a man-whore. And don't ever call me Kitty Cat again," she said just as her hand connected to his face. The sound of the slap was heard by everyone within earshot. Damon raced over to the scene and saw red.

Jansen, not to be outdone by a woman, balled up his fist and hit her across the cheek. Though she was shocked, she instinctively raised her knee and knocked him in the family jewels just as Damon came to finish the job. Damon pulled him up by the hair from his crouching position and hit him with a right cross to his eye. Jansen fell to the ground and looked like he had passed out.

Rose was there in a flash. "Call the police!" she ordered, and one of the hall's staff complied. She bent down in her silver dress and felt for a pulse on Jansen and for any signs of breathing. "Thank God he's breathing." Rose stood up and glared at Cat. "What the hell just happened?"

Mr. James arrived in time to hear the explanation as the rest of the guests crowded around the spectacle. Damon, still in protector mode, hovered over Jansen while having his arm around Cat. "I saw Jansen corner her, and by the time I got here, he sucker-punched her across the face and looked like he was going after her again, so

I hit him, and he passed out. He's drunk as a skunk; he shouldn't drive anywhere tonight."

"Catrina, is this true?" Rose questioned in an authoritarian voice.

"Yes. Jansen is very drunk, and he wanted me to come home with him. When I said no, he said something awful, and I slapped him. He retaliated by punching me, so I kneed him. That's when Damon came."

Rose looked angrily at Cat and then at Damon. She tried to compose herself when she addressed Mr. James. "I am so very sorry, Mr. James, for what just happened to your son. You can be sure we will take the matter to the authorities. If you wish to press charges, I totally understand." Cat couldn't believe what she had just heard! Rose was defending Jansen! Rose didn't call the cops for Jansen; she called them on Cat and Damon. What a bitch!

The sirens were heard, and the crowd began to disperse to let the cops into the smaller circle. The younger of the two cops, a woman, felt Jansen's pulse and confirmed he was breathing and rolled him over, at which time, Jansen threw up all over the floor. The guests near him jumped out of the way and started to leave the building.

The older policeman took statements from Cat and Damon while the policewoman took Jansen's. She got up and spoke, "Sounds like he wants to press charges against Dr. MacGregor for assault."

"What?" Cat and Damon screamed. "That's enough," she replied.

Her partner cut in, "That won't be happening since, as I see it, it was self-defense and protecting a victim of an assault. Dr. Mac-Gregor only threw one punch. If he continued to hit Mr. James, then there might be a case. But as I see it, Ms. Carneri has a case for assault on Mr. James. Ma'am, do you wish to press charges?"

At first, Cat was going to decline. The death stare she was receiving from Rose and the total embarrassment she was feeling was torture. She just wanted this night to end. Still, she knew that if Jansen was let go, he might continue to go after her. Was he an alcoholic? She wasn't sure, but he surely drank more tonight than she'd ever seen him drink before. Besides, she wasn't sure if Rose was ever going to let her live this night down even if she did decline to press charges. "Yes, I want to press charges." Then she looked over at Mr. James. "I'm very sorry, Mr. James."

The handsome man now looked sad and much older than when she had seen him earlier in the night. "Don't be sorry, Catrina. I am the one who is sorry. Sorry that I let him get this bad. I am ashamed that I raised a son who thinks it's okay to hit a woman. Are you okay?" His sad eyes changed to a look of concern.

"I'm just a little shaken up right now. I'm sure that I'll be fine."

Rose was stunned by the turn of events, but Cat could see this was far from over. The hall's manager came over with an ice bag for Cat's cheek; the police officers cleaned off what they could of the mess on Jansen's clothes and escorted him to the squad car. Mr. James talked with the hall management and the police to ensure that he would pay for anything that needed to be fixed or cleaned due to his son's actions. He apologized to Rose, but she wouldn't hear of it; she apologized back to him.

When the Jameses were gone and the mess was cleaned up, Rose came back over to Damon and Cat. "Do you need to see a doctor?" she asked. Perhaps Cat was wrong. Maybe there was some compassion there.

"Thanks, but I think I'm fine. I better get up and see what still needs to be done to close out the event." Cat started to walk but felt a little unsteady. Damon was right there to keep her from falling over. "Thank you," she said.

The reality was that there wasn't much left to do. The guests had already gotten their auction items, and the hall staff was already cleaning up the tables and decorations. The money and the credit card machine were accounted for and going back to the safe with the security detail Rose had hired to follow her back to her office to lock it up for the weekend.

When Cat was ready to leave, Damon had already picked up her cell phone and her clutch purse and was walking with his arm around her. Cat knew she needed to touch base one last time with Rose. "That's everything, Dr. O'Brien. I'm going home if that's okay with you."

"How's that bump on your cheek, Catrina?" "I'm sure it'll be fine. Just a little sore right now."

"Well, go on home then. We'll talk about this on Monday." Cat wasn't sure, but it didn't sound too promising. Still, she was extremely exhausted and just wanted to go to bed. Her nerves and her emotions were all over the place, and she was wiped out.

When Damon stopped, they were in front of his truck. "Where's my car?" Cat asked.

"I'm taking you home in my truck. We'll come back tomorrow for your car."

"I'm fine. I can drive myself home, Damon." She started to get a rise again.

"No. I'm driving you home tonight." There was no room for discussion in his voice. She realized that this night had taken a toll on him as well, and she was too tired to fight. No holding of hands, as hers was holding an ice bag to her cheek. There were no more words spoken.

At her apartment, they both walked silently up the back stairs, and when the kitchen light was turned on, he turned to see her and carefully pulled the ice pack from her face to see the damage. "Well, he cracked you good. The swelling is going down, but I'm afraid you're going to get a bruise."

Cat's temper was rising again. She didn't like the feeling that he was talking down to her, like she couldn't handle herself. "Thank you, doctor," she snipped and turned around to take off her shoes.

"What's that for? Why does it sound like you're mad at me?"

"Maybe it's because you felt like you had to 'take care of the little woman' instead of realizing I was doing fine on my own. He was already falling to the ground when you got there. Then you had to be the big hero and finish him off. Oh, and you almost got yourself arrested," Cat bit back.

"What is wrong with you tonight? I know you had it handled, but I'm the kind of guy who won't let another guy hit a woman. Period. I won't apologize for that. And another thing I won't apologize for is looking out for you. I love you, goddamnit, and I won't stand by when someone is going after you. I will protect you if you're in trouble. I do that with everyone I love."

His eyes were ablaze with fury and hurt. Cat knew she was handling this all wrong but couldn't seem to control herself. "Well, I was handling it, and now? Now I don't know what Monday's gonna bring. Will I have a job? Will Rose make it so bad for me that I'll have to quit? I don't know, maybe it was a mistake having you come to the event. This was a very important night, and it ended very wrong."

Damon became livid, and Cat's eyes went wide with concern. "A mistake for me to come? A mistake? What is with you, Cat? Ever since Devil's Lake, you've been pushing me away!" he paused, but she could see that he wasn't done. "No. Wait. Since you came to visit me and my family." He pulled his hands through his flaming red hair. "Shit. It's the missed condom, isn't it? You're mad at me for forgetting to put one on? You're afraid of being pregnant, aren't you?"

Pregnant. That word got through when the rest of them roared past her ears. "The condom? You think this is all about a stupid condom? Are you afraid you got me pregnant? Would that be a problem for you? Doesn't fit into your plans for our future together? You've got everything else so perfectly planned out, but an unplanned pregnancy would screw everything up now, wouldn't it?" Her hands were on her hips, and she had fire in her veins and vengeance on her lips. Damon was puzzled; she could see that all she needed was a zinger and she'd win this battle. And she had one. The mother of all zingers, coming up.

"No need to worry about the fucking condom, Dr. MacGregor, or any condoms for that matter. I can't get pregnant. I can't have children."

Damon's eyes went from puzzled to astonished, and then, was it compassion? Dammit! She didn't want compassion now. She wanted to fight. The blood left her head and she felt faint. He saw her waver and got her a chair, then pulled one across from her. Now the tears began to fall, and her old friend, the hiccups, began as she tried to explain, "Don't you see? It doesn't matter if you wear them or not. I can't have children. You want them. Four of them, to be exact. Your parents expect grandchildren. I can't give them any."

"Why didn't you tell me before? I thought you were mad at me because I was so careless. I thought you didn't want to be with me anymore. Why can't you get pregnant? How long have you known?"

Through hiccups and tears, Cat started her story. "When I was back in college, I had an opportunity to go overseas to do an internship with an international sea otter rescue. While I was there, I noticed that my breasts were leaking, and I knew I wasn't pregnant because I hadn't been with a guy in a long time. I went to several doctors and had lots of tests for six months. Turns out I have a small tumor on my pituitary gland." She saw Damon gasp and felt his hands clasp hers. "No, it's not cancerous. It's benign. But it makes my body already think it's pregnant. The last doctor who diagnosed me confirmed that I have a 95 percent chance of never getting pregnant."

Damon leaned forward to put his forehead on hers, and then he spoke. "Okay, so you mostly can't get pregnant. Then why was it such a big deal to use condoms? Why didn't you tell me?"

Cat didn't have the energy to get angry again, but felt like she wanted to, so she raised her voice again; maybe a little too loud. "Because you were supposed to be the rebound guy, okay? You were supposed to be the one to make me feel better. Have some fun. Get my confidence back and then say goodbye." Cat could feel the pain that was radiating from Damon's body. It was enough to ease her anger and calm down. Her compassion started to bubble up from the frenzied, murky anger pool she'd been wallowing in. She sighed, put her hands on either side of his face, and stared deep into his paler blue eyes. "But you turned out to be The Guy, instead. I went from feeling like this is just for fun to this is serious. He could be my future. He's the guy I want to marry. I want to have his babies. I can't have his babies." Tears started to roll down her face, which triggered tears to roll down his. "He wants babies. What if he doesn't love me enough to stay?" she whispered.

Damon put his hands on either side of her face, careful not to touch her tender cheek, and used his thumbs to wipe away her tears. "Catrina Carneri. I love you forever. That will never change.

We promised to be honest with each other early on. I am more upset that you kept this from me than the fact that you only have a 5 percent chance of getting pregnant. Why would you think that you couldn't be honest with me?" Damon's eyes searched Cat's.

"Because being a part of a big family and having your own is so important to you. I didn't think your love for me could com- pete with it."

"There are other ways to make a family, Cat. What you seem to be forgetting is that I want you in my family. I need you in my life, Cat. Nothing else matters. Whether we have no children or adopt a village, I can't see myself in a future where you aren't in it. It doesn't exist. You are my perfect family."

Tears came streaming down Cat's face, and her heart was beating so hard that she swore it could be heard outside of her body. Damon kneeled next to her and placed his head on her bosom while Cat lifted her arms and cradled his head. She could feel dampness growing on her dress where his face lay, and she knew he was crying with her.

"I'm so sorry, Damon. I didn't want to hurt you. I just was too scared to say anything. I've always wanted a family, and it killed me when I learned I can't do the one thing that only a woman is made to do." Damon lifted his face and looked deep into her eyes. She felt him searching her soul for something else.

"Cat."

"What?"

"Who else knows?"

"My family and Aurelie." He paused. Damon seemed to be choosing his words very carefully.

"And Jansen? Did you tell him?" Anger started to form once again in the pit of her stomach.

"Hell no! Why would you ask me something like that?" "Because you didn't tell me, and I thought we were pretty serious.

You were with Jansen for a long time, Cat. Why didn't it come up?" He was searching in her eyes again. This time, she was searching as well. Why didn't she tell him? She had plenty of opportunities throughout the years. Curious.

"If I had to guess, it was because I didn't fully trust him. Even though I didn't have full confirmation that he was cheating on me until a few months ago, I guess I always had a feeling, a kind of nagging concern that something just wasn't right for me to share that with him."

Damon paused again. Cat could feel him trying to find the right words again. "So, you didn't tell him because you didn't trust him. Correct?"

"Yes." She was not following him.

"Is it possible you didn't tell me because you don't trust me either?" The concern in his eyes and the hurt in his voice was palpable. She hated that she was the one who caused him this hurt. Cat wished she could take it all back, all the tongue lashings, the pushing away, the keeping of secrets from him. Now he looked like a frightened child, and she hated it. It was worse because she knew it was her actions, or lack thereof, that caused this.

"No. Not possible. I trust you, Damon. More than I've ever trusted another man who isn't a part of my family. The truth is, I kept the truth from you for a very different reason. I didn't want to lose you. I was very afraid, and if I'm truly honest, I still am, that you will leave me because the urge to be a father will be greater than your need to love and stay with me. I'm very fearful that you will stay in the beginning because you love me, but then you will resent me, and then you may stay out of obligation or leave me after we've already built a life together because you realize that time is running out for you to be a father."

This time, it was Damon who recognized how frightened Cat had become. She had exhumed confidence and strength earlier in the night, but now he was seeing her childlike presence and she could see his concern for her in his eyes. Damon put his hands carefully through her hair and then looked into her wide, golden-flecked eyes. "Oh, Cat. I don't know how to show you how wrong you are. Before you came into my life, I didn't feel anything. Paige had taken those teenager-crazy ideals about love and sex and used my feelings to manipulate me to be who and do what she wanted. When she dropped me, I put up a wall so tall and so thick that I didn't think it would ever come down. It took a lot of therapy and a lot of time to thin the wall a little bit and have it shrink down in size, but it was still there until Friday Night Live. That one kiss broke down that barrier. It came crashing down around me. I feel emotions now that I wouldn't let myself feel for so very long. I don't want to go back to that same man. He was hollow. He wasn't whole."

Cat blurted out, "But you won't be a father. You won't be whole if you're with me either."

"I can be a father and you can be a mother. We get to choose which kind we want to be, together. That's what matters most to me. Being a family together, building a life together." Cat felt him get up and then he brought her up next to him. Damon put his hands on either side of her neck, lowered his head, and carefully kissed her swollen cheek, and then planted light kisses down to her pouting lips. Next, he sucked the remnants of salted tears off her tainted lips and then pushed his tongue into her mouth. Cat's tongue found his and welcomed him fully. Now a new kind of stirring had reached the pit of her stomach and moistened her loins. She wanted him badly. He had been gentle with her, but she now felt she needed to be in control of the situation. So much of tonight was out of her control and she had handled it, but now she wanted something that she could move forward at her own pace and with her own body.

Cat stepped away from the embrace and saw that Damon looked perplexed and then saddened. But his looked quickly changed when she reached behind her neck and unsnapped the halter straps and let them drop over her heaving breasts. Then she slowly unzipped the back of the dress and let it gently fall around her hips to show Damon what she had promised him hours earlier. Underneath that shimmery flirtatious red dress was an equally sexy, strapless, scarlet corset set. The corset was made of satin and Venetian lace with a lace-up front that showed the deep "V" of her cleavage. A matching lace thong was already moist, letting him know that she wanted him. Cat smirked like a Cheshire cat when she saw Damon scan her up and down and then swallow. She left him speechless. Cat was pleased and wanted to show him how much more pleasure was in store.

Damon shadowed her like a zombie following its master. He followed her to the bedroom, where she lay provocatively on top of the cream satin duvet cover. "Take your clothes off, now," she commanded in a low, throaty voice. Damon's eyes were still wide, but he did as she commanded. As he reached for his tie and unbuttoned the top collar, Cat let loose her hair and let it fall around her face. Damon quickly unbuttoned the rest of the shirt and shrugged it off, along with his suit coat. This time, Cat took her hands and slowly brought them over her heaving breasts, with her middle finger following the deep "V" until it ended near her hips. Damon followed suit by unbuckling his belt, unbuttoning his pants and letting them slide down to the floor, revealing black silk boxers with a definite rise highlighting his appreciation for her seduction. Next, Cat took her hands over her hips and led her right hand to her pulsing mound and began massaging it back and forth while she bit her lower lip.

Damon's wide eyes became clouded with passion and hunger. He stepped out of his clothes, ripped off his socks, and leaned over the top of her. "No," Cat commanded. Damon was perplexed. She could tell he didn't understand what she wanted him to do, and he was anxious to get a signal from her what he should do next. Cat lifted her finger and placed it on his mouth. He opened his full lips and sucked in her finger greedily. "I want to be on top this time." He nodded and let her push him down on the bed and then begin taking off his boxers with her teeth, gently nipping his tender skin on the way down. Damon closed his eyes and moaned in desire and agony as she was within inches of his rock-hard shaft that was aching to be inside her.

When Cat was done, she left the bed and stood at the edge so that he could see her, but not touch her. She commanded again, "Watch me." Damon's eyes fluttered opened, and he gazed at his brazen lover who was shedding her thong and corset in a slow and lustful manner to tease his sexual appetite to its peak. She sneered as Damon's body was stretching and gyrating in symphony with every lace she loosened, every inch she shimmied her thong down to the floor, and when she turned around so that her perfectly cleft peach-bottomed ass was begging for him to enter her, his moan turned into an almost roar.

"Damn it, woman! I can't take much more of this. Get over here!"

Cat felt her sexual tension rising along with her confidence, knowing that he was dying to be inside her, and the only thing keeping him from it was her command. "Why?" she whispered, now facing him so he could see just how large and dark her nipples had become, like ripe Bing cherries, waiting to be plucked.

"I want you, Cat. Shit, I'm dying over here! I need to be inside you," he begged.

"I need to be inside you, what?" she asked. At first, he didn't get it. He was looking desperate.

"Please, Cat. Please, come over here and make love to me. I can't wait any longer." With his plea, she realized that she'd been playing with his emotions for long enough. It was just becoming an extension of what she'd been doing for weeks. That's not what she wanted to do tonight. She no longer wanted to be in total control but to lose control in their desire together.

Cat walked over to the side of the bed and straddled him. Looking straight into his eyes, she plunged down onto his engorged shaft until he was fully inside her. "Oh, God!" she screamed as Damon moaned and thrust up to have their hips meet. Cat started the rhythm and Damon matched her. She intended it to be a slow, sweet, lovemaking session. Instead, it was as if the beasts of hell were nipping at their heels and they had to quicken the pace. It was raw; it was ravaging as they grabbed for each other in what could only be explained as lustful desperation.

Cat accelerated the pace as Damon matched her thrust for thrust, and at the apex of Cat's emotional and sexual roller-coaster ride, she let go of a scream complex with anguish, anger, sadness, emptiness, and at the end, it left her with a sense of peace. She rolled off him and lay by his side with her healthy cheek against the soft auburn curls on his chest. Was it possible that he could still love her?

Cat sighed and then fell asleep with a new feeling—hope.

Overnight, a rainstorm rolled in and lulled Cat in and out of sleep. Then, as if she was awakening in a dream world, the smell of French toast and bacon wafted under her nose. She fluttered her eyes and saw Damon holding a tray of breakfast items for her with a cold can of diet soda, which sounded really good about now. She wriggled herself so that she was sitting up. Cat tried to smile, but winced a bit, remembered that she had a tender cheek to contend with. "Wow, that smells amazing, Damon. Thanks." He set it down on her lap as she noted his hair was every which way and his beard was a bit on the scruffy side. "Are you going to join me?"

Damon smiled a warm, familiar smile. "I already ate. You get my leftovers."

Cat giggled. She could tell that he spent a little extra time on her breakfast in bed but didn't want to argue. She was spent from last night. It was nice to just sit in bed a while longer and eat yummy food. Cat picked up a crisp piece of bacon while Damon cracked open her soda. "Mmm. This is so good, Damon. Thank you," she said as she reached for the diet soda and took a long, cool drink.

"How did you sleep?" He looked at her with concern in his eyes.

Cat took a minute to think about her answer thoughtfully.

"I seem to remember I had some crazy dreams on and off, but I don't remember what they were. I did hear the rainstorms come through, but it was more like a soft lullaby than a distraction. How did you sleep?"

Damon paused and then looked away for a moment. Enough that Cat stopped eating the slice of French toast she had on her fork. "Honestly, I fell asleep like a rock at first, but then I kept having weird dreams and waking up. I thought it was better if I just got up and start the day while you slept in."

Cat's eyebrows furrowed together. "What time is it?" "Almost ten. Why?"

"I promised my parents that I would pick up Mia by noon. I'd better get a move on."

"Let me get Mia. You take it easy. You worked really hard on that event, and with the shit hitting the fan afterward, you need to lie low today. Let me take care of you now. Okay?" Cat nodded as she was chewing on another slice of toast and finishing it off with a bit of bacon drenched in maple syrup. Boy, was she hungry!

"Okay. While you're gone, I think I'll go and soak in the bathtub. I have to get all this crap out of my hair and my legs are sore from wearing high heels all night long."

Damon turned back around and smiled at her, although it looked a little sadder than usual. "That sounds like a plan. I tell you what. On the way to your parents, I'll stop by the store and rent a movie and something easy to make for a late afternoon meal. "

"That's perfect. Thanks again, Damon, for taking such good care of me." And then the tears started to show up. "I am really sorry I screwed up so much. Can you forgive me?" Tears dripped down her face and plopped onto the plate and swam in the maple syrup.

"Oh, Cat," Damon sighed and lifted her chin. "I know you're sorry. I already forgave you last night. We both have a lot to process, but I don't want us to think about any of that for the rest of the day. We'll have to tackle it on Monday regardless, so let's just be lackadaisical for the day. If you want to stay in PJs, I'm all for it." And he smiled that dazzling smile she'd missed for so many days. How could she have tried to push him away? She needed him in her life; he gave her balance. He was her light.

"I love you, Damon. Thank you for making me breakfast, for picking up Mia, for making me relax today. Thank you for being in my life." With that, she reached up and kissed him with her sticky sweet and salty lips.

"Yum," he said as he took her tray away, picked up his keys, and left her to get settled into her bath.

Cat sauntered out of bed and began drawing her bath with lavender Epsom bath salts. Next, she picked up the trail of clothes and put hers in her hamper and in the dry cleaning pile. She folded Damon's and placed his on a side chair in the front room. She realized he must have packed an overnight bag because all his clothes from last night were here, on the chair. What did he have on? Ah, sweats and a T-shirt. Perfect. She felt like after all the days of hiking and working with Aurelie along with watching everything that she ate to get into that amazing dress, she wanted to give her body a break. Now she just wanted to relax. He loved her just the way she was. Even now, knowing her secret, he still wanted her. He proved that last night. He was desperate to be inside her. She felt the need to possess him and, in the end, he healed her.

When the bath was full, she slipped in and dunked her head under for a moment to feel the void when you're fully immersed in water. At the moment she lifted her face out of the water, she closed her eyes and just let the heated bathwater and salts caress her sore muscles. She was able to simply let her thoughts flow without judgment or emotion and allow the water to float them away.

Her mind felt lighter when she finished her bath. When the water began to cool, she woke from her meditative state and scrubbed her body of its leftover glamor and grime from the night before. It was an awakening. She was starting to feel like a new woman, and she realized it was all due to Damon. How could she have ever thought he would leave her? He had told her time and time again. He showed her in a million ways how he felt about her. How she made him feel. She could get through the next few days knowing that he'd be there for her. After she suffered the wrath of Rose. After she went to the police station for the next steps in convicting Jansen of assault. She was confident that Damon would be there for her. Cat was feeling a sense of optimism glowing through and giving her a new lease on life.

By the time Damon arrived with Mia, she'd already organized her clothes for the next day, put away all the items left astray the night before, and made the bed. In her puppy slippers, fuzzy pajama pants and top, no makeup, and her curls up in a messy bun on top of her head, she looked like a young college student.

Mia scampered up the stairs to meet Cat as if she hadn't seen her in eons. "Hello, little girl! Did you miss me? Grandma must have spoiled you at her house, didn't she?" Mia just answered with a great big kiss and a ton of butt wiggling with her tail going a million miles a minute.

Damon followed with a bag full of baked potato chips, caramel corn, a pizza, and *Wonder Woman* and *Justice League* movies, which neither had seen yet. He set everything on the kitchen table and set up shop. "I figure we can watch *Wonder Woman* now, take a break, and bake the pizza and then watch *Justice League*, then dinner and a movie."

Cat smiled and planted a huge kiss on his mouth. "Sounds like the bestest day ever!" Next, she strolled over to the television and plopped onto the sofa with fluffy blankets available for snuggling.

"How was your bath?" Damon asked as he took Cat's feet and placed them on his lap. Next thing she knew, he was massaging them, making sure he hit the pressure points just right to release tension.

"Mmmm. Good. But not as good as this massage. You're a genius," Cat said as she melted into the pillow on the arm of the sofa. They lay like that for the movie, while Mia lay on her bed. The rest of the day continued into that slow, mosey-like pattern. A bit of time in front of the television, a bit of time in the kitchen fixing something to eat. A little snuggling. Some gentler petting. A lot of quiet relaxation.

When it was time for Damon to leave, Cat felt a letdown. Not only didn't she want him to leave, but she also knew what she would be dealing with on Monday, and she didn't have the energy to handle that right now.

"Do you have to go?" she said as she hugged him in the kitchen. "Yeah, I have to. Sorry, but I got to get ready for work tomorrow.

Call me after work and let me know what happened. Okay?"

Cat looked up at him, pouting. "I know you have to go. I'm sorry I asked. It's just been so nice having you around today. I don't want to see you leave. And yes, I promise I'll call you tomorrow." Damon bent down and softly kissed her lips, lingering there before he said goodbye to his other best girl, Mia. Cat looked out the window as the headlights dimmed out of the driveway and veered onto the roadway.

Usually, after an event, she chose the most comfortable outfit she could get away with because there was always a lot of hustle and bustle to get everything back in order, along with processing the donations. However, she had a feeling that things were coming to a head with Dr. O'Brien, so she wanted to make sure she looked professional and competent to handle anything Rose would throw her way. In the end, Cat decided on a simple black pantsuit with a white mock turtleneck and flats. Flats were a must. Next, she went to the kitchen to plan out her lunch. Probably a salad since she ate all crap food today. It didn't sound very filling, so she also packed a string cheese and an apple, just in case. After letting Mia out one last time to do her duty, Cat took a quick shower and went to bed. She needed all the energy she could muster to get through the next twenty-four hours.

The next morning came quickly, and Cat didn't dawdle. She breezed through her morning routine; the only difference was that she intended to wear her hair up, but a bruise materialized over-night, so she chose to straighten her hair so that it was partially hidden. Cat kissed Mia goodbye, packed up her lunch, and was on her way to face the day.

At work, the usual banter that would happen after an event was not evident as everyone focused on the work to be done. Cat had plenty to do, making sure that gifts were entered into the donor database while Shelli worked on putting away the gala decorations and stored them for the next year. Around 10:00 a.m., Dr. O'Brien came into the clinic with a sense of being all about business. She nodded to her team and caught Cat's eyes in a staring contest, neither one budging. "Catrina, I'd like an update on where we are with the numbers and a list of the largest donors with their phone numbers before lunch. I'd like to call them personally to thank them."

"Of course, I can get that to you in the next hour." Not wanting to show any sign of weakness, she continued to stare at Rose until she turned to leave. Cat went back to her office, crunching numbers and entering gifts until 10:50 a.m. and then ran the reports Rose had requested. She gathered her papers and strode to Rose's office down the hall. Rose glanced over her reading glasses and motioned for Cat to shut the door behind her and sit down. Cat complied and then placed the reports on Rose's desk.

"As you can see, overall, we are 12 percent over last year's results, stemming from a very successful sponsorship campaign and an increase in our live auction donations," Cat pronounced. "I've also organized the donor report from the largest donor to the smallest along with both their phone and email information in case you cannot reach them by phone directly. Thank-you letters will be generated after lunch and should be ready for your signature by the end of the day." Cat felt confident that she had answered all of Rose's questions before they were even asked. Best to confront the attacker before they can attack.

Rose reviewed the reports and then took off her glasses and set them down while she looked at Cat's face, focusing for a moment on her bruised cheek. Cat felt the change in her confidence level coincide with the way she was being reviewed by Rose. "Thank you, Catrina. It seems that everything is in order. For all practical pur- poses, this gala has the makings of being one of our most successful events to date." Cat almost accepted the compliment; however, she felt uneasiness, and her stomach was tightening. Something else was going to be said, and it wasn't going to be good. "You are a talented grant writer and fundraiser. Unfortunately, I have to let you go."

Cat took a moment to take it all in. "Excuse me? I don't under- stand. We made money. We made more than last year. Why would you let me go?" Cat tried to keep her voice steady, but she was quickly losing it.

Rose sighed and looked straight into Cat's eyes that were now all perplexed. "Catrina, I work very hard at keeping this center up and running. That means I am responsible for every dollar that comes into our coffers, every animal that is treated, and every staff member that is hired. I have a great deal of responsibility, and that means that I am also the face and the brand of this establishment. I intended to run this center as a business with a focus on professionalism and integrity."

Cat interrupted, "I understand that, Rose. It's one of the reasons why I accepted this job. I wanted to be a part of something that made a difference, and people respect the work that we do here. I wanted to work somewhere where my skills were taken seriously, and I was treated as a professional."

Rose sighed again. "Perhaps, but you didn't act professionally. I have to let you go, Catrina. It's not easy for me because you have added value to this organization, but you do not act with integrity outside of these walls, and it's negatively impacting this center. I've worked too long and too hard to let your actions ruin what I've built."

Cat was astonished and totally flummoxed. "What do you mean that I don't act with integrity? I am always acting with integrity, inside these walls and out. Ask my neighbors, landlord, anyone."

"Really? Why are you forcing me to say this to you? You really don't know why you are being fired?"

"I guess you're going to have to spell it out for me. I really don't understand why you'd fire me if I do good work and make your center money. Unless you just don't like me as a person." Cat saw the change in Rose's face go from pity to fire. Things were not going well at all, and they were about to get worse.

"Seriously, Catrina? Whether or not I like you as a person is beside the point. Your personal life is damaging the image of this center. Instead of keeping business and your personal life separate, you consistently chose to intermingle them. Besides my better judgment, I kept you on even after you started to date one of our largest donors. Then you two broke up, and I felt I could give you another chance. Then what happens? You start another relationship with another one of our significant donors, Dr. MacGregor. Honestly, Cat, you disrespect me with your behavior. You're embarrassing yourself by forcing me to say these things out loud."

Cat was completely blown away. She was on the verge of tears. How could this be happening? It was Jansen's bad behavior at the gala. She had done nothing wrong. Why was she being made to feel that she had?

"Look, Cat, I respect your work. Therefore, I have written you a letter of recommendation. The reason I came in a bit late is I was working on your compensation package, which I believe is more than fair. If you are willing to take my advice, I recommend you hand in your immediate resignation, and then you being fired won't end up on your professional record."

Cat was in disbelief. She couldn't believe what she was hearing, especially the fact that Rose used her nickname. Cat was not prepared for this conversation. She fully expected a confrontation, but never in a million years did she think she was going to get fired. Trying to drum up some semblance of confidence, she replied, "Rose," since they were now on a more personal level, "I have always acted with integrity. Jansen accosted me. I did nothing to provoke him. You're making me out to be someone who uses her sex as a weapon to snare men, wealthy men. I'm not like that at all. It's not true!" Cat was almost crying now.

Rose's gray eyes iced over. "Seriously, Cat? How can I not consider that as your modus operandi? Two wealthy young donors. One smart, beautiful grant writer who is doing work that she sees as a stepping-stone to something bigger and better. Like her own ranch, perhaps, with her own horses to tend to. Why work for someone else when you can find a man who has the means to give you everything you've ever wanted? It happened once. I let it go. It happened twice. Now I have one of my largest donors in jail and all of Lake Country spreading the news via the gossip trail. Sure, we had our most successful event, but it may be our last. Our integrity is in the gutter because you couldn't say 'no' and keep your personal life and your professional life separate. I don't know what kind of long-term damage your antics have caused this sanctuary. I should have done this a while ago. I hope it's not too late for the fate of these animals and this organization to let you go now. I have to, Cat. The future of this center depends on me being strong enough to let you go right now." Rose started to melt her icy exterior when she saw the tears dropping on Cat's cheeks. "Cat, this is your last chance to leave here with your dignity intact and my offer to let you go out on your own terms."

Cat tried to make sense of the swirling emotions and convoluted conversation that was occurring. She saw Rose slide a piece of letterhead in front of her and place a pen next to it. Rose had printed Cat's resignation letter and was just waiting for her to sign it. Cat had nothing else to say. She had nothing left to fight with. She wiped away the tears, picked up the pen, and signed away the life she had created at the wildlife rehabilitation sanctuary.

Preview of

Canoodling Out West

— BOOK TWO —

Chapter One

Damon's day started at 3:30 a.m. when his phone alerted him that Angie was in labor. As much as he wanted to spend the day at the hospital helping his best friend and business partner, Pete, cope with everything, he knew the clinic needed him there in Pete's absence. Damon grudgingly climbed out of bed and got ready for the day ahead.

He arrived at clinic with a large traveling mug full of coffee and just enough time to connect with the staff before prioritizing the day's visits to make sure all the clients were covered. Though he was tired physically and mentally, it was a nice break to be going through his workday instead of dealing with his feelings and mulling over everything that had happened in the past seventy-two hours.

Before he knew it, it was 6:00 p.m., and the receptionist had closed off the clinic lobby while the rest of the team tidied up and checked on their equine patients for the night. While he desperately wanted to call Pete, he knew that it would be best to just let Pete call him. First babies tended to take the longest, and it might not be seen as supportive for him to be at the hospital. Damon checked his phone for an update and walked outside where he noticed a shadow by his truck. He looked up and saw Cat wearing a baseball cap, sunglasses, gray sweats, and her black tennis shoes. "Hey, beautiful. I didn't expect to see you today. What did I do to deserve a visit at work?" He tried to lighten the mood, but it wasn't working.

"Sorry to bother you at the clinic. It's just, I mean, I didn't know where else to go." Her voice was cracking, and she hung her head. Damon stepped closer and gently took off her sunglasses. What he saw shocked him. Her usually bright hazel eyes were bloodshot red and swollen.

"Babe, what's going on? Why are you crying?" He reached out, and she took a step back but then looked up at him; that's when the hiccups started.

"Rose fired me today."

It took Damon a moment to process what she had said. "What do you mean she fired you? What happened?" Now he took a step toward her and put both of his hands on her shoulders.

"She said that I used poor judgment and accused me of being a gold digger. She accused me of using my position at the wildlife rehab sanctuary to trap wealthy men in the hopes that I could quit and lead a life of privilege. With my own ranch. Riding my own horses."

"What? That bitch! She can't do that to you!"

"Damon, she did. She gave me the option to resign immediately and accept the severance package—three months' pay and benefits—or fire me and it shows on my professional record. I really didn't have much of a choice in the matter. Besides, what if she's right?" Cat looked up sheepishly at Damon.

"Cat, Cat. Don't you dare think like that! How can you believe in the crap that she unloaded on you?" His blood was boiling, and he wanted to hurt someone, someone who hurt the woman he loved.

"Think about it, Damon. I have been. All afternoon. The only two long-term relationships I've had are with guys who I met through work."

"But that's just circumstance. It's not like you sought me out.

That's not how it happened with Jansen, is it?"

"Okay, I get what you're saying, but she still has a point. I set myself up into a position where I have easy access to men who have means. I even have access to information about their wealth because it's a part of my job as a fundraiser. Just because I didn't accept the job with that benefit in mind, I can't deny that the only two real relationships I've had are directly connected to my work at the center."

Damon shook his head and lifted her chin so that she was forced to look into his eyes. It was then that he saw the tears.

"Cat. Did you go into that job specifically looking for a husband?" "No," she whispered.

"Did you come in early the day I met you because you knew I would be there with an injured animal?"

"No," she whispered again.

"That woman is envious of your talent, your intelligence, your beauty, and your youth. She was jealous when I paid attention to you and not to her, and she has found a way to get back at you. None of what happened Saturday night was your fault. Do you hear me?"

His heart was breaking seeing how hurt she was. Cat nodded in acceptance. He hugged her and rubbed her back to help calm the hiccups until they subsided. Just as they fell into a rhythm of breathing and slow rocking, his phone rang. He pulled it out of his pocket to see who it was. Pete. "Hello? Yeah? Congrats, man! How are Angie and the baby doing? Wow. Can't believe you're a dad now. What's her name?"

Cat gazed at Damon with a look of curiosity as he ended the phone call. "That was Pete. Angie had a baby girl today. They're naming her Rosella, after Angie's grandmother."

"Oh, wow. That's fantastic. At least there's something good happening today," Cat said, trying to smile, but it ended in a sort of a partial smile.

"Yeah, they want me to come and see them in the hospital. Apparently, everyone else has seen her earlier in the day, and they still want to show her off. Why don't you follow me to the hospital, and we can both see her?"

"Oh, I don't know. I look awful. Maybe I should just go home." "No, you don't. Besides, I bet you'll be looking better than Angie."

"Okay. It would be a nice distraction, anyway. Then I can go home and wallow in my pity party." "Cat, who else knows?"

"No one. I wanted to tell you first. I guess I'll have to let my family and Mrs. Romansky, my landlady, know next. Last but not least, Aurelie."

"Why is Aurelie last?"

"Because she'll want revenge. I need to get prepared to stop her from slashing tires, toilet papering the center, or whatever teenage prank idea she wants to do in retaliation for hurting her best friend." Damon laughed.

"What did she do to Jansen?" "You mean when he hit on her?"

"Is that what happened to make you two break up?"

"Yes. I mean, no. He fooled around on me throughout our time together. I only found out about the last one about a month before you and I met. Aurelie just told me he hit on her at a party." Cat smirked. "She grabbed his penis and he thought he was getting a handjob, but she almost ripped it off his body."

Damon yipped and brought his hands to his crotch. "Remind me never to get on her bad side."

"I will. Where's the hospital?"

"Waukesha."

Cat nodded and walked over to her SUV, and Damon watched her strap in before he put his truck in gear. His head was swimming with everything that had transpired over the weekend and now these new developments. He didn't know how Cat would handle losing her job and everything else that she was dealing with, like the assault by Jansen. Damon knew that he was struggling to keep up with everything. He agreed with Cat; the baby was a good distraction.

When they arrived at the hospital, the gift shop was still open, so they found a bouquet of brightly colored flowers in a ceramic baby block for Angie and a super soft pink blanket with a teddy bear hoodie for the baby.

Taking the elevators to the maternity floor, they gave the name Rossi to the volunteer, who handed them bright-pink nametags to wear, gaining them entrance into the secured birthing center. When they got to the room, Angie had just finished feeding Rosella, who was drifting off to sleep. Damon rapped on the door and heard Pete's tired voice say, "Come in."

As soon as Damon's looming silhouette entered the room, Pete's dark eyes brightened, and a large smile grew on his face. "Bro! So glad you could make it!" Then he saw Cat standing in the background. "Cat, glad he brought you! Come on in and meet our daughter!"

Angie had tidied up and a large smile came to her face as she reached out to give a hug to Damon. "We come bearing gifts for you, Beautiful, and your new baby girl. Congratulations, Angie. You are glowing!" He placed the flowers on her nightstand and welcomed the hug she was offering.

"So glad you could make it, Damon. It makes our day complete to see everyone who's important to us come and celebrate with us," Angie shared.

Pete encouraged Cat to come further into the room, and she presented him with a brown bag with pink tissue paper popping out. "Congratulations, Pete. Angie. Here's a little something for your new baby." Pete took it and ushered her closer to Angie in bed.

He let Angie open the present, who exclaimed, "Ooh! This is adorable! And so soft! Thank you, Cat. Thank you, Damon."

Pete gave Damon a great big bro hug and slapped him on the back. "Thanks, dude. It means a lot to me and Angie for you coming out tonight. I know I left you in a lurch today. You've got to be tired." Damon wanted to agree but just shrugged.

"You know I'll always be here for you and Angie whenever you need me."

"Good," said Pete as he walked over to the nursery bed where little Rosella was drifting off to sleep and carefully scooped her up into his arms. "Because we couldn't wait another minute before asking you to add Rosella to the list as your goddaughter."

Damon's eyes went wide, and Pete carefully placed the sleeping babe in Damon's strong arms.

"You've been like a brother to Pete for as long as we can remember. You've been there for us during good times and bad. We can't think of a better person to take care of our little girl if we can't," Angie piped in.

With that, Damon felt the warm bundle squirm to get comfortable in his massive arms. He lifted her up to his face, closed his eyes, and smelled the top of her head. And he was in love. He knew that this little girl had a piece of his heart forever. He'd do anything to protect her. Cat stood back, outside of his line of sight, stared at him, and recognized how quickly he had become attached to this tiny bundle. This new person. Whether or not he intended it to happen, Cat saw that his body and soul begged to be a father. Needed to be a father. Damon was so enthralled with this new life, building this new relationship, that he didn't see the tears streaming down Cat's bruised cheek and the sadness that clouded her soft hazel eyes once more.

After a few more minutes of catch-up, he noticed Angie's eyes fluttering and Pete's wide yawn. "Well, kids. We should get going. This is probably the only full night's sleep you'll be getting for a while."

Angie wanted to argue with him that tonight was just the start of their sleepless nights, but she couldn't stifle the yawn that came out instead. Damon bent down and kissed Angie on the cheek and shook Pete's hand in a final congratulatory action. Cat followed him out of the room and to the elevator. He didn't realize how quiet Cat had been in the room and was still processing everything when the elevator came to take them to the lobby.

When they walked in silence to Cat's SUV, Damon didn't think anything of it. When she turned around to see him, he thought that her eyes were glistening again, but then decided the gleam was coming from the bright parking lot light that she was parked under. "Thanks for being there for me, Damon, and thanks for bringing me to see the baby. She is gorgeous." Then she sighed, "Look, I know this week is going to be crazy busy for you with Pete out and all.

I've got a lot of things I have to get a handle on this week, so I'm thinking we just hold off on trying to see each other or call each other until the weekend. Say, Friday afternoon I can give you a call to see when we can see each other this weekend?"

Damon was in a stupor. He thought she would want to see more of him, not less. He was confused. Yet she had a point. Even with the temporary vet standing in for Pete, things were bound to be very busy at work with Pete absent. His brain was getting mushy with all of the things he was dealing with. Perhaps it would be a good thing for him to just focus on work and let her have some time to deal with all the crap that had been thrown at her. "I guess that would be all right. But promise me, Cat. Promise me that if you need me for anything—to talk, come over, a hug, whatever, you'll call me. Don't try to be strong just because you can. I want to be there for you if you need me to be. Got it?"

Cat nodded her head and whispered, "Got it." He reached out and hugged her and then tilted her chin so he could place a gentle wisp of a kiss on her lips. He watched her get into her SUV and then walked over to his truck, where he sat down and contemplated what he was feeling. How could he be feeling sad and elated all at the same time? Guys don't usually do that, but today proved him wrong.

All the way home, he kept thinking about how wonderful it felt to hold baby Rosella in his arms and how fantastic she smelled.

By Wednesday, Damon was getting darn right ornery. Lack of sleep and no break at work led to a very crabby and tired man. He and the contracted vet had full schedules, and then they were called in to handle an emergency breech delivery at 2:00 a.m. Tuesday morning. Then they got another call at 5:30 p.m. that one of their best clients had a mare that was in excruciating pain with colic and if they could bring her in. The surgery went smoothly; the patient handled it well. However, Damon's body was not happy with being on the go constantly and the lack of sleep that went along with it.

Thursday's schedule was a bit lighter, so he informed his team that he wasn't coming in until his first patient at 10:00 a.m. He decided to stop at the coffee shop in Delafield for an Americano to go. While in line, he heard a familiar voice say, "Damon? Damon MacGregor. Is that you?"

At first, he couldn't make it out how he knew the voice, and then it hit him. Like a cinder block being thrown from the roof of a building. He hung his head and sighed. Could this week get any more complicated? He turned around and there she was. As long and lean as she'd been in college. The hair was a bit different, a little shorter? A little more color? And she had her hands on the shoulders of a young boy with shaggy blonde hair and those big brown eyes that had melted his heart so long ago when he first saw them on Paige's face in their English Lit class.

"Hello, Paige." Damon sighed as he looked into her eyes. Still big. Still brown. A little tired, perhaps, but weren't we all by the end of the week?

"Samuel, this is my old friend, Damon. Damon, this is my son, Samuel." Paige beamed when she spoke about her son who was wearing a red-hooded sweatshirt.

"Hello, Samuel. Nice sweatshirt," Damon complimented.

"My name's Sam. Thanks. My dad bought it for me," he exclaimed crossly. Damon saw the look on Paige's face go from lit to sad.

Damon was able to place his order and wait on the other side. Far away from Paige. Unfortunately, she chose to stand close to him, along with her son, to wait for their beverages. "How've you been, Damon? Do you live around here now?" Paige asked inquisitively.

"Umm, no, I don't live here. Just getting a coffee before I see my first patient at ten." He didn't look directly at her because, quite frankly, he was afraid to. He didn't have enough energy to handle the day he expected to have, and now she had added to it. He simply had to cut his losses and try to diffuse the situation as much as possible.

"Oh. Patient? Did you become a vet as planned?" "Yeah.

"Americano?" the barista called. Damon walked up to the counter, grabbed his caffeine to go, and looked at Sam.

"Nice to meet you, Sam. Paige." He was already headed toward the door when he heard her call after him.

"Damon, wait up!" She grabbed her two drinks and scurried past several businessmen and women to get to Damon before he drove off. "Listen, it's been a while since we've seen each other, and I've just moved here. Maybe we could grab a cup of coffee another time?" She put on a sad puppy-dog face to make her point.

Shit. He certainly didn't need this now. "I don't think so, Paige. I don't think it's a good idea."

Sam was getting antsy, but Paige wasn't budging. "Samuel, why don't you get into the car? I'll be there in a minute." Sam grabbed his hot cocoa and left to go a few cars down to sit and wait for his mother.

"Samuel's a really good boy; he just gets a bit squirrely if he sits still too long," Paige offered.

"Sam looks like a good kid."

"I'm glad you think so. He started a new school last month. Still working on trying to make friends. He loves sports, so I'm looking into signing him up for basketball in the winter."

Damon couldn't quite tell why she was telling him all this, why she was stalling.

"Look, Paige, I've got to get going. I've got a hectic week, and I want to get through it all so I can spend time with my girlfriend this weekend." "There," he thought, "that should push her away."

"Oh, sure. I see. It's just, well, I'd hoped I didn't have to tell you in a parking lot," Paige shared.

He knew he shouldn't take the bait, but he was so overly tired he didn't have his defenses up.

"Damon, Samuel's my son."

"I know, you told me. You and Dr. Richards had a son. Congrats. Are you still together?"

"Umm, no. That's why I'm living here in Delafield now. I had to leave him. He's … he's not well. He drinks too much."

Damon didn't want to feel anything for Paige, but he couldn't help it. He felt sorry for her. "I'm sorry, Paige."

"Thanks," she sighed, and then she looked over at the car to Samuel. "I stayed this long because of Samuel. I really wanted to make it work, but he lost his teaching job at the university because they found out he'd been drinking on the job. Then it just got worse from there. Samuel doesn't know why we left, exactly. He just knows his father is sick. He's mad at me right now, but it's for the best."

Damon looked over at the kid and recognized he felt sorry for the boy as well. Every boy deserves a father. Tough break. "Jeez, I don't know what to say."

"There's more." Paige reached out and touched Damon's shoulder and looked into his eyes. "Damon, I got pregnant with Sam when I was twenty and had him at twenty-one. You and I were together when I was twenty. Samuel is your son, Damon. He's yours."

Damon's eyes bulged out of his head; his heart started racing, and he felt sweat beginning to wet his shirt. It couldn't be possible. She would have told him! Dammit, God! Why was everything happening right now? "It's not possible, Paige. We broke up because you were sleeping around with Dr. Richards. Sam is his son, not mine!"

"Oh, Damon, I'm so sorry I'm telling you like this, but I moved to Delafield to raise Samuel in a safe place and also to start looking for you, to tell you that you have a son. He's yours, Damon. "

Acknowledgments

As this is my first book, I had a great deal of help getting it ready to be published.

Thank you to the Canoodling focus group: Lu, Kristin, Nicole B., Maria, Tammie, Marcia, Julia, Donna, Erin, Kris, Joy, Nicole K., and Kathleen.

To the men in my life who held down the fort and made sure I always had the time and space I needed to write and edit, I recognize the sacrifices you made. Rich and Jonah, I am grateful for you, your support and love through this adventurous journey.

I will be forever appreciative to my friend, Melissa Blair, for her networking skills and social media tutorage. To Meg McCormick, professional photographer and friend, I value your generosity and your talent. Thank you for gifting me with the perfect professional photo for this book!

I owe a huge debt of gratitude to this group of individuals who guided me through the unknown publishing world. First, to the professionals who helped me understand the business of publishing: Kyle Danowski, Jim Morrow, Dave Hansen, Joel Beck, and Emily Pieper.

Finally, in this second edition of *Canoodling Up North—Book One of the Canoodling Series*, I want acknowledge my new publisher, Mike Nicloy, owner of Nico 11 Publishing & Design. Mike, I am excited to have you join me on this publishing journey.

Author's Bio

Shawn M. Verdoni is the author of *Canoodling Up North—Book One, Canoodling Out West—Book Two,* and her third book, *Canoodling Always & Forever—Book Three* (for release in June of 2024). She attended the University of Wisconsin-Whitewater for her degree in secondary education and the Milwaukee School of Engineering to complete her master's in business administration. Her best days are spent with her husband, two children, and two dogs just hanging out. She loves living in Wisconsin, especially in fall when you can find her in a pumpkin patch or an apple orchard collecting tart baking apples for her famous crumble crust apple pie.